The Children of the Nakba

Books by David Calder

REDEMPTION COVE
FIRE ON THE COASTAL ROAD
SHORTER JOURNEYS
SCENES FROM A LIFE

The Children of the Nakba

Based on a True Story

DAVID CALDER

My books can be obtained either through my website, David Calder Books, or from quality brick and mortar and online book retailers.

ISBN:
ISBN 978-0-473-32791-0 (Paperback)
ISBN 978-0-473-32793-4 (Kindle)
ISBN 978-0-473-32792-7 (EPUB)

"In a liberation movement, political policy springs from the mouth of the rifle, and we in Fatah are fighters in the political field as well as the military field. Each field serves and complements the other within Fatah's general strategic plan. Thus, we do not differentiate between political action and military action, and to emphasize this; we refrain from sending to the armed resistance-field any combatant who has not passed through our political organization."

- Khalil al-Wazir (Abu Jihad), 1976

'And God said as for Ishmael, I have heard thee. Behold I have blessed him and will make him fruitful, and will multiply him exceedingly. Twelve princes shall he beget, and I will make him a great nation.'

- Genesis 17:20

'For your fathers' guilt you still must pay.'

- Horace, Perseus Project Odes 3, Poem 6, 23 BC.

'Even Satan has not yet invented the revenge for the blood of a child.'

- Chaim Nahman Bialik, Israeli Poet Laureate

For Immensely. Thank you for these journeys.

PROLOGUE

The *Nakba*, or 'Great Disaster,' is the Arabic name for the departure of hundreds of thousands of their people from what had been called 'Mandatory Palestine,' during the establishment of the State of Israel from 1947 to 1949.

This is how it came about.

In February 1947, British morale in 'Palestine,' where it had been administering the remnants of the Ottoman Empire under a 1922 League-of-Nations charter, was in tatters. Exhausted by hatred and terrorist attacks from all sides, they said they were withdrawing, and all their troops would be out by mid-May 1948.

The U. N. which had taken over from the League in 1945, saw a dual opportunity. A chance to appear statesman-like, and a solution to the Jewish refugee problem in Europe. The diplomatic body set about dividing up the greater Levant into separate ethnic states.

British intentions, to offer both Arabs and Jews a population-based fair share of the land, were honorable but completely unrealistic. Their father-knows-best approach also worsened matters. Dark tales exist of drunks in tents with pens and rulers, toying with the lives of hundreds of thousands, and cackling after every line drawn. It's true that geographic features like the Jordan River were used as sole guidelines, regardless of the actual affiliations of the residing human beings.

Machiavellian politics were dominant. The Arabs spouted born-again nationalism and resentment of the Jewish settlers, while still taking Jewish Authority land-money under the table. The Jews created an efficient network of underground militias, directly under British noses. Arab leaders such as Transjordan's King Abdullah licked their lips at the prospect of greater empires. The British didn't want the responsibility any more, but wanted to retain bases in the Negev Desert. They knew they were far more likely to do so with the Arabs in charge than the Jews.

The British had laid the foundations for a particularly vicious civil war by teaching both Arabs and Jews, guerrilla warfare. They'd long used the Arabs as shock troops, such as against the Turks, under T. E. Lawrence. British unorthodox-tactics genius, Col. Orde Wingate had trained the Jews as desert scouts for their assault on Ottoman-Syria, and to defend themselves against Arab riots. The single most hated tactic of the war to come, obliterating resisting settlements after driving away the inhabitants, was begun by the British. Deserters and renegades from British forces fanned the flames of outrage with atrocities such as the first Ben Yehuda Street bombing of 1948. A key component of the British occupational-infrastructure were dozens of fortified police emplacements called Tegart Forts. These were dealt out to both sides like houses in a Monopoly game, ensuring there'd be brutal fighting for each.

A peaceful transition had been a pipe dream. On November 29th 1947, the U.N. confirmed the arbitrary partitions and violence exploded.

The Arab forces were initially rag-tag irregulars, led by nationalist fanatic Fawzi al-Qawuqji. But no-one doubted that a full-scale invasion by the surrounding, though bitterly divided, Arab countries, was inevitable as soon as the last British troop ship sailed out of Haifa.

The opposing 538,000 Jews included those militias, the Haganah-Palmach, Irgun, and Lehi, battle hardened after years of resisting British rule. They were soon swelled by volunteers from the WWII Jewish Brigade of the British Military, and more than 1,000 *Machalniks* (non-Jewish volunteers) from all over the world.

As the war quickly became barbaric, with no-quarter Arab assaults on outlying Jewish settlements such as Gush Etzion, and those trying to supply them, as well as the Jewish-youth manned convoys attempting to break the blockage of Jerusalem. Infamously, doctors and nurses in makeshift armored buses trying to relieve Hadassah Medical Center on Jerusalem's Mount Scopus, were slaughtered while British troops stood by.

Undisciplined Jewish forces in turn killed many civilians at Deir Yassin in the Jerusalem hills. Arab prisoners were executed after bitter fighting at Ein al-Zeitun in the Galilee, partly in revenge for a 1929 slaughter of Jews by individuals from the same town. Routine dynamiting of captured Arab villages occasionally caused further civilian deaths.

By the end of 1948, flamethrowers were in use amid such mutual loathing that the winner was never going to be magnanimous.

Hajj Amin al-Husseini, the Grand Mufti of Jerusalem, was certain the Jews would be overwhelmed when the Arab League arrived in force. He knew well the power of propaganda after four years of exile in Nazi Germany. His people bombarded the Arab civilians from mobile loud-speakers, with promises that if they got out of the way of the battle to come, they would soon return to claim the spoils.

Instead the Jews were ascendant, driving further multitudes driven south into the Egyptian Sinai, north into Lebanon, east into Jordan and Syria, or elsewhere by sea from the ports of Jaffa and Haifa. Mainly into squalid refugee camps where they became and remain, the political pawns of their 'brothers' running those countries to the present day.

Over 700,000 Arab men, women, and children were displaced during the Nakba, taking only what they could carry, their memories of their olive groves and citrus orchards, and their tales of a lost life that would become ever more idyllic in the telling over the decades to come.

This is just one story from the whirlwind that is being reaped from the wind, then sewn.

ONE

Surviving a grenade explosion, especially one so close, is very much up to the vagaries of physics. The casings of the little Russian bastards are segmented, you see, but the wad of TNT inside doesn't shatter them evenly. There can be big gaps in the shrapnel. That's what saved Yossi Hochman's life, though there would be times he wished it hadn't. But that's for later.

Tyre, Lebanon
Thursday, November 10th, 1977, mid-afternoon

A uniformed and heavily perspiring fighter from Fatah, the armed wing of the PLO, the so-called 'Palestinian' Liberation Organization, stood on a low wooden platform blinking out at the arrayed ranks of troops before him. He wasn't sweating from heat. The sky was leaden and the wind prowling the town square was icy. He was terrified. His face still bled from a gun-butt interrogation. His hands were bound behind him. The muzzle of a Kalashnikov assault rifle was jammed into the back of his tunic.

Captain Fouad Mansour was in no doubt that he was doomed. His rank, worn honorably these many months in Fatah's service, was no protection now. He'd seen many of these charades before, never imagining he'd one day participate.

"Isn't that true Fouad? You are a filthy Israeli spy!" shrieked Azmi Zrayir, PLO commander of South Lebanon. Tall and lean, hawk-nosed, and with the eyes of the fanatic, Zrayir wore a traditional Bedouin robe accessorized by Fatah's trademark black and white checked keffiyeh-neck scarf. His voice dripped exaggerated disgust.

Zrayir wheeled to address the ranks of uniformed troops arrayed across the square. Displaying his full *Juhayman*, the stern visage of the warriors of his wandering tribe, he waved the evidence of Fouad's apostasy on high. It was a miniature copy of the Druze bible, the 'Epistles of Wisdom,' confiscated from Fouad's bedding during a surprise barracks inspection.

The Sunni Arabs that made up most of Fatah's ranks hated the Druze for their friendly relations with the Jews. Muslims in general considered the Druze sect, the Fatamids founded by the Iranian mystic Darazi and whose prophet is Jethro, father-in-law of Moses, to be heretics.

"All Fatamids are filthy spies," Zrayir declared, turning back to face his quivering victim. "Admit it or I will have your tongue cut out!"

Fouad's lips were paper-dry. He knew it to be no idle threat.

"I.... no, my Colonel. Yes, I am of the *al-Muwahhidin*, but I have served Fatah well." He nodded vigorously at the witnesses, "These men will testify for me!"

Zrayir turned theatrically to 'those' men. They stood straight-backed, eyes staring ahead. He swept out a white robe-draped arm, relishing the role of Allah's avenger. "Is that so?" The tone was oily. He shouted, "Who speaks for this Fatimid? Come forward and join him!"

The only movement across the square was a swirl of dust on a malevolent flick of wind. Deciding he'd imparted enough of a lesson for the day, Zrayir gestured dismissively with one hand. The hapless Fouad felt a rifle muzzle touch the back of his head, but never heard the discharge. His life-essence splashed out across the cobblestones.

Just another ordinary day among the ranks of the vilest terrorist army ever assembled.

Yarmouk Refugee Camp, South Damascus, Syria
same time

Within the PLO's heavily guarded headquarters, Khalil al-Wazir-Supreme Commander of the PLO's military wing, Fatah, was at his desk. His office door was closed. He was taking time out from the business of killing people to worry about his own problems. The most pressing of those was a woman.

While Khalil was his given name, he preferred his Arabic war name, his kunya - traditionally preceded by 'Abu,' meaning 'Father of.'

It was the name by which so many knew and feared him. Abu 'Jihad', 'Father of the Struggle.'

Jihad un-steepled his hands and reached for his cup. Sipped from it and grimaced. The coffee was cold. He'd lost track of time. Glancing across at the *Cezve* bubbling aromatically in the corner of his office, he started to lift his portly body from his plush office chair to refresh it.

The door opened and his intelligence chief, Salah Mesbah Khalaf, who also went by a kunya, Abu 'Iyad', meaning 'Power,' entered.

Jihad slumped back down and glared. *I should just go sit among the souks (markets) and be pestered by the beggars!*

There's more," Iyad said.

"There always is. Can't it wait?"

Iyad said, "Just so long as you know Yasser was there yesterday. In Cairo. He heard it all."

"Well he'll plague us I'm sure," responded Jihad grudgingly.

"Already is. Don't worry. I'll keep him at bay."

"Most appreciated," gritted Jihad. "Now I did ask to be left alone. We will talk tonight as agreed."

Iyad nodded elaborately and backed away.

Back at Iyad's own desk on the same second floor, he returned to checking reports. They were from his army of spies across the Middle East. But after a moment, he set them down and thought about the infuriating man in the other room.

We've known each other 17, no 18 years. He's a vain, emotional, immoral monster. Why do I defer to him that way?

Could I run Fatah just as well? Of course!

Be as ruthless? Absolutely!

But it was the information in front of him that gave the PLO and Fatah its edge in the great politico-military game that was the Middle East. Their ability to bind together the factions that made up the anti-Israel Arab bloc depended on it. Without it, without him, the movement would fragment into isolated cliques within weeks, each suspiciously regarding the others. Paralysis would follow. Their great mission, their drive for a homeland for their displaced followers, would come to nothing. Iyad shook his head resignedly. He and Jihad needed each other. They might as well be conjoined twins. To serve the cause and that evil man was his calling. He looked at the next report in the stack. One of his men in Amman had overheard a Jordanian army officer venting frustration with his King's constraints against direct anti-Israeli activities. Perhaps the man could be spurred to renegade action. Ever the spider in his lair, he made a note in a margin to follow up.

Jihad, with a fresh cup of *Kahve* (Turkish coffee made thick and dark,) with a piled spoonful of treacly brown sugar well stirred in, lapsed back into deep thought about his problem.

Sex was at the root of it.

He had traveled widely in the west since co-founding Fatah 18 years before, tirelessly promoting the displaced-Arab cause and scouring relentlessly for sources of weapons. Those 18 years included all the 'Swinging Sixties.'

He well understood his rock star status among the young people of the Middle East. Regardless that his women-followers wore burqa cloaks and hijab veils, and could be stoned to death if caught alone with a man, he and the other powerful terrorist leaders lived like the Caliphs; attracting groupies like hummingbirds to nectar. It was a job benefit he treasured.

Not that the sex was flaunted.

Darkened trucks moved around the refugee camps late at night. Doors opened and closed. Lights flickered on and off. All repeated shortly before dawn. Conservative women raised their hijabs to eye level and kept their gossip within their closest circle.

Fighters and young progressive women kept their envy to themselves.

Given that the lives of his retinue were at his whim, he'd been completely certain not one word about it would ever get back to the powerful, conservative, and often highly religious regional leaders on whom his status, funding and flow of arms depended.

With this woman, he'd been completely wrong.

Losing his piece on the side wasn't Jihad's concern. Losing respect, which he craved above all else, most certainly was. He was accustomed to being feted by and mingling with world leaders at will, despite what wider society might think of him or his organization. Just weeks back, it had been the Soviets kowtowing to his delegation at their Kremlin: that wrinkled old man Brezhnev.

Who could have imagined the all-powerful leader of a 266 million-member empire would ingratiate himself to a grocer's son expelled penniless from Ramla by the loathsome Jews?

Never mind that I was in the company of that timid, albeit politically shrewd, little lizard Yasser.

It was MY power and might they were bowing and scraping to!

MINE!

Yet this... woman threatened all of that. He balled his fists in frustration edged with more than a little fear.

How can something as insignificant as a woman, in fact one less than half my age, threaten everything?

He gulped some coffee, wishing he'd thought to sprinkle in a pinch of hashish to calm his nerves. His thoughts switched to his marriage. His demure and compliant Intissar, ignorantly and comfortably domiciled on Damascus' fashionable, if any part of a slum could be considered such, Loubia Street, immediately came to mind. She was also his cousin, which, he abruptly realized, added a whole dimension of extended-family stress if the marriage were to collapse.

I hadn't even thought about Ali and her uncles. Sharmuta! They say Tunisian blood feuds go on forever!

And what of his sons, Jihad and Bassem, for whom he had such big plans? And his daughters, Iman and Hanan, whom he loved dearly? In another plunge into the emotional chasm, he saw himself ostracized on the world stage and ridiculed as a philanderer. Even worse, an incompetent one!

Why? Why?

Jihad knew very well why.

Though his family was a delight to come home to, he was a man with an enormous sex drive, adventurous tastes, and a conviction that when it came to fucking, enthusiasm was almost everything.

Intissar, the perfect Muslim wife, wouldn't know the meaning of either word.

Really, though, that was just background. It had been his stupid assumption that what happened in Lebanon would stay in Lebanon, which had led to this. He was omnipotent. A simple command that the woman wasn't to be allowed out of Lebanon would have saved him.

Instead, she'd turned up here at his Damascus headquarters in PUBLIC, demanding to be noticed. How long could he expect to keep the affair private after that?

His knees trembled under the table. His sphincter tightened involuntarily at the enormity of it all.

The caliphs used to execute adulterers that way, with the hot.... Allah save me! I need to do something, and swiftly.

Even the last resort of all men of power, bribery, hadn't worked. Dalal Mughrabi had turned down flat an offer of a political posting to Rome, weepily declaring she wanted to be a fighter like him. And with him!

He shuddered to the core.

Still, he had to say, in that there was at least some logic. She'd out-trained and out-shot every other candidate in her class while becoming a commissioned lieutenant in one of his brigades. She was quite a woman, in fact. Nineteen and voluptuous compared to Intissar's bag-of-bones build. A trained nurse also, and superb with the children at her post at Dbaiyeh, 10 miles northeast of Beirut.

And exhilarating on a mattress! Ah, the things she can do with that fantastic mouth! Not to mention being suitably subservient otherwise. If only she had stayed in her place, we might have gone on forever!

Jihad dragged himself back to reality. The cursed woman always seemed to have that effect.

Perhaps she's a witch!

No! The situation was untenable. He simply had to make it all go away.

Can I just have her shot? No. Not so soon after her visit. It has to be something more subtle.

But he had no more time to waste on this now. After all, he did have a war to run. And the crisis Iyad had been referring to, this new peace initiative between Egypt and Israel, might yet dwarf everything else.

TWO

Cairo

Wednesday, November 9th, previous afternoon

President Anwar Sadat, a small, nattily dressed 58-year-old with sharp features receding back into dark frizzy hair, drew a hush from the floor of the Egyptian Parliament when he rose to speak a little after 4:00 p.m. He looked beyond the spotlight, around the great circular chamber, at the several hundred delegates and guests. He noted the sprinkling of hijabs, Egypt having granted women the vote in 1956, and the unusually large proportion of high-ranking military officers in khaki uniforms with broad splashes of decorations across their chests.

An aide stepped to his elbow as he rearranged his notes and whispered, "They smell something in the wind.

They're staking out their positions, Sadat thought.

No matter. I'd be doing the same.

This joint parliamentary session was the 25th anniversary of the Second People's Revolution over the Egyptian monarchy. He'd played a significant part in that. He followed protocol and paid generous lip service, slipping in some financial matters he knew would be controversial if he provided too much detail. Then got down to the subject most on his mind.

"Brothers and Sisters, Members of the People's Assembly, the time has come to put an end to the conflict with our neighbors to the north, which has resulted in such bloodshed for so long, among the flower of our youth. And if not ended, will lead to our irrevocable financial ruin. I am prepared to go to the end of the world, and Israel will be surprised to hear me say this, even to their Knesset itself to argue with them, if it will prevent one more Egyptian soldier from being wounded, or one more Piastre being wasted on pointless war. Members of the People's Assembly, we have no time to waste."

The resulting hush extended into a stunned silence, eventually broken by applause that spread enthusiastically throughout the building. Astonishment was everywhere. Nowhere more pronounced than in the grizzled and acne-scarred face of a pudgy 47-year-old former civil engineer dressed in green fatigues, a black and white checked keffiyeh and scuffed combat boots. PLO Chairman Yasser Arafat was never one to primp for public occasions.

Arafat looked sideways at his senior adviser Farouk Al-Kaddoumi, who was Algerian.

"*Mon Dieu, Mon Dieu*," he whispered in wonder."*Monsieur Sadat qu'avez-vous fait?*' (Mr. Sadat, what have you done?)

He remained seated, head down on his chest, considering what this meant for his exiled people.

The applause was succeeded by the hurrying feet of press members scrambling for the public phones.

Jerusalem

later the same evening

"It's a ploy," said Israeli Defense Minister Ezer Weizman, a tall and rail-thin, brisk-mannered, 54-year-old-with a thick brush mustache and frizzy brown hair receding like Sadat's. "Plain and simple. He can't possibly mean it!"

The venue was purposely unimpressive: the second-floor Prime Minister's Offices on Kaplan Street, Givat Ram. Only a cheery fire broke the austerity. The four other men present said nothing for the moment. Each was mulling over, from his own perspective, the opportunities and risks of Sadat's bombshell announcement.

"He doesn't really intend to come here," Weizman expanded emphatically. "He's only saying that to look good in Geneva!" He paced a couple of steps before adding, "The Syrians wouldn't consider it for a start and a fragmented Arab bloc plays into our hands, not his. Nor will the PLO accept it. They will fear Jordan and perhaps Lebanon will follow and they'll be excluded."

"I'm not so sure," offered Yechiel Kadishai, the 55-year-old chief of the Prime Minister's Department. He looked at his boss, who was the only one seated. And in a wheelchair, at that. "Sadat is at least correct that this endless arms race will bankrupt us all if someone doesn't come to their senses. Remember, he also mentioned new taxes in his speech. They can hardly afford to keep up their numbers in Sinai, let alone mount another offensive. As for us, we'd be broke already except for the $3 billion a year from the Americans."

"And I don't agree with you at all, Ezer" said 63-year-old Moshe Dayan, the bald, eye-patched Minister of Foreign Affairs, smiling sardonically as if at some inner joke. "When you make war on a country twice and get your ass kicked both times, it's not weakness to seek peace. It's common sense. I know. I did most of the kicking. Sadat is a sensible man. I think he is sincere."

"You think?" retorted Weizman.

"My experience is when the Arabs say one thing, expect the opposite. Remember their ambush in 1973? I'd recommend we strengthen the borders."

There was a grunt from a barrel-chested man leaning against the mantelpiece. Fifty-one-year-old Yitzhak Hofi, known as 'Chaka' since his days in the Palmach back before he was a senior IDF General, was famous for being of few words and making each one count. He'd arrived late from Mossad's HQ on King Saul Boulevard in Tel Aviv, but quickly caught up with the conversation.

"You speak, Ezer, as if this is a military problem you can solve with troops. Besides, my department knew perfectly well what was happening previous to Yom Kippur. That's how we took out their air forces."

He stepped away from the fireplace to use his hands for emphasis. "This, it's a matter of clarity. I admit my men in Cairo did not see this precise peace initiative coming, but we all knew there were signs. As that American song goes, 'you don't need a weatherman to know which way the wind blows.' I say wait and see!"

"Well then... Chaka," Weizman sneered, reflecting the natural tension between the military and clandestine branches of Israel's defense forces. "If I have to do the waiting, you better damn well be doing the seeing!"

Stepping forward to the table between them all, Hofi lifted a cup of coffee from a silver tray, extending the moment just to taunt his rival. "I will certainly be doing that," he intoned as he brought it to his lips.

"Ahem." said a gravelly voice. All turned to 64-year-old, Polish born former lawyer, urban guerrilla and finally politician, Menachem Begin. A glance would have told anyone the man was severely unwell.

Begin had suffered a heart inflammation earlier in the year while leading his Likud party to power in a huge upset He was now on heavy medication: the reason his long-time friend Kadishai hovered so closely and concernedly.

He raised a hand and let it drop while surveying the group through round-framed, thick-lensed glasses. It seemed to have taken enormous effort, but when he spoke his voice was strong and precise.

"Whether it's a feint, as Ezer says, expedient as Yechiel suggests, common sense as Moshe feels, or something that needs more digging into as Chaka believes, I say it is an opportunity we must seize now! I will receive him." He fluttered a hand weakly. "Yechiel, please give me a date the Knesset is sitting. Not too soon."

Kadishai consulted a notebook. "The twentieth. Sunday fortnight."

"I will receive him then and we will talk peace. If it goes well, I will meet him again with President Carter." He paused for breath. “In the spring. Perhaps March. Yechiel please stay a minute and help me draft a statement."

"Yes 'Chem."

"Then I must rest or endure wrath. Doctors! Pah! What do they know?"

"A lot!" declared Kadishai.

The other three men bowed their respects and left the room.

Yarmouk
November 10th, evening

The evening of the 10th was abnormally cold for November. Also, murky and fetid with the smog from the central souks, which watered the eyes of the truck drivers, as it drifted across the Ibn al-Abbas highway, beyond to the Jebel Aannter hills, and then to Beirut, 55 miles to the west.

Jihad and Iyad observed the gloom through the bullet-proof picture window in Jihad's office. It mirrored their moods.

Both were rotund men, 43 and 45 respectively, with typically oval northern Arab features. A fly on the wall might have noticed Jihad, with his hands clasped behind his back, uncannily resembled a well-known portrait of Napoleon Bonaparte. Otherwise, from the severe cut of their suits, they might have been bankers instead of mass murderers.

However, it was fresh intelligence that was a little more concerning than red ink on a spreadsheet which had prompted the meeting. "If Sadat makes peace with Israel, at best we will be marginalized as nothing but another protest group, and at worst others will follow like dominoes."

Jihad nodded gravely.

"The Americans want peace desperately," Iyad observed, "particularly their Democrats. The Jewish American bloc values Israel's security through peace, above all else. They are crucial to Jimmy Carter's re-election in three years' time. He's a much liked, but weak man, and vulnerable on almost all other fronts."

Jihad pursed his lips, but made no comment.

"My contact in the Knesset says Begin will seek to meet with Carter in Washington in March," Iyad added. "If progress has been made on peace between Egypt and Israel by then, we can expect an all-out push by the Americans to advance the initiative. And the dominoes to tremble."

Jihad said quietly, "We must prevent that if we can, or at least steal the focus if we cannot."

"Yes."

"We will need martyrs," said Jihad.

Jerusalem
November 11th

Menachem Begin, looking worn, gave a live address from his office, on black and white television, the next afternoon. It was intended to reach in transmission and tone far beyond Israel's borders.

"Citizens of Egypt. This is the first time I address you directly, but not for the first time that I think and speak of you. You are our neighbors and always will be. We, the Israelis, stretch out our hand to you. It is not, as you know, a weak hand. If attacked we shall always defend ourselves. But your President said two days ago that he is ready to come to Jerusalem. It will be a pleasure to welcome and receive him with the hospitality you and we have inherited from our common father, Abraham. And I, for my part, will be glad to come to your capital Cairo for the same purpose.

No more wars.

Peace.

A real peace and forever."

Jihad watched glumly from his fortified villa at Yarmouk. His lips drew thin. His troubles were deepening. But so was his formidable resolve.

THREE

Yarmouk
Saturday, November 12th, afternoon
"Do you ever think about how all this started?" Jihad asked. "Deir Yassin?"

"I busy myself more with current events, Khalil," replied Iyad. "It's what you and Fatah pay me for. If I need motivation, I need only think of my youth in *Yafo*." He meant Jaffa, the old town part of Tel Avlv. "I was 15 when the mortar bombs started to come down, you know. I don't need other examples."

"Perhaps not, but the story we tell is important. We send so many young men to their deaths, you and I Salah. They need something to believe in. Whether it's true or not."

Iyad recognized the pensive mood and resigned himself to one of his boss's monologues. Though they were at least informative, due to Jihad's seemingly encyclopedic memory.

"On the last Monday of March 1948," Jihad said musingly, "While civil order was collapsing following the British announcing they were leaving, the leaders of the Irgun, Lehi, the Haganah and their sub-group the Palmach-the partisan groups fighting for a Jewish state, got together in Jerusalem to talk about Deir Yassin. Menachem Begin was there. He was head of Irgun.

Deir Yassin was an Arab limestone-mining village of about 600 persons and 144 buildings on a hilltop a short distance west of Jerusalem. Not large. Not small. Peaceful. They had no problems with the Jews. In fact, they'd signed a peace-pact with those same Jewish leaders. Or their *Mukhtar* (Mayor) had. Still, if the village was to rise up during the hostilities, everyone knew were coming, they could make it difficult for the settlements nearby. Even threaten traffic on the major highway below.

The Jewish militants decided to set an example by assaulting the village while simultaneously warning the residents to evacuate. The opportunity seemed ideal on too many levels to pass up. It would be great training for new recruits, proof that the Jews were serious people, casualties should be insignificant, and pictures of the Arabs fleeing their advance would make great press.

Soon after that planning meeting, Jewish confidence soared even higher after a lightning raid that seized the entire armory of the British Army camp at Pardes Hanna.

Well before dawn on Friday, April 9th, 120 Jewish fighters, including many newly deployed and non-Hebrew-speaking Machalniks, arrived in trucks and fanned out for the attack. At 4:00 a.m. a junior commander named Yitzchak Rav, from the Haganah, waved a Webley .455 caliber revolver, complete with a brand-new officer's lanyard, high in the air and said in an English cockney accent, "That's it, boys and girls, let's move!"

"Rav?" interjected Iyad

"Rav."

"Yes, I've heard of him. He and his men stood with their PIATs against the Syrian tanks in the Kinarot Valley. Can't have been many weeks later."

"Ah, so you do follow history," said Jihad curtly. "Well, that battle was a loss for our cause as well, and I wouldn't go repeating anything else that makes the Jews look good either. I'm sure there are many other tales, but just hear this one out."

Iyad knew better than to further irritate his notoriously short-tempered leader.

"But of course, there was no warning broadcast," Jihad continued. "Our recruiters say one was never intended, but the truth is the truck with the loudspeaker got stuck in a ditch, miles away. This was the first combined fight by the Jewish groups. The poorly trained attackers with their Enfield rifles - some still slippery with delivery-grease, and their Sten-guns and Mills grenades, had to figure it out as they went along. Advancing from three sides, they disturbed a sentry at about 4:45 a.m. and the shooting started.

But instead of fleeing as expected, the defenders put up a stiff fight, including some deadly sniper fire from the Mukhtar's house.

Due to the language barrier between the new foreigners and the locally born Sabras, and also the groups using different radio frequencies, command and control rapidly deteriorated into chaos amid the smoke, dust, roar of gunfire, and shrieks of bullets ricocheting from stone walls. The Irgun commander, Ben-Zion Cohen, was seriously wounded by friendly fire, and at 7:00 a.m. the Irgun wanted to withdraw in defeat, while the Haganah was reporting imminent victory.

But gradually the Jewish attackers regrouped and in the cold light of dawn began a crude but effective house-to-house advance through the village, throwing grenades through windows at the terrified Arab families sheltering within, then firing inside until the screaming ceased. By 8:00 a.m. there were many wounded civilians."

Jihad paused.

"You don't get involved in recruiting much, do you Salah?"

Iyad was affronted.

"My people keep your operations folks well informed of fertile ground. I keep in touch with it. But my job is a little more strategic than that, wouldn't you think?"

"Yes, and you do it well."

Iyad inclined his forehead in acceptance of the olive branch.

Jihad said. "It's just we don't mention this next part during our speeches. When the screaming of those wounded reached a crescendo, some invaders, again led by Yitzchak Rav, formed a protective wall and began carrying the injured from houses on beds."

"I can see why it doesn't come up," said Iyad.

"Yes, but fortunately for our propaganda purposes, it was only temporary," said Jihad. "Jewish senior commanders decreed there would be no mercy. The would-be Samaritans discontinued their efforts under a tongue-lashing."

“Shortly after that explosives were called up, and the attackers began blasting their way through the low brick homes, burying Arab fighters and cowering families alike. Finally, at around 10:00 a.m. a Palmach-manned armored vehicle arrived, and obliterated the last of the Arab resistance with some two-inch mortar rounds.

At a Jewish cost of five dead and 35 wounded, 107 Arabs lay dead. Among them were babes-in-arms, and children only one or two years old. There were also many wounded. Over 100 others had been taken prisoner.”

After another pause, Jihad added quietly, "They shot some of those too, you know. In a brick merchant's yard. That much of what we say is true.”

"The prisoners?"

"Yes. After they had been marched through West Jerusalem. It drew quite a crowd."

"The shootings or the marching?”

"Sometimes I wonder about your attention span Salah."

Iyad rubbed his forehead wearily. "Well, it's served you well enough since Algeria, hasn't it? That's what... 16 years now? God, we were so young!"

He pinched the bridge of his nose.

"No, I knew what you meant, and I'm sure it's compelling information also.

I must be just... getting a little tired."

"Then just do your job. Give me options. What about our European friends?"

Iyad knew exactly what Jihad wanted. Resources for this current operation.

"There aren't too many at the moment," he finally offered.

"What about the PFLP? Wadi Haddad and his Uruguayan. What's his, ummm...?" Jihad snapped his fingers.

"Carlos,” Iyad confirmed. “And he's Venezuelan. And probably in Yemen with Haddad, since the old man's leukemia has gotten worse. Or maybe in East Germany, under Chancellor Honecker's protection. That's all out of the question, anyway. The

PFLP is only waiting for Haddad to die so they can pick over the pieces. Probably George Habash will step back in."

"Habash just wants to play politics."

"No argument there."

Jihad turned his back to the window and leaned against the sill, hands braced at his sides.

"Couldn't we use some of their European proxies if Haddad's gone quiet? The PFLP's had success with that. Why can't we?"

Iyad scratched the back of his head.

"For a start, the Jews killed Wilfried Bose and Brigitte Kuhlman at Entebbe. They were the hard core of the Revolutionary Cells. The June 2nd group is out of play at the moment too. I hear Gabrielle Tiedemann and Christian Moller have an operation happening in Vienna."

"Vienna? Wasn't she there with your Venezuelan, when he seized the OPEC Ministers a couple of years back? You'd think she'd have the intelligence to stay away."

"Yes, she was. Killed two men. That's part of the problem. She's vicious and volatile. No one wants to work with her."

"What about the South Americans?"

"Well the Tupamaros are contracting out their work these days. They had a new French breakaway group, the Brigades Internationales, take out a Colonel Trabal for them in Lyon. A revenge hit for the Uruguayan government not releasing their leader, Jose Mujica."

"What about those Australians we had here in training?"

"The Croatian Brotherhood? Wannabees. That's mostly come apart. No help there."

"Well, there must be someone we can use?"

"No one I can think of, that we can be sure the Mossad hasn't infiltrated."

"What about Abu Nidal? Can we make peace there, just for one operation?"

Iyad snorted.

"That drunken maniac? You're joking, of course. He's been trying to kill me since '74. I'd get in first if he wasn't in Baghdad under the protection of General Hussein, who's running Iraq now by the way. No! Most certainly not!"

He rose from his seat and walked closer to Jihad, gesturing with his hands for effect.

"I'm telling you! There's no one reliable that I can be sure the Mossad isn't listening in on. Not Ahmed Jibril. Not Action Directe, that's the name-of-the-month the French group is going by now. No one! We will have to use our own people. What about Daoud?"

Jihad chewed on this for a few moments. Mohammed Daoud Odeh - Abu Daoud, was his top commander in the war that had enveloped Lebanon in the fire and horror of the last three years. "I can't spare him."

"Force 17 then." Iyad meant the original PLO bodyguard force that had kept Arafat, Jihad and numerous others alive during the Jordanian civil war. "Under the Red Prince."

Ah, the Prince, thought Jihad. Abu Hassan Salameh. The man the Israelis blame for the Munich Olympics massacre. As it happened, unfairly, since the planning had been done by Iyad and Daoud with Salameh a mere go-between.

"No, he's in Beirut, besotted with that Miss Universe woman."

"Georgina Rizk." Iyad grinned despite himself. "There might be worse things to be obsessed with."

"Yes, I hear he plans to marry her, and when he's not with her he's looking over his shoulder for Mossad. Now he has something to lose, he's lost the heart for anything else."

The conversation dwindled into silence.

Jihad turned back to his gazing from his office window, at the jumble of spires and square tiny-windowed buildings casting long shadows across the maze of narrow stone streets that was south central Damascus. A minute passed. Two.

Then all hard-edged again, Jihad said, "Now I must think more about our dilemma with Egypt. Please let me know when there is anything more that's important."

"I most certainly will," said Iyad dryly, and left Jihad to his brooding.

FOUR

Yarmouk
Saturday, November 12th, evening

Jihad already had in mind a working plan for thwarting this Egyptian-Israeli peace initiative.

It required a direct attack on Israel's civilian population: the one thing guaranteed to divert Israel's eyes from the world stage, force it to look inward and recognize its vulnerability, and remind it what would happen if the displaced-Arab issue was not foremost in everything it did.

He considered himself a master at this. His last masterpiece took place in 1975. What the Israelis had called the Savoy Operation: a ruthless foray into the beach-side area of Tel Aviv that had ended in blood and flames with the destruction of an entire hotel.

Despite his verbal sparring match with Iyad, he'd already known he'd have to find his resources close at hand.

That was always the challenge.

Finding people to carry out his psychopathic dramas.

You just didn't find disciples willing to slaughter people for a cause, and die in the process if necessary, on just any street corner. Not even in this dangerous part of the world.

And once you found candidates, what attributes are you really looking for? Are the best and brightest, the most likely to go the distance? Or will they simply think too much?

Not that intelligence is necessarily incompatible with brutality. The PFLP terrorist leaders Haddad and Habash are both medical doctors.

Perhaps the worst and dumbest are a better choice, on the basis that anyone else will know better. Would they have sufficient intelligence and imagination to find their way through Israel's land or sea defenses? And what about leadership? Do you promote on merit?

Jihad rid himself of those negative thoughts.

None of this would be simple or easy.

In his favor, the most fertile terrorist recruiting ground ever known: the Lebanese Civil War, lay all about him. His organization, in fact, had started it two and half years earlier in April 1975. Fatah fighters had attacked a Beirut church, setting off a seemingly endless cycle of alternating Christian versus Muslim reprisals.

Conveniently, the war was in a state of uneasy calm. For some weeks, violence had only seemed to break out when one group interfered with travel on a highway controlled by another. Surprising, really, since he knew of more than twenty-two armed groups operating within the country. Sometimes it seemed every enclave, suburb and town had its own militia, aligned according to the ethnic or religious breakdown of the population. Still, things were quiet, with none of the rural atrocities that had marked 1976, such as the butchery at Aishiyeh and Damour.

Territorial boundaries were also fairly static, with Jihad's Muslims entrenched in West Beirut and the Christians dug in on the other side of the no-man's-land called the 'Green Line.' Travel near the fronts was safer than it had been in months. All the better to cast his net among all the Muslims involved in the conflict, not just Fatah alone.

While the senior commanders of those militias weren't directly under his command, but from the regular armies of their sponsoring countries, the junior officers were invariably displaced-Arabs and in no doubt that Fatah was the big dog on the block. Regardless of affiliation, the groups were generally happy to cooperate unless the objective conflicted with their own specific goals. That would never be the case with an attack on the universally hated Israel.

He recalled a Time Magazine article, in which a reporter interviewed an Arab fighter near the Beirut front lines. The man had said he was a sniper working on top of a bombed-out apartment building and had taken the reporter up to show him. There he had a Dragunov sniper rifle, a sandbag to rest it on, a box of bullets and a piece of chalk. When asked what the chalk was for, the man said every time he shot some woman or child scrounging for food in the rubble, he would make a mark on the parapet and an officer would come around and pay him one Lebanese pound, a few American cents, for each. The horrified reporter asked, "Why don't you make the marks, throw away the ammunition, and spare the lives?" The offended man drew himself to his full height, and snapped, "Of course not! I am an honorable man!"

Such were the twisted minds of many in the fight, but Jihad needed operatives with greater clarity of mind than that; the dedicated but not the fanatical; a team... no, teams that he could bind together by their shared hatred of Israel.

And there was plenty of hatred to go around.

If you were of displaced-Arab descent and one of the *Fedayeen,* those who sacrifice, two things drove you. *Sharifa* (national pride,) and an abhorrence of Israel rooted as Jihad's was in al-Nakba. For a whole generation of children coming of age in the 1970s, the stories passed down from their parents had morphed into a truth all of its own, engendering a zealous loathing of all things Jewish. Of course, there were always hardcore jihadists who saw the world only in terms of Islam against everyone else, and others who were simply adventurers or mercenaries doing a job. But for most, a hunger for a 'Palestine' that had never in fact existed, and an enduring and unreasoning hatred of Israel for taking from them what they had never had, obsessed every bone in their body, every moment of every day.

Jihad lifted his head, wondering if he should have coffee to break him out of all this deep thinking. After all, the important thing was the 'what,' not the 'why'. He needed to start reaching out quickly. Who knew how fast this situation between Egypt and the Israelis might escalate?

Overall approach confirmed in his devious mind, Jihad began extending feelers out to the militias operating around

Lebanon. The centers of such operations were the displaced-Arab refugee camps.

The largest of those were; Shatila-which occupied most of the Beirut suburb of Sabra, Burj Barajneh-further south near the shell-cratered airport, Dbaiyeh on the northwest Lebanese coast, and Rashidiyeh-at Tyre on the southwest coast.

The regional telephone system, though degraded by two years of war, still reached most areas. In some cases, when he had additional information to disseminate that wasn't safe from Israeli spies if spoken aloud, he dispatched couriers in small convoys of Toyota Hilux pickup trucks with .50-caliber machine-guns mounted on the beds.

The basic message was the same for all. He was looking for volunteers of displaced-Arab extraction, with front-line experience if possible, but with sufficient basic military training if not, and above all the desire to strike Israel at its heart. That it was almost certainly a one-way mission went unspoken.

This all underway, he placed a final call to his senior leader in South Lebanon. That man, Azmi Zrayir, was beneath only Abu Daoud in the Fatah command hierarchy, with over 1500 Fedayeen under his command. It wasn't a call he'd looked forward to.

Jihad considered the devout Zrayir a zealot, known to execute errant fighters for trivial infringements-sometimes by dragging them behind trucks. But he was a fierce and effective commander, and Jihad had no choice but to tolerate him.

When Zrayir came on the line, Jihad first had to listen through numerous "Allah-be-praiseds," at which he wrinkled his nose. He'd often found obsequiousness a sign of hidden ambitions, and long believed the ascetic Lebanese would one day become too big for his keffiyeh. But that was a matter for the future. For now, he needed the man.

Jihad explained roughly what his plan was, ending with, "I will be relying on you for logistical support for the mission, including training and launching facilities, as well as weapons and equipment."

"Allah bless you for bestowing this trust, *Effendi*," effused Zrayir.

"I have told you before Azmi, we are all equals under the banner of Fatah."

"Forgive me, Eff... I will not let you down!"

I guarantee you that, promised Jihad to himself.

"Why at my headquarters, I have such a man now," offered Zrayir. "A fisherman's son from Batroun, Mahmoud Ali Abu Naif. Only 22, but a capable man and a good leader. He's recovering from minor wounds."

Well, he at least knows men. Something to consider, anyway.

"I will take your suggestion under consideration, Azmi, and perhaps meet with this man when things are clearer. Keep him around your camp for now."

"As you wish, Effendi."

Jihad sighed in irritation, but let it pass.

"And I do. Now, in the meantime, please consider my needs and send details of any suitable candidates to me in Damascus."

"Allah be with you, Effendi."

"And you Azmi."

Regular military affairs kept Jihad occupied most of the following week. But before getting down to business at the regular end-of-week round-table meeting, he asked Iyad to update him on what his spies were hearing about Egypt and Israel.

"You will recall we fired some rockets over the Lebanese border into Nahariya the week before last. Word is they caused some casualties, but there's been no significant retaliation."

"Very good," said Jihad to nods all around the table. "If we have the ammunition, we should keep that up."

"We might want to be a bit careful, though," Iyad added, "Weizman threatened in the Knesset on Monday to carpet bomb our launch area if we do it again."

"Let's give it some time then. What about the TV appearance you were talking about?"

"Yes. Walter Cronkite had both Begin and Sadat on his CBS News Hour by satellite link on Monday night. They spoke of negotiations with, quote, 'no prior conditions.' You know what that's shorthand for!"

"Yes. Throwing us on the scrap-heap. What about the hawks and doves in the Knesset?"

Iyad pursed his lips, knowing his boss was about to be displeased.

"One thing before that. On Tuesday Begin sent a formal invitation to Egypt for a Sadat state visit. My man in the Israeli President's office saw the document himself. It's been accepted, but they're keeping it quiet. Juggling the timing around their holy day, the *Shabbat*."

"*Ebn El Sharmuta!*" (Son of a whore,) Jihad spat. "I was hoping it was all just talk. What date?"

"Nineteenth."

"*Khara!* (Shit!) That's tomorrow!"

"Sorry. Only learned that this morning. We could organize a reception..."

Jihad thought about that. "No. Not enough time."

"Okay. Anyway, hawks and doves. Weizman is being a hard-ass, of course. So is their Army Chief of Staff, Gur. He accused Egypt Tuesday of a secret buildup of forces. It's not true as far as I can tell. Dayan was on the radio on Wednesday, saying Israel should applaud the Egyptian change of position after 29 years of hostility. Overall? Not good."

What's that American saying? Jihad thought. *La Khara Sherlock?*

"Well, keep me advised."

"I will do that."

Jihad's fears were compounding, but his plan was on track and he thought he had time to spare. He shifted his attention to other operational matters while waiting for his orders to begin delivering results.

FIVE

South of Tel Aviv
Saturday, November 19th, dusk

As a third and Shabbat-ending star blinked to life over the Sinai Desert, a series of events began, which many watching from below had believed they would never see in their lifetime.

An Egyptair Ilyushin IL-62 passenger jet entered Israeli airspace unmolested. The six MIG-21 fighter jets escorting it flashed their wing lights and peeled away to the south. An equal number of Kfir C.2s took formation on either side for the rest of its historic journey north.

Within the hour, while Jihad in Damascus stared sullenly at his television, the aircraft touched down at Tel Aviv's Ben Gurion airport and taxied to a place of honor. Anwar Sadat augustly descended a ramp of stairs to the tarmac and was embraced by Menachem Begin. Crowds cheered. Brass bands blared. A 21-gun salute thundered.

The next morning Begin, in the Knesset in Jerusalem, acknowledged Sadat like a long-lost friend, declaring, "We welcome you here today and honor your courage. Everything can be negotiated and must be negotiated."

Over the next four weeks, things for Jihad and Fatah deteriorated from farce to fiasco.

Iyad's regular verbal bulletins described a river of congratulatory and conciliatory messages flowing between Egyptian officials and anyone who mattered in Israeli politics. Opposition Leader Shimon Peres, President Ephraim Katzir, and even Golda Meir despite her famous saying, "We will have peace when they love their children more than they hate us," and the illness that would take her life a year later; joined in.

On November 23rd, on Israeli television, Foreign Minister Dayan proposed new Egypt-Israeli talks in Geneva to build on the disengagement agreement signed after the 1973 Yom Kippur War. He hoped other Arab leaders would participate.

Within three more days, Sadat was offering open discussions in Cairo as soon as the 3rd of December and lobbying Syria, Jordan, and Lebanon to be involved. The U.S. enthusiastically chimed in, asking that the talks be delayed to increase the chances of more nations attending.

By the 28th, Begin had formally agreed to attend, in a letter to Egyptian acting Foreign Minister Boutros Ghali. President Jimmy Carter and his Secretary of State Cyrus Vance kept the momentum going with positive statements on the 30th and December 6th. Vance also announced a Middle East visit to both countries, to take place the second week of December.

The promised conference began on December 14th with only Egyptian, Israeli, and U.S. delegates attending, but Begin made a surprise visit to Washington the same day to plead Israel's case to Carter.

It was Jihad's worse nightmare become real.

Whatever else might be said of him, he was not a felon, and had never enriched himself from the millions in foreign aid Fatah received. Though he was feeling some pangs of regret about that.

In his mind's eye, he could see the comfortable, respected dotage he'd always imagined, basking in the glow of having secured a homeland for his people, shrinking down to a miserable existence in a 100 peso a month Cuban tenement, looking over his shoulder for the icepicks like Leon Trotsky.

On the afternoon of Sunday, December 18th, Iyad was summoned to Jihad's office. He found his boss reviewing files at the large conference table. Each had a large photo pinned to the cover. He waited nonchalantly, until Jihad looked up and growled, "Tell me some good news."

"There isn't much unless you are counting on the UN to be practical, in which case you probably also believe in djinns," Iyad replied mildly.

"Oh? What's their latest fantastic plan to solve the world's problems?"

"The usual number soup. Resolutions 32/20 and 32/40. Full recognition of our rights would you believe?"

"Really? And they plan to invade Israel to impose those, of course?"

"The resolutions will die in the Security Council from a U.S. veto, as always."

"What a surprise!" snarled Jihad, clearly even testier than usual. He gestured at the stack of paperwork. "Anyway, I wanted your view on these."

"That's your shortlist?" asked Iyad, moving closer.

"I'm calling it Operation Kamal Adwan."

The name needed no clarification. The former PLO spokesman, killed in a 1973 Israeli commando raid on Beirut, had been close to both of them.

Iyad indulged his boss by pulling over the pile of dossiers and rifling through them, though he already knew every detail of each fighter, since everything crossed his desk first whether Jihad knew it or not.

"I don't see the big Syrian, Ahmadi."

"Killed at Jounieh last week," said Jihad, referring to a Lebanese coastal town that marked the northwest boundary of Fatah territory.

"Pity. How about the South American, Rodriguez?"

"He's crazy. Threw a grenade at a couple of comrades during a squabble at a roadblock. I'm having him shot."

Iyad slid the paperwork back across the table. "The rest look okay. Except one. Some I know fairly well, like that big Kuwaiti camp guard at Shatila and the Jordanian boy Ramez.'

Iyad picked up a picture of the slim, cold-eyed youth, then tossed it back. "I was at that meeting. An emotional youth, as I recall. But he does do cold blooded work!"

"Good to know," Jihad commented. "The two Gazans and the West Bankers look capable. I'm not sure about the boy from Ramallah, from those riots, but I'll look at him just the same. Which one worries you?"

Iyad's jaw set rock hard. "You know which one, Khalil. He's been nothing but trouble. It's all I can do to stop scar-faced Mohammed from cutting his throat in an alley!"

"Well, I knew his parents," said Jihad. "I put him into intelligence with you because I believed he had promise. He did well enough in Tel Aviv, didn't he?"

"Yes, he did," admitted Iyad.

"Well, this will solve your problem, then won't it?"

Iyad conceded that point also.

The morning of Monday, December 19th, dawned drizzly and gray in Beirut.

The night before, Jihad had traveled by small military convoy along a circuitous and closely guarded route from Damascus to Shatila Camp.

While the city was waking up, dressed in the dark double-breasted suit that was as much his trademark as Arafat's fatigues, boots, and black-and-white keffiyeh, he had himself chauffeured to a row-house, on a less-graffiti-plastered street than most in the Sabra District.

With his driver holding an umbrella over his head, he climbed the spider-cracked steps in front and knocked. It was almost quaint. He probably hadn't knocked before entering in 15 years.

A middle-aged woman named Louha Mughrabi answered. She immediately swept her black shawl over her head and bowed. A number of dark-haired children, playing in the lounge, got up and ran giggling from the room.

Mrs. Mughrabi called out deeper into the house and stepped deferentially aside. A hallway doorway opened a few inches and a young woman's face peered out. Jihad marched to the door and closed it behind him.

Dalal Mughrabi stood illuminated by a pale light leaking in through closed lace curtains. She was wearing a long nightgown. Jihad sat down on the foot of the rumpled bed and looked at her.

Dalal was about 5' 6", with an attractive face framed by wavy dark hair in a pageboy cut. Her intense, almost black eyes, seemed to Jihad windows, into a spirit of he knew to be of uncommon determination.

The shapeless nightgown couldn't conceal hints of fitness and strength. He remembered also, the small breasts with pert upstanding nipples, the curves of her thighs and the soft woman parts between them, her movements; writhing beneath him, and her cries of love in the night.

A part of him even now wondered how he might maneuver her onto her knees before him.

Aware of his blunt appraisal, and remembering his curt dismissal last time they had met, she stared back defiantly.

Jihad said, "How are you little one?"

"I am well Umri," she replied, using the endearment 'my life' as she always had when they were alone. "But I miss you."

"I understand," he said.

"But circumstances..."

"I want to be with you," she blurted.

"Alas, you cannot."

"You would rather be with that... woman?"

"Intissar and my children are not something we can speak of, little one. They are part of me and cannot be separated."

She flared. "Am I not part of you too, *Umri*?"

He raised a hand calmingly. "We have had much, little one. But it must end now as I told you in Damascus when you came unannounced."

"I needed you! I had to see you!"

Jihad sighed. "Little one, I deal with powerful men. Conservative men. They would not understand."

Dalal sobbed.

Jihad said, "I am a leader. I must suppress my own needs." Then added the sop, "Though it breaks my heart to do so."

He stood and continued more firmly, "And I must think of my children. They will be leaders too, if given the opportunity. My son Jihad will replace me someday, Allah willing."

Dalal saw that the argument was lost, so said huffily, "I only want to serve the cause and fight the Jews beside you, and in your..."

"That has ended!" Jihad said flatly. Then softened. "But if you truly wish to fight the Israeli dogs, you can do so with your training, your leadership, and your resolve. There is a way. An operation is planned."

She brightened slightly. "I will serve you any way I can."

"Then that is the way you shall do it. I will send for you when I return to Damascus. But this, what we had, must be behind us now. Do you accept that?"

She looked at the floor. Eventually she said quietly, "Yes."

"Again, so I am sure."

"Yes."

"Good. I will send for you. Be ready." He turned and opened the door and went out.

Dalal Mughrabi broke down and slumped on the bed, weeping abjectly.

Life can be very strange.

SIX

Shatila Refugee Camp, Beirut, Lebanon
Monday, December 19th

His personal problems dealt with for now, Jihad concentrated on interviewing the candidates for Operation Kamal Adwan.

He was a frequent visitor to North Lebanon. There were garrisoning levels to review. Points of weakness on the part of the opposition to exploit. Opportunities to mount an offense, to be taken advantage of.

While there, he normally divided his time between the northern Fatah strongholds of the refugee camps of Shatila; Burj Barajneh and Dbaiyeh. The southern base at Tyre was too regularly overflown by Israeli warplanes for his liking, so he generally delegated matters there to Azmi Zrayir.

In anticipation of his meeting with Dalal Mughrabi, he'd sent orders to the commanders of those three northern bases to have their people on his list summoned to see him that evening.

One candidate arrived at Shatila camp shortly after dark. A baby-faced, slightly-built, but hard-eyed 18-year-old Jordanian named Mustapha Abu Ramez. It was his work Iyad had complimented.

The man had been guarding an arms-warehouse at Sahet al Najmeh near the Beirut docks until half an hour previously. Then been driven in a truck with barely glowing headlights, the three miles south through a warren of bullet ravaged alleys and disarmed at the gate.

Ramez' father had been a minor hero during the 1948 war, from the famous village of Al-Ghubayya al-Tahta, southeast of Haifa. To break the ice and see how open the stubbly bearded young fighter might be, he commanded, "Speak of your family."

"*Alhamdulillah* (Praise be to God), my father Ibrahim fought for Fawzi al-Qawuqji, a great soldier."

Jihad noted him down as possibly religious, a problem if overdone, while agreeing, "Great indeed."

"Then he came home to his village during a break in the assault on the kibbutz of Mishmar HaEmek. The Jews had counterattacked behind and dynamited it. His first wife and baby daughter were dead amongst the debris."

"*Inna lillahi wa inna ilayhi raaji'oon* (surely we belong to Allah and to him we will return,)" sympathized Jihad.

"His first wife's name was Talya, and the child Kanz, which means 'Treasure' as you know," Ramez said with brimming eyes. "They were as alive in our household when I was growing up in Amman, as my own mother Shahirah and my two brothers. We would pray for them during *Salah* (daily prayers)."

Ramez began recounting other stories of Israeli brutality and injustice, universal among men of Ramez' background and repetitive after a while. Jihad directed him back to his personal life story.

At 17 he'd heard the call to Jihad at his local mosque and drifted on the fringes of the militias until he'd been recruited into the Jordanian backed Qadisiyya militia at Al-Jiza, west of Amman International Airport.

As he talked, Jihad reviewed the military record he'd been given in advance of the meeting.

Ramez was a natural with any kind of weapon, had risen quickly to body-guarding several senior PLA figures, taken part in a number of village cleansings in East Lebanon, and when ordered had killed a traitor unmasked at a PLA-Fatah meeting, right there at the table.

On the downside, the young man tended to insecurity. A margin-note by a former commander warned that his temper flared at the least insult. Yet despite the emotion he'd displayed, he was a fervent Jew-hater and a stone-cold killer. One hundred and fifty pounds of viper-like viciousness. Jihad decided he would serve his purposes perfectly.

In parting, he asked young Ramez to choose a kunya for the mission.

He chose Abu 'Rami,' the 'Gunman.'

Jihad thought that an enlightened choice.

Before Jihad could meet with any more prospects, however, Iyad arrived in Beirut on a covert mission to visit his spies in Prime Minister Rashid Karami's Lebanese Government. They met in Shatila's Fatah offices the next morning. The first topic was public knowledge.

"We seem to be having some wins in the U.N.," Iyad said.

"Not that it matters," Jihad said, becoming irritated as he always did at the mention of the monumentally ineffective world body. "The Americans squash them all."

"I did say seem. But one, at least, might have some durability. The Israeli resolution against terrorism finally came to a vote on the 16th."

Jihad mused a moment. "They've been pushing that a long time. It's not in our interests either."

"True,' responded Iyad. But immediately before the vote the Arab bloc, backed by our friends in Moscow, put in a clause excluding any 'national liberation movement.' That's us."

"Yasser will be delighted," said Jihad. "But how is it going in Washington?"

Iyad shrugged. "Begin announced another round of talks on 'Face the Nation' with Bob Schieffer on the 18th. At Ismailia in the Canal Zone this time. They start Saturday. Hopefully just another talk-fest that won't come to anything."

"I wouldn't be so sure," Jihad said morosely. "The more they talk, the greater the risk they'll agree on something."

"We'd better speed up this operation of yours then."

"That's why I'm here in Lebanon."

Iyad said, "There's one other on the U.N."

"Anything important?"

"Hard to tell. They passed a thing called resolution 32/17 on the 19th. It declares all Jewish activities in the occupied territories illegal, particularly new settlements."

"They'll ignore that."

"Yes, they will. Anyway, what matters most is stopping Egypt and Israel from signing a peace agreement without giving us our own country first. Begin stopped off last week in Britain to talk to their Prime Minister, Callaghan. Now he says he's going to these meetings in Ismailia. Begin's getting a little too proactive for my liking. We need him back home, focused on his own backyard."

"I said I'm working on it," growled Jihad.

The next morning as the outskirts of Dbaiyeh came into view from Jihad's Mercedes, he reflected that he'd always liked this camp in the relatively peaceful far northern part of the country. It was where he'd met Dalal Mughrabi.

The first of the day's interviewees was a coarse-featured Gazan, Zukhair al-Massri. At over six feet tall and weighing more than 200 pounds, he was unusually large for an Arab.

His file listed a date of birth in 1957 in Khan Yunis, which made him 20 and an actual 'Palestinian' since that year was between Egyptian occupations of the Strip.

"Tell me of your youth in Gaza City."

"The Jewish *khan-zeers* (pigs)," Al-Massri replied in slum Arabic, "would patrol on Omar Mukhtar Street. We would meet them in the Palestine Square. There were many stones left over from *An-Naksah*.'"

He was referring to 'The Setback,' as the 1967 Six Day War was known in the Arab community.

"Sometimes we would hit one and cheer. They would fire their rubber bullets. My friend Khan had his ribs broken that way. Sometimes they'd catch and beat us with truncheons and rifle butts. We would meet them again the next day, same time and place. That was my life in Gaza City."

"How did you escape?"

"After 17 they would no longer beat you but take you away to a camp. My father did business with a Bedouin who knew the way across Sinai and paid for my use of a tunnel beneath the wire to reach his camp by night. I traveled first to Cairo, then on a boat to Cyprus, then here."

"Your commander says you are experienced and have fought in the countryside."

"I was nearly two years with the *Ain Jalut*." A Syrian aligned militia whose name was synonymous with rural atrocities. "And yes, I've been to the villages and killed the *Masiheyin* (Christians). Now I am with Fatah."

"Why are you here? I mean today. Volunteering."

The big Arab grinned evilly and made an over-arm motion. "I would like to throw stones at the Jews again. I am a much better shot now."

This was a brutal thug. No doubt about it. But Jihad had met many like him, and they were often staunch to the end. "And so you shall," he said.

Al-Massri chose Abu 'Jalal,' meaning 'Seeker of Glory,' as his kunya.

Even thugs can have aspirations.

Jihad's second candidate of the day was more on the brains than the brawn side of the equation, though not enjoyably so.

Nineteen-year-old Amer Ahmed Amreya was a European-looking Arab from Judea & Samaria-the West Bank of the Occupied Territories to some. Slim, with a Zapata mustache, straight light brown hair and unattractive rat-like features. His eyes revealed cunning and a hint of fiery zeal.

Jihad wondered immediately if he might also be too clever by half for the operation. His file read like a job application.

Amreya had been a history student and activist at Birzeit University in Ramallah, in 1977, when the Israeli Religious Zionist movement began breaking ground for an expansionist settlement four miles north of campus.

Amreya's student cadre had fought the Israeli Border Police to a standstill over three riotous days. On learning he'd been specifically targeted for arrest or death; he'd escaped across the Allenby Bridge into Jordan.

"I thought I might go to Germany and join the Red Army faction, or Italy to the Red Brigades," Amreya announced.

"Is that so?" Jihad replied. The self-absorbed little applicant totally missed the sarcasm. Jihad had been friendly with the jailed RAF leaders Baader, Ensslin, and Raspe before their suicide two months previously. They had been serious people and would certainly have sent this little wannabe packing.

"Yes, but I went to Yarmouk instead and joined Fatah," Amreya added, as if it was some great gift he'd bestowed. He then launched into a diatribe on his political ideology.

Jihad had heard all the political-philosophy he would ever need, but he let the man prattle on for a while. Amreya ended imperiously with; "Now I am a sniper at Youssef Souda. My post is on the roof of the Hotel-Dieu de France Hospital." That location was well inside Phalangist territory. While Jihad thoroughly disliked the man, that and his notes said Amreya was at least fearless. In the end, everything else could be managed.

Jihad was baffled initially, when Amreya chose 'Tariq' as his kunya. Then the little shit couldn't resist showing off, by explaining that it was after Muslim General Tariq Ibn Ziyad, who had defeated Rodrigo, the last Visigothic King of Spain, in the year 711.

What is it the Americans say? Jihad thought. *Whatever floats your ship?*

SEVEN

Dbaiyeh Refugee Camp, North Lebanon
Thursday, December 22nd

The following day it was another Jordanian, Mohammed Hussain al-Shamri, 18, who had been released from garrison duty for consideration.

He had the swarthy, thin-faced appearance of many city-melting-pot Arabs, bushy eyebrows that pinched together in the middle of his forehead when he frowned, and stuttered when nervous; which seemed to be most of the time.

From a prosperous Amman family with roots in Judea & Samaria, he'd rebelled after the death of a beloved father, and spent his childhood living on his wits in the souks. Assumedly he'd been a capable thief, since he still had both hands.

Too young to get caught in the 'Black September' near-annihilation and expulsion of the PLO by the Hashemite Authorities in 1970-71, al-Shamri had heard the call to Jihad around the Mosques in his teens. Earlier in 1977 he'd joined up with a small Iranian-aligned militia called the *Amal*, to fight the Phalangists in East Beirut. For his pains he'd received a ticket to Beirut, a battered wooden-stocked AK47 with a magazine of corroded-looking rounds, and found himself manning a roadblock without any training whatsoever.

The Amal information was a surprise to Jihad, given the enmity between the two fundamental sects of Islam since their acrimonious split over the line of succession of the Prophet Mohammed.

"Ye-ye-yes, they are followers of Ali and I of Abu Bakr as the first Caliph," al-Shamri acknowledged defensively.

'Possible zealot. To be watched,' Jihad noted down.

"Bu-bu-but the Quran tells us both to strike down all *kāfirs* (unbelievers,) Allah willing, and the enemy of my enemy makes a good friend. But ye-ye-yes there was... sssssstrain, so I came to Fatah two months ago and am training here as I'm sure my Lord knows."

"I am not your Lord!" rebuked Jihad. "I am your Supreme Commander and you will address me as such."

Then softening, said "I see you know Sister Dalal?"

"Yeeeeees the sister and I know each other. I see her with the camp children. She is kind. I watch over her when I can."

Jihad smiled. His plan was coming together even better than he could have hoped.

Though the camp commandant had described the youth as a quiet, resentful loner without much initiative, every operation needed solid worker-bees. Particularly with something extra to offer.

Al-Shamri's kunya for the operation was taken from his middle name, Abu 'Hussain.'

Two more prospects awaited Jihad when he arrived back at Shatila two days later.

The first was the highly recommended 18-year-old Khaled Hussein from Jihad and Iyad's discussion, an oil worker's son over six feet tall, shambling, gangly and raw like an overgrown boy, with thick lips, and scruffy facial hair.

Most within Fatah wore their checked keffiyehs rakishly. A badge of honor. Hussein wore his in a formally as a turban and sat reverently during the meeting.

While he considered himself Kuwaiti, Hussein's family had actually moved to Tulkarem, Judea & Samaria, immediately after the 1967 war when he was seven. To a villa, since the family had some savings, but inevitably Khaled had hung around the refugee camp with kids he knew.

There he'd observed frequent examples of IDF brutality, soaked up the tales of al-Nakba and the related Israeli evils depicted in Fatah recruiting materials, and joined Fatah at the age of 16.

Having served at the Green Line and spent the last few weeks with the local garrison, he'd heard about the coming operation from loose talk around the camp and eagerly applied.

Jihad decided, after questioning him for a few minutes, that he was a dim-witted man, but his record was steady and he'd likely make a good follower.

Apparently lacking the imagination to think of anything else, Hussein chose his first name, Abu 'Khaled,' meaning 'Immortal', as his kunya.

The second prospect was another hulking, blunt-featured Judean & Samarian from Jericho, in the mold of the newly named Abu Jalal.

Fawzi al-Ramez carried his 225 pounds with brooding menace, had an upper arm wound, though the dressing was dry and it didn't seem to bother him, and some missing front teeth, but again apparently for some time.

At 24 he was the oldest prospect Jihad was due to see, and the most experienced fighter on the list. He also had some serious Israeli prison time behind him, having started out as a stone thrower, also like Jalal.

He would have been what? Thirteen when the Jews annexed the West Bank? Who from that time and place wasn't heaving rocks?

But apparently, he'd been too stubborn or inept to escape before reaching imprisonment age, unlike Jalal and other luckier Fatah recruits.

"So, they seized you?"

Al-Ramez' eyes glittered. "Yes. I got one as they came at me, though. Between the eyes."

"Where did they take you?"

"Camp Ofer. Indefinite detention."

Jihad pictured the barbed wire, rough prefabricated buildings, and harsh climate of the notorious camp near Giv'at Ze'ev in the occupied territories near Al-Quds (Jerusalem).

"Tough place at seventeen."

The big man shrugged, his response to anything unpleasant. "The Jews called us *Metmurds*. (Intransigents). Twenty-four hours a day in a cage. They enjoy the *Falaka* at Ofer too."

Jihad shuddered. Beating of the soles of the feet until raw. Excruciating. And crippling.

"I used to dream of getting my hands on one of them, just once, but they wouldn't come close enough of course."

"Never?"

"We used to save our Khara." The big ugly man made a throwing motion with his right hand.

Jihad's stomach churned. *The final defense of the completely defenseless. Throwing your own shit at your enemy.*

"Not even to feed you?"

Al-Ramez' eyes darkened to blackness. "Three would come. Twice a day. Two with riot shields. One with buckets of wheat slush. There was a long channel, like for rain on a house. They would pour the buckets in the channel. Then lift that end with a stick so it ran down to us. The way you would feed a pig. Thirty of us in a cage. Ten cages. We would scoop it out with our fingers. The weak did not eat often."

"Water?"

"They would turn on a hose twice a day too."

Allah's mother.

"And you were released in the prisoner exchange in 1976?"

"Yes. I crossed the *Urdunn* (Jordan) and volunteered."

He mentioned a well-known Fatah officer at Karameh, still a Fatah base despite being largely destroyed by Israeli tanks during the famous confrontation that put the PLO on the political map in 1968.

"He sent me to Beirut to kill the Masiheyin. They say I am good at it. I've certainly done it enough. Believe me, they are no substitute for Jews."

"What would you like to be called? Your 'Abu?'"

"Ramz. Just Ramz."

Symbol of Freedom.
"Very well."
"*Insha'Allah.*
When do we begin?"
"Soon. Very Soon."

A crisis within Fatah flared the same evening Jihad signed up Ramz at Shatila.

There had been a meeting the previous August at Chtaura, in the relatively neutral Bekaa Valley, to talk about a possible army-policed buffer zone in refugee-swollen south Lebanon. The PLO, Syrians from the Arab Deterrent Force, and emissaries from the Lebanese government-whom Iyad's spies reported greatly feared another Israeli invasion, had attended. The last thing Jihad wanted was restrictions on his fighters' free movement near the Israel border, so he'd stayed away.

Suddenly it seemed the buffer zone might actually go ahead. Jihad had to leverage all his contacts in the Syrian Government to forestall it.

Fortunately, the Lebanese got the message within a matter of days and he could again turn his attention to Operation Kamal Adwan.

Immediately he was interrupted by an almost apoplectic Iyad. Things between Egypt and Israel had gotten even 'worse.'

"Begin has pulled... what's that basketball term? A full court pressure? He's turned up at Ismailia with Dayan, Weizman, his Attorney General, and other aides, bearing proposals endorsed by President Katzir."

Jihad was immediately worried.

"And?"

"It has worked. A joint Egypt-Israel statement has announced military and political committees to convene by mid-January."

Jihad immediately abandoned plans to travel anywhere for more interviews. Time didn't allow it. Three of his four remaining candidates, a Yemini and two Egyptians, would have to be checked out by people further down his chain of command. He'd have to rely on their judgment.

The Yemini was at Dbaiyeh having arrived there too late to be seen by him personally. One Egyptian, the inexperienced one, was at Karameh, and the other at Nahr al-Bared, a coastal outpost north of Beirut.

Jihad sent word to the three locations requesting early feedback.

That left only one man on Jihad's list of operators, one he already knew only too well. The same man Iyad had objected to.

Abdul Salaam, a 19-year-old Lebanese from Tripoli on the north coast, was a fisherman's son about 6' tall; slim, charming and roguishly handsome, with a Charlie Chan mustache and a pretentious Afro.

He was said to cut quite a figure under the revolving silver balls of Damascus' Al-Hboubi district discotheques, in his tailored flared jeans, and expensive silk shirts unbuttoned enough to show off his smooth chest. Unfortunately, he was also an arrogant, womanizing, pain in the ass, no matter how good he was at his job as an analyst with Iyad's intelligence group.

Abdul's large family, like Jihad's own, had been expelled from Ramla, southwest of Tel Aviv in 1948. Jihad had known them well and stayed in touch, even though most had gone north to Lebanon rather than south to Gaza. At the end of 1976 when Abdul was in his first year of studies at the University of Tripoli, his father Bilal had been killed while entering Judea & Samaria on a family visit, in what the IDF termed an accidental shooting by a clumsy army conscript.

Abdul had immediately quit school and begged his 'uncle' Jihad for a job. Showing a knack for languages, he'd received some Hebrew language training in Damascus, then been inserted under forged papers into Tel Aviv for a month's reconnaissance. He was currently doing propaganda work and money-collection in the building right next door to Jihad's HQ.

Unfortunately, his interpersonal skills weren't a match for his smarts. He'd alienated everyone in his section in record time and capped that off with an affair with the wife of one of Jihad's mid-level commanders. He'd volunteered for this field-operation to get out of town, He'd certainly have been found dead in the street otherwise.

But he was the only man on Jihad's list who was both Hebrew-speaking and had vital experience inside Israel. If he could be made to fit in, he could make all the difference to the operation. As a bonus, Jihad had already decided the operators would go in by sea, which assumedly the man knew a little about.

Jihad sent word he was to stand by for the operation and noted on his list he would simply call him Abu 'Salaam.' He then turned his focus to the leadership of the operation.

He'd decided there would be two field commanders. Leading independent teams working side by side. This would provide redundancy of equipment and give the operation its best chance of success if disaster struck either team.

As for one leader candidate, Azmi Zrayir, for all his tyrannical ways, was generally a good judge of men. His recommendation of the man named Naif he was holding in Tyre, sounded a reasonable option for one leader, subject to meeting the man of course.

For the other, there was only one option. He hoped to Allah, he could make it work. It was such an elegant solution to many things. His thoughts went back to a famous series of events from 1970.

A young woman from the PFLP named Leila Khaled had captivated the western news media by hijacking a TWA Boeing 707. It had been flown to Dawson's Field north of Damascus and blown up on the ground after the passengers were offloaded. Leila Khaled had then brazenly bargained her way to freedom. And after plastic surgery to change her appearance, she'd tried again but been caught.

Still, her charisma and contempt of western authorities had shown the world what a woman was capable of doing for the cause.

That was the commitment and impact Jihad needed to derail the Egypt-Israel peace initiative before the Americans became so deeply involved there would be no stopping it. If he aimed to accomplish through Operation Kamal Adwan what Leila Khaled had achieved, though the plan bore no resemblance, Dalal Mughrabi was the perfect stand-in.

Which all shrank to insignificance when he thought of her being out of his life forever! He knew the woman! She was tenacious beyond belief. She would never let him have a life without her. Certainly not the life of unadulterated power he had now.

Jihad leaned back in his office chair in satisfaction.

Looking down, he noticed a speck of lint on his finely tailored Savile Row suit.

He flicked it off.

Good.

Very good.

Within days, Jihad also had the reports he'd requested on the remaining three operational candidates.

The Yemeni, Akram al-Assadi, 18 years old, was the son of a minor warlord of the Al-Matheel tribe from the wild mountains south of the capital Sana'a. He was described as having the typical appearance of men from those deep desert tribes; wiry build, beak nose, wispy beard, and dark curly hair growing out of control. Also a *Zebiba*, the friction mark from frequent contact between forehead and prayer mat of the extremely devout

Yemen is believed by many to be the cradle of humankind: the place where the Ark settled after the great flood, and the original home-place of all Arabs. Yemenis are a proud and often ferocious people with the world's highest ratio of guns to population.

Maturing among such fierce fighting men, it must have seemed natural to young al-Assadi, to find his own path in the ways of war, with the militias in West Beirut, fighting for Allah in the nationalist cause of the Muslims against the infidels. Perhaps he saw it as some kind of OE (overseas experience,) the way British Commonwealth youth view a year or so in London. He'd spent most of 1977 in the guerrilla forces of a renegade Jordanian Army Colonel named Said al-Muragha, better known as ‘Abu Musa,’ at that time cooperating closely with Fatah.

The officer providing the report had concerns about the prayer scar, which suggested al-Assadi might be too religious, since most Fatah fighters were not. And felt he was a loner, still clinging to his tribal roots, since he'd attended the interview wearing a *Jamiyah* (decorative Yemeni dagger.)

But knowing the Yemeni fighting reputation, Jihad was glad to have him. He noted al-Assadi had adopted one of the 99 names of the Prophet Mohammed, Abu 'Ahmed,' as his kunya.

The Egyptian at Karameh had also impressed his interviewer with his willingness and enthusiasm, despite his inexperience. Barely 18, Mohammed Raji al-Sheraan was slight of build, and self-effacing in nature, with a deluge of dark hair, a bulbous nose, and thick lips.

From a family of field workers expelled from the orange groves of *al-Majdal Ascalun* (Israeli Ashkelon) during al-Nakba, he'd attained trouble-making age in the Cairo slum of Imbaba where his father had a stall at the souk. Working his way north on a coastal vessel, he'd become briefly involved with the Lebanese Arab Army before realizing he really wanted to fight Israelis, not Christians, and volunteering at a Fatah recruiting center at the Mohammad al-Amin Mosque in West Beirut's Martyr's Square. Training at Karameh the previous few months, he'd been awaiting a posting when his commander heard about the operation.

He wanted to be called Abu 'Wael,' the 'Rescuer.’

The last, the other Gazan named Hussein Fayadh, also just 18, hadn't been interviewed at all because Azmi Zrayir hadn't had time to get to Nahr al-Bared.

Jihad had to go off his original information, which described a small, slyly clever, unkempt boy with a size complex and a perpetually shifty expression. Born in Khan Yunis, but raised like Wael in Cairo, he had been deeply affected by the seditious writings of Jihadist philosopher and founder of the Muslim Brotherhood, Sayyid Qutb.

Trying to overcome his sense of inferiority, Jihad supposed, he'd run away to Beirut and given 'family-reasons,' for joining Fatah earlier in 1977, a common code for an upbringing filled with horror stories of the Nakba.

That he was serving in Nahr al-Bared, as far from the action as it was possible to get, might have given him away as a thoroughly dislikeable young man, and Jihad would probably have rejected him outright if he'd met him.

Instead he was accepted, with plain 'Fayadh' as his kunya.

The core of the operation was in place.

For better and worse.

EIGHT

Yarmouk
Saturday, December 31st

The following Saturday was bitterly cold in Damascus, with a light sleet driven by a sharp northerly, and crusty ice littering the sidewalk and steps outside Fatah's headquarters.

Fatah Lieutenants Mahmoud Ali Naif and Dalal Mughrabi shivered as they climbed down from a brown Unimog truck in their olive-green Lebanese battle fatigues, combat boots, and keffiyehs. Mortality was on their minds, knowing this summons almost certainly meant their violent deaths.

Stamping the circulation back into their feet, they surrendered their Kalashnikovs and Makarovs at the guard station, and clumped up a staircase to the second floor.

A meeting was wrapping up in Jihad's office. They waited while topographical maps were put away, and the attendees except Jihad and Iyad dispersed.

Jihad waved them in. It seemed almost as cold inside as out, and the terrorist commanders wore greatcoats over their suits. They felt shrewd eyes appraising them. Mughrabi adopted the semi-formal military stance she knew was expected, and after a moment's hesitation Naif followed suit.

Jihad, hands clasped behind his back, circled them slowly, something he did habitually to disconcert visitors. After a few seconds he grunted as if in approval, emerged in front of them and said brightly, "Very good!" Though actually he wasn't pleased.

Dalal appeared to have put their past behind her, holding herself erect, staring ahead expressionlessly. But the taller Naif seemed to Jihad to lack substance and appeared almost to be smirking. Only a fool with a death wish would do that openly here.

Plus, Jihad had been hearing things about Naif. Azmi Zrayir may have been impressed with him, but others were not, though he could see how the man might make a good first impression. Tallish, broad-featured, and unusually fair-haired and blue-eyed for an Arab. perhaps from his father's Phoenician lineage. He also seemed built strongly enough and must have performed satisfactorily to have been made an officer.

Jihad mentally reviewed the man's background. His family was originally from the small olive farming village of Beituniya, 12 miles north of Jerusalem on the West Bank. When the troubles began in 1947, they took shelter with extended family in a village outside Haifa. That village rose against the Jews after Deir Yassin. Joining in cost the men of the family their lives on the afternoon of 21 April 1948, during the brutal fighting at Wadi Miamr. The next morning the British evacuated Naif's mother by sea to Batroun in north Lebanon. There she later married a fisherman, Adnan Al-Naim, Mahmoud's father. The officer conducting his interview for Fatah had noted that as an only son, Naif had felt bound to reclaim those olive groves he'd heard so much about as a child.

The word from his peers, however, was that Naif's-devil-may-care attitude and constant joking around, combined with a pitiful desire to be everyone's friend, masked deep insecurity. He also sulked when caught in one of his frequent lies. None of these traits was useful in a leader.

Still, he'd been proposed, and he was there and Jihad was out of time. And he did have sea-faring experience. Who knew how he might shape up in advanced training? That had certainly happened before.

Jihad brushed aside his misgivings and got to the point. "I have brought you here to tell you about a great opportunity to serve the cause, and offer you the chance to lead in it."

Patently hollow words. Fatah never 'offered' anyone anything.

Dalal and Mahmoud already knew that well, so showed no reaction.

"I understand you know boats." he directed at Naif.

"Hard not to if you want to fish for bream in 60 feet of water," Naif said with a grin.

Jihad stopped stock still. The man had no situational sense at all. For a moment he considered having Naif shot out of hand. He let a long silence hang in the room while he glowered.

To his credit, Naif immediately added, "Yes Sire! My father was a fisher, and I went with him many times. Often I would operate the boat on our return while he prepared the catch."

Jihad made himself relax.

"Good good, because we plan to strike a blow at the Jews' own hearts, from the sea. But Mahmoud," he used the man's first name, disarmingly. "Do not call me Sire. We are all brothers in the cause here."

He paced away a couple of steps and turned back. "We have selected a force, two teams, and we plan to deliver them by ship under your joint command, off the shore of *Yáfa*." (Tel Aviv.) "From there you will sail to shore in smaller craft, where you will seize a large building, perhaps a hotel. And hostages you will trade first for foreign ambassadors, and then for some of our brothers in Jewish jails. Also, for your freedom to return home to the honors that will be due you."

Jihad was a mesmerizing orator. He had them in the palm of his hand after only a few sentences.

Dalal and Mahmoud's eyes had traveled to Jihad's face, but snapped straight ahead again when he addressed Dalal directly. "Sister I require much of you. You will be my Warrior Queen and strike a blow for all your sisters. They need to know it is not only our men who bear our flag, but all of us equally. Will you do that for your sisters?"

Dalal nodded vigorously, yet again under Jihad's spell.

But even beyond that, he had re-awoken the dreams of her childhood. She had imagined this every day since being commissioned. This was her chance. She would not let the cause down.

Naif had also drawn himself up an inch or two, swelled with pride. Here was his chance at heroism, to be honored by his peers. "We will not fail you," he said, throat tight with emotion.

"Good, good, let me show you," Jihad said.

Maps were brought back out again, while Iyad advised, "My sources tell us, the Zionist pig Menachem Begin plans meetings in America with the dog Carter within the next few months. Certainly before *Bahá.* (Late March.) They believe this may encourage Sadat to further betray our brethren. We wish to show the pigs that they can speak with whom they wish, they will never be safe in their beds until our demands for nationhood have been met."

Jihad prodded at the maps while sketching out roughly what he had in mind. One map was of the Tel Aviv waterfront.

"We don't know this place," commented Naif.

"One of your team members has been there, and will show the way,' reassured Jihad.

Sensing encouragement was more important than information, Jihad rested a hand on Naif's shoulder and spoke to the man's obviously enormous ego.

"I am honored to serve with you. Mahmoud, you will be our commander while at sea, and lead our brave warriors to the Zionists' shore, where we will strike!" He punctuated the statement by punching his right fist theatrically into his left palm.

After all, words are cheap. Actions will decide all that in due course.

To Mughrabi, he announced grandly, "Sister Dalal, you will be our flag-bearer when on land, and hold it high into the dens of our enemies!"

She beamed rapturously. Naif looked ready to explode with pride.

"Comrades, I know you will not fail me or the martyrs before you. We shall call the operation 'Kamal Adwan' after our comrade lost in Beirut these five years past. You will begin training within days. Your men are on their way to join you. There is no god but Allah, and Muhammad is his messenger."

He made a dismissive motion and the enamored pair filed from the room, eyes gleaming brightly.

Naif and Mughrabi left Yarmouk immediately for Lebanon to wait for travel orders in a Chevy Caprice because the weather had worsened too much for travel by open truck. But within minutes Jihad realized he hadn't asked them to choose kunyas and sent a messenger after them.

He soon had his answers back.

Naif wished to be known as Abu 'Hiza'a,' which showed some imagination.

Khirbet Hiza'a was a fictional Arab village from the time of al-Nakba, made famous in an expose of Israeli brutality by the nonconformist Jewish writer S. Yizhar.

Naif might be a lightweight, but he wasn't illiterate.

Dalal Mughrabi preferred to be called, simply, 'Sister Dalal.'

Jihad immediately began thinking about a place for training the operatives in Lebanon.

Fatah had numerous training camps there, but he assumed the Israelis, from their cursed incessant reconnaissance over-flights, knew every one of them. Somewhere new, easily camouflaged, and above all: secret; was needed. A possible location leapt quickly to mind, and the next morning he summoned Iyad to discuss it.

On the morning of January 20th, 1976, a unit of PLO-aligned forces had swooped down from the eastern hills, and assaulted a Christian township that straddled the coastal road 15 miles south of Beirut. The attackers, including Jordanians commanded by Abu Musa and Syrians from the *As-Sa'iqa* (Thunderbolt Brigade) under Zukhair Mohsen, who would ever after be known as the 'Butcher of Damour,' for his work that day, overwhelmed and executed the town garrison. Then they rounded up the townsfolk, all 582 men, women, and children, and machine-gunned them against stone walls.

The immediate attraction was that the area around the town was under Fatah control and the PLO had begun repopulating it with

Muslim refugees from the cities. This would be Ideal cover for any new activity, particularly from Israeli air-strikes.

Iyad enthusiastically agreed.

"Damour? I know it well. The Masiheyin defenders had built a barracks and training area in the valley between the highway and the hills. Only the fence was destroyed during Mohsen's glorious victory. That could be rebuilt quickly, and with the refugees moving in, those housed there could be easily passed off as guards, or even social workers. A perfect location I would say."

"I will advise Zrayir to make it so," said a pleased Jihad. "And what about other matters?"

"Things seem quiet, Khalil. Just the usual political posturing going on."

Iyad was lying. A dangerous practice around Abu Jihad, but he had good reasons.

Anwar Sadat's peace overtures had caught the Soviets by surprise and threatened their Middle East influence. The KGB had responded by holding a meeting in Baghdad on December 15th. Both Abu Nidal, an independent terrorist leader known to be a crazy drunk, and Ilich Ramirez Sanchez, the famous Carlos, had attended.

The KGB head, Yuri Andropov, had offered a huge sum for Sadat's assassination. Iyad's spies said Carlos had considered it a suicide mission and immediately flown back to his safe-haven in Algeria. But Nidal had taken the money. It was yet to be determined whether his group had the resources to do the job, but he was certainly insane enough to try.

Iyad wasn't keeping this from Jihad because it wasn't confirmed, but because it would bring out the worst in his boss. Iyad had long managed this aspect of the Fatah leader with great care.

Jihad would rub his nose in the fact that Nidal was willing to do something Iyad wouldn't. Next, he would sulk that he hadn't been informed directly. Jihad thought of himself as feted and respected, and of the USSRs Defense Minister Andrei Gromyko as a close and intimate friend. Then he would drive all those around him to distraction with his schemes and counter schemes.

Better to keep him focused on this Israeli venture, which Iyad was beginning to think might bear fruit.

So-what if Abu Nidal was to succeed? In present circumstances that could only be good for Fatah so long as their fingerprints weren't on it. And if world events shifted, and it looked to be unwise? Iyad was sure he had the means to derail it in plenty of time.

He and Nidal had been the worst of enemies since the split between Fatah and Nidal's forces in 1974. Nidal had since made at least three attempts that kill him.

Come to think of it, I might even disrupt the operation just to spite the man.

"Well, please keep me informed of anything you hear."

"I certainly will," Iyad said, and left Jihad to his plotting.

By that time the last day of December 1977 on the western calendar was turning into a long day for Jihad. But he still had one important decision to make.

At that very moment, the best man in the Fatah organization, who wasn't an indispensable commander, was supervising a crucial arms delivery into the Beirut docks

Mohammed Mahmoud Abdul al-Raheem Masameh was 29, almost an old man in Fatah circles. Also, a true 'Palestinian' born in Yáfa before al-Nakba. Over 6'2" in height, all in proportion, his Adonis-like good looks were blemished only by missing the tips of two fingers from his left hand; an injury suffered during the 'Black September' fighting in Jordan in 1971.

Raised in Damascus and recruited personally by Jihad, Masameh had spent his entire adult life fighting the hated Jews. First as a team leader within Fatah's elite commando force, *Al-Asifah* (The Young Lions,) and then commander of Force 17-Yasser Arafat's own personal guard. When his experience became too valuable to waste on just any battlefield, he'd been pulled and sent for extensive ideological training in China, Russia, and North Korea.

Since returning, he'd been Jihad's personal troubleshooter, and a roving trainer at a number of camps, working with experienced fighters to raise their skills to the next level, or weeding out recruits who had no chance of making the grade.

Inconvenient or not, Jihad knew if he wanted the best results, he'd have to invest the best resources. Masameh was really the only man for this job,

He sent Masameh detailed orders telling him what was expected of him, and to contact Azmi Zrayir for transport to Damour well ahead of the trainees.

Then he leaned back in his chair and considered all he had accomplished.

He'd assembled a fighting force with a real chance of derailing the Egypt-Israeli-US peace talks before the train could even exit the station. And what a varied force it was.

Eleven men, as well as a woman in a leading role in a society where women were more often second-class citizens. Five men from the 'occupied territories.' Three West Bankers and two Gazans. Multinationals also; two Lebanese, two Jordanians, a Kuwaiti, an Egyptian, and a Yemeni. And young! Aged 18 through 24. Some vastly experienced at war, and one yet to even taste it. Three seemed religious zealots, but two were moderates, and seven had no religion at all as far as he could tell, except the sermon of the gun.

And all were bound together by the blood in their veins and the hate in their hearts. They were the true children of the Nakba.

All they need is the right training and let Allah help anyone who gets in their way.

Then he cut two further sets of orders, to be delivered overnight and actioned without delay.

One was to Azmi Zrayir to have the Damour training site repaired, provisioned, and otherwise made ready for immediate use.

Another went simultaneously to an apartment nearby within Yarmouk Camp, and a barracks near Shatila Camp in Beirut.

Operation Kamal Adwan was officially under way.

MAPS

Israel
Lebanon
Ain Ebel
Nahariyya
Acre
Zefat
Carmiel
Haifa
Shefaram
Tiberias
Bat Galim
Nazareth
Atlit
Neve Yam
Afula
Zichron Ya'akov
Ma'agan Michael
Tanninim
Jisr Al-Zarqa
Or Akiva
Katzir
Beit She'an
Jenin
Hadera
Olga
Netanya
Havatzelet HaSharon
Tubas
Taibe
Nablus
Kfar Saba
Glilot
Sharon Station
Tel Aviv-Yafo
Ariel
Tel Aviv
Maale Efraim
Ben Gurion Airport
Jaffa
Rishon LeZion
Ramallah
Karmei Yosef
Ashdod
JERUSALEM
Bet Sheme
6
Ashkelon
Sorek Stalactite Cave
Efrat
Kiryat Gat
Judea & Samaria
Idhna
Hebron
Gaza City
Gaza
Netivot
Rahat
ad-Dhahiriya
al-Qarara
Rafah
Beer Sheva
Arad
10mi
20km
Egypt

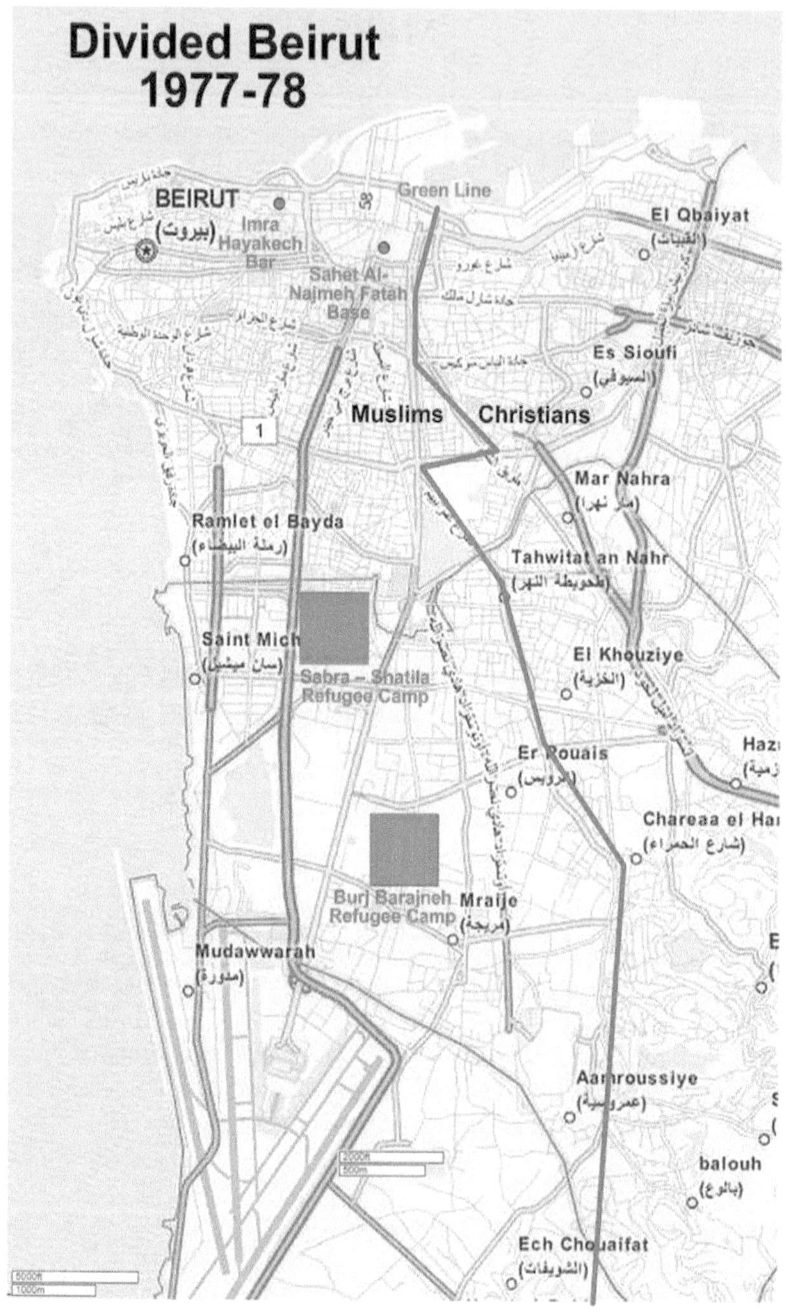
Divided Beirut
1977-78
BEIRUT
Imra
Hayakech
Bar
Green Line
Sahet Al-
Najmeh Fatah
Base
El Qbaiyat
Es Sioufi
Muslims
Christians
1
Mar Nahra
Ramlet el Bayda
Tahwitat an Nahr
Saint Mich
Sabra – Shatila
Refugee Camp
El Khouziye
Er Rouais
Chareaa el Ha
Burj Barajneh
Refugee Camp
Mraije
Mudawwarah
Aamroussiye
balouh
Ech Chouaifat

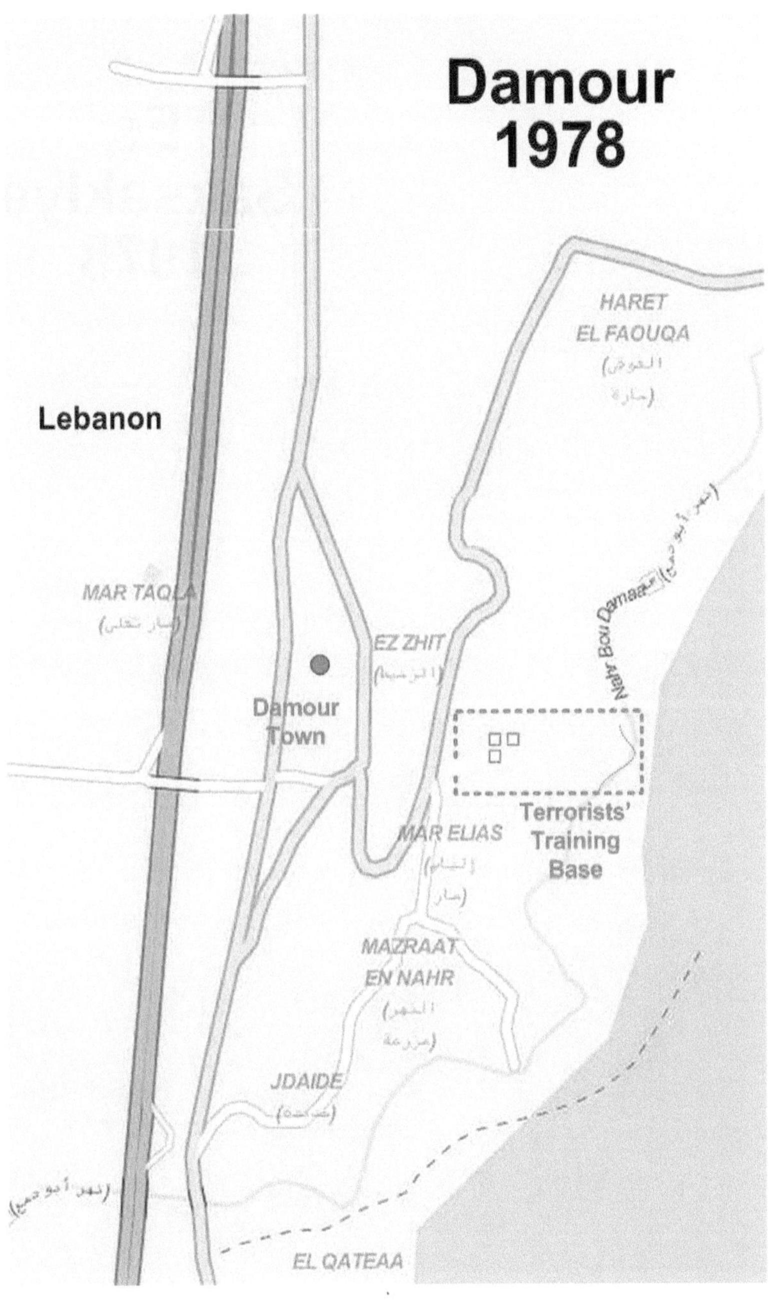
Damour
1978
HARET
EL FAOUQA
Lebanon
MAR TAQLA
EZ ZHIT
Nahr Bou Damaa
Damour
Town
Terrorists'
Training
Base
MAR ELIAS
MAZRAAT
EN NAHR
JDAIDE
EL QATEAA

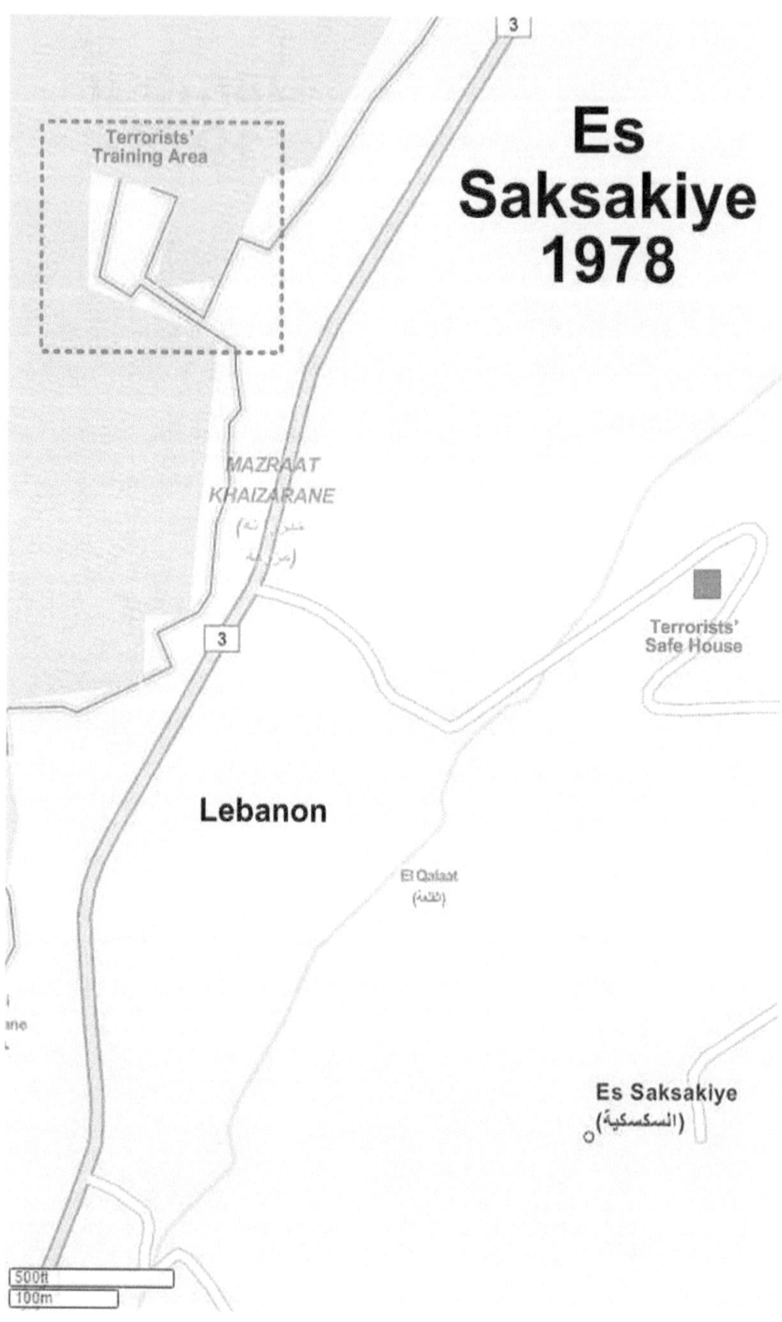

Es Saksakiye 1978
Terrorists' Training Area
3
MAZRAAT KHAIZARANE
Terrorists' Safe House
Lebanon
El Qalaat
Es Saksakiye
(السكسكية)
500ft
100m

Journey to Israel
9-11 March 1978
Es Saksakiye
Tyre
Sansato
Lebanon
Shlomi
Nahariyya
(נהריה)
Acre
(עכו)
70
85
Tamra
Kiryat Motzkin
Haifa
(חיפה)
79
Tirat Karmel
Atlit
Daliat el Karmel
Zodiacs
Yoqneam Illit
73
66
Kibbutz Ma'agan Michael
Tanínim
Zichron Yaakov
Or Akiva
Umm el Fahm
Harish
Israel
Hadera Power Station
Hadera

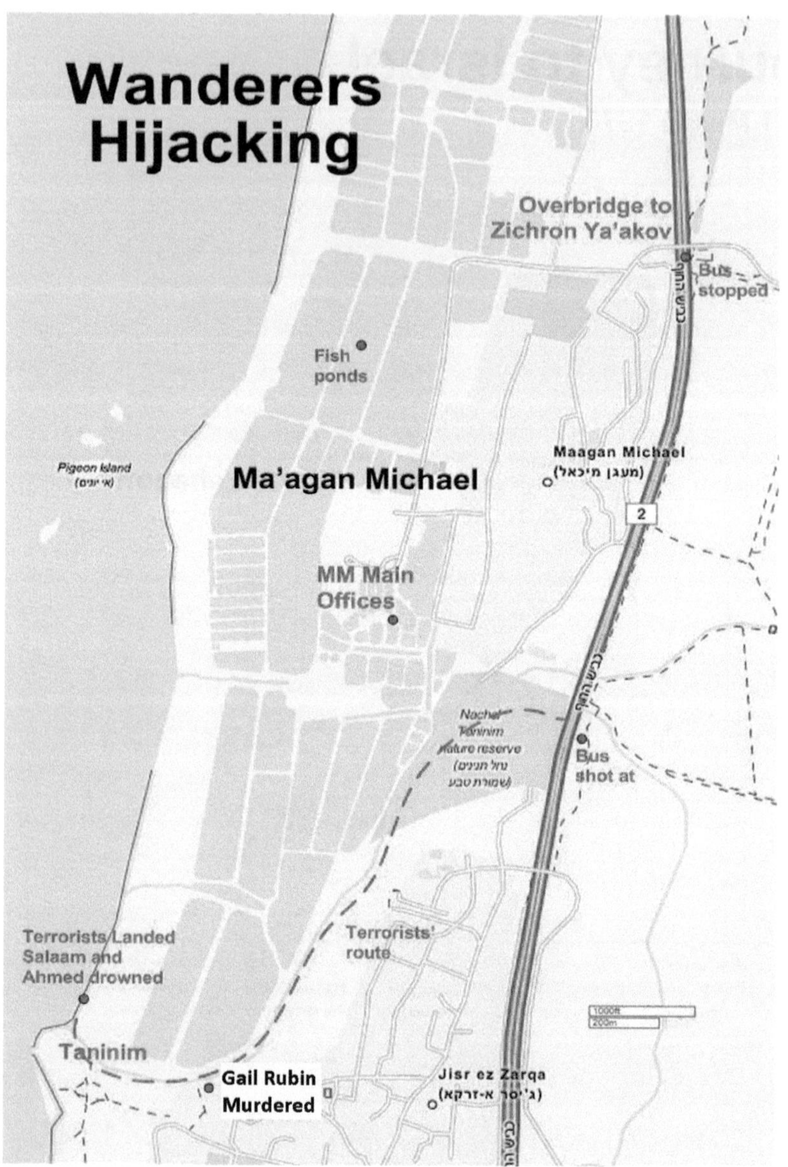
Wanderers
Hijacking
Overbridge to
Zichron Ya'akov
Bus
stopped
Fish
ponds
Ma'agan Michael
Maagan Michael
(מעגן מיכאל)
2
MM Main
Offices
Bus
shot at
Terrorists Landed
Salaam and
Ahmed drowned
Terrorists'
route
Taninim
Gail Rubin
Murdered
Jisr ez Zarqa
(ג'יסר א-זרקא)

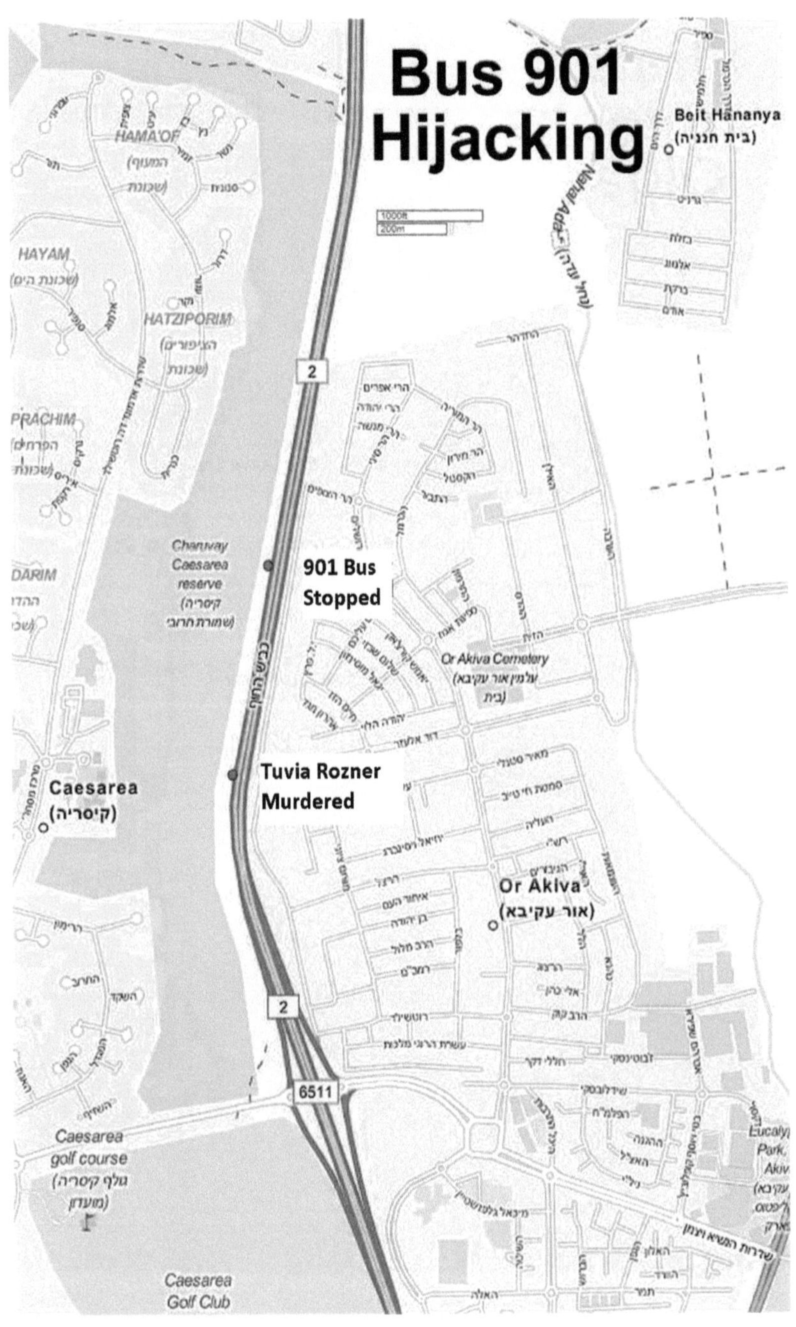
Bus 901
Hijacking
Beit Hananya
(בית חנניה)
1000ft
200m
Nahal Ada
HAMA'OF
HAYAM
HATZIPORIM
PRACHIM
DARIM
2
Chanuvay
Caesarea
reserve
901 Bus
Stopped
Or Akiva Cemetery
Tuvia Rozner
Murdered
Caesarea
(קיסריה)
Or Akiva
(אור עקיבא)
2
6511
Caesarea
golf course
Caesarea
Golf Club

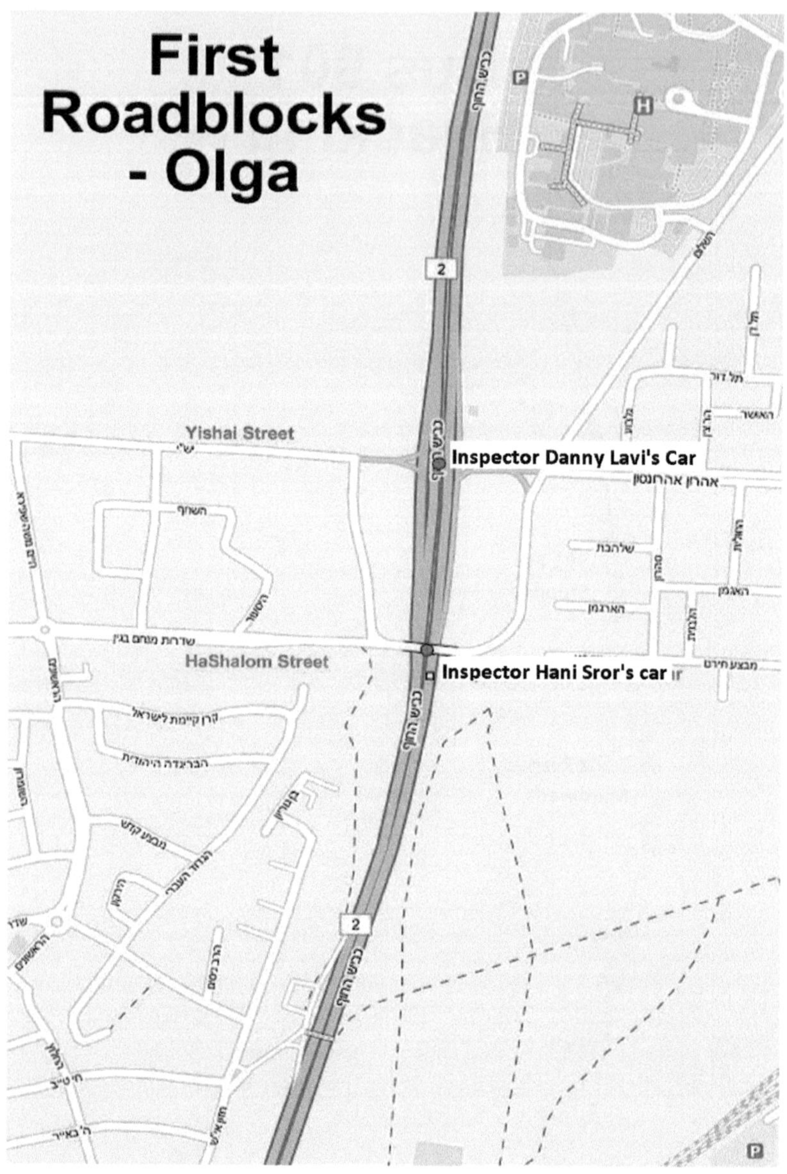
First Roadblocks - Olga
Yishai Street
Inspector Danny Lavi's Car
HaShalom Street
Inspector Hani Sror's car
2
2

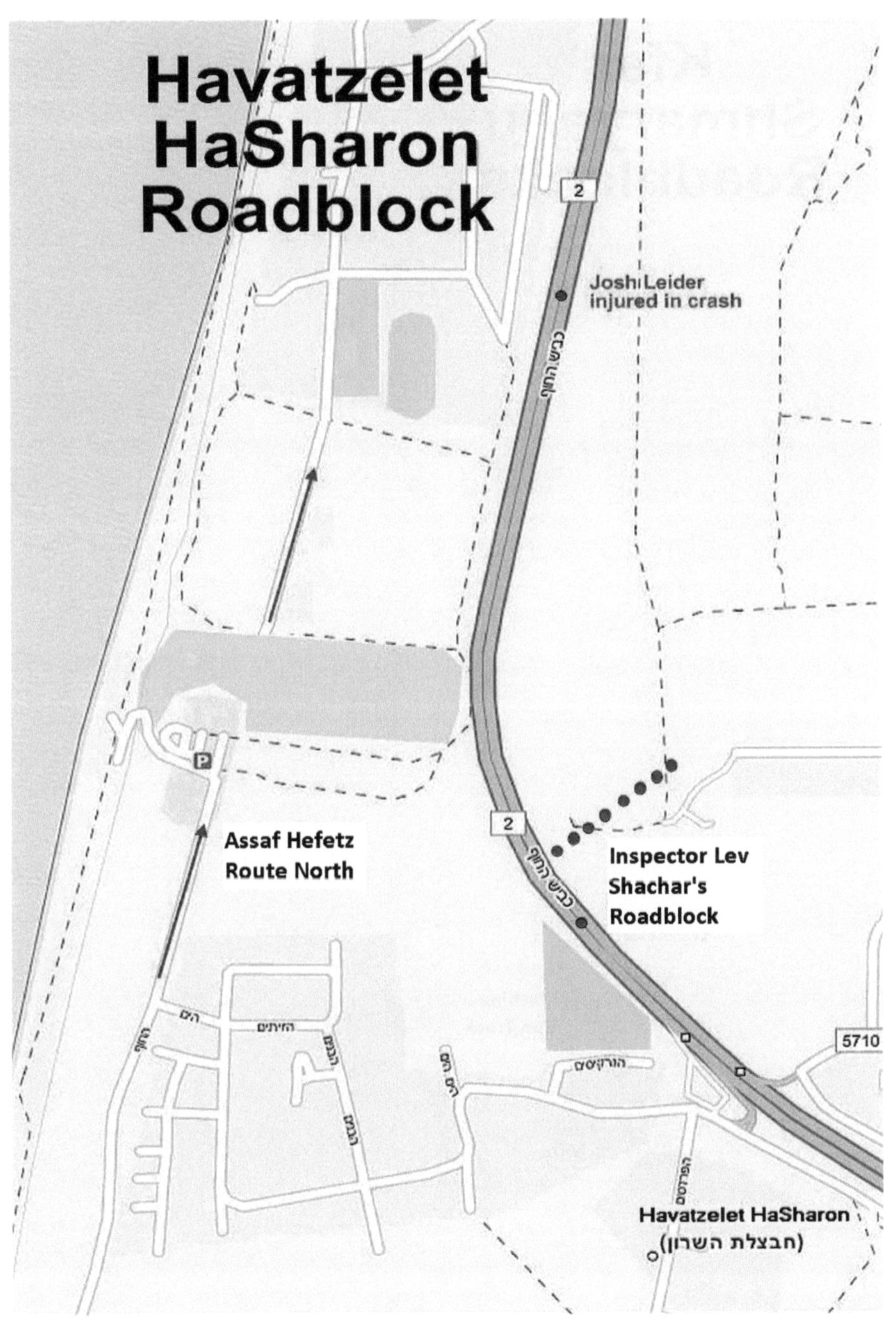
Havatzelet
HaSharon
Roadblock
2
Joshi Leider
injured in crash
Assaf Hefetz
Route North
2
Inspector Lev
Shachar's
Roadblock
5710
Havatzelet HaSharon
(חבצלת השרון)

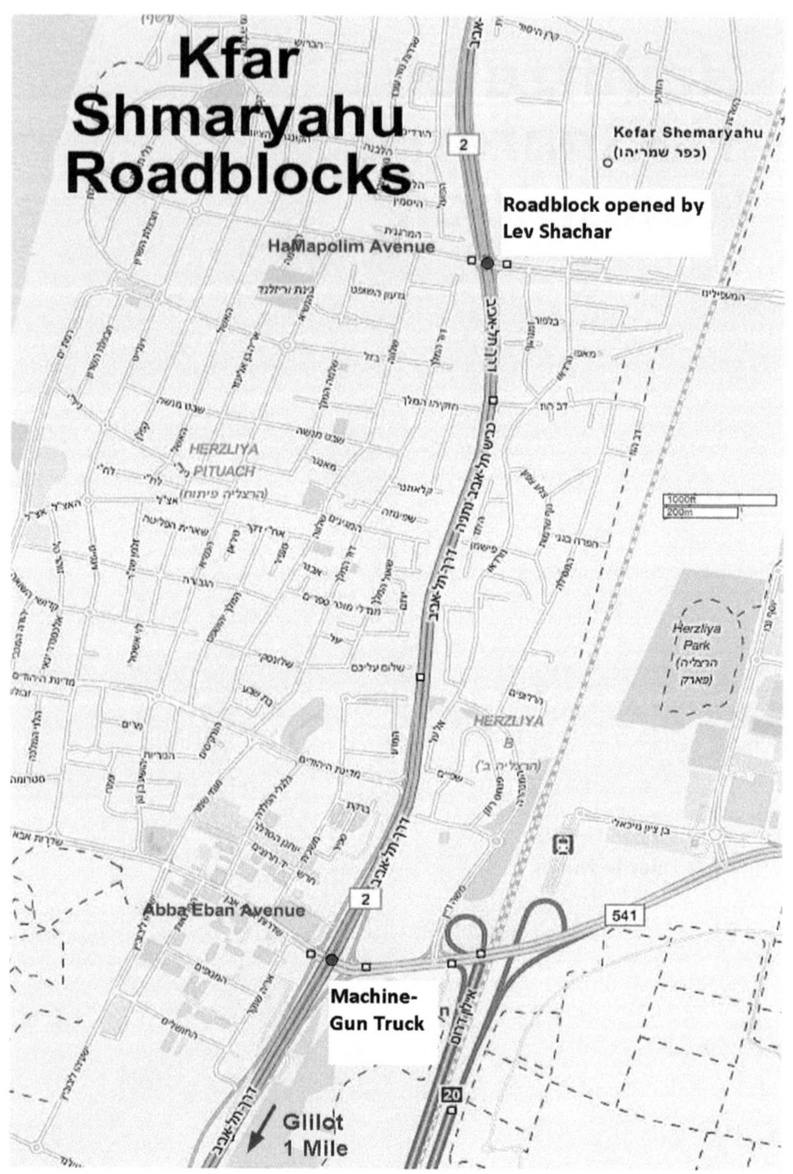
Kfar Shmaryahu Roadblocks
Kefar Shemaryahu
(כפר שמריהו)
Roadblock opened by Lev Shachar
HaMapolim Avenue
HERZLIYA PITUACH
(הרצליה פיתוח)
Herzliya Park
(הרצליה פארק)
HERZLIYA B
(הרצליה ב')
2
541
20
Abba Eban Avenue
Machine-Gun Truck
Glilot
1 Mile

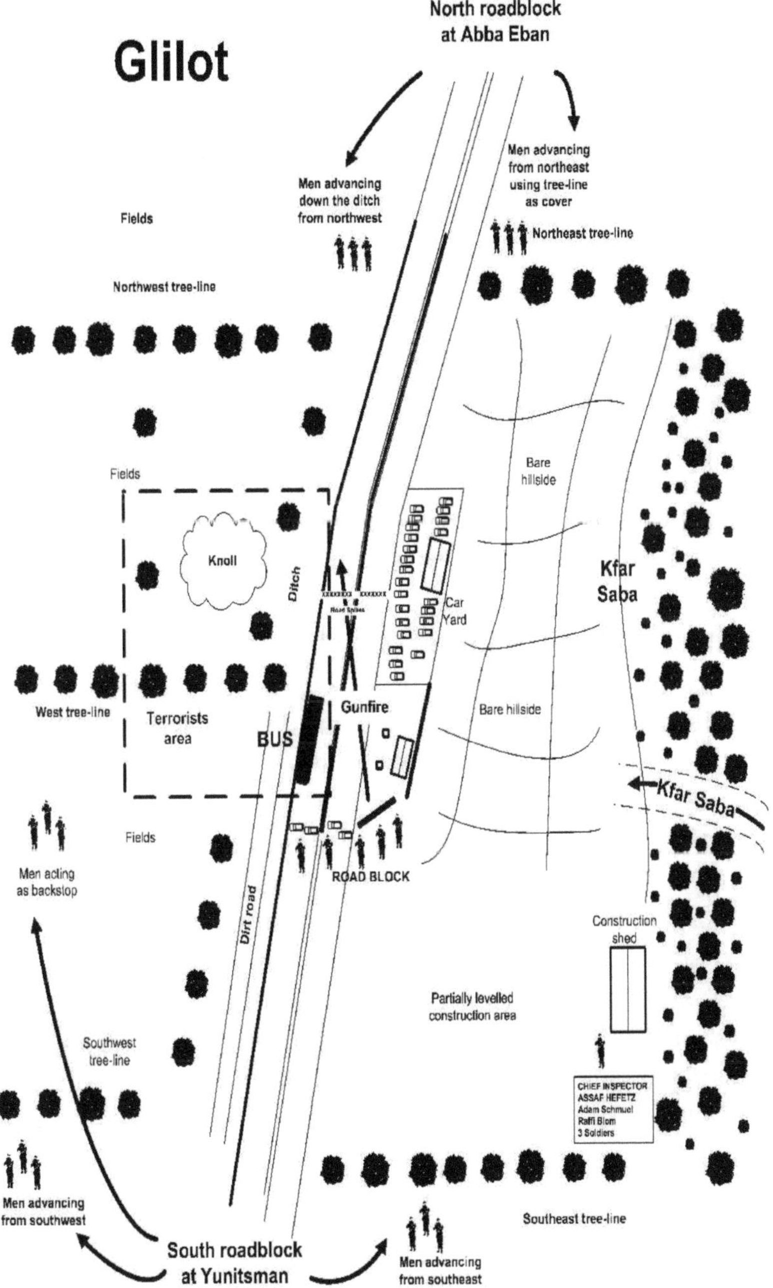
Glilot
North roadblock
at Abba Eban
Men advancing
down the ditch
from northwest
Men advancing
from northeast
using tree-line
as cover
Fields
Northeast tree-line
Northwest tree-line
Fields
Bare
hillside
Knoll
Ditch
Road Spikes
Car
Yard
Kfar
Saba
West tree-line
Terrorists
area
BUS
Gunfire
Bare hillside
Kfar Saba
Fields
Men acting
as backstop
ROAD BLOCK
Dirt road
Construction
shed
Partially levelled
construction area
Southwest
tree-line
CHIEF INSPECTOR
ASSAF HEFETZ
Adam Schmuel
Raffi Blom
3 Soldiers
Men advancing
from southwest
Southeast tree-line
South roadblock
at Yunitsman
Men advancing
from southeast

NINE

Damascus
Sunday, January 1st, 1978

Nineteen-seventy-eight dawned icily bright, but quietly, across the Middle East. Devout Muslims, or those for whom it is wise to appear so, don't celebrate Christian New Year's Day. Their equivalent day, *Muhurram,* had been the 12th of December.

Therefore, Sunday was just another working day around Yarmouk, and Abu Salaam was in bed in his second-floor apartment on Palestine Avenue, planning on escaping the embrace of a young girl whose name he didn't care to remember, and walking the 300-yards to his Fatah office. Then he heard boots on his stairs.

Similarly, Abu Hiza'a was asleep in a barracks near Shatila when he was shaken awake around the same time, 8:00 a.m., and told to get ready to leave.

By mid-afternoon the pair was on their way to Latakia, a port 200-odd miles north of Damascus, where they arrived late in the evening, at an amphibious training base that occupied a heavily guarded group of warehouses on the Al-Orouba docks.

They were shown to a dormitory where they disturbed a dozen or so men already sleeping. Among the grumbling, Salaam's ear for languages picked up at least half a dozen, including Turkish, Croatian, and Irish and Australian English, before everyone settled down again for the night.

Latakia, Northern Syria
January 2nd

The next morning the two men met with the facility commander, a squat, balding, 40-ish, Syrian naval-officer named Galal Abdalla Ali.

His instructions were to keep quiet and concentrate on their own business, which would take a couple of weeks.

Then they were shown to cavernous building equipped with chairs, a blackboard, and a row of water tanks in which outboard motors were mounted, each motor with a line going down to a portable gasoline tank.

A hands-on training session was already in progress. Five of the men from the dormitory were standing by the tanks, where several of the motors were puttering. The building reeked of oil fumes. Two instructors were directing, one Arabic-speaking, the other English, both with thick eastern-European accents.

Their turn came, and they began two days of instruction on a Russian military-issue two-stroke outboard motor, a primitive but functional, pull-started device weighing about 110lbs, gray with the wording Mockba-M16HP in darker letters along the side of the lift-off engine cover. They learned to strip it down and reassemble and restart it in poor lighting. Also overcome challenges, such as too much oil to the gas tank, and a bucket of water poured through the workings.

After two days, both men were confident they could operate it in almost any conditions.

The following day they were taken to a beach next to the docks for group training in the Czech made *Zverokruh* (Zodiac,) inflatable boat.

This weighed about 125lbs in a zipped carry bag. Once inflated by hand pumps each craft was about 14 feet in length, 6'6" wide, and drab gray with a double layer of black plasticized fabric on the outside. Each seated up to seven men, and could carry up to 1650lbs total weight, including cargo in zipped 'dry' bags secured down the centerline.

Training was in teams of six. In whispers, since open conversation drew shouts of abuse from the supervising Syrian sailors, they learned their comrades were two Turks from the THKO, an Italian from the Red Brigades, and a Kosovan from some unpronounceable Muslim separatist group.

Each team had to show they could carry the empty boat by ropes strung through loops along the sides, 100-yards at a run without stopping, before moving on to launch-and-recovery training; using davits attached to the dock to simulate the crane of a mother-ship.

Also, before operating the boats under power, they had to know how to handle them using only the three pairs of collapsible oars. It was a bad-weather week in the northern Mediterranean, with a cold wind and strong waves, causing numerous capsizes.

Salaam found himself far too often picking up the slack for Hiza'a, who liked to lord it as the lead man, as long as it didn't require showing an example.

Still, the Tripoli fisherman's son made the best of the situation, and by the end of two more days they were deemed, "*Tisbah kafya*" (Good enough.)

During the week or so of sea exercises that followed, the boats proved stable and nimble under power. The Soviet engine was thrifty; using only about a quart and a half of gas per hour at a cruising speed of 15 knots.

They ranged wider as confidence grew, practicing navigation by compass under starlight on fortunately now placid seas.

Their final exercise wasn't boat related at all, but a 200-yard night swim from offshore to the docks in full clothing. Salaam managed it with ease despite the bitterly cold water and still had enough energy left to go back and help the struggling Hiza'a ashore.

Back in civilian clothing the next morning, they humped their equipment into the back of an unmarked Bedford produce truck, covered it with bags of winter vegetables in case of border inspection, and began the 126-mile journey south along the M51 to west-central Lebanon.

Damour, West Central Lebanon
Thursday, January 5th

Meanwhile, the other Kamal Adwan operatives had arrived at their training base.

They trickled in in in twos and threes over several days, in unmarked trucks and cars, wearing civilian clothes and carrying nothing that would give them away as fighters on the move. Those who had to cross borders carried legitimate papers issued by officials either bribed or coerced into Fatah's service, declaring they were farm-workers.

Ironically named after Damoros, the ancient Phoenician god of immortality, Damour was an uninteresting place with none of the cedar-clad beauty of much of Lebanon. The town part was nothing more than a half-mile-long sprawl of bullet-pocked and alley-riddled stone houses in a fork in the Old Saida Coastal Road, guarded north and south by barbed wire and machine-gun nests.

But their precise destination was down in the valley between the town and the inland hills: a military installation of maybe 10 acres enclosed by a tall fence topped with shiny-fresh barbed wire. Barracks-stood on three sides of a rolled-earth parade ground. Out wider were a firing range backed by an earthwork berm, and an obstacle course entwined with the scrubby trees along a stretch of the Bou Damaa stream. A number of shot-up vehicles, including the shell of a bus, perhaps left over from the slaughter in the town, were scattered across the rest of the open ground.

Three camp orderlies and a cook supplied by Azmi Zrayir were there to greet them. Mohammed Masameh hovered in the background evaluating each new arrival, as did two muscular-looking men, there to assist with physical fitness. Each new arrival was directed to a cot in the bunkhouse that could have slept more than 40 in rows down both sides, then to get some food in the mess hall and wait for further instructions.

Since there were only about 3,000 active Fatah fighters at any one time in Beirut, it was inevitable some men would know each other from convoys and roadblocks, but none well, only that they were there as comrades on a joint operation. Those hard men who knew who Masameh was, bowed respectfully in greeting and kept a healthy distance.

Dalal was the last arrival other than Salaam and Hiza'a. She'd been given a little extra time to say goodbye to her family, to whom she was close - particularly to her beloved younger brother Mohammed.

She caused more than a ripple.

The more religious men, Ahmed and Wael, and to a lesser extent Rami, Khaled and Fayadh, were shocked. They weren't used to a woman, particularly one with an uncovered head, being among them, let alone being treated as an equal.

A marked exception was Hussain, her friend from Dbaiyeh. He greeted her warmly and kissed her on both cheeks, further raising the hackles of the extremists.

She was aware of the looks and whispers being exchanged. She'd been through it all before and knew how to deal with it. So did Masameh, who kept her in his sight in anticipation.

Leaving a small bag on a bed in the bunkhouse which she'd chosen deliberately because it was in the middle of others already occupied, she went looking for something to eat.

Several others were seated in the mess hall, and Ahmed and Khaled were carrying plates when she passed them near the serving counter. Close enough to hear Ahmed murmur something that roughly translated to "slut."

Dalal grabbed a metal tray, wheeled, and smashed it against the back of Ahmed's head. Then she put her full force into kicking him as he lay dazed and bleeding on the floor, punctuating each thud of her boot with terse words.

"Do not... Speak... Of me... That way!"

In Dalal's experience, respect was made up of equal parts rapport, admiration, and fear. If she couldn't immediately have the first two, she would start with the last.

Then she walked unhurriedly to the counter, helped herself to some steaming rice and vegetables, and withdrew to a corner to eat, chewing slowly and deliberately.

Ahmed got to his feet and staggered toward the ablutions area to clean himself up.

No one else made eye contact or said a word.

Later that night, Masameh summoned them to the classroom building, for what they expected would be a welcoming speech.

The gathering visibly tensed when he entered. He was an impressive sight, with wild tangled long hair, a chiseled physique, and beautifully symmetrical features discernible even beneath a short, ragged beard.

He commenced with a blunt statement.

"You will call me *Baba'a* (Father) and I will chastise you like children if you fail to carry out my instructions instantly and to the syllable. If you persist in failing me, I will kill you."

There were no complaints. They respected toughness and would most surely need to get through the training regime ahead.

Baba'a then introduced Dalal, pointedly calling her *Mulazim* (Lieutenant.) He made clear that she and another man who would join them later would be the ranking officers under him.

Dalal immediately extended an olive branch by insisting she be called "Sister" instead. There were a few encouraging nods of approval around the circle.

The meeting ended with some housekeeping rules around cleanliness, eating, and sleeping times and the like. Nothing they hadn't heard before.

Afterward, everyone made their ablutions in the bathrooms at each end of the bunkhouse. There was no running water, but large washing bowls were provided.

The flush-toilets, over a septic tank, had to be hand-filled. Then the devout put down rugs and knelt facing to the southeast for late prayers, before everyone settled in for the night.

Dalal could already sense a growing deference, confirming she'd done the right thing by making an early stand. She intended to build on that, as she'd always had to do, with single-minded determination and professionalism. At least now anyone who resented her knew it would be smart to keep it to himself.

And when she heard the rhythmical rustling of hands under the covers that night and on many nights to come, she smiled and kept that to herself in turn.

Breakfast was served at 8:00 a.m. in the mess hall. Yogurt and pocket bread with fillings such as beef, onions, spicy bean-paste, pine nuts, and a savory sauce. And urns of strong coffee.

When they returned to the bunkhouse, a large truckload of equipment had arrived. Each drew their own supplies, including boots, changes of cheap civilian clothing for blending in with the civilian population when moving outside of camp, and incongruously garishly colored, plasticized-fabric backpacks for hauling their ammunition and other tools of war.

Also, their personal weapon: a Czech-made Kalashnikov AKM 7.62 x 39mm caliber fully automatic assault-rifle, an upgraded version of the ubiquitous AK-47, which they were to keep loaded and within hand's reach at all times. Each gun was grease-caked. They spent the rest of the morning cleaning those and sorting out their other items.

As the day proceeded, some, particularly the big men, turned to individual exercise to combat the growing tedium. The fitness trainers made suggestions as to what might work with each man's body type.

It crossed the minds of some that this might be an easy posting, not realizing they were being scrutinized for any sign of emotional or physical weakness.

That easy day was the calm before the storm. Word came at dinner time that formal training would begin on the parade ground at 5:00 a.m.

TEN

Damour
Friday, January 6th

The Kamal Adwan operatives' daily routine over the next month began with a run that became progressively longer each brisk early morning, followed by calisthenics to cool down.

Breakfast was 6 to 6:30 a.m., then an hour of water fetching, washing, cleaning, and other camp duties.

At 7:30 a.m. they met in the classroom-building for general discussion, which became personal instruction time as they individually developed.

Between 9:30 and 10:00 a.m., they could do what they liked. The devout caught up with prayer.

A single scheduled prayer time was right away a problem for Hussain, Ahmed, and Wael. They expected five; Fajr, when the first white light appears in the east, Dhur at noon, Asr, when a thing's shadow is the same length as its height, Maghrib at sunset, and Isha'a at around midnight. Baba'a's secular encouragement, however, soon had them catching up when they could.

Ten till noon was further fitness training. Everyone seemed to have come into camp in reasonable shape, and soon could easily complete the obstacle course. Fighting in a war was, after all, no cake-walk. Even Hiza'a and Salaam, who had joined the main group later, their conditioning sharpened by their days of boat handling at Latakia, came up-to-pace quickly enough.

Hiza'a, however, had other problems fitting in. Some knew him by reputation as a fool for his inappropriate behavior around various camps. While he wasn't actually shunned, it was questionable whether they would follow him into battle, which didn't escape Baba'a's attention.

The food served during the noon -1:00 p.m. meal break, by local Muslim restaurateur spared in the 1976 massacre, was surprisingly good for such limited facilities. Typically, a lamb or beef stew with a lot of starchy side dishes and heaped plates of freshly baked *Man'ooshe* pita bread.

Then came two hours of weapons re-training, a mixture of classroom instruction and practice on the range. A new feature of their Czech-made AKMs was a selective fire lever with 3-shot burst capability as well as single-shot and fully automatic. Once they had the hang of that, all the operatives were effective with the weapon, including Dalal, who had qualified during her Lieutenant's training the previous year. Jalal, Ramz, and the big and steady Khaled were particularly good. Rami was in another class entirely, to the point of showing off, being equally excellent left-handed and right. The only shortcoming was frequent jams due to the poor-quality Chinese-made ammunition. Baba'a promised to ask Azmi Zrayir's people for something more reliable.

Dalal, all the while, marveled at how childishly the men behaved with their toys. Muslim children are taught that overt physical gestures such as high-fives are appalling manners. That sticks with many of them. But these were constantly catcalling, hooting and cheering at every success. Disobedient little boys, was what they really were, she realized.

Very dangerous little boys.

Guest instructors were brought in after the first week to teach heavier weapons skills, beginning with the Chinese Type 69 rocket-grenade launcher. This used a 12lb re-usable launch tube to send a 9lb grenade accurately as far as 200-yards. Jalal, Ramz, and Rami were already skilled, but soon all could hit a 55-gallon oil drum at 100-yards, at first with inert practice rounds, and then with warheads that shredded the thick steel like paper, and would be deadly to anyone within 20-yards.

Another major weapon was the Kalashnikov RPK light machine gun, which shared many of its parts with the AKM, but had a longer barrel, bipod, and a 75-round drum magazine. They trained with these in two-person teams until all were capable of pouring large numbers of accurate rounds into the berm at the back of the range.

They also practiced a lot with the Russian made F1 hand grenade. The little dark-gray segmented globes weighed only a little over a pound, but were devastating to anything within a 10-yard radius. Carrying them loose in backpacks proved clumsy and not a little dangerous, so every operative was issued a webbing vest to clip them to.

One special session was devoted to stripping, reassembling, and firing, three weapons they were likely to encounter in Israel, in case they should capture and have to use one; the lightweight, fast firing and easily handled, Uzi 9mm submachine gun; the Israeli.223 caliber Galil assault rifle, and the same caliber American Colt M16 carbine.

Assault training using live fire involved the collection of old vehicles, particularly the bus. All learned how to back each other up in stopping, boarding, clearing and reloading passengers as hostages.

You never knew what you might have to do.

Ahmed and Wael trained also with Semtex, a Czech supplied explosive that smelled like almonds, came in 1lb plastic-wrapped blocks, and could be molded harmlessly like builder's putty. They learned the different fuse types, and how to use delayed timers for booby-traps. Practical work involved running out from behind shelter at the back of the firing range, slapping a wad of explosive against an oil drum, poking in and lighting a 10 second fuse and racing like lightning back to cover.

There were also occasional sessions, depending on who was present and available, on first aid, CPR by the Holger-Nielsen method, radio communications, and general cross training on anything anyone thought might be useful.

Two hours of training from the chin up began at 3:00 p.m. daily.

The operatives' minds had to be conditioned to carry out the goals of the operation completely. This meant extensive ideological and psychological training. Jihad had seen the effectiveness of that first hand during a visit to North Korea in 1963, and Fatah became one of the first armed groups in the Middle East to seize on and train for it.

Fatah fighters including Baba'a had received extensive indoctrination in China, Vietnam, East Germany, Czechoslovakia, Bulgaria, and Yugoslavia and returned eager to pass on the knowledge. In turn, members of the IRA, Red Brigades, Red Army Faction, South Moluccans and many other groups had been indoctrinated in Fatah camps.

Baba'a however, didn't have the mesmerizing personality required, so a specialist was brought in daily, from Beirut, in the back of a chauffeured black 1964 Citroën DS-21.

The specialist was a stubby, chain-smoking, toad-faced, 48-year-old French woman by the name of Shezia Heinrich-Mamatow; a three-times-divorced former political science professor and close associate of French anarchist Daniel Cohn-Bendit, Danny the Red. Since losing her tenure at the Sorbonne for participating in his 1968 riots, she'd been hanging out on the fringes of the Middle Eastern conflicts and was glad of the work.

Ms. Heinrich-Mamatow entered the training room for her first session wreathed in cigarette smoke, arms full of newspapers and books, which she unloaded onto a couple of empty desks. The magazines were copies of the PLO monthly newspaper *'Filistiniya Nida' al-Hayat,'* ('Our Palestine, the Call to Life,') and the Arab 'National Covenant.' Also, articles by terrorist leaders like Dr. George Habash of the PFLP and Nayef Hawatmeh of the DFLP, famous for a 1974 event known as the Ma'alot attack. The books included Arabic translations of Castro, Guevara, Chairman Mao, and the North Vietnamese' Ho Chi Minh and General Giap. Even a collection of excerpts from Hitler's 'Mein Kampf'. The eyes of Tariq, the group's wannabe intellectual, lit up.

She plomped down a large ashtray and two blue packs of Gitanes on a desk that had been turned around to serve as a podium. She surveyed the group while tapping out a fresh one and lighting up, and took a large drag before expelling the smoke off to her left. Then she slapped her hand down flat on the desk with a crack.

"The point of terrorism," she shouted, "is to frighten people out of their minds!"

The action jolted the twelve trainees upright.

Jabbing a fat finger, she demanded to be told what generated the greatest fear in adults. When no one responded she snapped, "Threats to their children!" with another of her trademark slaps on the desk.

Over and over, and over again, she drove home that uncertainty creates fear, and hostages must never be given information of any kind, to heighten that uncertainty. Physical discomfort and humiliation increased this, so hostages must not be allowed the use of toilets or even to stand and stretch. Or comb their hair, or wash, or apply makeup.

Hostages' self-confidence, esteem, and sense of identity had to be broken down at all costs. "Choose one who stands out. Make an example! Be brutal. It will keep the others in line, I promise you!"

She knew her topics intimately and argued them compellingly. After each hand-slapping pronouncement she would cackle huskily, and invariably light and draw deeply on yet another cigarette. Two hours a day and often longer, six days a week, she preached Marxist-Leninism including the Communist Manifesto, Imperialism and the Arab Reaction, Revolution and Counter Revolution, all against a backdrop of Islamic history, the displaced-Arab cause, and the evils of Zionism.

One statement was repeated many times. "Terror must be terrifying! Making people half afraid means nothing! They must be certain that their lives are in danger! Then they never forget!"

When Ms. Heinrich-Mamatow's black Citroen had departed at around 5:00 p.m. the trainees were allowed an hour to themselves before supper.

The evening meal was always preceded by bowls of hummus and plates of pocket bread. The main was usually

Mujaddara; a chicken dish with lentils, rice, pine nuts and chick peas, with fried cauliflower and a big salad, topped off by *Baklawa,* a sweet sticky baked dessert of nuts and fruit.

The first two-person, two-hour night watch began at 8:00 p.m. and rotated through to 4:00 a.m., with everyone getting one unbroken night's sleep in three.

By the end of a solid month of training, every member was in peak condition. Physical activity was then dialed down into maintenance mode, with an hour of calisthenics morning and evening, and a circuit of the obstacle course alternated with a session on the firing range with all the weapons, every other day.

Mental conditioning, however, continued daily for as long as the team members remained at Damour.

ELEVEN

Yarmouk
Thursday, February 2nd

"So how do you think that helps us, Mr. Spymaster?" Jihad sneered from the comfortable chair in his office.

Iyad shifted uncomfortably in his, mystified by this response to the great news he'd just delivered. He'd been sure Jihad would be elated that the Egyptian-Israeli talks had gone badly for the Egyptians and Israelis, and therefore very well, for the displaced-Arab cause.

"Khalil perhaps I wasn't clear. I'm saying President Carter tilted massively in our direction. God knows why. His Jewish supporters must be outraged."

Jihad asked, "And they call this the 'Aswan Formula'?'"

"Yes. Carter is saying a formal peace treaty, ratified and supported by the U.S., must include the two things we want most. Israel pulling back to pre-1967 borders, and a 'Palestinian' solution.' Surely that's great news?"

Jihad's body language signaled the opposite. Slouched in his seat, he had his palms together in front of his chin. And he never slouched.

"Look, this is what you wanted, right?" Iyad probed tentatively.

"Maybe. Maybe." said Jihad. "What about these problems with the press Sadat is having?"

"They have turned on him like a nest of cobras. They say he's selling us out too cheaply. That has to be even better for us."

"Perhaps." Jihad settled even lower in his chair. "But what is Sadat's response?"

"Trying to appear much tougher at the moment. But never mind him," Iyad rushed on. "It's all on Israel's shoulders now. What can Begin say? He has to give ground in our direction."

"I have a problem that he and Sadat are even having dinners together," Jihad said morosely.

Iyad gaped at his boss.

This is unfathomable. This breakthrough represents more progress toward our own homeland than our entire three decades of armed struggle has achieved.

But fearful of igniting one of Jihad's tantrums, he kept his voice level. "We have an unprecedented opportunity here. Never has so many powerful forces been aligned in our favor."

Staring straight ahead, Jihad absently, "But the Egyptians have pulled their delegation from the Political Committee Meetings. Correct? I suppose that's something."

Something? What does the man want?

"Temporarily, I think. To take the pressure off Sadat at home from those who say he's giving in too easily. But the other signs favor us."

"Favor." Jihad stared at the center of the table as if it was a pit he was considering throwing himself into.

Iyad threw wide his hands exasperatedly. "Yes favor! Khalil, I don't get it. We are on the brink here. How can this not be a great day? Our struggle may be ending. Our homeland in reach. All that stands in the way is Begin saying yes! Are you so afraid he will say no that you don't want to raise your hopes?"

Jihad stared at his friend of 18 years as if he was a complete stranger.

Is he really such a fool? We've been building up Fatah since, what, 1959? All those years! It's the reason for our existence! Or is he so naïve he can't see what all this means?

If Egypt and Israel make peace, it's the end of everything?

No more Fatah.

No more power!

Left alone again, and with his whole life's work under threat from, of all things, Fatah's own success; Jihad vowed to focus entirely on Operation Kamal Adwan. It was no longer just about derailing peace talks. In the dark recesses of his mind, it had evolved into a pure exercise in hatred and revenge.

He'd been receiving progress reports from Baba'a via Azmi Zrayir, most recently on January 22nd, to say the trainees were pulling together satisfactorily. But now the operation had become all-consuming that was no longer sufficient. He needed to get the information firsthand.

He called for transport. Within an hour he was on his way to visit Damour, accompanied by Iyad and Zrayir, in a gray Mercedes Benz W123DI touring car guarded front and rear by armed-fighters-filled pickup trucks.

Baba'a, alerted in advance by a runner from the town, had the operatives waiting in the classroom.

Jihad swept into the room in his tailored black suit and what he fondly believed was a trendy mustard tie. He was flanked by Iyad in similar but better coordinated gray dress, and Zrayir in his flamboyant traditional Bedouin robes. The operatives shot upright into stiff military stances. Jihad motioned them offhandedly to sit and then moved behind the desk at the head of the class.

"Each of you has been chosen for a mission of penetrating into Yáfa from the sea. This is why you have been trained in boating, sea navigation, and urban assault. You are here because of your special talents and because the organization has trust in you."

He swiveled his head while pausing a second for effect. None of the audience appeared surprised. He was momentarily annoyed.

They all know this because Hiza'a knows this, and the man is incapable of keeping anything to himself! But I suppose, given their training, nothing else makes sense anyway.

"After we strike the main objective, Allah willing, we will close off the streets of Yáfa. On one street, for example, we might hold 500 hostages. Five hundred people at once at gunpoint until our demands are met. Will they not bargain then? At any moment we can destroy everyone! Blow up their buildings, no matter how many people are there. Our dagger will be a poisoned dagger in our enemy's heart, and we will take down as many as possible!"

He watched the movement of heads as the fighters glanced around at each other, studying body language for any wavering.

"When we land in enemy territory, Allah willing, we will set up our fortress and begin to fire on our enemy. We will dig in his throat and heart. We will turn the Yáfa day black!"

He leaned forward and put his hands down on the table, firmly in emphasis. Unfortunately, it wasn't squarely on four legs and rocked, spoiling the gesture slightly. Still, he saw with satisfaction he had them in his spell.

"We will turn the Yáfa day into destruction, Allah willing. We will turn the Yáfa day so it will be remembered through history as Black Saturday. Black Sunday. Yáfa will be closed those whole days with blood and destruction!"

Heads were nodding. He felt a flash of pride at his speaking skills.

Jihad gestured to them to approach the large table in the corner. All brothers under the sun. Iyad unrolled some topographical maps he'd brought. In the shadow of the operatives, the terrorist leaders appeared even more diminutive.

Speaking alternately, the three visitors added as much flesh to the bones of the operation as they could at this early stage. They described where they would probably be dropped off to motor in by themselves, the seaborne approaches, and likely points of reference such as the clock tower on the headland above Jaffa harbor, south of the beach area.

"You will be in two teams, each in their own zodiac boat," Jihad said. "Comrade Hiza'a will be the overall sea captain responsible for getting you ashore and will command one team. Sister Dalal the other. The breakdown of the teams will be decided after your final sea training."

Dalal asked, "And the... exact target?"

Jihad's finger moved across the map of Tel Aviv to an area of the foreshore around Hayarkon Street and Ben Gurion Boulevard, then circled a cluster of hotels, including the Dan Beach Hotel.

"Probably one of... these! It will be confirmed closer to the time."

He brought Salaam into the mix and let him point out landmarks he remembered. Lighthouses, markets, wharves and beach breakwaters. Just enough to plant the seed they wouldn't be going in completely blind.

It was Hiza'a who addressed the elephant in the room. "What will be our exit plan?"

Others murmured in chorus.

Jihad lied smoothly and convincingly.

"The hostages you will take are to be traded for a smaller and more manageable group of foreign ambassadors. In turn, you will trade those for a number of our jailed compatriots and air transport to freedom."

He felt spirits lifting around him.

He closed by congratulating them on their hard work so far, about which he had heard, "Only good things."

It was another lie. He knew from Baba'a there were at least potential problems with the team dynamics. The real reason for this visit was to find out details of that.

The terrorist leaders and Baba'a then met in private, speaking English, which Baba'a had learned during a Jesuit Catholic upbringing, and Jihad was fond of practicing whenever he could.

Baba'a began by saying how much Dalal had impressed him and quickly gained the respect and confidence of everyone, with her determination and 'follow me or don't: it's your call!' attitude. Which she'd always back up with another demonstration of her competence.

He then repeated the misgivings mentioned in a previous message to Jihad about Hiza'a. "The man is militarily capable and I understand he did well enough with Salaam in boat training, but he has no social radar. He wants to be liked too much, never takes anything seriously, and is most certainly not a leader. Were we a larger operation, he might make a useful second in command to someone else, but that is not our structure.”

"Alternatives then?"

"I would have said Tariq because he has some leadership experience, but he thinks he’s cleverer than is the case. Or Rami, but he’s a lone wolf by nature. A fearsome wolf, but still a loner."

“How are the rest doing in general?”

Salaam liked to dress the part a bit too much; always wearing his webbing festooned with grenades, even when others were lounging around the camp in jeans and tee-shirts. But the more experienced ones had proven their mettle. The others were performing up to their lesser potential.

Jalal and Ramz, the two thugs, had taken on extra fitness training when it had been slackened off for others. Tariq, Fayadh, Ahmed, and Hussain, the ones most inspired by Ms. Heinrich-Mamatow's teachings, had a sort of study group going on where they discussed political theory.

The most devout members, Hussain, Wael, and Ahmed-and others as the mood took them-had established a prayer routine that worked for them.

The only truly restless one was again Salaam, but he still did his duty without question, knowing Baba'a would accept nothing less.

"You believe they are ready to be tested?" Jihad asked.

"Yes," replied Baba'a. "It is the only way to be sure. It may answer our other questions also."

"Then I will see it is arranged, agreed Jihad as the leaders got up to leave.

"In the meantime, continue working within the current command structure. I will consider your views and decide what should be done. *As-Salamu Alaykum*."

"And may Allah be with you also," Baba'a responded.

Jihad left Damour encouraged, but also troubled. He saw a decision looming that he really didn't want to make.

TWELVE

Yarmouk
Sunday, February 5th

During the three weeks prior to meeting the operatives at Damour, Jihad had been reaching out through agents into the docklands of Beirut, seeking a ship for the operation. Entirely unsuccessfully. There were good reasons for this.

Two years prior, Fatah had attacked the Savoy Hotel in Tel Aviv, also using Zodiac boats launched from a coastal freighter. Eleven Israelis, including a Special Forces Colonel, and all but one of the terrorists had been killed when the hotel was destroyed by a suicide bombing. The ship that delivered the attackers off the coast had been captured by the Israeli navy. The crew was currently doing hard time in Ashkelon Military Prison. That outcome was well known within the Lebanese shipping community.

Jihad's chief agent called him the day he returned to Damour, profusely apologizing that all approaches were still being met with refusals. Jihad told him to double the money on offer and try harder, or expect visitors at his door.

That same Sunday evening at Damour, as the operatives were bunking down for the night, their big test was thrown at them.

A little after 9:00 p.m. a canvas-sided truck came down the access road and was let into the camp by Baba'a's assistants.

First to climb down from the back were eight bearded, grimy, and stinking Fatah fighters. The trainees emerged to investigate the commotion.

Jalal and Rami knew several of the visitors and called out greetings. They were ignored as shouting and the thrusting of gun muzzles began forcing a group of captives down after them.

There were 18 prisoners of both genders and a wide range of ages.

Eight were middle aged or older. Two such men had priest's collars, and three of the women wore nun's habits. Some adults' faces showed signs of abuse. The elder of the two priests had his nose smashed flat against his bleeding face.

There were also ten young people, teen-aged and younger, down to a girl around seven. All the captives were confused and extremely fearful, cowering and staring wildly around.

The prisoners were taken to the classroom and held under guard while the operatives followed Baba'a's orders to put on their work clothes and boots and gather their AKMs. It occurred to several while they were dressing that there might be a connection with another event that day. Shortly before dusk, a yellow earth-moving machine had rumbled down from where it had been doing road repair work in the town, and was now parked by the berm at the back of the firing range.

Just as everyone was finishing dressing, Baba'a came into the bunkhouse fully armed, closed the door and stood with his back to it.

In a voice dripping menace he said, "Did you think you would just wave your guns at the Jews and they would give you what you want?"

Baba'a scanned their faces, judging their reactions, and made an expansive motion with his free arm. "Did you think their women and children would line up to be bargained for by the Zionists that lead them? That they would bow and sweep wide their arms and say, 'but of course you can have back your olive groves! Here! Have this piece of land we stole from you and build yourself a fine house!'"

He stepped closer, looking balefully into their eyes. Lingering an instant on each before moving on to the next.

"No! This is how it will be. These kāfirs were taken today in a house of their foul God in Chiyah." He meant a Christian suburb of Beirut close to the Green Line.

Looking purposefully at Ahmed, Wael and then at Hussain, Baba'a said, "Perhaps it is Allah's will." Then at a shout, "Tonight you will show me that you are capable and worthy of the mission that has been given to you! Now follow me to the firing range!"

Everyone understood as soon as he said the last words. A line was about to be crossed. This was the real thing. Everyone knew it was a test that must be passed.

For some of whom Shezia Heinrich-Mamatow's statements about inducing fear in hostages and the necessity of execution as motivation, had been only words; they had suddenly become a stark reality.

Outside, the mob moved by starlight and a quarter moon toward the rear of the firing range, with the captives being driven ahead by blows and shouts.

Stomachs churned in some operatives. Bile burned in throats. Blind willingness in the abstract and flying on the wings of a great adventure was one thing. Committing mass murder to demonstrate their level of dedication was something else.

At the berm a generator clattered into life, and arc lights blazed down from poles. The captives were forced into a huddle beneath them, threatened by gun-muzzles on all sides.

Baba'a gave a command, and a nun was dragged from the group and shoved to where he was standing. She stood blinking confusedly under the brightest light near the earth-moving machine. Baba'a drew a pistol and shot her in the side of the head. Then leaned over and fired a second shot into her upturned face.

No orders were given or needed. Two more victims were shoved forward, young girls this time. Jalal shouldered his way forward and fired his AKM on fully automatic into their bodies at a range of a foot or so. The bullets ripped dirt into the air from the mound behind them. Baba'a again supplied the coup de grâce to each.

Then the bloody-faced priest was pushed into the open, holding a set of rosary beads to his lips and muttering in Latin. Rami stepped forward firmly. Baba'a waved him back, and pointed at Wael, who'd become something of a team mascot.

Wael stepped forward confidently enough, then doubled over and vomited on the ground. Baba'a shouted, and when that had no effect pulled the youth roughly upright and made him lift his weapon.

Wael blindly pulled the trigger and missed, but corrected and sent the man down shrieking, to be silenced by Baba'a. Wael lurched away into the darkness.

This went on for ten more minutes.

The third nun tried to stop two of the young people being separated out and was killed before them. Otherwise the captives went to their deaths almost numbly as they realized there was no hope. All the while, as the operatives waited to do their job, they were aware of Baba'a's glittering eyes on them.

Rami, Ahmed, Khaled, and Hussain all did as they were told perfunctorily and then stepped away, faces impassive. Dalal also, after shooting one of the adult men. Ramz sprayed two prisoners with automatic fire where they huddled and finishing the job with single shots to the head with no compunction whatsoever.

Salaam, however, missed his victim with his first two attempts, and then kept the trigger pressed until his gun was empty. Tariq for all his firebrand revolutionary rhetoric was nearly as useless. Likewise, Fayadh.

Finally, Hiza'a proved all suspicions correct when his big talk deserted him. Unable to step forward until shouted at, he then couldn't hold his weapon steady. After clumsily completing his task, he too stumbled off retching.

As the group straggled silently back to the bunkhouse, they heard the earth-mover growl to life behind them, ensuring that no evidence would remain come daylight.

Baba'a was thoughtful in his bunk that night.

Yes, some performed well, but enough did not to put the operation at real risk. I must let Jihad know that as soon as possible. Something will need to be done to shore things up.

"Our training here is done," said Baba'a to the operatives sitting on cots or leaning against walls around the bunkhouse the next morning.

Few had attended breakfast, and most seemed subdued after the events of the previous night.

"There is more to be done, but not at this place," he added. "You may have a ten-day leave to do as you wish. Transport will be provided to take you wherever you choose. Not all at once, but over the next days. But you must advise the nearest Fatah commander where you will be at all times and be ready to rejoin the operation immediately when called."

Not everyone took advantage of the opportunity.

Big Khaled, Fayadh who was almost as disliked as Hiza'a, Tariq with his nose in his books on armed struggle, the taciturn Ramz, and Jalal-who to the best of anyone's knowledge had never had a friend and it was doubtful if he'd even had parents, were content to stay in camp.

Of those who accepted leave, Salaam wanted to be anywhere else and find himself a woman. He requested transport to Tripoli. Dalal wanted to spend time with her family in Beirut. Hussain, Rami, Ahmed, and Wael wished to be taken to Shatila to spend time at the mosque on the square. Hiza'a wanted to go anywhere he could impress someone.

Those staying were pleased to see Hiza'a go. They were heartily sick of his affecting airs from old American movies, though he wasn't clowning so much at the moment.

Those leaving were told to take everything with them, including their personal weapons. As they were packing, Baba'a advised them curtly, "You are not to disclose anything about this operation to anyone, even family or lovers. Anyone who does will be immediately delivered to Azmi Zrayir as a traitor, for his judgment."

They began dispersing that evening and the next, exactly as they had arrived, in civilian clothing and with their weapons concealed under piles of innocuous cargo.

The following morning, leaving his staff to cater for those remaining, Baba'a climbed aboard his own transport bound for Syria.

That same morning, Wednesday, February 8th, sixty miles away in Yarmouk, Jihad sat through yet another of Iyad's briefings on Middle Eastern events.

Sadat had been talking with Carter, trying to get the peace initiative moving again on terms favorable to Egypt. He had also published a reassuring letter to the American Jewish community in the Miami Herald. Those efforts had restarted the joint Egyptian-Israeli military-committee meetings, and one had just concluded in Cairo.

In Israel, an uproar had broken out. A radical right-wing group called the *Gush Emunim* (Bloc of the Faithful,) had broken ground for an illegal settlement near the archaeologically important, ancient Judean & Samarian city of Shiloh. Arguments for and against this were dominating discussion time in the Knesset.

But a greater threat to Fatah was that the U.S. was trying to sweeten any Middle East peace deal with their customary bribe. Weapons. Warplanes, in fact. Israel and Saudi Arabia would be receiving F15s and F16s, while Egypt the much lesser performing F5s so as not to tip the strategic balance. For Fatah, this meant going cap in hand to the Soviets for the latest missiles to counter them.

But the matter of the ship was far more pressing. Jihad was back on the phone by mid-afternoon, haranguing his Beirut contacts about their lack of progress.

At least if a ship could be found, Jihad knew there were plenty of crews for hire. The Eastern Mediterranean shipping circuit of Cairo, Limassol, Latakia, Istanbul, Tripoli, and Beirut, had been a haven for sailors looking for work, for centuries. But the sailors had no ships, and those who did, didn't want to lose them.

Time was getting truly short, because Jihad had already decided on two alternative dates for the operation: the Saturday nights of the 3rd and 10th of March.

He wanted the operatives to come ashore on the Tel Aviv beach-front as the Jewish Shabbat was beginning at sunset. Iyad had assured him traffic on the streets would be at its lightest, as many workers traditionally went home early to their families to light candles, bless unleavened bread and share Aruchat Shabbat, the sacred meal served on the family's best crockery over a Mapah Lavanah, the traditional white tablecloth.

Between outbursts at his ship-seeking envoys, the Fatah leader had also been completing arrangements for the final training phase of the operation. Baba'a had said he needed another solid week for joint boat training at a new location.

That was to be a safe house at the Fatah-controlled fishing village of Es Saksakiye, 40 miles south of Beirut. The place had been used before to launch clandestine missions, but not recently. There was a marina nearby, with a beach for training with the Zodiacs and a wharf able to berth a coastal-size ship.

Most importantly, it was sufficiently far from the border, that if the operatives moved in quietly and kept themselves invisible by training only at night, they should be safe enough from Israeli air-strikes.

Then on Thursday afternoon the 10th, like an answer to a plea to Allah, a vessel finally fell into Jihad's lap. He immediately sent a couple of followers to look at her.

She was named *Sansato.* Perhaps after the mountain in China. But perhaps more aptly because it means 'sensible' in some Arabic dialects, and a sound and sensible vessel she was.

Cypriot registered, but Norwegian built, she was a dual gasoline and diesel oil carrier plying the coastal-marina trade. Right then she was berthed at basin three, quay 11 at the Beirut docks, minus a crew, waiting out a spike in spot diesel prices. Her hard-up offshore owners, blissfully unaware whom they were dealing with, were glad to earn such a handsome income off her in the meantime, no questions asked.

Those looking her over weren’t seamen or engineers, but to them she seemed quite serviceable.

Thirty-three meters in length and with a draft of three meters, her Volvo-Penta 550hp diesel engine appeared well enough maintained, and a chart in the engine room said she had a cruising speed of better than 10 knots at 50 liters per hour. The swing-boom hoist amidships looked ideal for small boat launching. Accommodation was adequate in two four-bunk cabins forward and an eight-bunk cabin aft, plus there were hooks for hammocks in the ceiling of the below-deck passageway. Even her colors were ideal for Fatah's purposes: a black hull and gray superstructure that made her almost invisible in the night with her running lights off.

Jihad hired her immediately for a one-month rental, to be returned to the owners at Larnaca, Cyprus, her home port. The rate was $5,000 American dollars a week, not counting the extra cost of a crew yet to be found.

The operation had overcome its last apparent obstacle. It had its ship.

THIRTEEN

Yarmouk
Friday, February 10th

Baba'a arrived in Damascus on an unseasonably bright and warm Friday morning, having spent the previous two nights at the Neolithic diggings at Joub Jannine in the Bekaa Valley, sharing the tent of a large-breasted and almost albino-blond German archaeological student.

Lying in her camp bed the previous evening, as she traced the scars of the wounds, he'd accumulated during his 12-years within the struggle, he'd been full of doubts. He'd questioned his self-worth and felt an overwhelming sense of mortality. Not even her skilled efforts, in bringing the fine young warrior of her overseas study interlude to yet another shuddering climax, could dispel his feelings of dread.

Now late in the Friday afternoon, he was in Jihad's upstairs office with the ever-attentive Iyad also at the table.

Jihad began the meeting beaming from having secured the ship, but sobered rapidly as he listened to Baba'a's report on the teams' status and its performance the previous Sunday night.

Baba'a concluded with, "I still think they will do the work, but with only Sister Dalal to drive them, they will need to stay in one group."

"Out of the question!" fumed Jihad. "We've been lucky in the past getting teams ashore, but we can't depend on that forever. Besides, the objective requires a pincer approach. There are two main entrances on different streets."

"You asked for my opinion," Baba'a huffed, "There it is."

"I know. I know," Jihad placated.

Earlier in the day, there'd been another of Iyad's intelligence briefings.

Sadat was in the U.S. having talks with Jimmy Carter at Camp David. An overnight joint press release had confirmed the Aswan Formula as the basis of any prospective peace agreement. Despite his continued savaging in his country's press, Sadat had promised to resume direct talks with Israel on his return home.

Cyrus Vance supported his boss and Sadat by saying that Israeli settlements in the Sinai "should not exist." Begin's testy reply reminded the Americans that the Israeli-US conversations at the end of December hadn't mentioned settlements at all.

The twin tides of history and world opinion might be turning against Israel, but all present at the Fatah briefing were unanimous that the planned short sharp reminder was still needed.

That those of displaced-Arab heritage were here. And they weren't going anywhere.

But as usual, of late, Jihad's and Iyad's priorities had not been the same. A scowling Iyad said, "Don't you think we should be worrying more about this arms sale Khalil? The numbers are enormous! Israel will be getting 15 more F-15s and 75 F-16s. The Saudis 60 F-15s. Egypt only 50 F-5s. The Jewish air force will become practically omnipotent. The F16 is a fine ground attack aircraft, capable of untold damage to our emplacements in South Lebanon. We need at least shoulder-fired SA7s if not vehicle-mounted SA8s to prevent that. Shouldn't you be talking to your Soviet Foreign Minister friend Mr. Gromyko?"

Jihad had hardly more than grunted.

Now, as he looked at Baba'a, Jihad's emotions were conflicted.

With its ship on hand, the operation wasn't dependent on anything except a reasonable chance of success. And this tall, powerful man represented that best chance. But the loss of Baba'a's operations skills to Fatah and Jihad personally would be devastating.

Where will I find another like him? Still, the operation was his masterpiece. *What choice do I have?*

"Mohammed, I need to call on you for something more," he said carefully.

"I know," said Baba'a.

"You do?"

"Yes. I have thought it through. I want to do it."

Jihad rocked back in his seat.

He'd been steeling himself to be persuasive. Not this.

"You... know the risks? He waved his hands to dismiss the words. "No. We have been comrades too long not to speak directly. You know the almost certain outcome?"

Baba'a's reply was firm. "Khalil, I am not one of the children you have sent me many times to make ready for the fight. I have fought in your ranks for many years. Sent many men on your behalf to their deaths, their ears full of words of the homeland to come. Of regaining our green fields. Our mountains. Our homes."

Baba'a studied his maimed hand for a few moments while he sought the right words.

"It is time I struck a blow again personally, or I am nothing but a *munafiq* (hypocrite). For all the men I have trained and lectured and sent away. I must do my part. Myself."

"Mohammed, I don't know how I can bear to lose you. And I have never said that to another man."

"It shall be as Allah wills, and as you know I am not a religious man."

Jihad stared out the window at the far, sun-soaked hills, struggling with an unusual feeling he abruptly realized was regret. Then he dismissed the moment of weakness from his mind.

"Yes, it shall."

The Lebanese Civil War was not being fought at sea, though many had. This was the North-Eastern Mediterranean after all, which had seen countless offshore battles between the founding Phoenicians and invading Persians, Greeks, English Crusaders, even Napoleon's French. All the way back to the ancient Natufians, probably. Fighting in coracles like dodgems at a county fair, but with bronze swords instead of ice-creams.

But in 1977-78, the fighting was inland where the Christians were sandwiched between the Fatah's forces in the west and the Muslim Syrians in the east. Therefore, the coastal maritime trade had been remarkably unaffected. In fact, was protected by Fatah, which received the majority of its arms that way. There was no particular shortage of sailors looking for work. The trick was to find the right kind.

Therefore, since February 9th when the Sansato had been chartered, Fatah's agents had been inquiring surreptitiously among the labor exchanges, bars and other hangouts around the Port of Beirut, for a ship's Master.

This was a simple and straightforward piece of work. No-one conducting the inquiries thought; given Fatah's reputation, there would be any problem enforcing a suitable contract. Therefore, they weren't really looking for the best man available, just one qualified enough to satisfy the Beirut Harbormaster. And one certain to be discreet.

On February 15th, their search took them to an alley smelling of rotting fish and crowded humanity, and lined with illegal food and trinket stalls, off Ibn Sina Avenue, three blocks from the Beirut docks.

In a Turkish-themed basement bar called *Imra Hayakech,* they asked the barman to point out a purported ship's master named Karem Osman. They found the 46-year-old Turk in a back room acrid with cigarette smoke, playing *Pişti*, a card game similar to 'Snap,' for a pound a point.

Osman was a slovenly man with a big belly under a greasy tee shirt, a comb-over, and short stubble covering his entire throat. But he was able to show them a current Captain's ticket.

Over strong coffee for the Fatah men, and numerous glasses of milky colored *Raki* for the Turk, they felt him out sufficiently to decide he could be trusted to keep quiet. Then offered him a princely sum, for a couple of week's work, dropping spies off the coast of Israel.

He seemed untroubled by the risks.

They took him to see the Sansato.

He assured them he could get her underway on a couple-of-days' notice and agreed to supply an equally discreet engineer and some deckhands.

A down payment changed hands at Tariq's old dockside base at Sahet al Najmeh, with the balance due when the ship departed Lebanese waters with the spies on board.

Present were half a dozen conspicuously armed fighters, so there was no doubt of the consequences if Osman reneged or told anyone of their agreement.

Es Saksakiye, South Coastal Lebanon
Saturday, February 16th

The following day, transport quietly collected the operatives from various locations around North Lebanon, and delivered them to their final training base. It took only a day this time. Their fate assimilated; the now eager operatives were literally waiting at their front gates.

They found their southern Lebanese quarters, much more cramped than at Damour. Their base was a five-bedroom, two-bathroom house on the northwest fringe of town, on a bend in a winding gravel road that ran down to and crossed the coastal highway, and ended at a small marina with a wharf.

The house was set back in some trees, away from prying eyes. At the rear was a black Datsun pickup truck concealed by a tarpaulin, for shuttling them and their seafaring gear, the 500-yards or so, to and from the marina.

One bedroom was already occupied by equipment, including two large bags containing the deflated Zodiac boats. New arrivals drew a sleeping bag and mattress each from the equipment room, and staked out some floor space in one of the other bedrooms.

"We will be here at least two weeks, so make the best of it," said Baba's on the morning of February 17th, commencing their welcoming instructions.

"The Fatah forces in the town have not been informed of our purpose, only our presence. We wish to keep it that way. And there are civilian residents in the town, our people to be sure, here to protect against air-strikes, but the Zionists have spies everywhere so don't show yourselves or any equipment outside during daylight. Other than staying fit and keeping yourselves and your equipment clean, your days are your own. Fresh food will be delivered nightly and you will prepare it yourselves. There is a 6:00 p.m. to 6:00 a.m. curfew on the town, so after dark we will have boating training. Every night until we have it right."

Not that night, however, because in the evening Jihad and Iyad, along with Azmi Zrayir and a half dozen bodyguards, arrived equipped with maps and other props to give a further briefing.

"My brothers and sister," Jihad said when they were all gathered cross-legged in the sparsely furnished lounge, "I have come to give you important news, and further details of your mission."

He indicated Iyad, who had no idea what this news was.

"Our intelligence says the Zionists may be better prepared than we thought, and the journey by sea more difficult, so it has been necessary to strengthen the operation. Comrade Baba'a will be joining you in overall command while on the ship. He will also be an equal commander with Sister Dalal when on land. This will allow our strongest seaman, Comrade Hiza'a, to be our navigator at sea and see you safely ashore."

Baba'a stood and nodded, then sat back down again.

Salaam knew he was the best seaman, and might have reacted at the insult. Instead, he heard only that he would no longer have to follow the other man's orders. He shed a sigh of relief and said nothing.

Mollified by the compliment he'd been thrown, and perhaps a little relieved knowing what those around him thought of him, Hiza'a said nothing either.

There was a murmur of approval from the others. In their minds, this greatly increased their chances of survival.

Jihad then began the fine-tuning of the operation, beginning with finalizing the precise timing.

He was determined to launch the mission on his first chosen date, meaning they only had 12 days to complete boat training if they were to board the Sansato on the 1st, be inserted off Israel on the 2nd, and strike at the planned time of 7:00 p.m. on the Shabbat, Friday the 3rd.

"We must strike before the pig Begin travels to Washington. We know only that he will do so in March. He must have his country's vulnerability foremost in his mind when he meets with the American Carter!"

The Sansato would drop them not long before dawn, 25 miles off Tel Aviv's shores. That timing would give the Sansato time to escape due west toward Cyprus. The operatives would then need to bide their time before heading to shore, because 25 miles was only about four hours of motoring in the Zodiacs.

"You will be safe enough unless an Israeli gunboat accidentally finds you," Jihad insisted. "Your small boats will be invisible to their radar."

"If one does?" Fayadh ventured.

"Then you will fight!" replied Jihad, punching a fist into one palm.

The plan from there was that Hiza'a would navigate them in by compass when the timing was right.

When they got close to shore, landmarks such as the lighthouses north and south of the Tel Aviv beach-front would guide them into the Tel Aviv beach-front. If time allowed, they were to booby-trap the boats before making their rush inland across the 200 yards of sand to Moshe Lahat Promenade, which paralleled the shoreline at that point.

Their primary target was the prestigious Dan Hotel, the most luxurious on the beach-side strip and not far south of the northern lighthouse. The distinctive building occupied an entire block between Hayarkon Street and Moshe Lahat, along Frishman Street. It should be full to the brim for the weekend, having been recently renovated and had the 266-foot King David Tower added.

Salaam said he would recognize it. Moshe Lahat Promenade arched over a distinctive low bluff just to the north of it. He was given photographs anyway to help him pick it out in case the skyline had changed since he was there.

The assault would require boldness and good timing. One team would have to run up Frishman to Hayarkon and block the lobby entrance to prevent escape. The other would wait and then shoot their way in via the staff entrances on the lower level.

But in case that objective could not be located, or they came ashore too far south for capturing it to be practical, their secondary target would be any heavily populated building. There were many. They were cautioned, however, to avoid the ferociously guarded U.S. Embassy, which also stretched between Moshe Lahat and Hayarkon only a few hundred yards south.

Most importantly, during the movement over the beach and the assault up through the lower floors of the hotel, the group was to kill every Jew they found. Once in control of the hotel, they would seize as many hostages as possible, then demand to exchange them. First for some designated foreign ambassadors, then for imprisoned comrades plus transport by plane from Sde Dov Airport three miles to the north, to Damascus.

If those demands weren't met within four hours, the estimated time the Israelis would need to mobilize their forces and get ready to take back the hotel, the hostages were to be killed. Then they were all to commit suicide by standing in small circles and holding grenades to their chests.

There would be no alternative evacuation plan.

No one said a word at this, but when Jihad and his contingent departed, a number of operatives remained where they were, wrapped in their thoughts for some time before somberly setting about their bedtime tasks.

FOURTEEN

Es Saksakiye
Saturday, February 18th

The following morning at Es Saksakiye began with envoys from Azmi Zrayir nearly beating down the door.

They brought warnings to be vigilant. The Abu Nidal group had assassinated Egyptian Cultural Minister, close friend of Sadat, and renowned Islamic novelist. Yusef Sibai; in Nicosia. An Iyad spy on the Cypriot Police Force had said it was the start of a region-wide campaign to shift the balance of power toward Nidal's Iraqi sponsors.

Iyad, in Damascus, was beside-himself with fury. If Nidal having ANY kind of success at all wasn't enough, a crackdown on displaced-Arabs in Egypt was certain, restricting the flow of information from his spies.

But the news had little effect on team preparation. They cleaned weapons and other equipment and meticulously weighed everything on a small set of bathroom scales. Also undertook as much boating instruction from Salaam and Hiza'a as possible without actually inflating the Zodiacs. As dusk drew near, they made ready to move to the beach beside the wharf for their initial night of training on the water.

At the shoreline, after inflating the two boats with the crude foot pumps provided, and fitting and test starting the engines, the operatives broke into their separate teams for the first time.

Boat balancing and weight distribution was crucial.

With 13 of them, and considering the change in command structure, Dalal as the lightest person on the mission was moved into Hiza'a's boat, which would be in the lead. Raml was repositioned at the left front, where he could cover the approach to any shore with his AKM.

The seven operatives in her boat, plus the motor and an eight-gallon plastic tank of gasoline, totaled 1343lbs. An additional 120lbs of weapons and ammunition would be strapped in place down the centerline, leaving them safely 187lbs below the maximum of 1650.

The six in the other boat, with Baba'a in the right front, Wael on the left, and Salaam at the controls, only totaled 1238lbs. The bulk of the heavy weaponry, including the two RPK machine-guns and a case of Semtex explosive fuses taped to the outside, made up an extra 300lbs of load, while still leaving plenty of water-line clearance.

They trained in that configuration for the next nine consecutive nights, despite the seas roiled by persistent spring *Khamsin* winds. The 20th and 21st were particularly stormy, but all admired the stability of the little boats, both in ocean rollers and the nasty inshore chop.

They worked on recovering and re-launching from the shelving beach in case they came ashore in the wrong place in Israel and had to put to sea again. And arming themselves quickly in case they were caught by Israeli gunboats at sea. That proved trickier than expected. The solution was dividing the weaponry into two 'dry' bags, strapping the bottom bag of less needed equipment down first, then securing the light weapons bag with bungee cords so it could be accessed swiftly. Around 11:00 p.m. they would deflate the boats, pack them and their engines in their tough rubberized carry bags, and be back at the safe house not much after midnight.

In the mornings everyone would sleep late, then ate leftovers from the last night's meal. After that, each operative spent the day according to his or her own nature.

There was always someone in a corner practicing sit-ups or press-ups, competing for the most impressive count in one session. Those with the physique, like Jalal and Ramz, or the vanity like Salaam, spent time working with weights.

Beneath their sweating bravado the air hummed, with the unspoken awareness their lives would soon rely upon the strength and endurance these workouts were building up.

There was an almost continuous game of *Tarabish,* a Lebanese version of the addictive American game '500,' going on at the kitchen table. Khaled seemed always on the triumphant team, no matter whom he partnered, and hooted loudly while snatching up the winning hands.

At sacred times, the prayer group now included everyone except Dalal, Jalal, Ramz and Baba'a. All met with their mats at the prescribed times in one of the bedrooms and knelt facing southeast. The new members followed along or haltingly re-conjured prayer chants from childhood. "... All praise is due to Allah, Lord of the world. The beneficent, the merciful. Master of the Day of Judgment..."

Then on Sunday the 26th came a couple of severe setbacks.

Karem Osman had found a crew for the Sansato in Beirut, Greek deckhands by the names of Xavos and Tomaso, and a fellow Turk named Hasan, as ship's engineer.

Hasan immediately noticed a leak in the engine's cooling system. The repair wasn't major, but the engine had to be dismounted for access. Hasan could do the work-with some help from the two Greeks, but it could take a number of days.

This made it impossible to get the Sansato to Es Saksakiye to rendezvous with the operatives by the evening of March 1st. Since there was no chance of getting another ship, the operation had to be delayed a week.

On top of that, the Sansato's draft had been checked against the depth of water beside the marina wharf. The water was too shallow for her to come all the way in. On the night the operatives would board her they would have to inflate the boats on the beach and motor out to the ship, rather than carry them aboard over a gangplank.

This meant they would be exposed much longer than was wise considering the Israelis' regular surveillance over-flights, but couldn't be helped. At least these problems had been found in time to make allowances.

Iyad heard this news at Yarmouk on the 28th. His day had already been ruined by the announcement, that all displaced-Arab's rights-of-residence in Egypt had been canceled by Sadat, in retaliation for his friend Sibai's murder. When he had to tell Jihad of the delay in the mission while the ship was repaired, it drove his mercurial boss into a rage.

At Es Saksakiye everyone had been counting on one more night of boat exercises, last prayers and meals, final equipment preparation, and then being on the water. This turn of events threw everyone off badly.

The operatives moped. The safe house stank from cigarettes being chain-smoked to combat the lingering disappointment and increasing boredom.

But they were lucky; not for the last time.

Israel was too busy complaining about the U.S. arms sales to its enemies to worry about peace talks. Ezer Weizman had been on television hinting at taking Israel's air bases in the Sinai off the peace table. Only Foreign Minister Dayan seemed to have his eye on the ball, saying the lack of peace-progress was understandable. Iyad's spy in the Knesset had kept him well informed of regular contact between Carter and Begin, but nothing yet pointed at a firm March date for a summit. The backup dates of a March 9th departure, and a strike at Israel on the evening of the 10th, looked like they would work equally well.

Wednesday the 8th began with a look that lingered a little too long. By mid-afternoon many more glances had been exchanged in a kind of sexual semaphore, since the two had not yet touched or even spoken intimately.

By evening, the tension between them was apparent to anyone with a sense of atmosphere.

Well yes, of course, but how with so many around and no privacy?

I will make a way, was her response.

By late in the afternoon, even the slowest of the operatives, knew Sister Dalal had chosen Salaam as her lover for her last night in Lebanon.

After the velvet settling of darkness, Wael, Fayadh, and Ahmed took their mattresses and blankets into other rooms. Salaam was lying on his back when Dalal came in and lay beside him.

She was barefoot, and wore a rumpled linen blouse without a bra, and baggy *Sherwal* trousers of soft cloth with a string for a belt. She smelled of shower soap. Salaam drew it in like the scent of summer in Kashmir's fabled Mughal gardens of Nishat.

He had not changed his mode of dress as much, though the leaf pattern on his wash-softened fatigues was barely discernible.

Salaam had enjoyed many women. But oddly, his sexual drive wasn't strong. His craving had a deeper motivation.

If he was desired, he existed.

If not, he dwelt in a pit of self-loathing, and fought to hide that fact every waking moment.

Like most deeply insecure men he was prudish and shy, unable to articulate his desires even if he'd had the self-awareness to know what they were.

None of his previous encounters had been anything like this.

He was accustomed to eyes admiring him from the souk-stalls, and to luring those behind them away to assignations. Or taking home tarty teenage girls who couldn't keep their hands off him in nightclubs. Neither type made any demands of him beyond lying beside his sculptured body and letting him have his way.

Well, perhaps, in one or two affairs with married women, who generally knew what they wanted, He'd felt hints of this invisible force, this raw need, but never like this.

He was aware of her eyes studying him. He had no idea how he should react.

Dalal had doubts and uncertainties too, but not about fucking. Naturally adventurous, on being exposed to the engorged testosterone of the often half naked fighters at Dbaiyeh, she'd taken to sex like a flower to a summer's day. Reveled in the primitivity and sweatiness of it

She'd also learned what men liked. And what she liked. And tonight needed.

Celibate since that explosive day at Yarmouk that had exposed her and Khalil's relationship for what it was, she needed carnality. To have it envelop her. But also touch and gentleness. To be acknowledged as a woman again for perhaps the last time.

Salaam broke the ice by clasping his hand on her shoulder. She flinched. His hand was coarse and hard from weeks of physical activity. Not what she had fantasized about all day. He clumsily scraped it along her back under her blouse and she recoiled again, but let him explore. Surely tenderness would follow.

He groped her breasts and then reached lower, toward her cleft, without finesse.

She slapped his arm away. "Don't maul me! You are not playing with your cock now! Don't you know anything?"

Salaam jerked as if pricked with a knife. For a moment the room was dead and cold.

Dalal looked into his awkwardly hanging face. It was lovely, with full almost feminine lips and a nose that wouldn't have shamed Michelangelo's David. The face of a guileless boy.

"Here, let me. Lie back," she whispered.

She doffed her cotton top, then unbuttoned his shirt and put her hand on his stomach, moving her fingers soothingly, caressing the corrugations. She wondered how a body could be so hard. So arrogantly male.

He writhed in tune with the movement of her hand and made a soft sound. Her petulance was gone. Replaced by a warmth between her thighs. She adjusted her thighs and felt the slickness spreading between them.

Her hand moved in gradually growing circles. The bottom edge brushing rhythmically against his waistband, then began slipping more and more easily underneath. His breathing became hoarse.

She separated his buttons and her fingers encircled his hard, pulsing cock as naturally as time. It was thick and strong and quite pink in the lamplight. A faint sheen of fluid coated the engorged tip. She gently stroked for a few seconds, enjoying the feeling of pure control. Then moved to pleasure him as women have pleasured men since time immemorial.

Feeling him shuffle a pillow under his head so he could watch her, she smiled. His musk filled her nostrils, pungent and sweet at the same time. The taste of him filled her senses. It was the taste of... oneness.

The moisture between her thighs became a small flood. With one hand lightly playing beneath, she began slipping him in and out of her mouth. His hips moved in time with the bobbing of her head. His gasping was ragged.

She tried to prolong their pleasure, but control had switched. His right hand grasped her hair tightly as he groaned from the depths of his belly and arched. She clamped tight, luxuriating in the joy of the most intimate act a man and woman can share.

While they cooled, she thought of his powerful hands in her hair, and how she'd been so repulsed at first by his roughness, and yet how that masterful grip holding her at the moment, had been so fulfilling.

Salaam stirred, recovering. His hand entwined gently in her hair. She shivered.

Beside her elbow, his maleness twitched as it hardened. She lifted her head to see his eyes.

"*Khadhani.*" (Take me!) She said playfully.

Salaam shook his head, not understanding.

" Khadhani!"

He pulled her face to his, and they kissed. Long and hard. Sharing tongues. She thrilled, knowing he didn't care where her mouth had been, only about possessing her. Her head fell back in ecstasy.

What will he do? Force me to my knees and use me again? Wrap my tits around his cock and make me lick the end of his cock while he thrusts?

She loved hearing in her head those English words she'd learned in the camps. So excitingly, deliciously, dirty.

"Sharmuta," came from his lips.

Yes, I will be your whore!

Salaam pushed her away to tear at her lower garment and maneuvered until he was between her legs.

He was at her entrance, spreading her wide.

She moaned, *"Nekni ana! Nekni ana!"* (Fuck me! Fuck me!)

Salaam lifted her with every delicious thrust, until there was only the taste in her mouth and their scent of their sweat, and the feeling of being stretched ever wider.

Their cries soared, before trailing away into paralyzed gasps as they subsided to heaving rest.

She was owned. Therefore, she must be worthy.

FIFTEEN

Es Saksakiye
Thursday March 9th 7:45 p.m.

Next evening, the rumbling of the Sansato's anchor chain sent the seabirds roosting on the rough ground around the marina shrieking into wheeling flight. Three flashes from a light out at sea meant the waiting was over.

Baba'a and Ramz had been shuttling the operation's equipment to the marina for more than half an hour. The others, after eradicating all evidence of the group's presence at the safe house, had chosen to walk the few hundred yards down the gravel road.

As he passed the dawdling operatives on the way back to the house for the last of the gear, he called out "*Yalla! Yalla*!" (Hurry up!) They steadfastly ignored him, intent on making this last walk at their own pace. All except Dalal, who glared, signaling the two of them were now equals under the gun.

On Baba'a's return to the marina, a convoy of dimmed-headlight vehicles lined the road. Silhouettes of armed men cragged the skyline. The stubby figure of Jihad hovered on the fringe of the pools from the wharf-lights, watching Ramz, Hiza'a, and Salaam inflate the second boat.

When everyone else arrived, they gathered to hear their leader's parting words.

"If anyone wants to withdraw, let him speak," Jihad said.

Surprised eyes flickered to the fighters close by, knowing they would be taken aside and shot if they spoke up. No one got this deeply into a Fatah operation and walked away. Nor did any of them think that unfair. They were fighters in the cause. Violence was their calling card. There never had been any going back.

After that it was an unceremonious parting.

Jihad gave Baba'a a paper in Arabic and Hebrew, listing the prisoners in Israeli jails to be released. He didn't glance at it, but if he had, he would have noticed one name was Musa Juma al-Tallka, the sole survivor of the Savoy Hotel attack. Fatah didn't know he had already died in custody more than a year before.

Other items passed over included money to pay the captain. Also, a cheap Japanese waterproof watch so he could keep time aboard ship. And a small two-way radio. Taped to it was a list of frequencies Fatah HQ would be monitoring.

Jihad had nothing more to say except, "*Fi Amanullah*," (May Allah protect you).

"*Insha'Allah*." (If it is Allah's will,) replied the operatives in chorus.

The Zodiac boats then transported the operatives and their hand-belongings out to the Sansato.

On arriving at the ship's side, they found the crew had thrown down a cargo net, an unusual item to find on a coastal tanker. Another clue, extra hammock hooks below decks signaled the Sansato had a not-so-innocent past in people smuggling. Not that her latest passengers cared.

Eleven of them clambered up the net while Salaam and Hiza'a returned to the beach to collect the dry-bags of weapons. Finally, the Zodiacs were hoisted aboard with ropes and carefully lowered onto the deck once the engines were swung up and locked in place. The bags of weaponry went below and the cargo net was heaved over the boats as camouflage. The Sansato grumbled her anchor back aboard.

A little before 8:30 p.m. with all running lights extinguished, she turned away from the shore at gathering speed on a south-south-westerly heading.

In the wheelhouse, Karem Osman had been shrewdly observing. If he hadn't known from the beginning whom he would be taking aboard, seeing their equipment dispelled all doubt. The outlines of weapons were distinctive, even inside sealed bags. Spies didn't require those.

He was also well aware that the ship's crew from the Savoy Operation of March 1975 was suffering indefinite hard labor sentences in an Israeli prison. Therefore, he had a survival plan. He intended to make sure the Sansato came nowhere close to any ships of the Israeli navy.

What he didn't know was there was actually no danger of that at all. By coincidence, the World Youth Yachting Championships were taking place off Tel Aviv over the next few days. The sailing event was important on the Israeli tourism calendar and warranted every protection possible. The Israeli Navy's VLDR radar on top of Mount Carmel had seen bad weather developing to the west. Even as the terrorists were boarding, the IDF was ordering all their offshore patrol boats to relocate south to provide search and rescue support if needed.

But unaware of this, during the previous week's engine repairs he'd had Hasan disconnect the ship's speedometer and odometer. If anyone had asked, he would have said there had been no time to get them working again. He'd also calculated precisely how far, or rather the least distance he'd have to motor south, before he could plausibly tell his passengers to launch their boats.

The drop-off point he had agreed with the Fatah agents, 25 nautical miles north and west of Tel Aviv, was about 98 miles from the Es Saksakiye. About 10 hours steaming at the Sansato's regular cruising speed. Osman had no intention of going anywhere that dangerous.

He believed, correctly, that Baba'a, whose orders he'd been told to obey, would know the distance and planned drop-off time from briefings and maps. But the terrorist commander would have no ability to relate engine pitch to speed in the dark.

Osman intended to motor much more slowly and on a subtly zigzag course. That would make the actual drop-off point only 65 miles south of Es Saksakiye, somewhere west-south-west of Haifa. He also planned to work his way quite a bit further out to sea, so the lights of that port wouldn't give him away.

He also had one more trick in his bag for covering his treachery. He'd spoken to the two Greeks and told them to keep their eyes out for an opportunity.

Around them the sea was calm and the sky above clear. If Karem had noticed there'd been no red sunset that evening, it hadn't registered on him. Not that it would have mattered even if he'd known his betrayal would put 13 lives in danger. All Karem Osman cared about was collecting his money and saving his skin.

At 1:46 a.m. on Friday, March 10th, by which time ship was well west of Haifa, Baba'a woke troubled. Concern that they had never practiced launching at sea had been eating at Baba'a, and he wanted to take advantage of the glassy seas and have a full dress-rehearsal. He shook Hiza'a and told him to wake the others. Then he found his way on deck and to the bridge.

The younger of the two Greeks, Tomaso, was at the wheel. Baba'a told the man to wake the captain. Osman emerged bleary and slightly drunk and strongly argued against this new plan before gloweringly shutting down the engine.

Baba'a was determined the rehearsal should be real life, so all the weaponry was brought up from below. They did run-throughs for over an hour, with the equipment-filled boats being lowered over the side and the terrorists clambering down the cargo net to board. They even practiced taking the crucially important compass headings while motoring in circles around the drifting Sansato.

After the boats were aboard again, they left everything exactly where they would need it later. Then they all went below to eat a cold meal before catching a few more hours sleep.

No one saw Xavos sneak on deck, and following his captain's orders, remove an item from each boat, and drop them over the side.

Baba'a was awakened by Tomaso again at 4:00 a.m. and told to go to the bridge.

Karem pointed to a place on a chart and said they were about 30 miles off Tel Aviv, on an easterly bearing toward the drop-off point. Estimated ETA was in half an hour. Baba'a knew no better. He paid the man and headed below deck to join the others.

Within the final half-hour the operatives ate again, put dark slickers on over their military garb, and made ready to launch. Everything about the boats seemed as they'd left them. All they had to do was lift up the hulls and lower the motors.

But the way the first Zodiac swung side to side once lifted, showed immediately the weather had deteriorated. Baba'a went to the railing and stared out into the darkness. Into a keen wind, and over a rollicking swell.

Nonetheless, the launch in the lee of the ship's tall black hull went like clockwork. Within five minutes, the operatives were all aboard the bobbing inflatables. Baba'a was the last over the side after paying Osman, who waved only a dismissive hand in parting.

With the engines running well, they drew away from the Sansato's side in trail formation. Behind them, they heard the sound of the ship's engine revving up rapidly as she turned toward Cyprus, 100 nautical miles to the west. The stars were gone, replaced by a dome of unbroken darkness, but as yet the wind was only about 10 knots, not quite enough to form whitecaps. Adrenaline levels were so high no one yet felt vulnerable. While a three-foot swell kept the two boat captains' hands full, it seemed they would manage.

Then Hiza'a gave a shout, echoed a few moments later by Salaam. The compasses were gone. The significance was swift to sink in. They had no way to navigate.

A hubbub of voices broke out. After a short exchange with the two captains, Baba'a shouted. "Save your energy! The wind is from the west, so downwind is Palestine. At dawn we will motor away from the sun until we see the lighthouses of Yáfa."

The engines were shut off to save fuel. The carry-ropes through the loops on the boats' outer hulls were un-looped and used to tether them together. Oars were assembled to keep the boats in line with the swells through the rest of the night.

They tried to use the radio to alert Jihad of their predicament, but heard chattering Hebrew voices on all the channels they had been given. Sometime in the night water shorted it out, and they never got it working again.

Eventually a sunless dawn arrived. Just a watery glow that quickly became bright in every direction, dashing their hopes of navigating by it. Soon it was replaced by uniform grayness, dimmed frequently by drenching squalls. At least the seas didn't get much worse.

Noon came by Baba'a's watch, by which time almost everyone was violently seasick. The adrenaline-laced excitement of the launch had long degenerated into dogged misery.

Salaam offered his best advice. "Drink a lot of water! Try to keep your eyes off the sea, and on something that doesn't move!" But everything was moving.

Still, the Zodiacs dealt with the surging waves as comfortably as could be expected and took aboard remarkably little water for the conditions. Most that did accumulate was rainwater. They took turns scooping it out with a tethered canvas scoop.

By 4:00 p.m. most could keep down some food, but it was obvious there was no chance of an attack on Israel that evening. They would have to wait out the night and hope visibility had improved enough by the morning to get their bearings.

The light faded, and they were again alone in darkness on the heaving sea.

The second morning did bring a lot more visibility, varying from 100 yards in squalls, to a few miles in between. All of it empty sea.

They were irritable and argumentative from the stultifying monotony, and suffering salt sores where constantly wet clothing chafed. Also starving now, and no one had more than a quart of water remaining.

Both boats started their motors and headed away from the sun at a slow but steady speed. But they still had to bide their time.

All aboard prayed to Allah for his grace in bringing them in sight of land as close as possible to dark. Coming into sight of Tel Aviv's popular beaches in busy broad-daylight, even on the Shabbat, would be fatal.

SIXTEEN

North Coastal Israel
Saturday, March 11th

Many miles west, Israel was waking up to an overcast and drizzly Shabbat morning.

A woman at a coastal Kibbutz fed her children while her husband showered.

A German-born Jew in Tel Aviv laid shirts out on a bed in anticipation of a sea trip that evening.

North of Haifa, a huge ex-soldier dressed, disappointed that his wife wouldn't be with him on a day-excursion.

At a vegetarian *Moshav* (collective community) in the far northern hills, an acclaimed young musician practiced notes on a clarinet while his family readied for a trip home to Jerusalem.

Two full-of-life teenagers from Haifa, who didn't know each other at all, woke up in modest hotel-rooms on downtown Tel Aviv's Dizengoff Street.

Adults fondly believed themselves in control of their destinies. Children blissfully began the last day of their young lives.

By 8:13 a.m. at the Bus Terminal at Bat Galim on Haifa's foreshore, Egged Social club members, who called themselves the *Navads* (Wanderers,) were gathering at their place of employment for a social-club bus excursion. Mostly owner drivers with their families. They were bound for the newly discovered Sorek Stalactite Cave near the township of Beit Shemesh, southeast of Tel Aviv.

Wanderers' expeditions were always festive events. Mothers had bags of toys and clothing changes for their children. Also, contributions for an eagerly anticipated bring-and-share picnic lunch. Every trip they said they'd take less, but always seemed to bring more.

Their company bus, a perk of their employment, waited at a passenger island, glowing brightly in in the Egged fleet's new colors, red with white trim. The company emblem, Hebrew letters stylized into the wings of Mercury, gleamed proudly on the grill. One of the newer 'Intercity' models, registration number 88-191, it was a sturdy vehicle with bodywork built over a Swedish Scania chassis by Yochelman Merkavim Ltd. in nearby Hadera. YM had done good work, using heavy steel framing and thick plywood flooring overlaid with Formica veneer, all encased in a shell of 16th inch sheet steel. The 52 seats were of steel tubing padded with kapok and trimmed in pleasant pastel-shaded plastic. Access was by two sets of concertina doors on the boarding side, operated by levers beside the driver's right thigh. Before the day was out, it would be significant that the front doors were connected via linkages, while the rear ones were hydraulically operated.

There were no *Haredi* (Orthodox Jews) among the travelers, but otherwise they were a typical cross-section of Israeli Society. If asked, 8 out of 10 would have said their Jewish identity was culturally all-powerful, but not religiously so.

They were mindful of the holy day, but delighted the *Oneg Shabbat* (enjoyment of the Sabbath,) commandment in the *Torah* strongly encouraged eating, singing, and spending joyful time with family and friends. They planned to do plenty of that.

Some came in small cars and parked in the employee area behind the wash bays.

One such was Amnon Drori. He was early, to be sure of a seat with legroom. The ex IDF paratrooper was enormous. But his beloved Dutch wife Ruth wasn't with him. She'd woken him early at Kiryat Haim, one of the townships comprising the coastal Krayot district northeast of Haifa, to say their youngest daughter Danila had a fever. He'd pulled her close, bent down to put his face in her hair, and said in her native language, "*Je zal in mijn hart totdat ik terugkom, mijn liefde*" (You will be in my heart until I return, my love).

A number of families, all close friends, had car-pooled or caught early buses; another perk of the job.

Monique Ankwa, a fervent outdoors-lover, was talking gaily to other early arrivals, Leah and Avner Geffen, about recent walks she'd been on. Monique's husband, Haviv, had his attention on their four excited children. Two-year-old Galit, 'Missy' as she was better known (who would be the youngest child aboard) toddled happily between the families. Nearby, the two Geffen children, including bright and bouncy five-year-old Efraim, settled into seats.

Lavan and Joseph Hadani were chatting with Gil and Shoshana Gal-on about child rearing. The youngest children of each family, five-year-old Naama Hadani, and Liat Gal-on, just six, were notorious for bad behavior on a long day-trip. But everyone adored Naama's infectious little giggle, while Liat had elfin features and a smile to melt any heart.

The Meshkels, Ben and Rachel, had arrived typically late, bringing their two boys, eight-year-old Issac and his irrepressible six-year-old brother Benjamin, known as 'Junior.'

Further back sat the Hochmans, Joseph, who preferred 'Yossi,' and Rebecca. An unofficial club cheerleader with her two small boys, Roi and Ilan. on her knees, Rebecca was chatting with Lily Glotman. Yossi was discussing the latest driver's roster with Lily's husband, Shim'aon. Neither man was happy with his assigned shift. With Rebecca deeply involved in the affairs of their kibbutz, Neve Yam, Yossi liked to have his days off in groups so he could assist with the kids.

The Zaits were there, Judith and her driver husband Solomon, known to all aboard as 'Shlomo,' and their two young ones.

There were also squabbles. The Bosknitzs, Dov, a 36-year-old former Captain in the IDF regular forces, and Rina, a 34-year-old nurse at Haifa's Rambam Hospital were resolving a minor disagreement they'd brought from home, while also trying to settle their two boys. The surrounding people were used to it. They knew how devoted the bickering couple was, even after 12 years of marriage.

By the scheduled departure time there were 62, generally boisterous and joyful people aboard. Predominately couples up to their 30s and 40s, with their children, but also a number of singles like Amnon Drori. Also, some pairs, like 38-year-old Abraham Shamir, with his teenage daughter Marie. Many of the 22 children aboard wriggled excitedly on their parents' knees as they waited to start moving.

Long experience had taught the parents to keep the bench-seat across the back open; room for children to color in their books, and to play on, when they got bored.

At 8:30 a.m. the designated driver, 36-year-old Gid'on Haas, made sure his wife Judith was comfortable, then strolled up the aisle slapping seatbacks and announcing he was ready to go. Carry bags were quickly zipped and stowed.

Gid'on made sure the short curtains bracketing the side windows were open for maximum visibility, then closed the doors. He eased the bus out of the depot on to Retsif Aharon Rosenfeld Avenue, then followed the waterfront anticlockwise along Hubert Humphrey Drive, toward the entrance to Highway 2.

Also called the Coastal Highway, this route south hugged the Mediterranean for most of its length, ending where Tel Aviv began. From Tel Aviv they would swing inland and travel south to Beit Shemesh on Highway 4, before making the final climb to the Sorek Cave.

As the company passed Tirat Carmel and the open road commenced, Rebecca got her first song going: Chana Malhina's anthem, *'Yerushalay'm Ba'or* (Jerusalem in the Light.)

Yerushalay'm ba'or
Kama chom avnech mefitza
Betchilat a'boker u've redet ha'yom fading light
Kmo she'halev sheli zoher ee'tach.

Eer kdosha, bhira u'moo'eret
Hamkom hakdosh shel leebi

Or eretz Israel, ha'echd ve'hayachid
Le'chekech hakadosh tekarvi o'ti.

Jerusalem in the light
How warm your stone glows
In early morning and fading light
As my heart glows with you.

Holy City, burning bright
Temple fountains of my heart
O'er Eretz Israel you shine unmatched
To your sacred bosom, draw me close.

The Wanderers' tradition of juicing up gentle songs had everyone stomping along.

Fifty miles out in the Mediterranean at that moment, Fayadh was the first to see one. Or at least its snout and mischievous black eyes. They rose from the water to study him, before the creature squeaked to its pod-mates, and dived again.

Unsure if it was delirium, he sat upright and rubbed his eyes. By then frolicking bottle-nosed dolphins surrounded them, chattering as if as surprised at the encounter as the humans were.

The terrorists gazed in wonder, especially the inland Arabs, to whom the creatures were as marvelous as unicorns. The pod re-grouped and undulated away.

Fayadh shouted, "*Bel hew 'elamh!*" (It is a sign!)

Heads nodded.

The engines roared to life and the cold and wet men set out to follow. Though inside a minute the dolphins had vanished, the boats continued on for hours, up one side of the swells and down the other; keeping the glow of the sun behind them until all directions were equal.

Then they plugged onward by instinct.

A little after 2:00 p.m. the terrorists glimpsed a tall tower through the coastal haze. It was a chimney of the Hadera coal-fired power plant, not that they had a clue. It was soon lost to view again.

The slight Mediterranean tide carried them north. Shortly white patches appeared on the horizon. They made out surf beating at areas of beach and rocky outcrops. The boats aimed for one of the broadest areas of surf, north of a low headland. Through the haze, there seemed to be buildings beyond the headland, and high ground farther away.

Gradually the mouth of a sandy bay took form and the distant high ground solidified into a buttress of mountains. They made out a curious man-made structure on the right-hand side of the beach, just to the left of what appeared to be the mouth of a stream. It might have been part of a roadbed. They were seeing the remnants of a stunning ancient engineering achievement. A Roman aqueduct built by the Emperor-Engineer Hadrian.

The beach appeared their only chance of survival. They must avoid veering south at all costs, where an area of seething dragon-toothed reefs reached out hungrily.

About two miles offshore, the engine of Hiza'a's inflatable spluttered to silence as its gasoline ran out. The boats were tethered again and Salaam's took over the lead. That got them a mile closer to the coast before its tank also ran dry. Then they broke out the oars and paddled apprehensively toward shore. at areas of beach and rocky outcrops. The boats aimed for one of the broadest areas of surf, north of a low headland. Through the haze, there seemed to be buildings beyond the headland, and high ground farther away.

Gradually the mouth of a sandy bay took form and the distant high ground solidified into a buttress of mountains. They made out a curious man-made structure on the right-hand side of the beach, just to the left of what appeared to be the mouth of a stream. It might have been part of a roadbed. They were seeing the remnants of a stunning ancient engineering achievement. A Roman aqueduct built by the Emperor-Engineer Hadrian.

The beach appeared their only chance of survival. They must avoid veering south at all costs, where an area of seething dragon-toothed reefs reached out hungrily.

About two miles offshore, the engine of Hiza'a's inflatable spluttered to silence as its gasoline ran out. The boats were tethered again and Salaam's took over the lead. That got them a mile closer to the coast before its tank also ran dry. Then they broke out the oars and paddled apprehensively toward shore.

SEVENTEEN

Sorek Cave, Beit Shemesh, South Israel
12:22 p.m.

The Sorek Cave, discovered during explosions expanding a limestone quarry, was a relatively new tourism attraction in Israel.

Getting there involved a serpentine highway up through pine lands to a terraced parking lot, then a five-minute zigzag hike down a hillside with a spectacular northern view, to a cheerfully lit reception center.

Behind steel doors, the cave was a pleasant climate controlled, 80-yards deep, by 50 in width. The tour guide led them on a half-hour footway journey, meandering among pillars and cones and past fantastic and surrealistically color-lit shapes. He explained the science and pointing out macaroni, fried eggs, an ice-cream cone, Snow White and the Seven Dwarfs, even a realistic lion.

The Wanderers were enchanted. Families clustered to gape and gasp at each wonder before moving excitedly along to the next. Afterward, some tagged along with the following tour party. Emerging the second time with faces still aglow.

Everyone then gathered blankets and food. They filed back up to a flower-bedecked natural amphitheater in the hillside and spread out sumptuous leftovers from last evening's Aruchat Shabbat festivities. Also, containers of water and fruit juice, plus a few flasks of something stronger.

When children were off playing, the adults commenced a club tradition: *Seypevr Heyy'* (Life Stories,) where members took turns speaking about their histories and experiences.

Amnon Drori immediately towered up from where he'd been occupying an entire blanket. He shared stories of his military service in Colonel Rafael Eitan's 35th paratroopers on the Gaza Front in the 1967 war, where his nickname was 'Big Fish.' He'd qualified at the maximum weight a silk canopy could carry. Despite his appetite, his unit was glad to have him. He could carry a German MG42 heavy machine-gun las if it was a plastic toy.

Switching to family life, he described meeting Ruth at a Rotterdam shipyard social-club dance, while working as a welder in Holland. Then bringing her back to Haifa, where she had supported him through his tourism studies at the Ort Institute, before he'd joined Egged as a tour guide. He had them in belly laughs describing how she made his clothes when they were not so well off. The audience knew the story and was happy to hear it again.

"Ruth buys canvas. Holds it against me and says, 'this will look nice! Trust me!' Friends I have trusted her always, since she first laid her cheek against this piece of granite that I call my face. *Ashety at hheyyem, shel!*" (My wife, my life!)

Next, Rebecca Hochman rose and described her life at Kibbutz Neve Yam. Her grandparents were founding-pioneers of the Gordonia Zionist Youth Movement, and her husband Yossi, her childhood love.

Neve Yam occupied a piece of salt-marshy shore-land just over an arched bridge from the Atlit Detention Camp, built in the 1930s by the British to detain refugees seized from ships beached by the Haganah, back when they were trying to hold back the tsunami of displaced European Jews.

Little did the British know Neve Yam was a stronghold of the *Palyam* (Jewish resistance' Navy.) Those cheerful, suntanned young people in their khaki shorts and shirts, greeting the guards while passing by the camp, were on their way to smuggle supplies and messages under the wire.

With the capricious weather and the land useless for agriculture, it wasn't the wealthiest settlement on the coast. A road from the fish processing plant at Neve Yam's center led through dunes to a small harbor.

There the fishing boats were launched every morning by a rusty Massey-Fergusson tractor and recovered each evening. The children would flock like seagulls to see the precious cargos of tuna and bream.

The rest of the time the children made their own fun, beach-combing for miles along uninterrupted sands, or riding bicycles around the inland area. Often, they'd ride up to the peaceful and beautiful town cemetery, on the hill beside the bridge, to play hide and seek.

A few Wanderers, listening all these years later, nodded and smiled at Rebecca's portrait of endless sunlit summers. Some version of her carefree childhood was a common theme among kibbutzniks. Many also knew how passionate Rebecca was about the affairs of the kibbutz, having been accountant and treasurer.

Then she surprised them by announcing, "I'm giving that up. I've enrolled to learn literature at the University of Haifa this fall."

Which brought the handsome and outgoing Shim'aon Glotman to his feet. He was also studying part time for English and German degrees at the Open University. He hoped Rebecca would find as much *geshmack* (satisfaction) from her studies.

He stayed on his feet to tell his own life story. Born in Moldova but expelled with his parents to Transnistria by the Germans at age seven, Shim'oan's background was hugely varied.

A talented jazz pianist, some had heard him play at work events, he also loved soul and classical music, painting, sculpture and writing poetry.

"You might have seen my picture of Lily and the kids." He said. Of course, they had. He was the company paymaster, and they often made visits to his desk.

"Sixteen years we've been married next month, and I love that woman more each day. I hope to have my book of poems, showing just how much, finished this year. But some of you new ones may not know that story of this." He tapped his right leg.

"I went right into the *Gad'sar Golani* (Special Forces) at 18. Did my three years. Twenty year later I'm with Egged, and its *Milhama Yom Kippur* (the 1973 war) and I'm called back up.

Not so young then!" He grinned ruefully. "Anyway, first jump, there goes the leg. Compound break."

He'd spent two years in rehabilitation before he could walk again, with Egged all the while keeping his job open. "That's the Co-Op (as Egged employees refer to the company) you are with, friends. We take care of our own. Be glad."

The next speaker, 44-year-old Avner Geffen, was well liked for his generosity and willingness to swap shifts on short notice if anyone was stuck, but also prone to depression over relatively minor issues.

Perhaps understandably. His early life-story was tragically all too familiar to Jews from the Diaspora. Born in Vsondovic in Poland, he'd been orphaned at the age of seven, one afternoon in 1941. A truckload of Waffen SS troopers had pulled up in the street where his father and mother were walking to the market. They were out to make an example, after the throwing of a Molotov cocktail at a Wehrmacht motorcycle dispatch rider. The troopers seized 10 people at random, including his parents, and shot them against the nearest wall. along with other families, seven-year-old Avner and his nine-year-old brother had been forced to wash away the blood.

After that the young brothers had survived the last two years of the war in Silesia's forests, until among many thousands of others, being rescued by the Zionist 'Youth Aliyah' movement. He lived with his wife Leah, their shy 11-year-old daughter Ronit, and son Efraim, who could hardly have been less so, in Kiryat Tivon, nine miles southeast of Haifa.

Last to speak was 38-year-old Haviv Ankwa, a strongly built and square-jawed, Moroccan born Jew with dark features and kindly almond eyes. His tale was all the more interesting for the catch in his throat, when he spoke of the Arab family who'd taken him in when orphaned young. Haviv and his brother were helped to immigrate by Youth Aliyah, and relocated to Haifa in 1952. After discharge from the regular IDF in 1966, he married Monique and lived seven years in Eilat on the Red Sea. His fluent Arabic had earned him a tour guide's job with Egged, and he'd stayed on with the company after moving back to Haifa for better schooling opportunities for his four children.

But by then, adult Wanderers were being pestered by bored offspring. With the sun starting to wane, the day was cooling fast and lingering showers still stalked the hills. It was time to re-board the bus. Blankets were folded, carry bags repacked, errant young people corralled, and infants changed for the homeward journey.

Gid'on Haas drove down off the hill just after 2:00 p.m. and set a course to skirt Tel Aviv and see them safely home to Haifa via coastal Highway 2.

Meanwhile someone else in a vehicle, 31-year-old Shaul Weizman, son of the present Defense Minister, fighter-ace and war-hero Ezer, was speeding down off the Judean hills from Jerusalem in his BMW 5-series. He was on his way to a meeting far less social. In fact, it concerned the security infrastructure of the entire nation.

Shaul had been pensive on arising that morning. He would bitterly disappoint someone, today. The circumstances brought Shakespeare to his classically trained mind.

Macbeth, in fact. '*If it be done, twere well it be done quickly.*'

Trepidations regardless, he'd taken his time over brunch on the patio at the family compound in Kiryat HaYovel, a leafy and prosperous suburb in the hills of Jerusalem. Though he'd declined a third cup of coffee offered by a white-dressed server. He was looking forward to the journey and didn't want to get too hyped up. Shaul felt he did his best thinking while driving.

To him, the root of Israel's problems was the unique intermingling of the country's political and military universes. Nowhere else were those powerful threads so intertwined, or did so few layers separate the respective roles. Politicians interfering in matters of defense, and soldiers impinging on politics, was commonplace.

It went right back to the founder of the nation, David Ben Gurion, someone Shaul thought of as a grandfather figure. As a small boy, Shaul had played on Ben Gurion's knee at his home in the Negev, near where his father had been based as an air force squadron commander. The great man had set the trend in 1947, by personally recruiting Canadian fighter ace George 'Screwball'

Beurling to fly P51 Mustangs for Israel, only to have him die in a transport-plane-ferrying crash in Rome. Then by bringing in U.S. Engineer-General Mickey Marcus the same year. Marcus had completed the 'Freedom Road' to Jerusalem before being killed by a nervous sentry on the final day.

But that had been wartime. Perhaps understandable.

For Shaul's taste, though, politicians still got involved far too often in tactical military matters. Only recently, Prime Minister Golda Meir had approved Operation 'Wrath of God,' the retaliation by Mossad against the perpetrators of the 1976 Munich Olympics tragedy. Of course, she had little choice. If she hadn't, Mossad and the Special Forces chiefs would have proceeded anyway, and the political wing would have gotten no credit.

He sighed. There just seemed to be no accountablility.

The reason was, of course, that such meddling didn't do the harm you might expect to powerful careers. For instance, his father's boss, Menachem Begin, had long wielded political and military power with the same hand. As head of Irgun during the British occupation, he'd planned the July 1946 bombing of the King David Hotel in Jerusalem. Ninety-one had died. Shaul also knew for a fact Begin had tried to assassinate German Chancellor Konrad Adenauer in March 1953, killing a German army disposal specialist instead. It hadn't stopped him from becoming the 14th Israeli Prime Minister.

The fact was, politicians and generals routinely washed each other's hands.

You couldn't even get elected Kibbutz Toilet Cleaner without the support of powerful military figures. It was quite standard for Generals and Admirals, with even a glimmer of charisma, to be helped along the path to political power at the end of their uniformed careers.

Such things required money. But didn't everything? And it was always in short supply.

The U.S. dictated what equipment they used. The rise and fall of senior officers depended on who got that funding. Whole internal empires could be built and then wiped out in an instant with a wriggle or slash of the budget pen. It seemed the military marched, not on its stomach, but on a constant flow of money requests.

More personally for Shaul, the thus-empowered military could override even the most solemn of political promises. One of those promises had been made to the person he was going to see today. Someone he had enormous respect for. He wasn't relishing being the one to break it.

But that was his job, he reminded himself. He was a political middle-man, and a master at it. Considered a hero in military circles, he'd paid a devastating price. His climb up the uniformed ranks, purely on his merits, had been stellar. He'd been mentioned as a future General, even Chief of Staff, while still in his 20s. But it all ended with the crack of an Egyptian sniper rifle during the 1970 Sinai War of Attrition that cost him a lung and damaged his larynx.

Yet the bullet hadn't taken away his keen judgment of men. These days he used his mind gathering facts, discerning whether funding was justified, and generally passing up to the powers-that-be, whatever information they needed to make hard decisions.

And yes, passing back down the bad news. Regretfully, that was often. The brutal fact was Israel simply couldn't afford parallel streams of anything. One size had to fit all. Which brought Weizmann directly to his problem of the day.

The matter stemmed back to Ma'alot in 1974.

On the night of Sunday, May 13th, an action-unit from the so-called Democratic Front for the Liberation of Palestine (DFLP), had crossed the Lebanese border, and entered the development town of Ma'alot, only three miles south. A busload of children on a school trip from Safed was dossing down in the school gymnasium. Barely believing their luck, the fighters seized 85 children and 5 teachers and began making demands. Dozens of troopers from the *Sayeret Matkal* (General Staff Reconnaissance Unit,) the Israeli Army's elite anti-terrorist force-had flown in by helicopter, tasked with a rescue-assault. Unfortunately, the incident was heavy on assault and light on rescue. A sniper bungled a shot, allowing his target to warn the other terrorists. One terrorist made it to the classroom containing the hostages, opened fire before throwing a grenade, and 26 mostly young lives were lost.

An outraged press pilloried all involved, who in turn blamed it on the military being overstretched.

The fact was, for all their finely tuned lethality, Israel's elite Special Forces units, which included the Air Force's Shaldag (the equivalent of the U.S. Delta Force) and the Navy's Shayetet 13 (Navy Seals), were useless at saving lives.

A public inquiry concluded the *Magav* (Border Police) should have its own special forces-type capability, emphasizing live rescue. A new unit called the *Yeshida Meuchedet Mishtartit* (Police Special Unit) was formed. It soon became better known by its acronym, Yamam.

A highly decorated, just-retired, 31-year-old *Rasan* (Major) of the paratroopers named Assaf Hefetz, was appointed leader. He was given the equivalent police rank of *Rav Pakad* (Superintendent,) and solemn promises he could do it his own way, and that the unit's role as the primary domestic hostage rescue force would be absolutely sacrosanct.

Hefetz modeled the new force on the German *Grenzschutzgruppe 9 der Bundespolizei* (GSG-9), with whom he had trained extensively during his military service. Ironically, the GSG9 owed its own existence to the poor performance of regular Wehrmacht commandos at Munich during the horror of the 1972 Olympics massacre. GSG9 made their name by rescuing 86 passengers from an aircraft hijacked to Mogadishu in October 1977, killing every hijacker without a single innocent loss.

The difference between them and Yamam was that Hefetz set higher standards and trained his men harder. They ranked with the best in the world.

But expecting the military to give up their internal defense role to the border police purely on an edict had proven a pipe dream. The Sayeret Matkal, boosted by their success in rescuing 256 hostages in the raid on Entebbe, had re-trained and reclaimed their lost space.

Yamam found itself relegated to an on-call unit for local events the regular police couldn't handle, which weren't many. After numerous complaints that went nowhere, Assaf Hefetz had requested a cabinet review of the situation which had been delegated to Weizman. Hence the news he was on his way to deliver.

He glanced down at his watch, obsessive about being on time for meetings. He'd promised to be in Netanya by 3:00 p.m. He'd allowed plenty of time, but...

No need to dawdle. Things to do.

Weizman pressed down on the accelerator and felt a thrill as the sporty little coupe rocketed forward.

By 2:30 p.m., passengers bound for Haifa on Egged's scheduled 2.45 p.m. non-stop route 901, were arriving at the Central Bus Station at Neve Sha'anan, in Tel-Aviv's southern suburbs.

Some were older people, so the ticket attendant graciously pointed out their transport, a more elderly Leyland than the Wanderer's Scania, and invited them to board at their leisure.

Some had attended quite unconnected Bar Mitzvahs the night before, including a beautiful long-haired girl accompanied by her mother, and a guitar-carrying, tomboyish teenager. Also, a 66-year-old Syrian-born Jewish man who'd taken a rare few-days off work at Haifa's bustling Talpiot Markets to see a much-loved grandson come of age.

Other travelers included a vivacious young woman taking her new boyfriend home to meet her parents at Nahariya in the far north, and a German-born man on his way to catch a passenger ship from the port of Haifa to Manchester, England to buy goods for the family business.

And a care-worn matron, known as, 'Princess' to her many Haifa friends, and a 73-year-old grandfather who was grateful to settle into a seat after the bustle of visiting some of his nine grandchildren.

In all, 30 passengers, an average number for a Shabbat, were aboard 901 when their driver, 34-year-old Avriham 'Avi'

Perets, a small and cheerful man with a square face framed by curly hair, bounded up the steps.

Avi was dressed as usual in black pants with sharply ironed seams and a starched white shirt. He greeted the passengers cheerily as he settled into his seat.

He was followed aboard by a short, muscular, prematurely balding 46-year-old man named Zvi Eshet, who made up for his shiny pate with an oversized drooping mustache.

One of Egged's most popular tour guides, Zvi was an emotional man, but greatly respected for his tremendous historical knowledge and deep love of country. This day he was riding as a passenger, home to his wife Rita and their two children, Gal and Emit, in Haifa's Krayot district. An enthusiastic Wanderer's Social Club member, Zvi would have been with his friends on the Sorek Cave trip had he not been showing a group of tourists around Tel Aviv the previous day.

On a previous excursion, during Seypevr Heyy, he'd spoken falteringly of his parents' escape from Warsaw in 1933. He'd been a babe in his mother's arms as the ghetto began crushing the city's Jewish families together-eight to a room. Fortune then smiled, as they were able to make their way out of Poland, and immigrate to Israel from France just before the British halted such travel.

He'd ended his speech vehemently with, "*Aney l'evelm la alek lemvevt shely kekh, kemv tesan letbh!*" (Never will I go to my death like that, like a sheep to the slaughter!)

Zvi settled in the back to doze away a slight hangover,

Avi gave out a hearty "*Nesi'ah Tovah!*" (Let's have a great trip!), let off the air-brakes with a distinctive pop-hiss, and at 2:51 p.m. drove out of the depot and headed for Highway 2.

And destiny.

EIGHTEEN

Or Akiva, West Coastal Israel
2:51 p.m.

At that time of nearly ten-to-two, north of both buses and a couple of hundred yards from Highway 2, a devoted couple, 49-year-old Katia Sosensky (Katy to her many friends,) and her 56-year-old husband Joseph, were at their daughter Maya's kitchen table. Joseph's sister Batya was there with them.

They were chatting gaily in a mixture of Hebrew and Yiddish (Katy's preferred language,) and relishing life as only those who have lived through the utmost in horror and privation, truly can.

Joseph and Batya were Dolghinov Jews, from the last 221 survivors of that town in eastern Belarus, who had trekked to safety across hundreds of snowy miles of East Russia in the deep winter of 1942.

Now Joseph and Katy lived in Ashdod, south of Tel Aviv. Yosef was an oil refinery technician with the Sunol Gasoline Company, and Katy a homebody who made quilts and crafts and was locally renowned for her citrus preserves.

On this pleasant late Shabbat afternoon in March, they were with family, making plans to drive north later to the Talpiot night markets in Haifa, which would open when the Shabbat ended with the glowing first stars of dusk.

Aboard bus 901 most of the 30 passengers had settled into the quiet reverie of people with time on their hands and no urgency. One was just a schoolboy, but as the ticket agent at the Tel Aviv Bus Station had noticed, a number were older people. The likes of Else Shwin and Simcha Cohen, matrons traveling separately.

Also, Josef 'Joe' Kheloani, a 66-year-old still with a full head of dark hair, Mathilda Ashkenazi, sitting with her hands primly folded over the carpet-type handbag on her knees, and 'Princess' Malkah Leibwitz.

Haifa was home for most of them, but Russian-born carpenter, Otari Mansharov was going home to Acre, and Moshe Abergil planned to take a break from his stressful sales job in Tel Aviv, at his apartment on Mount Carmel.

In fact, as were the Wanderers, the passengers were a true cross-section of Israel, and had many tales they could have told. Joe Kheloani was Syrian-born. His family had been Rabbis protecting the sacred Cave of Elijah at Jubara near Damascus, for more than 40 years. He'd immigrated to Haifa to support his fast-growing family. Initially by working on building sites and tarring roofs in the Middle-Eastern sun. A religious man, he wouldn't ordinarily be traveling home on the Shabbat from visiting one of his 10 children, except he didn't want to miss a day at the job he loved: working at Haifa's Talpiot markets.

Sixty-eight-year-old Matilda Mizrahi was returning to Haifa and her husband Albert, after a solo trip to see their only son Bilha. Born in Sofia, Bulgaria, with every imaginable advantage, she'd attended a *Yeshiva* (Jewish elementary school,) and a French high school. Then attained a college degree; an amazing achievement for any woman in the 1920s, let alone a Jewish one.

Princess Leibwitz, 58, was quite the opposite. From Kodiist, Romania, orphaned when only a month old by the Spanish influenza pandemic, she'd received no formal schooling at all. After marrying Yechiel Leibwitz, they'd fled to Iasi on the Moldovan border to escape abject poverty; barely surviving repeated Nazi pogroms. In 1959 they finally made it to Haifa and built a life working often poorly paid jobs. But loved by many for her generous spirit, she too was on her way home after visiting a son and grandchildren.

A number of people aboard 901 were returning from Bar Mitzvahs: Jewish coming of age ceremonies.

Like 73-year-old Meir Segal, a fifth-generation Sabra born in Safed, homeward bound from his grandson's. A dignified, barrel-chested man, he was happily nodding off in the window-glass-magnified warmth of the western sun.

Likewise, 14-year-old Revital 'Tali' Aharonowitz was tall and lovely, with stunning long brown hair, and a beatific smile. She had a sketch-pad in her lap with some drawings of dresses. That morning she'd persuaded her mother Chaima, now sitting beside her, to let her visit the fashionable end of Dizengoff Street. She was excited about showing what she had seen to her *chaverim* (best friends), Ruth and Shona.

And 18-year-old Na'omi Alichi, traveling alone, with a cased guitar and a black backpack resting beside her. Cheerful and tomboyish, with a halo of frizzy hair, she was a senior at Ha-Reali High School in Haifa's eastern suburbs. Assured of receiving her *Te'udat Bagrut* (diploma) at the top of her class come June, she was excited about being inducted into the IDF for two years of national service. But she was mostly beaming brightly at having indulged her real love: music. Just that morning she'd gone to Old Jaffa's 'Second Aliyah' Wharf where the buskers gathered and joined in with her guitar on a few songs.

Others traveling for family reasons included an attractive young couple holding hands and frequently staring enraptured into each other's eyes: Leah Tavor and Gilad Gantz. She was taking him up to Nahariya on the Lebanese border for family vetting and approval.

Thirty-two-year-old, German-born, Yehuda Basterman; stood out for his business attire and worried face. That morning at his parents' condominium on Yefet Street in Old Yaffa, he'd gazed anxiously at the weather beyond the famous Ottoman-era clock tower, while laying out shirts for a trip to Manchester, England, to buy goods for the family retail business. He was prone to seasickness, which nothing seemed to help, and his passenger ship was leaving that night from Haifa's Old Port.

Seasickness would be the least of his problems.

The road straightened as the lake-shore fell behind them, and the bus gathered speed past the distinct white limestone escarpments of the Sharon Plain.

At that same time, just a few dozen miles north and a hundred yards off the Taninim Stream-mouth, Baba'a slouched low in his Zodiac. He glanced at his watch for the hundredth time. The terrorists had been at sea just 42 minutes short of 36 miserable hours. They indeed looked like coming in at a relatively safe place; that strip of beach just north of the stream-mouth, cluttered only by that ancient piece of brickwork. On either side of that haven, combers crashed against reefs.

The tide had peaked and the current now pulled them south. Disregarding Hiza'a's feelings, Baba'a hollered to both boats, "Row harder. To the left. Left!"

Signs of habitation were visible onshore by then. Muddy football fields, fortunately empty, bordered the stream. Beyond those were the blocky concrete buildings, and unpaved streets and alleys of a substantial Arab town.

Hostile or not, who knew? But had he known, he was coming onshore just hundreds of yards south of the aquaculture Kibbutz of Ma'agan Michael, which most certainly was.

He knew one thing at a glance. They weren't anywhere near Tel Aviv.

Seventy-five yards from the shore, the surf's grip began bringing them in. Baba'a ordered the boats un-tethered, and the oars pulled aboard except those the boat captains were used to steer. He ordered the dry bags untethered and unzipped so all could arm themselves for the landing.

There was an immediate problem on the second boat, the one carrying fewer people and more equipment. The bag of RPK machine-guns and explosives had been placed on top. The men struggled to get at AKMs and grenades underneath, distracting from keeping the boat straight. Salaam finally freed his weapons. His webbing was soon festooned with grenades, ready for anything lying in wait.

The boats were coming in line abreast through turbulent white water 50 yards or so out. Men began steering with only arms over the side. A giant wave swelled beneath the Zodiacs and shot them like surfboards toward shore, 15 yards or so apart. Everyone gripped anything they could with the hand not holding a weapon.

Then, at the edge of the surf-break, the wave rode something on the sea floor. Water thrust up violently. The right-hand boat reared, then broached. Those on its right side were flung high and clear, to splash down into chest-deep water. On the left-side, Wael, Ahmed, and Salaam were thrown out sideways. The wooden butt of Ahmed's flailing AKM thudded against Salaam's head. The weight of the man's vest pulled him under. The flipped Zodiac came down on Ahmed, knocking him out or worse. It trapped Wael, exhausted from two days of retching over the side of it.

Those simply tipped out were faring much better. Hiza'a, also wearing a heavy vest but able to handle the weight, also Jalal and Tariq, found their feet despite the powerful suction of water and began wading ashore.

Fifty yards up the coast, the other Zodiac had beached safely. Its occupants clambered out, shouting. They hauled their craft free of the waves and rushed to help.

As they reached the overturned boat, the rescuers saw Ahmed's body, out of reach, being carried face down out to sea. They grabbed the heaving boat to steady it while Khaled ducked beneath. He grabbed two hands-full of battle-dress and hauled Wael out into the open air. Ramz helped hoist the limp body onto the upturned hull of the Zodiac. They all dragged the boat ashore.

Dalal was at the water's edge, shouting, "Do something!" And in fact, the rescuers had gotten to Wael in time. After a few minutes of crude CPR, during which he spewed a great deal of seawater, he was breathing again on his own, though barely conscious. Only then everyone collapsed.

Dalal wept openly. No one believed it was out of grief for the lost Salaam. He'd just been a warm, hard body when she'd needed one.

In HaTikva, South Tel Aviv, 37-year-old Avraham Luzia helped his beloved wife Tzyona in through the sliding side door of a white Mercedes L206 taxi-van. He whispered, "You look fine, my dear!"

She truly did look radiant in her sundress with its orange, red, and yellow flower pattern. Her cloud of hair beautifully curled. That morning she'd paraded before her husband in every dress suitable for the child's birthday party they were attending in Haifa, to let him pick just the right one.

The door-to-door shared shuttle service between Israel's two largest coastal cities, already had seven passengers. The couple moved to the rear and made themselves comfortable on the bench seat

This was an important event for the Luzias. This would be the first gathering of the tight-knit extended family, since the recent *Laveyah* (funeral) of Avraham's adored mother. On that day, clasping her sobbing husband as his mother's casket was being lowered beside that of her late husband, Eliza had whispered also.

"At least how beautiful. Couples going to rest together. Perhaps we will too one day!"

Little did she know how soon she'd be proven correct.

The van driver, Jivan, a young Armenian student in his mid-20s at the Open University of Israel, cheating on his student visa to pay his bills, looked at them expectantly.

"Daniel Gardens!' Avraham called out cheerfully. "We will show you exactly where, when we get close."

Jivan smiled, ticking them off his booking sheet. All drop-offs in the same central area. The best kind of trip. He accelerated gently away toward Namir Avenue, a main northern thoroughfare out of the city.

By 4:06 p.m. on the beach, the terrorists had recovered sufficiently to get up off the sand, turn over the second Zodiac, and set about re-arming themselves. Immediately there was another setback. The RPK machine guns and explosives, unsecured during the chaotic landing, were now at the bottom of the sea.

The RPKs were no particular loss. Their purpose had been to defend a captured mid-city hotel, which now looked an unlikely goal. And only Ahmed and Wael had been trained with the explosives Ahmed was dead and Wael in no condition to play with things that blew up.

But they had plenty of everything else. Each boat had carried enough Kalashnikovs for everyone, though some were AK47s distinctive for the foldout bayonet under the barrel. And enough ammunition and grenades, including rocket propelled.

Everyone found their AKM where they'd laid them down or drew new ones, took grenades they clipped to their chests, plus as many banana clips of ammunition as they could carry. Ramz, Hiza'a and Jalal seized a grenade launcher and a three-pack of projectiles each.

As soon as Rami had his gun loaded and cocked, he trotted off to scout around the corner along the bank of the stream. They would obviously have to follow it inland. At the first bend was a national park sign. Seeing the Hebrew wording jolted home their predicament.

Indeed, the terrorists were not alone.

A couple of hundred yards upstream from the beach, a woman stared intently through the lens of a Leica 35MM, into a bush on the far bank.

Gail Rubin, an attractive, New York born-and-raised, 38-year-old Jewish woman; was in a blue windbreaker, canvas-leggings and overshoes. There was a second camera, a telephoto-equipped Canon, on a sling over her shoulder. She was trying to get a bead on a quite rare, Waterside Warbler.

Back in the U.S. her nature photos were starting to feature regularly in prestigious coffee-table magazines. She was eager to supply her agent with fresh ones.

And this was the best place by far, Taninim Nature Preserve: one of the last fragments of coastal wetland till in its natural state. She'd grinned on learning that 'Taninim' meant 'Crocodile.' There hadn't been any of those in Israel since the Kabarra Swamp, of which this had once been part, had been drained a hundred years earlier.

It was close to her home in Caesarea, and this was the perfect time. Right after a storm, when stream-birds were still sheltering, and seabirds rested on the headland after the heavy weather.

She twisted the lens adjustment, then sighed as the Warbler hopped to a different twig. *If only this damn bird will sit still!*

If only some Angel from God had whispered into her ear, “Look over your shoulder, Gail. And run!”

In a minute, Rami was back with the other terrorists, on one knee hissing, "There is a woman! With a camera!"

While recovering, Dalal's grief had become an angry determination. She was fed up with living in Baba'a's shadow. Jihad had appointed her a leader, and she intended to lead. Here was her chance to grab the initiative.

Tucking the ‘Palestinian’ flag she was wearing as a scarf deeper into the vee of her battle-jacket, she grabbed her AKM, racked the slide, and ran along the hard sand above the waterline. Splashed across the shallow stream-mouth. Crouched down. Then crept slowly until she could peek left around the bend.

Gail Rubin was no more than 100 yards away.

Dalal broke into a run.

Gail heard legs swishing through the grass almost immediately. She turned and stared blankly, until it dawned on her that the approaching woman with the brightly colored, bulky scarf around her neck was pointing a rifle.

She glanced frantically about, but there was no help.

Dalal called out, "*Awqif! Awqif!"* (Stop! Stop!) Though Gail wasn't moving. She knew it was some command in Arabic, but wasn't sure what. She barely knew enough Hebrew to get by.

When the two women were only a few feet apart, Dalal stopped and spouted a stream of accusations. Gail didn’t understand a word and wasn't being given time to answer, anyway. Then Dalal realized from Gail’s mode of dress she was probably a westerner, so switched to badly accented English before stopping for a reply.

"This is Taninim." Gail replied in bewilderment, lifting the camera. "I am here photographing birds. Please!"

"Which way Tel Aviv?" Dalal demanded

"There." Gail pointed south down the coast beyond the headland. "A long way!"

"Where you from?"

"America. I'm a nature photographer."

"How you get here?"

"I drove. I have a car. Please. Over there!" She pointed upstream, where its orange roof showed above bushes on the bank.

Nothing Gail said was placating this angry woman. She pointed upstream and blurted, "There's a highway. Please don't hurt me. Please!"

Dalal advanced a couple of steps, rifle held low and menacing, as if to spear the American woman with it. "No," she shouted, "How you get here? To my land! This is MY land, not yours!"

"They... they... this is Israel," Gail said abjectly. "I am Jewish. They gave me a visa!"

Dalal's rage fully erupted. She fired three times. The sounds were sharp even in the broad open space. The rifle's muzzle jerked viciously. The first shot hit Gail in the torso, the second high in her chest, and the third passed over her shoulder.

The American woman made a soft cry and fell.

Dalal didn't look down, but wheeled and headed back to the others.

Nothing was said.

The terrorists returned quickly to the boats, where Wael lay half conscious and coughing, to gather the rest of their deadly tools.

NINETEEN

Highway 70, 15 miles north of Haifa
4:23 p.m.

On a northern highway in the balmy Shabbat afternoon sunshine, another tight-knit family was approaching the highway confluences of north-central Israel. And grave danger. They were a musical family beloved by thousands.

The father, Hanoch Tel-Oren, was at the wheel of their Ford Fairlane 500 station-wagon. A large car by 70s Israeli standards, but being immigrants from Portland, Oregon, they liked what they knew. They'd Hebraized their family name to 'People of the Mountains,' after their home-state, as is common among American Jews settling in Israel.

Hanoch had been a prodigy at Julliard and was currently the First Flutist in the Jerusalem Symphony Orchestra. His wife Sharona, beside him, was also a renowned flutist, and daughter of a famous Hebrew poet and novelist, Avraham Regelson.

And dozing in the back seat in space hard-won from two of his brothers, was a family member who, but for the impending cruelty of fate, might have had a career to pale that of his parents. Omri Tel-Oren, a slightly-built 14-year-old, was the star clarinetist of the Jerusalem Youth Orchestra. Sleepy from jet lag, he'd recently returned from a triumphant tour of Europe.

The family was returning from the mountainside vegetarian *Moshav* (cooperative community) of Amirim in the Galilee hills, after a three-day break, a treat after Omri's trip. And what with the late start, getting gas and a separate toilet stop, Sharona felt they were running well behind schedule.

The boys have sports practices tomorrow, and we haven't even reached the Coastal Highway yet. We won't be back in Jerusalem until past the children's bedtimes.

Aboard the converging Wanderers' vehicle, now 25 miles north of Tel Aviv, children had become fidgety. Rebecca Hochman's sons were being particularly rambunctious.

She made eye contact with her husband Yossi in a separate row, then passed Roi over to him so she could give Ilan a quick diaper change.

At 29, a year older than Rebecca, handsome and long-haired Yossi adored his boys and for a powerful man; had an angel's touch with them. He'd been bulkier 10 years ago with the IDF commandos. These days on top of his Egged owner-driver's duties, being a part-time semi-professional footballer for the Zichron Ya'akov Eagles, maintained his washboard-stomached physique. He was, in fact, missing an important league game there today to be with family and friends.

Some toddlers-and-up, used to Egged buses from previous long trips, were using the secret world beneath the seats to play a game of I-can-see-you-but-you-can't-see-me. Offenders included slight, 10-year-old Ytzak Ankwa, livewire little Liat Gal-on, cherubic 9-year-old Mordechai 'Moti' Zait, and serial offender Junior Meshkel who was into every kind of mischief. Forts had been made from carry-bags. Eyes peeked from under blankets. Giggles were being kept to a minimum to avoid alerting the evil, spoilsport giants above.

But they were

But they were captured anyway, and the uprising quelled as a safety measure. The culprits were banished to the rear-row to play with books. Or toys. Or anything.

Some chance. Grinning faces left no doubt they'd be back underneath in minutes.

With order restored, Rebecca got another song going. Dov Mankiewicz' ode to the kibbutzniks, '*Ha'adama Hageu'la,* The Land Redeemed.' A club signature tune it was sung with gusto, and accompanied by much tapping of feet and slapping of hands on seat-backs.

Me'mir Kiryat ha'reach na lemata
Atzey ekaliptus ba'a'vira shel hasharon
M'Emek Ha'chula derech ne'har ha'yarden
Le'chof Ha'kineret U'me'ever
Ha'rea'ch Ha'meo'rav shel odmat hageu'la

Mi'pisgat Ha'Tavor eynay gomo't
Ha'mordot ha'medoragim ve'hasadot ha'shchookim
Ha'hitnachlaluyot ha'amitzot ne'erachot
Ganigar, Geshar, Shemer, Nitzanim
Re'tzu'at ha'adama hageu'la

Ani shom'aa et ha'ag'vanim musharim, ani ro'ee et ha'Hora nirkedet
Merim et koli u'milarbev itam
U'vaboker, ani Boker Tov!
Ho'el et magafay u'menif et ha'kova
U'meaarbev st Ze'ata im ha'adama hageu'la

From Mir Kiryat the scent drifts down
Eucalyptus scent on the Sharon breeze
From the Hula Valley across the Jordan stream
To the Kineret shore and on beyond
The stirring scent of the land redeemed.

From Tabor's crest my eyes drink in
The terraced loam, the fretted fields
The brave settlements arrayed, Ginegar
Geshur, Shemer, Nitzanim
The girded belt of the land redeemed.

I hear the *Gvanim* sung, watch the *Hora* danced
Raise my voice and whirl along
And in the morn, I'll *Boker Tov!*
Don my coat and hoist my tools
Mix my sweat with the land redeemed.

What a perfect day it was to be alive and free.

Katy Sosensky in Or Akiva had just refreshed her lipstick in Maya's little bathroom and walked out into the lounge to collect her purse. There was no one there. She heard the doors of their car being opened in the driveway and increased her pace.

The sky had cleared, and promised a lovely evening to go north and pick around the stalls at the market when it opened at the end of Shabbat, for *Kholov* cheese, *Banitsa* pastries, *Achva* cakes, and all the other treats. She was sure the *m'arm'l'ad* wouldn't be as good as hers, which was prized all over Ashdod.

Maya was going to drive. Katy looked at Batya in the back seat. *Ww'ás s dy yyaln?* (What's the sudden rush?)

Batya made a "You know, Joseph..." rueful grin.

Katy grinned too, as she climbed in.

What a schlemiel! We have all the time in the world. The market won't open for ages!

The problem for the terrorists on the beach at Taninim, once bristling with loaded weapons, was what to do about Wael. He was recovering, but not yet able to walk. They couldn't leave him or shoot him like a crippled dog, though that might have crossed some minds. They couldn't debate it long either. People, alerted by Dalal's shots, were peering down from the high-rises on the hill. Someone might come down soon to investigate.

Baba'a assembled a pair of oars. He peeled off Wael's fatigue-jacket and his own, and they rolled their comrade onto the makeshift stretcher. He and Khaled picked up the man's gear and went to take ends.

But Dalal wasn't done cementing her authority. She insisted on everyone gathering in a group. "Kamal Adwan," she shouted. "Deir Yassin," the others responded. A tradition begun at Damour and entrenched at Es Saksakiye. Slavery to the cause.

Then they formed a small procession, splashed around the corner from the beach and set off along the bare riverbank toward the highway indicated by the American woman.

They felt naked. Even the right-handed terrorists bore their AKMs left-handed, covering the open ground on their right.

In an outbuilding of Kibbutz Ma'agan Michael, no more than 500-yards to the north, a large, disgruntled-looking man sat at a desk holding a yellow highlight pen and poring over documents. He looked highly overdressed, because he wore a suit and the desk was in a corner of a packing shed cluttered with scoop-nets and smelling of fish-food pellets.

Reserve Army *Aluf*(Major General), Yuri Dubinsky, was two days off his 55th birthday, and the Knesset Member for the political party, Coalition for Change. He'd retreated out there for peace and quiet, to work on a bill he was presenting when the Knesset was next seated, but privacy had been hard to come by.

Dubinsky was a quite famous Israeli citizen, having been one of the founders in 1949, of this same kibbutz, the largest by area in the country. But he was also famously irascible and hard-headed. He'd once been sacked as Army Director of Operations by an infuriated David Ben Gurion by conducting a test of the emergency mobilization system without bothering to tell anyone it was a drill.

And sure enough, he'd been disturbed almost immediately. Someone had imagined they heard shots.

"Well you better go look," he told the greenhouse attendant who'd interrupted him.

"Take Shem. And Aaron, if you can find him. It's his job. It's probably those kids from the Arab village with fireworks or something. Take an Uzi, though."

"Yes sir," said the worker. A minute later the man was armed and wending his way, along with a binoculars-carrying companion, through the scrub that separated the kibbutz from the sea.

A few moments after the investigators went out of sight, a door opened in a nearby accommodation block, as Aaron Eshell, a moon-faced and seriously overweight 40-year-old security guard, left his sister's unit after a late lunch.

A heavy smoker, Aaron had been dying for a fag for more than an hour.

He was determined to walk to the pedestrian overbridge that arched over Highway 2, and then all the way to the Zichron Ya'akov shops if he had to, for a pack of Dubek Filters.

By 4:32 p.m. the terrorists, following the Taninim stream east toward Highway 2, had reached Gail Rubin's parked car. A glance said it was useless. Gail had liked sporty little vehicles. This was a Fiat 850 hatchback. It might have carried two of the men, if one had his head out the window.

There was a small child's stuffed toy on the front passenger's seat. It would seem a curiosity later, to those who knew Gail had no children. But not those who knew she had a row of them on her mantelpiece in Caesarea. Ramz smashed the back window spitefully with the butt of his AKM before they moved on.

The stream-bank became scrubbier and swampier the further they walked. Wael was trying to sit up, but still wasn't talking coherently. Baba'a ordered him to lie still, and he and Khaled continued carrying him east. Finally, they emerged from the scrub on the west side of Highway 2 where the Taninim flowed under the highway and crouched down to get bearings.

Israelis drive on the same side as Americans. Traffic from the north was coming down a long slope from their near left. What little traffic there was. It would be an hour-and-a-half before devout Jews would begin driving around. But the terrorists weren't aware of that, only that things were quiet. The highway's lanes, one each way, were separated by a narrow strip of gravel. The terrorists on the west side of it had their backs against a low limestone bank. The east side dropped off into brushy, open land. Due east again were the outskirts of the Arab town of Zamarin, and then Zichron Yaakov's burgeoning townhouses and villas.

A short distance south on their side of the highway was the Arab village of Beit Hanania, and without knowing the name, they had tramped right past Jisr Al-Zarqa. And of course, over their left shoulders, north, was Kibbutz Ma'agan Michael with its many acres of fishponds splashing with Tilapia.

Wael was now begging to be let up. Baba'a and Khaled put the stretcher down by the side of the road. He clambered upright and shakily took back his equipment. Dalal barked orders, and Hussain, Jalal, Ramz, and Rami ran across the highway, weapons cocked. Hussain and Jalal went and knelt in the center divider.

The others spread out along the near side, gazing uphill.

As Dalal sank down in a crouch there also, she thought of the American woman.

How could she walk the beaches of my homeland when I'm forbidden?

On top of the stress of exerting her authority within the operation, it had made her blood boil. She felt a pang of shame, but instantly switched it off.

Yáfa is our mission. Our everything. All she had time to think about.

Baba'a was also reacting rather than planning. There was no strategy any more, except to seize vehicles and hostages and head south where that woman had pointed for Tel Aviv. They would have to see what came along and respond accordingly.

They had been blockading the highway, less than a minute, when there was a low, deep sound growing in the air. The engine of a large vehicle droning up the incline from the south. In a few more moments they could hear the rumble of tires on the roadway. Then above that, the faint sound of voices singing in a foreign language.

When the Wanderers bus was close enough, the two terrorists kneeling in the center-divider raised their weapons. One in sweat-slick and shaking hands. The other with grim determination.

Hussain opened fire first, with the characteristic thuh-thuh-thuh-thuh of Russian-designed weapons.

TWENTY

Highway 2, Taninim Bridge
4:35 p.m.

Little Naama Hadani ran petulantly up the aisle again toward the front of the Wanderers' bus.

Her mother was ignoring her, making voice noises with all the big people. Worse, she'd been sent to the back where the other kids were drawing and coloring and they'd ignored her too! It was unbearable! She intended to run until she got some attention.

Lavan reached down her right arm and snared her. Pulled her daughter upon her knee in the first row right behind driver Gid'on Haas. Pressed her face against the Naama's and murmured endearments.

Naama chuckled with delight. Wriggled her legs. *Much better. Mommy loves me after all.*

Gid'on squinted ahead at an unusual sight. Then growled to himself. *What the hell are these people doing on the road? Some people have absolutely no sense of safety! Should be jailed!*

The windshield glass in front of him imploded.

Hussain had forgotten his training and fired an entire 30-round clip on fully automatic.

The rounds had riddled the upper area of the windshield, then gone on through and shattered the rear glass as well.

Baba'a, kneeling near Dalal by the southbound lane, cursed under his breath.

How many times did I tell them to shoot low?

The bus zigzagged drastically, but straightened out, and seemed would carry on. But the terrorists didn't have time to watch it.

A blue Volkswagen Kombi van had appeared in the southbound lane. The white-faced driver saw weapons. He frantically sped up. Khaled and Tariq leapt onto the road. Then jumped back as the van blasted by.

Dalal fired several shots that had no effect. She clicked to fully automatic and emptied her weapon. So did Baba'a. Everyone else was blocked. The van swerved violently. Its tires screeched with each change of direction. But it too straightened and kept going.

The terrorists glared after it, ears ringing. The sour smell of cordite hung in the air. Everyone turned their attention back to the northbound lane. To their delight, the bus had stopped in the center divider 200-or-so-yards up the highway. People were spilling out. Distant voices clamored.

Dalal ejected her empty magazine to clatter on the road. She jammed home a replacement. *The bus is Allah's gift. The hostages it holds will give us a bargaining position we couldn't have hoped for just minutes back.*

All the terrorists stared at it hungrily, like hunters watching a downed bird which still has some life in it. *How can we get to it before it flutters away?*

Yuri Dubinsky's two men sent to investigate possible shots, raced back gasping and panting into the packing shed at 4:36 p.m. Dubinsky turned irritably to see why. Their words stopped him in mid-motion.

"There are..." said one.

"Boats." said the other.

"Where? What kind?" Dubinsky demanded.

"In the bay, just this side of the stream," said the first.

"Zodiacs," said the second.

Dubinsky hurried to a wall telephone and dialed a number from memory. While it rang at an up-scale, five-bedroom unit in Kfar Yona, a dormitory suburb of Tel Aviv, Dubinsky noticed the two men were fidgeting. "Yes?"

"We also heard.," said the first.

"More shooting," said the second.

Then in chorus, "Just now over by the highway!"

But the general had clapped his hand over his free ear when a deep voice came on the line. His hearing was poor anyway, from ruptured eardrums back when he'd been deputy commander of the tank corps. He'd missed the men's words.

Dubinsky said who he was into the phone.

General Zvi Bar, commander of the *Magav* (National Border Police,) replied, "Ah Yuri! How are you general?"

"Look, Zvi, some of my guys have found boats. Those rubber ones the Arabs use."

"Really? I'll have my people in Haifa get down there immediately!"

"I knew you would. That's why I called you right away." Dubinsky noticed his two men still hovering, looking awkward. He vigorously waved them away.

"Good good," said a pleased General Bar. An opportunity to get one up on the other agencies was never to be missed in these days of tight budgets.

"Shall I give the local police a call too?" Dubinsky asked.

Bar chewed his lip. *No sense in sharing the credit.*

"Let's ah, keep it to ourselves, hey? No need to cause a panic. Just keep your people indoors, hey? My boys won't be long!"

Within a minute Dubinsky was back reviewing his important document. The Knesset was in session the coming Tuesday.

Gunfire had torn all around Wanderer's driver, Gid'on Haas, ripping at his clothing and lashing him with glass fragments. Now he clung to the heaving steering wheel with all his strength.

Miraculously, he'd been hit only twice, flesh wounds in the right arm and shoulder. They were bleeding freely, turning his good white shirt crimson, but so far painless from shock.

Behind him was devastation.

Naama Hadani, moments ago balancing joyfully on her mother's right knee, had been shot in the face and fallen forward without a sound into the aisle. Several rows back Rina Bosknitz was lolling in her aisle seat, her face also a red mask. Elsewhere passengers were clutching at arms and shoulders, or shedding fragments of broken glass from faces and hair. Trying to grasp what was happening amid the whirling of loose objects blowing about.

Many hadn't realized they had been shot at: the sound of Hussain's firing had so intermingled with the crashing of the windshield caving in. The possibility of a terrorist attack had been so remote in their minds, most believed they were in a traffic collision, or something off the back of another vehicle had flown through the windshield.

Gid'on knew.

Virtually blind from the buffeting wind and splinters of glass in his eyes, he sensed rather than saw where he was going.

Ahead, Aaron Eshell, on his way to Zichron Ya'akov to feed his nicotine addiction, stood frozen on the Highway 2 overbridge. Convinced the juggernaut careering toward him would take out the pillar beneath him and hurl him to his death.

But gradually, with the upward slope assisting, Gid'on got the vehicle pulled up, half in the center strip. Then the pain hit him and he leaned forward, groaning over the wheel. His wife Judith rushed from the back, lifted him out of his seat and sat him down in the well behind.

Someone pushed the lever to open the side doors. Passengers began getting off, still looking baffled or asking one another what had happened.

Aaron gawked at the frontal damage to the bus which was actually quite minor apart from the shattered windshield and rear window, then came running down from the overbridge to help.

Back at the shooting site, the terrorists heard vehicle noise. They turned to look south and saw, right in front of them, the answer to how they could reach the bus. A large van falling into their trap. *Surely another sign and gift from Allah.*

Jivan was enjoying the drive, with the Mercedes shuttle-van pulled strongly up a long hill. One of his university courses was in Hebrew. Eavesdropping on his passengers' conversations was one of his guilty pleasures as well as good practice.

The couple in the back was going to a family birthday party. The child was turning seven. He smiled. He had cousins that age. Sweet kids.

In the rear mirror, the Jewish lady showed her husband the corner of a gift-wrapped dress. She was going to treat all the party guests to pizza. *Mmmmmm.*

He looked ahead and noticed figures on the highway, and a lot more activity in the distance. Then the figures had all his attention.

They were waving him down at gunpoint.

The terrorists wrenched open the van's doors.

The seven people who climbed out were obviously Arab, even if they hadn't been jabbering in that language. The terrorists waved gun muzzles and let them run away down the highway, while calling out to each other to bring all their equipment.

Then Baba'a ducked his head inside and saw a man and woman in the very back. They looked Jewish. They were clinging to each other in bewilderment and didn't seem to comprehend anything said to them. *A bonus!*

Baba'a kept his gun on them while hollering, "Yalla!" at his companions. The terrorists piled into the van with everything they had.

Ramz seized the wheel, and they roared up the highway after their prey.

The vicinity of the Wanderer's bus was utter confusion.

About 40 passengers had spilled onto the roadway. Most had crossed to the west edge of the blacktop. A group of eight or ten had collected around Aaron Eshell by the foot of the overbridge steps. Some were sitting on the grass verge. One was Lavan

Hadani, stricken with anguish, hugging Naama's small blood-soaked body.

Among 22 who'd stayed aboard were Dov Bosknitz and his youngest boy, 10-year-old Eran. His oldest, 11-year-old Danny, had been swept outside with the flood of exiting people. Dov was kneeling in the aisle attending to Rina, who was lying between two rows of seats. Her skull was deformed by a serious bullet wound, but she was half-conscious and gasping for water.

Four small passing vehicles, two from each direction, had stopped to investigate.

One southbound car was driven by Jeffrey Shapiro, a 29-year-old sales representative returning to Tel Aviv. He was now among the crowd, trying to comfort some most distressed.

The second vehicle had contained a couple in their late 20s, named Eliezer Kroitoro and Vanessa Schwartz. They had seen the injured and returned to look for a first aid kit Monica thought they might have.

The first northbound car belonged to 60-year-old Pinhas Kopel, no less than the retired 3rd Commissioner of Israeli Police, heading to a reunion in Haifa from Kfar Bin Nun southwest of Jerusalem. He'd driven around the crowd of distracted terrorists thinking they were infuriating idiots. Luckily, he hadn't shouted at them. At the bus, he'd finally grasped the situation and was trying to call for help on his CB radio, except this seemed to be a reception dead-spot.

The last car contained the four Sosenskys from Or Akiva, who were just then crossing the northbound lane to offer help.

Into the middle of this melee arrived the terrorists.

Baba'a had harangued them during the 45-second race north. "Let no one escape! No one!"

Ramz skidded the van to a halt near the bus's rear door. The terrorists launched themselves out of the van like demons from *Gehenna* (hell.).

Ramz aimed his AKM in the air and fired a short salvo. Then leapt up the back step and fired more shots down the aisle. The bullets passed inches over the people attending to Rina Bosknitz and Gid'on Haas, sending them sprawling. The passengers still in seats huddled down in terror.

The terrorists had rehearsed this scenario numerous times at Damour. The rest split up. Half ran round the back of the bus. The rest charged straight ahead to come around from the front.

Rami, in mid stride, looked to his right and saw the Sosenskys in the roadway. At the same instant, the four Israelis realized these were armed Arabs. They wheeled and ran back toward their car.

Rami sprayed fire in their direction.

Joseph and Katy were struck multiple times and knocked down on the roadway. Batya was hit high up on her right shoulder, and Maya was struck in the wrist, but they managed to get behind the car and drop flat.

Kopel watched, amazed, as the small terrorist opened fire so viciously and accurately. Then he flopped down on the front bench seat of his car and steeled himself for a storm of bullets to come through the door.

Nothing happened.

For some unaccountable reason Rami didn't press his advantage: just followed his fellow terrorists out of sight.

Ramz' and then Rami's fusillades, though blocked from view by the bus-body, alerted everyone standing along the left edge of the road.

The group talking animatedly with Ma'agan Michael security guard Eshell by the overbridge staircase, among them Danny Bosknitz, instinctively hunched down, staring around wildly for the threat. Then bolted for cover when the terrorists appeared and fanned out.

They were only yards from the scrub bordering Ma'agan Michael. As they melted into it, gunfire followed, wounding several. One was a woman who staggered south until through the brush before falling, then crawled back to the roadside.

Families were torn apart. Numerous children, including young Danny, had no chance to say goodbye to parents and brothers and sisters they would never see alive again.

Eliezer Kroitoro and Vanessa Schwartz, rummaging in their glove compartment for medical supplies, took one look at the terrorists, and ducked down in the front seats. But the passenger's door was open, exposing them. They quickly wriggled through and lay down beside the car, hardly daring to breathe.

Miraculously, like Kopel, they were overlooked.

Everyone else around the bus stared in dread and dismay at the guns trained on them, then lifted their hands or pulled children close.

With the tall wild-haired terrorist leader shouting unintelligibly at them, the captured Wanderers began shuffling together like corralled animals.

TWENTY-ONE

Highway 2 beside Kibbutz Ma'agan Michael
4:40 p.m.

The terrorists had seized 49 civilians, including Samaritan Jeffrey Shapiro, who right then was wondering what in hell he'd gotten mixed up in.

Unfettered power immediately brought out the worst in them. They whooped and catcalled jubilantly, while prodding the helpless with the sharp-beveled muzzles of their AKMs. Grinning made Tariq look wolfish and Fayadh fiendish.

Noise was constant. Little Missy Ankwa cried loudly in Monique's arm. Little boys howled while their mothers tried to calm them. Lavan Hadani screamed as she was forced to leave Naama's body lying on the road.

Most captives felt they'd been cast into a hideous nightmare and couldn't shake themselves awake. They abjectly obeyed, shuffling their legs by rote. Some men were distraught, like Lavan's husband Joseph. But not all. Others stared balefully at their captors, though careful not to endanger their loved ones by outright resistance.

Except Amnon Drori, the huge ex-paratrooper. He clenched and unclenched his fists, eyes blazing furiously at the humiliation of his friends.

Then he glared angrily at Jalal. Perhaps the big Arab remembered Ms. Heinrich-Mamatow's words about making examples.

Jalal advanced on Amnon. Jabbed him repeatedly in the ribs to force him back and into the open. They locked eyes for another long moment, then Jalal sent half a dozen bullets into the Israeli's broad chest.

Screams and shouts immediately broke out, but were quickly beaten down.

Jalal spat on the body, then calmly rejoined the others.

Pre-cut lengths of nylon rope were pulled from backpacks. The able-bodied men's hands were tied, leaving a tail. Then in a surreal re-enactment of horrors that will never be long enough in the past, they were forced back aboard and lashed into the window seats, spaced out as human shields.

Once anyone who looked like they might resist was secured, the old, the frail and the women and children, were packed in around them, in some rows five or six for every two seats. Dov Bosknitz was dragged away from Rina and pushed to the rear. The Luzias from the shuttle van were also jostled aboard.

Then the terrorists took firing positions, Rami and Hiza'a armed with grenade launchers. The curtains were pulled across every side window that wasn't a firing port. Some were positioned at intervals down the aisle, swinging their AKM's menacingly back and forth.

While this was happening, Dalal and Tariq were demanding to know who'd been driving.

On learning it was Gid'on Haas, who could now barely stand, they press-ganged the nearest capable looking candidate. That was Shlomo Zait, despite his wife Judith's pleading.

The remains of broken glass were kicked out of the front and rear window-frames. Shlomo was made to start the bus, turn it around to face Tel Aviv, and wait again in the center divider until all evil tasks were complete.

There was absolutely no plan other than to head south where Gail Rubin had pointed, but the Arabs remained gleeful: waving rifles and grenades with the pins removed, at the already terrified. It didn't seem to matter that their predicament hadn't changed.

All except Baba'a. He was restless. They'd been stationary far too long, though it had been less than seven minutes since the first shots. He walked to the rear exit and stepped down onto the highway.

Immediately he heard a vehicle. He swung north and aimed his AKM up the hill.

The Tel-Oren's station-wagon crested the rise beside the Ya'akov Zichron off-ramp, just before 4:40 p.m.

Sharona was the first to notice anything amiss, as the magnificent Sharon Plain opening up before them. First the sparkling from heaps of glass near the hulking bus straddling the divider, then the haphazard way cars were parked along both verges. Suddenly she realized the red-splashed mounds scattered around were bodies.

She was rocked forward against her seatbelt, as the brakes came on hard and knew Hanoch had seen it all too.

Her window had been down to give the boys in the back some air. With the fine-tuned hearing of a professional musician, she made out babies crying. Her eyes followed the sound to the bus, then went wide. A tall, bearded man in military dress was pointing something at her. It spat flame.

She heard the station-wagon's windshield shatter, and the hammer blows of bullets hitting the front of the car as one ragged rolling sound.

Hanoch yelped. His right hand dropped loose off the wheel. His arm spurted blood. A bullet had struck an inch above the elbow, breaking bone and tearing apart the median nerve. A terrible injury for a right-handed professional musician.

Not realizing how seriously he was hurt, Sharona relievedly let out a deep breath. The rest of the gunfire had seemed to pass harmlessly between them. Some as close as through her seat back. Then she looked behind and shrieked. Omri's face against the right rear upholstery was a disfigured red mask.

Somehow Hanoch kept control of the car one-handed and got them safely to a stop in the middle of the southbound lane. He got out, clasping his maimed arm to his midriff. While he found a towel to suppress the bleeding, Sharona scrambled into the back.

"No, no, no, no..."

She gathered her beloved son in her arms.

There was movement also, on the outside of the lanes, as if a trance had been broken.

The couple, Kroitoro and Schwartz, and the two surviving Sosensky women stood up by their cars, and Kopel inside his own. They stared in horror and disbelief at the carnage.

Batya and Maya Sosensky ran straight to the side of Joseph and Katy. Batya had seen violent death many times. There was nothing they could do, and they were in need of a doctor's help themselves. She dragged her niece with her uninjured arm, to the driver's door of Kopel's car and pleaded through the glass for help.

The prolonged lull in the traffic had also ended. Vehicles were arriving; the people rushing over to help the fallen. Someone called out that Naama Hadani was still breathing. She was carried to a car that screeched off north. The Sosenskys climbed into Keitel's car and he accelerated in the same direction.

Sharona Tel-Oren helped Hanoch back in the car, and yelled chokingly to her oldest son, Noam, to get in front and drive. She knew from her and Hanoch's early days at nearby Kibbutz Mesilot, the nearest hospital was south at Hadera. But going that way meant following the bus.

Noam steered around the milling people and, with his mother still babbling instructions, U-turned north also, toward Haifa's Rambam Medical Center.

At 4:44 p.m., Yuri Dubinsky cursed at the sound of feet echoing off the concrete floor of the shed, and got up to reprimand whoever it was this time.

A minute later he was saying, "Poppycock Aaron! Terrorists don't land on beaches in northern Israel to attack the south. What are they going to do, walk? Their target has to be Haifa. I've notified the best authority to deal with that.

He looked over the distressed, babbling, mostly barefoot crowd Eshell had with him. Dubinsky's selective hearing had picked up "*taoonah*" (traffic accident.)

Zvi will be infuriated if I spoil his coup and call in the police after giving him the heads-up. His people should be here any time. I'll let them handle it.

"So, they've been in a bus accident. No, I'm not going to get the police worked up over that."

Eshell went to protest, but Dubinsky held up his hand in finality.

"That's it. Enough! Aaron, it's your job to keep these people out of here. Do your job!"

"I saw it with my own eyes!"

"I don't want to hear it. There is enough going on down at the beach. I'm expecting visitors any minute. Now get these people out of here and do what you have to do!"

"But..."

"Now Aaron!"

Eshell shepherded the people outside. "Wait here!"

He ran as fast as his bulk would allow, for his sister's unit a short distance away.

Short, swarthy *Shoter* (Constable) Hamid Ba'asha, at the Zichron Ya'akov Police Station, at 4:46 p.m., put every ounce of his frayed patience into speaking politely.

"The city people will come and fix your pothole soon, Mrs. Mayer."

"Yes, I'm sure. And I'm sure they will do a good job. But please call 106 for that next time."

"Yes, I'm sorry they are closed on Shabbat."

"Bye now."

He banged down the front counter phone.

Zichron Yaakov was a busy station, having been a British Tegart Fort prior to the 1948 war: big enough to have housed hundreds of prisoners from the captured coastal Arab town of Tantura at one point.

Hamid's annoyance, though, wasn't with the woman trying to get her road fixed. He felt abandoned by his workmates. *Mamzers!* (Bastards) *Those guys should have been back to relieve me fifteen damn minutes ago!*

Hamid's curse was he hated soccer, so he always got stuck running the station on game days. And this was the big one. Beach United versus the local Eagles. Almost the whole town was there. As was every other officer on duty, to keep the peace of course.

In fact, he'd been hearing firecrackers, lots of them. That still wasn't a reason to leave him stuck with everything else. The phones had been going crazy. He'd taken two minor emergency calls in just the last five minutes that he couldn't do a thing about. People up on the hill reporting an accident involving an Egged bus down on the Two.

Those damn guys better get back here soon!

The phone rang yet again. "Constable Ba'asha!"

"There's been shooting on the coastal highway!"

"Who is speaking please?"

"Aaron Eshell. I'm a security guard at Ma'agan Michael. Please..."

"That's an accident site, sir, we've already had calls. Some officers will be over there shortly."

"I am telling you its terrorists!"

Hamid sighed. *Why me? Overreacting citizens. Sheesh.* He summoned his last reserves of patience. "I'm sure you're mistaken, sir. Look, don't worry about it. We'll be over there soon."

"But..."

"Look sir, I have to keep the line open. We appreciate your call."

A minute later, the officers Hamid had been waiting for sauntered in, looking pleased.

"About time," said Hamid. "Fireworks keep you busy? Anyway, there's some accident on the Two by the overbridge. Go over and have a look, would you?"

As the two officers walked out to their car, one looked sideways and raised an eyebrow. "Fireworks?"

His partner grinned back. "Must have been outside the ground. I couldn't hear a thing for the cheering. What a great game!"

Before another minute passed, there was a screech of tires and the clattering of car doors. Hamid looked up, startled. The front swing doors crashed open and a middle-aged couple helped a woman inside. They lowered her onto on the waiting room bench seat. Her left side was scarlet. "Help us please. She's been shot. We found her beside the highway."

Hamid's eyes widened to dinner plate size. He fumbled under the counter for the radio hand-piece. Held down 'transmit' and bellowed, "Zee-arr seventeen. Zee-arr seventeen. It's a terrorist attack. Acknowledge seventeen!"

It was the first time those words were spoken on the police communications network that day, but not the last.

Hamid hurdled the counter and helped get the injured woman, write with blood loss and in considerable pain, on the floor with her legs elevated to conserve blood flow to her vitals. Then found a hand-towel for her rescuers to compress against her wound.

Moments later he had the laminated emergency-procedures and notification-numbers list out on the counter, a phone in each ear, and was taking turns talking tersely into each.

Aboard Egged's route 901 express bus to Haifa, northbound on Highway 2 south of Beit Hanania, driver Avi Perets was carefully observing the posted speed limit of 90kmph, and warily watching the highway ahead. Wondering what was causing approaching vehicles to flash their lights at him.

A blue Kombi van had even swerved vigorously left and right to get his attention. A speed-trap, no doubt, though this reaction seemed a little extreme. *Fair enough though I suppose, the Meeshtarah (traffic cops) have their job to do as well, even on Shabbat.*

He caught the glint of the sun off broken glass, up near the overbridge, before realizing it was a fellow Egged bus facing him in the center divider. Had to be in some sort of trouble. Maybe it had collided with the white van parked crookedly beside it.

Then prickles of adrenaline rippled the backs of his hands. A figure had stepped down from the bus. The banana-shaped magazine of the Russian AK-type weapon in its hands was unmistakable. The figure swung away from him. Instantly there was smoke from gunfire going the other way.

Avi's mind blared, *terrorists! I'm carrying passengers*!

He lifted his foot off the gas. An area of packed gravel between the road lanes, to allow northbound vehicles to turn left onto the Arab town, was just ahead. Avi braked hard, hauled his wallowing vehicle in a half-circle, and pounded the accelerator to the floor.

TWENTY-TWO

Southbound on Highway 2, south of Ma'agan Michael
4:48 p.m.

Aboard the hijacked Wanderer's bus, the terrorists' basest instincts now knew no restraints.

They had 48 helpless and terrified souls under their control, time on their hands, and nothing to restrain them. Their elated grins morphed into cruel sneers. Shezia Heinrich-Mamatow would have been proud.

When the hostages were being crushed back aboard, Dov Bosknitz had seemed completely broken by the twin horrors he'd suffered: his horribly injured wife and his missing son Danny, who he was certain had been murdered in the shooting outside. His hands hadn't been tied. He'd just been forced into a rear aisle seat. But he'd pulled himself back together and was desperate to reach Rina near the front, where she still moaning for water.

Dov got out of his seat. Ramz shouldered him back into place. But when the big Jerichoan Arab turned away, he got up again and made it two steps up the aisle.

The brute shoved him down in the aisle and fired a short burst of shots into the Israeli's back, setting his cotton shirt smoldering.

The hostages nearby shrank away in horror. Mothers turned their children's faces from the ghastly sight.

Ramz swung a boot into Dov's twitching body, then smirked at Hussain and Tariq nearby and said, *"lin llam yakun alddarae ' ela alaql 'an-takun tahdhira."* (If not a shield, he can at least be a warning.)

They grinned back, and the three shouldered weapons, picked up the bloody body and threw it into an empty window seat at the back.

Then shouts came from the front, and the terrorists' mood changed mercurially yet again. There was another bus ahead, this one blue and white. It was swerving, trying to get around some traffic.

Consternation immediately replaced surprise. Another load of precious hostages was potentially getting away. Baba'a rushed to Dalal's side at the front, where she had her gun jammed into the flesh of Shlomo Zait's neck.

She yelled at him to speed up. When he was slow in responding, Baba'a mashed his foot down on Shlomo's, flattening the gas pedal on the floor.

On the highway ahead of Avi Perets, the traffic had just become impassable. With the Wanderer's Scania in his rear-view mirror and a dawdling van ahead, he had only one option. He veered hard left across the divider into the temporarily empty northbound lane, praying they wouldn't bog down.

There were cries of terror among his passengers, who had only been murmuring until then about the reversal of direction. None had seen the Wanderers bus ahead before the turn. Now they knew something was terribly wrong.

It also brought bleary-eyed Zvi Eshet reeling up from where he'd been dozing in the back, to the seat opposite Avi. The two Egged men exchanged a few words, then Zvi reached for the tour-guide's microphone fitted to all Egged buses.

"We saw trouble and are avoiding it. Please hold on to your seats!" he said over the speakers in the eaves. He tried to think of calming words and failed. "Thank you everybody. Hold on!"

But the madcap wrong-way race was already over, really. In a moment the Scania was behind them again. With traffic speeding toward him head on, Avi had no option but to steer back into the right lane. There, with traffic bunching up again, any hope of escape was gone.

The windshield-less Scania swung from behind the Leyland, left wheels on the divider. Jalal waved his rifle from a window. Avi ignored him grimly.

Baba'a jammed his own AKM even harder into Shlomo's ear and made him steer the Scania as far left again as he could. Jalal unleashed a storm of bullets at the left side tires. He hit his mark, but a good deal of the gunfire also went high as usual. It raked along the side of bus 901.

There were gasps and cries inside 901 as passengers were hit.

Otari Mansharov, the harmless 37-year-old carpenter heading home to his family in Acre, slumped sideways dead in his seat. Moshe Abergil, the 26-year-old vacationing salesman, doubled over nursing an exit wound in his belly. Numerous others were grazed by glass and metal chips.

Avi's steering wheel juddered in time with the whop-whopping of flapping rubber. He tried to steer into the Scania, but the Leyland wouldn't turn. He had no choice but to slow down.

When the speed of both vehicles dropped to walking speed, Baba'a, Rami and Hussain jumped down and climbed aboard 901, fingers poised on the triggers of their guns.

Across Israel, word of the terrorism calamity on its hands, was finally getting to people who could do something about it.

Constable Hamid Ba'asha in Zichron Ya'akov, was urgently relating his still developing tale into the phones.

National Head of Operations *Nitzav Mishneh* (roughly an army light Colonel,) Haim Avinoam, at the National Police Headquarters in Jerusalem, had been summoned to hear it.

Fifty-year-old Haim was well suited to respond. He'd seen a lot of violent death. Thirty years before, as a young Lieutenant of the Haganah, he'd participated in one of the notorious tit-for-tat events that set the bloody tone for the War of Independence.

On the morning of December 30th, 1947, renegade Irgun members threw grenades into a crowd of Arab day-laborers queuing for employment in the single entranceway to the massive British-owned Haifa Oil Refinery, killing 6 and wounding 42.

The hate-filled attackers either didn't know, or care, that the refinery was a 24-hour operation. A work-shift including many Jewish workers was inside. Arab workers went on a rampage, killing 41 Jews and injuring 91 before British troops could intervene.

Jewish Command, while cursing the unruly Irgun and demanding suitable punishment for those Jews responsible, felt bound to retaliate. Haim was present the following night at the village of Baladh al-Shaykh in the Mount Carmel Highlands. The town was revered by Arabs as the shrine of a hero of their own 1935 uprising against the British; Izz ad-Din al-Qassam. After a Deir Yassin-like assault, 17 lay dead among the ruins. Relations between the sides never really recovered.

The brisk and highly efficient Avinoam had come up rapidly through police ranks after joining as a beat-cop after his military discharge on Armistice Day, July 20th, 1949.

On this occasion he wasted no time on irrelevancies. "Terrorists at Ma'agan Michael?"

"On the highway near there, yes sir!" confirmed Hamid.

"What have you done about it? Sent a car? Good."

"Yes, but they found nothing, except some abandoned vehicles and a lot of cartridge casings. Seven-point-six-two short."

"Not a surprise!"

"No sir,' affirmed Hamid. "There's a lot of blood there too. We're checking with the MDA (Magen David Adom) ambulance people and the local hospitals on that. Our men have headed on to the kibbutz to talk to a witness. A witness called us from there."

"Who else have you advised?"

"I'm letting South-Western HQ know right now," Hamid said.

That headquarters, just known as 'Sharon', was at Kfar Saba, 13 miles northwest of Tel Aviv, where the two main north-south highways, the Two and the inland Four, ran parallel. It oversaw the entire coastal plain between Tel Aviv and Hadera, except the beach city of Netanya.

There, *Pakad* (Chief Inspector-roughly the rank of an army Captain) Levi 'Lev' Shachar, concentrated hard on Hamid's voice coming in on a desk-speaker. The slim, youthful-looking, 29-year-old, was traffic commander as well as station second-in-command.

Lev's high rank for his age owed much to his competence, but also a lot to the 'New Policing' wave sweeping Israel. The initiative had been the pet project of the last Commissioner, Shaul Rosolio, and was being rapidly advanced by the present man, Haim Tavori. It was sweeping out the non-technically-savvy, senior dinosaurs, who imagined they still wore the wooly black fez of the British mandate-era police. Also, those running all-too-common miniature empires within their stations.

The new police were to be far more inter-cooperative, flexible in their roles, and have much better public relations. And closer aligned with military procedures as being pushed at the top by future Commissioner Herzl Shafir. With better communications than the present short-range radios and scattered phone lock-boxes, and more modern arms than the WWII era M1 carbines and .38 revolvers still in use.

But Lev, a native English speaker whose parents had emigrated from Australia when he was already a late-teen-ager, was having to concentrate hard to follow the thickly-Arab-accented Hamid. What was clear: the situation was serious.

Behind Lev, his boss, 37-year-old *Sgan Nitzav* (Chief Superintendent) Alisha Nadav, a sturdily built, no-nonsense, do-it-by-the book officer with prematurely graying hair, had arrived and picked up an extension.

The two men acknowledged each other without speaking.

Hamid was describing the highway scene. There was a lot of confusion. The hijacked vehicle was travelling north and while there were a lot of tire tracks, there was nothing to prove it had changed direction. Then Hamid said, "Hold one second," and broke away. They heard him speaking quickly in the background.

Back on the line again, he said, "My men are at Ma'agan Michael and have talked with some passengers, who are distraught. The bus was full and they have family still aboard. They don't know which way it went either, but the senior man at the kibbutz, a reserve Aluf, says some rubber boats have been found on the beach, and he's called out the Magav."

Oh crap, thought Lev. *Nothing quite like having another agency crawl over your patch in a crisis.* He looked across the room and got a similar reaction from Nadav. Plus, the border police thought they were more closely linked with national security, and were inclined to throw their weight around.

How the hell were they going to handle this?

On Highway 2 on the outskirts of Or Akiva, Avi Perets had accepted the inevitable and opened both side doors of bus 901, rather than provoke more shooting. He heard the boots of the terrorists hit the rear steps even over the last rumbling and shuddering of them coming completely to a halt. Meanwhile the red and white chasing bus nosed menacingly up almost against his rear.

Avi turned off the engine and kept his hands high on the wheel. Praying they would overlook his trying to run them off the road. He looked sideways where Zvi Eshet also sat still with his hands above his shoulders. Steeled for death, they waited out what might be the last moments of theirs, as well as all their passengers', lives.

But the terrorists simply ran up the steps and began shouting. Avi knew enough Arabic to know they were ordering the passengers off. He stood up, hands high, calling on his passengers to obey.

One of the terrorists began kicking a small individual as he cowered in the aisle with his arms protecting his face.

He believed they'd captured a uniformed soldier. Anyone with a glimmer of understanding of Israel would have known otherwise. Solomon Polak was obviously just a youth. Though 17, he looked even younger, and IDF National Service doesn't begin until 18. And the 'uniform' barely resembled the IDF's.

Solomon was a student at the Technion: Israel's Technical University in Haifa. Epaulettes and beige coloring were the only things the clothing-sets had in common. Before boarding, after visiting an aunt in Tel Aviv, He'd let her talk him into having a photograph taken in his school shirt.

Leaving it on would be the worst decision of his life.

Zvi Eshet watched this brutality with cold anger, but could do nothing to help. Under the gun-muzzles he could only go along quietly with everyone else. He prayed his opportunity would come later.

When his feet hit the ground, passengers were streaming from the back doors on his right. There was even less chance of escape now. A wall protecting the wealthy residents of Caesarea from unpleasant road noise flanked the highway. Escapees would have to run fully exposed either up or down the road: certain death in either direction.

More terrorists pointed guns and waved all the passengers toward the rear. One was little Fayadh, strutting like a gamecock. Princess Leibwitz was trying to ease her arthritic hips down to the ground. Fayadh swung at her with his AKM butt to hurry her along.

Out of the crowd came pugnacious little Avi, all five feet four of him. He breasted the slim terrorist. "Don't!"

Fayadh was amazed. *One of these is challenging me? These thieving Zionists?* He leveled his AKM. But he would also be firing into the backs of valuable hostages.

That wouldn't be popular. He hesitated.

Wael saved the moment by arriving and prodding Avi backward, then allowed the older people to climb down.

Avi went with the flow.

There was a sudden tumult of gunfire. Rami guarding the southern approach had seen two vehicles coming and opened up.

The one in front kept going at a normal speed as if the driver hadn't noticed. The second, a van, took several hits on the side and started swerving, then drove off the edge of the highway and rolled from sight.

Within another minute, all the occupants of 901 were standing outside. The dead and injured men had been left where they lay.

Once again, some captives cowered and cried. Others, Matilda Ashkenazi and Meir Segal among them, maintained their dignity. Still others were more confused than scared.

Then when the terrorists began splitting the men off from the group, Joe Kheloani protested. Khaled swung his rifle butt against the elderly man's back. Avi shouldered through the crowd and confronted him.

"They are in my care. Mine. Don't touch!"

Khaled didn't understand a word, but drew back anyway, nodding in respect at the angry little Israeli's courage.

The 901 passengers were crammed into the Wanderers' bus. The men's hands were tied yet again, even the harmless elderly. Avi Perets was bound into the last-seat-but-one on the right side. Eighty-eight people were now crammed into a bus built for 52.

The terrorists were positively chortling at this second huge victory. Moved by the moment, Dalal took off her flag, leaned over Gid'on and tie it to the bus's wing mirror as a streamer. But the cars Rami had fired at, however, had created a sense of danger.

Rami, Hiza'a, and Jalal loaded a rocket launcher each and took position at the rear side windows. Baba'a belatedly had the surrounding seats cleared to make space for the weapons' back-blast. The hostages were crammed even tighter into rows further forward.

Amid their brutal pushing and shoving, the terrorists didn't notice the small forms of Ytzak Ankwa and Liat Gal-on hiding below.

It was 4:51 p.m. when all was settled. In response to some furious gestures from Dalal, Moshe backed up and pulled out onto the highway.

Immediately the terrorists at the portholes began shooting at traffic. Several rocket grenades were fired with far more visual than destructive effect. But the sight of the explosions caused numerous vehicles to veer off the highway, onto the verge already scattered with stopped vehicles. The occupants joined those who'd already escaped afoot.

But one was still occupied.

The driver, 53-year-old Tuvia Rozner, was an Egged manager of all people.

Having previously run depots at Nahariya, Acre, and Beersheba, he was presently in charge of the Bat Galim depot in Haifa. Heading south with his wife Carmela for a visit with family in North Tel Aviv, he had gotten caught up in the panicked traffic ahead of the mad chase. When he'd realized it was two Egged buses, he'd immediately pulled over.

Sense of responsibility aside, it wasn't in Tuvia's nature to run away from danger. If any of the terrorists imagined trying themselves out against the best the IDF had to offer, it was probably a younger version of Tuvia they had in mind. He'd been a warrior most of his life. A veteran of WWII with the British and then a founder of the IDFs Carmeli Brigade Battalion 21, he'd fought in virtually every major battle during the Israeli War of Independence.

For the last few minutes, he'd been watching the transfer of the hostages, from what had felt like a safe distance, peering over the rim of the rear windshield, getting the best information he could for whichever authority he could then find.

Now the Scania was moving again, and Tuvia realized they weren't safe at all. His arms prickled with adrenaline. He grabbed the ignition key of the small Renault he was driving and cranked furiously. It wouldn't start. This had been a problem over the past week, and he'd intended to get the car in for service right after the weekend.

Those bearing down on him were now only a couple of hundred yards away. He thought of ducking down in the seat beside Carmela, but what if he'd already been seen? He kept cranking.

Finally, the engine caught. Tuvia had his foot awkwardly on the clutch pedal. It slipped off. The car jolted forward a couple of feet and stalled.

No point in trying to hide now.

He frantically started it again, jammed it in first gear and planted the accelerator pedal.

Baba'a and Dalal both called out, "Car ahead. Shoot! Shoot!"

Rami leaned out a side window, saw the moving Renault, and fired off-hand at it, kicking up dust-spurts off the road. His second attempt riddled the car, killing Tuvia and wounding Carmela. The Renault swung left, bounced off a parked car and stopped clear of the southbound lane.

The terrorists exulted as if their team had scored a winning touchdown at the Superbowl.

Wael broke into a song, the martial anthem 'The Mawtini-My Homeland.' Stumbling over the first few words, he settled into the better-known second verse, which was taken up by others. They sounded like a tone-deaf Russian men's chorus singing backward.

Mawtini mawtini
As-sababu lan yakilla hammahu an-yastaqilla aw yabid, aw yabid
Nastaqi mina r-rada wa lan nakuna li-l-ida kal abid, kal abid
La nurid La nurid
Ḏullana al-mu'abbada wa ʿaysana al-munakkada
Ḏullana al-mu'abbada wa ʿaysana al-munakkada
La nurid bal nuʿid
Magdana t-talid magdana-talid
Mawtini mawtini

My homeland, my homeland
The youth will not tire, 'till your independence
Or they die
Or they die
We will drink from death
And will not be to our enemies
Like slaves, like slaves
We do not want, we do not want
An eternal humiliation
Nor a miserable life
We do not want
But we will bring back
Our storied glory, our storied glory

My homeland
My homeland.

Their vehicle raced south toward crowded and unsuspecting Tel Aviv.

TWENTY-THREE

Sharon Police HQ, Kfar Saba
4:49 p.m.

Chief Superintendent Alisha Nadav and his 2IC, Lev Shachar, were still in the Sharon operations room, trying by phone to coordinate a response to the threat with the other west-side stations.

It was going badly so far.

"Haifa station is waiting for direct orders from on high," Nadav said sourly. "*Yahweh* (God) maybe. Or an actual sighting. But might come south and take a look at the hijack-site. Maybe."

Lev shrugged. "Well, that's Karel."

Both knew the man in charge of the city police in Haifa, Commander Karel Kohler, sidelined pending retirement, was a ditherer who couldn't delegate.

Lev said, "By the way the constable from ZR says his men have been roped in to the Magav's search along the coast. So, they're no help either."

"Does Jerusalem Operations know about all this?" asked Nadav.

"Yes, and Haim Avinoam is notifying Commissioner Tavori. No word back yet."

"Well, looks like it's down to us for now."

Which isn't bad except for numbers, Nadav thought. He had huge confidence in all his senior staff. His Operations Officer, 29-year-old *Mefake'ah* (Inspector) Daniel 'Danny' Lavi was another capable new-wave man. The third member, Inspector Hani Sror, who ran his Uniformed Division, was a real up-and-comer at 25. If they weren't both out on calls, they'd all be here dealing with this.

"At least there's consensus that the hijackers went north. No-one lands in north Israel to attack the south. Either the Magav or Kohler's people should find them pretty quickly. Then all we'll need to do is back them up, mmm?"

"Yes, but they're wrong," Lev said emphatically.

He crossed the room to the full-sized operations-wall map.

"Fatah will be behind this, and just like the Savoy Hotel attack, they will want to make the biggest splash. That's Tel Aviv. To the Arabs, TA represents us as a nation. I promise you they are headed south!"

He tapped beside the blue grid of the Ma'agan Michael fishponds a few times, thinking. After a few seconds said, "Supposing. It will have taken them a while to subdue their hostages, maybe ten minutes or so."

He glanced down at his wristwatch.

"Four-fifty-two now so they might have made it to about... here."

He circled an area north of Caesarea with his finger.

Nadav said, "That's under the jurisdiction of Hadera Station." Then he remembered the problem with that.

Hadera's 'New Policing' readiness review had found money missing. Also, an atmosphere of ill-discipline condoned by the station commander. That officer was now on leave pending court-martial. A top-tier Commander, 63-year-old Daniel Shrof was in there trying to clean up the mess. But the ongoing hunt for culprits had destroyed morale. They wouldn't be much help, no matter how perfectly strategically placed they were. It confirmed Nadav's sense he should trust his men and go it alone until others could catch up.

"Yes, I know," said Lev, echoing those thoughts. "We'll have to run the show from here with some help from Netanya if we can get it. Anyway, here's my plan!"

He circled two intersections on Highway two at Olga, 14 miles south of the original conflict. The major crossing at Yishai Street, then a smaller one, 100-yards further south again at HaShalom Street.

"We need to get Danny Lavi and Hani Sror to here and here, before the Arabs, and set up a main and a backup block."

"That's if they're heading that way," said Nadav skeptically.

"I'll stake my life on it. Tel Aviv's the target!"

"Can our men make it in time?"

"Already on their way." Lev tapped a spot at North Netanya at the 2, and Pardes Hanna on the 65 due north of the proposed ambush point.

"It's a ten-minute run either way, give or take. They'll round up what resources they can by radio as they go."

Nadav broached the obvious. "And if they don't get there in time, or can't stop them. What then?"

"Then we'll keep trying until we do. Letting these people anywhere near Tel-Aviv on a Shabbat night is out of the question!"

"And you, Lev?"

"I've got a backup plan. But let's see if Danny and Hani can find and stop them first."

"Okay. Keep me advised, please."

Right then, the Hadera police were being drawn into the situation whether suited or not.

Pinhas Kopel, with his two distressed and bleeding women passengers aboard, had driven right past the Zichron Ya'akov police station. It hadn't existed in his policing days. Instead he looped south and west to the station he'd once commanded, located between highways two and four, roughly half-way up the country.

At Hadera he demanded to speak to Commander Shrof.

Hamid Ba'asha's calls over the last 15 minutes had reached only a busy signal. The sergeant on duty had no clue there was an emergency, or who these people bursting in were, and besides, he was busy. He took his time looking up.

When he did, and realized Batya's injury was a gunshot wound, he shouted for assistance.

Shrof, there only by chance, came out of his office, took one look, and spluttered, "In God's name, man. Don't you know who this is?" he shouted. "Get these women to the Medical Center! And I want a full emergency turnout. Now! Nehemia, come into my office please. Details, sir! Details."

Within five minutes, while the harassed desk sergeant tried vainly to reach other stations for assistance, Shrof had his men on duty in police cars, heading to Ma'agan Michael. But instead of via Highway 2, where they would have found what they were looking for, they retraced Kopel's route.

It was a vital opportunity lost amid the developing shambles.

They found only a pair of MDA ambulances with drivers who knew nothing except that they had been called out to a traffic accident.

The policemen tried radioing in but heard nothing but squelch on every frequency. The senior officer cursed, looked up and down the road, and ordered his men to follow him. North.

At that instant there were four searches underway in western Israel, three completely in the wrong direction, by two agencies, neither in contact with the other.

And in the way of the blind men asked to identify a donkey by feeling only one part, the police from Zichron Ya'akov and the Magav, Haifa, Hadera and Sharon, were making assumptions based only on their own slim information.

It was a fiasco, and Israel would pay a dreadful price for it.

With the smoke from Tuvia Rozner's Renault curling up behind them, the terrorists hurtled on southbound, swaying dangerously as they took the long right-hand curve bordering the Caesarea Golf & Country Club.

The stress aboard had been too much for many. The bus stank of urine and worse body matter, mixed with fear and residual gun-smoke. At least the wind-tunnel effect flushed the worst of it away in their wake.

But a bizarre change had come over the 11 terrorists. Caught up in the hubris of their second success and their seeming invincibility, they were smiling and slapping each other's backs. Even attempting to befriend their captives.

Khaled and Hussain offered around blue packs of Gauloises Caporal unfiltered cigarettes. The hostages remained poker-faced, but several older people accepted, even though they had no means of lighting them, rather than trigger more violence.

Avi Perets had one put in his mouth. He spat it out and crushed it under his shoe as soon as Hussain turned his back.

Baba'a and Dalal even seemed relaxed. He leaned against a seat-back with a neutral expression. She held her weapon loosely on Shlomo, rather than trying to puncture his skull with it.

But with Dalal it was a facade. She was restless.

Leaving Shlomo in Khaled's hands, she moved down the aisle, navigating spilt blood, loose cartridge cases, and empty magazines; that made passage treacherous.

She brushed past Wael, Ramz, Hussain and Fayadh, all with their AKMs slung, to where Rami, Jalal and Hiza'a guarded the rear in a murderous semi-circle. There discovered she had nothing to say to anyone.

Turning to go back, she glimpsed down low, a small face with wide eyes, framed with blond hair. She stooped and saw six-year-old Liat Gal-on, all the way under one of the seats.

Memories of peaceful Dbaiyeh flooded her mind. A joyous time when she was fresh from her nursing training, the camp children played gaily by her side each day, and her relationship with Jihad was new and exciting; adding to her life rather than taking everything from it.

In one of those twilight-zone moments when all human morality stands on its head, she felt in her jacket pocket for a Nestlé candy bar she'd been saving since they'd been at sea, and offered it. The girl took it in her tiny hand.

Dalal rose self-consciously, afraid others might have seen what she'd done, and in this world gone mad, judge her for the act of kindness. But they were all scanning the roadside for threats.

She returned to her station slightly behind Shlomo Zait and touched him with her gun-muzzle to remind him not to do anything adventurous.

Meanwhile Tariq had noticed the tour guides' mike and audio controls and moved forward with glee. Delighted with the opportunity to lecture a true captive audience, he played with the switches until he heard sound hissing from overhead speakers.

"We are here to fight for our beloved homeland, but also for oppressed people everywhere. You Zionists cannot keep us from our lands forever. We will fight you and eventually we will win!"

He launched into a rambling summary of his ideology, namedropping every warrior-philosopher's name he could remember. If he'd paid attention, he'd have noticed that only a fraction of the audience could understand a word. Even if they could have heard it above the wind.

But then, being realistic had never been Tariq's forte.

A sense of surreal horror had pervaded many hostages.

Rebecca Hochman, holding her two young boys close, had her right arm back through the gap between her seat and the wall, comforting Eran Bosknitz in the seat behind her. She had a clear view of the boy's mother across the aisle on her back between seat-rows. Rina's eyes were open and staring. The couple had been among her best friends. Seeing the grief their orphaned son was suffering was almost worse than their loss. Tenderly squeezing his hand, Rebecca whispered, "Please be strong. We will get through this!"

Lily Glotman was separated by several rows and across the aisle from her precious warrior-poet husband, Shim'aon. At least their children, 14-year-old Anat and Eitz, two years younger, were in the seats behind him. She could see their hands on his own, which were still tied behind him. *Oh, my love, my love.*

In a window seat right behind the back doors, Zvi Eshet seethed with anger, but managed to keep his face impassive and his body language subdued. He'd been working on the knots behind his back. He was sure he could work them loose. *Maybe then there will come a chance. Just a chance!*

The calm was suddenly shattered by shouts and the chattering of Rami's and Jalal's AKMs. Buildings were flying by on both sides. An intersection, occupied by the first real threat the terrorists had had to face, was coming up on them fast.

A few minutes before, at 4:56 p.m., Inspector Hani Sror's knuckles had been white on the wheel of his Ford Cortina police car, as it raced along an unsealed road parallel to the main highway, the final few hundred yards to the southern of the two Olga crossings.

From the few words he'd exchanged with Danny Lavi over the swamped and virtually useless car-radio network, he knew Danny was heading just as fast for the usually busier northern crossing.

Whether they would be in time to close Highway 2 before their quarry passed was anyone's guess. But it wouldn't be for lack of trying.

Hani kept on trying to push the accelerator pedal through the floor.

Inspector Danny Lavi had actually made slightly better time. At that moment he was rounding the last bend on Aharon Aaronson Street, with the Yishai crossing just ahead.

He breathed out empathic-ally. He wouldn't be alone in this. There was a Hadera black-and-white nosed up to the highway. The calls he'd made for support from any officer in the vicinity had been heard.

The intersection had traffic-lights and the dark-blue-uniformed officer was out of the car, waving at intersecting traffic to stop and back up. Drivers were obeying.

Danny drove around the officer and placed his car right in the middle of the empty intersection. He got out, intending to talk to the other officer and make some kind of plan. He hadn't taken two steps when the Hadera officer's eyes widened and stared north. Danny swung to look in the same direction.

A strange sound was quickly growing louder: part wind-whistle, part engine-roar.

A red and white Egged bus, missing its windshield and trailing a Palestinian flag from the driver's wing-mirror, was bearing down on him at terrifying speed. What might be rocket launchers; jutted from side-windows. Figures inside were holding weapons.

In the name of... God!

Danny's mind flashed: he was going to be found with his .38 revolver still in its holster. One of those surges the brain has when suddenly flooded with adrenaline.

Then the bus started to swerve to avoid his car, adding protesting tires to the cacophony. Gun muzzles poked from the left side windows. Bullets tore overhead.

They broke the spell. Danny dived away; aware the other officer was doing the same.

When he lifted his head, the terrorists were heading away.

He could hear cheering.

Hani had only a little more time to prepare.

He heard shooting even before he was stationary in the HaShalom intersection. By the time he had his pistol out, the bus was already coming at him. He ran around the back of his car and ducked down.

He caught the briefest of glimpses of faces staring from windows as it went past. Some full of horror, others framed by unkempt beards and filled with anger. He got an impression the vehicle was packed, though most of the windows were by curtains.

Belatedly, he realized his .38 was in his hand, and he lifted it, before lowering it again. His heart pounded like a drum in his chest.

One minute later, after a terse conversation with Sharon Station, Hani was putting his car-radio hand-piece back in the car when Danny drove up and got out.

Danny's face was stark white.

"What?" Hani asked.

"I thought I was a dead man!"

"I imagine," said Hani, managing a grim grin. "Anyway, base says we follow. Not too close. Report in when we can. They think radio coverage will improve."

"Let's go."

Waving to the Hadera police officer to follow them, they got in their cars.

The three vehicles headed south on Highway 2 in fast pursuit.

TWENTY-FOUR

Kfar Saba
5:01 p.m.

"They got through," said Lev Shachar dejectedly. "I've told Josh and Hani to follow, and that we'll pull out all the stops down here."

"Fuck!"

"Yuh really! It's serious. That was our best chance. Sure, we've found them, but now they've got momentum and we're playing catch up. If they get as far as Tel Aviv, on a Saturday night, people out driving. Shopping in the markets. Walking with their kids..."

"I know that, Lev," Nadav said gently. "Believe me. So where is the next best place?"

"Nothing really, until near Netanya." Then Lev thought for a moment. Walked to the wall map.

"Actually, there are a couple of places around Beit Yanai." He pointed at the open area beside the lake of that name, south of the coastal power station. "But we can't be sure of getting there in time."

"How about FROM Netanya?"

Netanya Station was another one in turmoil. Many of the officers, including Chief Superintendent Samir Hanina, were new transfers and Lev had no idea of their competence level.

"Let's bring them into it by all means, but not to the north. Say to provide backup roadblocks... say around here!"

He circled a place south of the major coastal city. The next major southern crossing, Sha'ar HaYam Street in Kfar Shmaryahu, the northernmost suburb of Herzliya. Any shooting westward would be over open country around the Crusader-era ruins of Apollonia. Not completely safe for civilians, but saf-er.

Nadav could see the logic. The problem was, Herzliya was only 10 miles north of Tel Aviv. Risky. “You said you had a Plan B for yourself?”

“Yeah,” Lev, “I'm going to take everyone we can spare from here to where the highway curves back to the coast and doglegs south again. At Havatzelet HaSharon.”

He indicated just north of Netanya.

"There's a line of trees that hides what's around the bend, if you're coming south, until you are right on it."

"Sounds good," said Nadav, though with little confidence. But even if he’d been a micro-manager, this was decidedly not the time for it. He had to trust his men.

“You'll need to handle comms if you will,” added Lev

"Right."

"Ask Netanya to get their people on the way south. Tell them they are looking for a red and white bus with window curtains. And we'll need to get out an all-points bulletin. Maybe Jerusalem Ops can do that. Tell them we need any armed personnel, army, navy, air force, policemen. Anyone on leave, with a weapon and the training.”

“Right.”

"Tell them to come here so we can squad them up, or go to the end of the Two where Namir Avenue T-bones with Yunitsman Street. We have to stop these bastards or we'll have a bloodbath on our hands."

"I'm on it," Nadav said.

Aboard the Wanderers’ bus charging south with the high-rises of Netanya rearing up in the distance, the mind-state of the hostages had turned foreboding.

The 64 adult hostages seemed hypnotized into glum acceptance, while the eyes of their 24 children expressed only uncomprehending fear.

There'd been no further attempts by anyone to communicate with their captors, something that only Moroccan-born Haviv Ankwa and perhaps Syrian-born Joe Kheloani could have done effectively, anyway.

To an observer who didn't know the Israeli spirit, they might have appeared a cargo in transit, cowed into submission and hoping they were a valuable enough trading commodity for their lives to be saved.

That perception would have been wrong.

The 11 terrorists' mood, on the other hand, had darkened the further south they went. The traffic was thinner now as word spread to avoid Highway 2. This gave them fewer targets to blaze at to relieve their anger, and more time to consider their predicament.

The countryside was becoming more urban. They were passing villages with increased regularity as they drew closer to Tel Aviv. It had sunk in to whoever hadn't gotten it before, that they had no better plan than to invade the belly of the beast, and see what they could win from what would inevitably be a one-sided battle. And all they had going for them was their bottomless hate and capacity for violence.

The stress of this began truly bringing out the evil in them.

Desperate to micro-control the situation, Jalal and then Ramz, in particular, began striking out at every opportunity. If a leg stuck out too far, say as a result of three grownups crammed into a pair of seats, it was kicked out of the way. If an infant cried out for water or the toilet, both the child and mother were bashed. Every human foible or variance from total submission was met with instant and crushing brutality.

Then Fayadh paused gloatingly alongside weeping Solomon Polak.

Like a bully playing get-your-cap-back-if you-can in a school playground, or a sadistic child with an insect, he began tormenting the boy. He lifted his gun high to strike where Polak's brow was bleeding from an earlier assault. When the lad covered his face Fayadh hit him in the chest.

Other terrorists sniggered.

After a couple of rounds of this game, Fayadh realized he was holding an AK47 with a bayonet. He unfolded it and pricked the helpless 17-year-old boy in the upper shoulder.

Polak shrieked.

Fayadh stepped back, guffawing and looking around so the others could enjoy the moment.

Dalal turned and watched the road ahead. Baba'a steadfastly stared out the side window. Most of the rest shuffled in their stances, laughing uncomfortably, though Tariq's eyes glittered.

Fayadh jabbed again, harder. The bayonet-point deflected off the big arm bone and penetrated the thick axillary artery it protects. Blood spurted.

Polak screamed and fell into the aisle.

Fayadh went mad with blood lust. Stabbing and ripping at the fallen boy. His finger slipped into the trigger guard and the rifle fired, killing the boy and jerking the bayonet back out of the body with the recoil.

The horror of it was too much for Avner Geffen.

Despite his loving wife Leah's strong grip around his upper body, he screamed. And kept on screaming.

Rami was closest. He stepped over to Avner and poked the muzzle of his gun in the man's face. But Avner had dissolved mentally out of fear for his family. Rami reversed the AKM and hit Avner with a swinging blow that also battered Leah. It made no difference. Avner's screams were piercing and constant.

Rami reversed his gun again, and held it on its side like a modern-day Crip gangsta holds a .45. Bullets ripped Avner's chest apart, also grazing Shim'aon Glotman's left calf in the row behind. Leah Geffen's screams replaced her husband's, but were quickly smothered by several friends.

Then there came an unusual noise. A woman's voice, low, first clearing itself, then growing in confidence. Rebecca Hochman. She spoke the first line of the 'HaTikva,' the 'Hope,' the Israeli national anthem. A song the Wanderers had sung dozens of times. She spoke it tonelessly. Like a statement.

"*Kol'od balevav penimah.*" (As long as in the heart within.)

Then she turned in her seat as far as Roi clinging on her lap would allow, made an up-up motion with her hands, and said the phrase again emphatically.

Judith Zait joined in halfway through, then Lily Glotman across the aisle, then one or two husky men's voices.

The next line, *"Nefesh yehudi homiyah,"* (A Jewish soul still yearns,) began raggedly but ended strongly. The following line roared, even over the wind. *"Ulefa'atei mizrach kadimah, Ayin letziyon tzofiya"* (And onward, toward the ends of the east, an eye still looks toward Zion).

Everyone punched the chorus hard.

Od lo avdah tikvateinu,
Hatikvah hannoshanah
Lashuv le'eretz avoteinu,
La'ir bah David k'hanah.

Our hope is not yet lost,
The ancient hope.
To return to the land of our fathers.
The city where David encamped.

For long moments the terrorists stared incredulously, then their faces hardened, particularly Ramz, who was standing nearest to Rebecca. He snarled and reversed his AKM, but before he could strike, she pushed Roi aside and turned in her seat to confront him.

"Yes? You big bully! You're going to beat me now? Shoot me too? You will never break me. Never!"

Zvi Eshet made his move. He pulled his feet under him and sprang, bringing his hands around in the same movement. He grabbed Hussain, who was only four feet in front of him with his back turned, looking at Ramz. Spun him about so they were face to face and grappled for his AKM. Hussain had the gun pointed downward with his hand off the pistol grip, so Zvi grabbed it there, and leaned back, pulling the gun upward. When the gun-butt was between their faces and the muzzle somewhere around their waists, Zvi twisted the gun so it angled away from him, prayed the action wasn't on 'Safe', and hauled back on the trigger. The gun fired, a muffled stutter, before the vertical recoil twisted Zvi's finger away. Long enough to fire five bullets into Hussain's groin and upper right thigh.

Hussain groaned and sank down and away, leaving Zvi holding the AKM awkwardly with the butt near his face.

Zvi got the gun level and frantically swung the muzzle around to point it at... who knows? And for what? There was no direction he could fire that would harm a terrorist without also hurting a friend. Perhaps Zvi intended to order them to drop their guns.

There's no way to know because Ramz had no such qualms.

When his gun aligned on Z, he pressed the trigger and the stream of bullets cut Dov down.

Ramz roared unintelligibly, slung his gun over his shoulder, and easily lifted Dov's body like a sack of grain. He walked the five or six steps to the back of the bus where the terrorists there parted.

He hurled Dov out through the rear window-space to bounce away brokenly in the slipstream.

TWENTY-FIVE

Highway 2, Northern fringe of Or Akiva
5:04 p.m.

On the side of the highway on the northern outskirts of Or Akiva, Haifa Police Commander Karel Kohler and a procession of his people, had found the abandoned 901 bus. An MDA ambulance was also there.

Kohler, a portly man, alighted and positioned his gold-braided cap precisely on his balding head. Buttoning his blouse, he followed one of his sergeants aboard the bullet-torn Leyland.

The interior was littered with discarded belongings. A shape draped with coats occupied a window seat. Kohler gently turned back the coverings for a moment. Beneath were the slack features of Otari Mansharov.

Moshe Abergil was flat on his back in the aisle, midsection stained orange by Mercurochrome. Kohler guessed his girth may have saved his life, since belly fat plugs wounds. There were towels under his bloody back. One paramedic was holding a compress to his stomach, while another fetched a gurney. He seemed alert enough for the moment. Kohler asked the paramedics for a moment, and his sergeant to take notes.

Abergil remembered, the veering from lane to lane, the Thor's hammer-blows against the bus-body, then being struck.

"Do you remember stopping?'

"We were going slowly. They jumped aboard."

"How many?"

"Three or four."

"All of them?"

"No, I think there were just as many still on the other bus."

Other bus?

It wasn't much to go on, but there wasn't time to learn more. The man's pain was extreme. He needed hospital help. The paramedics insisted the police leave.

Kohler went back to his car and tried to reach Sharon station, as he'd promised if he had news. The radio channels were still choked. At least they knew which way the hijackers were travelling.

He waved an arm to his other men standing beside their cars. A big swooping circle to point ahead. The cavalcade mounted up and continued south.

At the Netanya Police Station, on Reuven Barkat Street just off that city's main east-west thoroughfare, five other officers were hurriedly getting ready for the road.

They were individually competent enough. They included 41-year-old Druze Sergeant Major Hamzah Arslaniyyun; perhaps the most experienced NCO in south Israel. Also 28-year-old Sergeant Ben Soshan and two bright and willing junior constables. But due to recent rapid staff turnover, they were new to each other. Worse, leader, Inspector Daniel Shiller, a 36-year-old, felt intimidated by the forthright-mannered Arslaniyyun.

A more assertive man would have been present when Sharon Chief Superintendent Nadav had briefed them by phone. Instead, he'd delegated to Arslaniyyun and hadn't directly heard what they would be looking for. That lack of leadership would prove disastrous.

Just the same, they were soon turning south onto Highway 2 at its busiest on-ramp, travelling in two cars with Arslaniyyun and Shiller riding together.

Immediately Arslaniyyun pointed excitedly at a vehicle ahead. "That must be it!"

"What? Where?"

"The red and white bus!"

"How do you know?"

"They said it has curtains."

Shiller could indeed see a large modern tour bus crawling along in the midst of a small flock of slow traffic.

"Okay let's get in front of it!"

In Jerusalem, Commander Haim Avinoam had also been busy.

All stations now understood what was happening. The weight was all on Sharon, but they had some help available from Netanya, and a plan underway to stop the terrorists north of there.

He'd also broadcast the all-points bulletin over Kol-Israeli Public Radio for volunteers.

Now he was trying to get them some help from entirely outside the area: Yamam, in Beit Shemesh. This required an airlift by the military if they were to arrive in time to do any good. Which meant a possibly prickly conversation with Major General Rafael Eitan.

Avinoam chose his words extremely carefully.

"Yes, I know General. But I'm looking at a copy of your memorandum of the 4th saying you wanted all transport requests to go through you."

Eitan cursed his misfortune.

Though only acting Armed Forces Chief of Staff at that moment (the appointment wouldn't be official until April 1st,) it was his job to watch the pennies. Airlifts were expensive. The Israeli Medal of Courage winner was far more comfortable approving requests from the field than blocking them. But budgets had been slashed, and what they had left had to be carefully rationed.

"Don't they have their own transport?"

"Yes sir," Avinoam replied, "But for training purposes only. They have an *Anafa* (Bell 212) but it only carries eight. Not much of a force in these circumstances."

Indeed, thought Eitan. *This could get big. No one wants their career ruined by taking a sickle to a harvesting contest. But money was money.*

"What about unit Two-Six-Nine?"

Ah, the Sayeret Matkal, thought Avinoam. *You prick. I've got lives at risk here!*

He was expecting the military man to bring up the military's 'best of the best.' It still pissed him off. *Why did there always have to be this turf-battle in times of crisis?*

He forgot his caution.

"General we are talking less than an hour. I repeat. One hour before that bus passes the Yunitsman corner onto Namir Avenue. And then Sir, it will be in North Tel Aviv and we will have bloody chaos on our hands! Do you understand me, General sir? I don't care if we have to teleport the entire Golani Brigade here in the next ten minutes, and it costs a billion Shekels. If we let these people loose in the city, we will be seeing the faces of bereaved mothers in our nightmares forever. Understand that General Sir?"

Eitan wasn't used to being told the facts of life. Especially by a policeman with the rank-equivalence of a paltry half-Colonel. But the new thing was to be nice to the police. He was careful with his tone.

"Commander, you are insubordinate. However, ahem, I will see what can be done."

"General it's a simple request," Avinoam pressed. "I'm told there's a *Yas'ur* (Sikorsky CH-53 'Petrel' heavy transport helicopter, which could ferry an entire platoon,) at Sde Dov."

Sde Dov was the small dual-purpose civilian and military airport, just northwest of the Tel Aviv city limits.

He thought but didn't say, *Herzliya has a private airport close to the two. In fact, they can land on the fucking road if they have to. If he'll just give me the damn support!*

At least Eitan seemed to be considering the matter. Avinoam looked at his watch. Almost 5:08 p.m. *Yehoshua!* "General we need it now!"

"I have said I will see what can be done!" Said Eitan. "Now carry on!"

There was a click as the call disconnected. Avinoam stared at the handset angrily.

Carry on? What in hell did he think we'd be doing?

He slammed it down on the cradle.

In the lounge of a condominium in Bnei Brak, a quiet suburb of Tel Aviv, a cropped-haired, slim but sinewy-looking 26-year-old Police Inspector named Adam Schmuel, sat with his feet up on an ottoman and his nose in a voluminous paperback.

It was 'Trinity,' by Leon Uris. The book about the Irish troubles. It had just become available in Israel. Adam's English was excellent, and he had a keen interest in history. It was making fascinating reading.

Around him was dominated by an array of workout equipment that wouldn't have shamed a commercial gym. Adam liked to keep his tools close.

There were two radios on in the room. A regular transistor broadcasting soothing music from Kol-Israel, and a police-band scanner periodically blurting out mostly garbled transmissions. Adam kept the first going because music was good for the soul, and the second because he was hoping something might pop up on it, to solve a work crisis he was having.

Two years before, in early 1976, he'd been applying for police positions after completing his IDF service as a *Segen* (Lieutenant) of the commandos. Someone mentioned a new unit called Yamam. This was to be a centrally based, first-call unit for all domestic security issues. With his 'A' type personality and hunger for action, it sounded the perfect opportunity.

He'd gone for a *Gibush* (tryout) at the Wingate Center near Netanya, through which candidates for any form of Israeli Special-Forces unit, had to pass. A fitness fanatic who never missed a 2-hour morning workout, he'd eaten up every challenge thrown at him. After being accepted, he'd quickly risen to his present position of 2IC to the unit's charismatic commander, *Rav Pakad* (Superintendent-roughly Colonel,) Assaf Hefetz.

But lately, despite his fierce loyalty to his boss, his physical workout had become the high point of his day. No real opportunities had come Yamam's way.

This was unfathomable to Adam, since their capability was far ahead of anything he'd seen in the IDF. Yamam wasn't even training with the IDF Special Forces any more. It chafed so much he was seriously considering quitting. But one always tried to have hope.

Therefore Adam, a caffeine addict also, had a coffee machine bubbling in the kitchen and the radios going. You never knew what the day might bring.

Just then he heard a low, excited voice speaking on the scanner. He listened intently. The few words he caught told him something unusual was happening traffic-wise north of Netanya.

Not that it was his business. Protocol required an approach from a regular police unit before his unit could get called out, but still...

He laughed at his eagerness. *Don't be crazy! What are the chances of some action dropping in my lap, right now when I'm off duty?*

He went back to the folks of Ballyutogue, Donegal, who were keeping the fairies at bay while laying old Kilty Larkin beneath the sod.

Tribal rituals. So many parallels with this place.

He hummed along with a song playing by his other ear. Mid-song, he heard the emergency radio-tones. He dropped his feet to the floor and listened. A voice spoke in precise Hebrew. Adam came right out of his chair.

It was an All-Points Broadcast. A threat was moving south on Highway 2 from Ma'agan Michael, which he knew wasn't far south of Haifa. A detailed set of instructions for all available and armed security personnel followed.

Adam grabbed the phone and dialed a well-memorized number. While it rang, he carried the phone over to a cupboard and one-handedly began dragging out his combat equipment.

In Ramat Gan, East of Tel Aviv, Rafael 'Raffi' Blom, a bearded 27-year-old English immigrant, had also heard the broadcast on the radio.

Raffi was a big man and a hard one; toughened by responding to "Jew-Boy!" taunts from the skinheads around Clapham Junction train station as a teenager.

And more recently by his service as a sub-lieutenant of the mostly Druze, elite IDF Unit 300 (Sword) Battalion. In that unit, a log on the shoulders of every six men taking the morning two-mile run was just part of the fun.

These days he was another ranked member of Yamam, but at this moment couldn't possibly have less resembled a *Mefake'ah Mishneh* (Sub-Inspector.) A closet biker who loved to look the part on his days off, he was in leather pants and a Harley-Davidson tee shirt with the sleeves torn off.

He'd just retrieved a fresh quart-bottle of Goldstar from his well-stocked beer-fridge, popped the top, and was cross-legged on the concrete floor of his basement garage, poring over a page of a mechanic's manual.

A dish of solvent beside his knee, containing the small parts of the carburetor, of a Suzuki GS750 motorcycle up on its stand nearby.

He reluctantly put the beer bottle down and squashed the top back on with his left hand. The motion made the tattoos on his thick upper arm dance.

"Well fook," he said.

Raffi got up and headed at a trot toward a closet for his gear.

Upstairs, a phone began to ring.

At his apartment in an up-scale block in North Netanya, the commander of both men, fought to keep the anger out of his voice, "So that's it?"

"Yes, afraid so. Status quo for now," replied Shaul Weizman, feigning cheerfulness equally poorly.

"Status quo?" said Assaf Hefetz incredulously, then broke off and stared out the picture window overlooking the tennis courts.

There was no point in mindless anger or a shouting match over this. He tried to think reasonably, a frame of mind that didn't always come easily when politics was involved. Perhaps find some reasoned rebuttal that might turn the tide in his favor.

Besides, it wasn't this young politician's fault. In fact, he had a soft spot for the huskily voiced, piercingly intelligent Weizman. It probably wasn't even the fault of the man's powerful father. The downgrading of Yamam was simply the collateral damage of budget issues combined with the military's superior clout.

I screwed up when I trusted the bastards. There are too many insincere politicians in this damn country.

He'd simply lost. And it was his men who would suffer. And that hurt. He wasn't used to losing at anything.

A broad-shouldered, bull-necked man with a close-cropped dome of a skull and a jutting jaw, the enormously physically gifted 34-year-old Assaf radiated strength and fitness. Good enough to have played the professional tennis circuit in his teens, he'd put his country first and chosen the regular army instead. These days he was a single-digit-handicap golfer, a skill-set at which he was getting far too much practice, trying to persuade the dick-heads who ran the country to see what was in their best interest.

And it was hard to let this go without a fight.

"Look I was promised," he said, hating himself for sounding plaintive. "They came to me! Said we would be first up for all internal security issues. Not second after Two-Six. First."

"Times change," Weizman said, shrugging.

"Be damned they do! They came to me and said they needed one force to handle all terrorist situations inside the borders. I built that force and it's the best in the world."

Weizman didn't doubt it. He sympathized with the policeman's frustration.

"Not the point, Assaf. No other country has our peculiar ties between the military and politics. Most of our politicians were soldiers. You think they forget who put them there? And who can bring them down? My friend you have simply been outvoted!"

Assaf chewed his lip sullenly. He'd had high hopes for this meeting. Only two weeks earlier he had given Weizman the full treatment at Beit Shemesh, inspections, exercises, the whole deal.

He'd had his arguments down pat, and his men had excelled. He'd asked Weizman only one question: What would it take to get Yamam its own role, to get a policy change certifying his group as the go-to force for all internal terrorist actions? Exactly what?

This answer was a bitter pill to take.

The fact was, there was only one thing that could change the balance of power he was being shut out of. Just as wars were good for promotions, only a serious terrorism attack at which Yamam were front and center, proving their competence and getting mentioned in the same breath as the damn Sayeret Matkal, could change policy.

Publicity had created Yamam. Only publicity of the right kind could cement home their value. Otherwise, they would wither awhile, then get caught on a real budget crush and be disbanded; his talented and highly skilled officers sent back to the beat.

As soon as he thought that, he felt revulsion that he could even think of a violent assault on his beloved country as anything other than an evil thing.

The phone rang.

Assaf's first reaction was to ignore it. He wasn't in a mood to talk with anyone. He needed to finish this meeting as graciously as possible and go beat some tennis balls to death.

The phone stopped.

Then his wife Deborah appeared in the entranceway to the kitchen, wearing a flour-coated apron and holding the hand piece against her. "Adam," she mouthed. "Urgent."

A half minute later Assaf was acknowledging Adam's words, while watching the belt pager he only turned off for meetings; come to life. He roared in anger at the flood of codes scrolling across the orange display.

He cut Adam off. "I'm going north. Round up anyone else you can find and get yourselves ready as a backstop down here. Anything changes radio me in my car on Channel 16."

“A chance to show them, hey?” persisted Adam.

“I hope the hell so!”

Inside three minutes Assaf was running down to the car-park under the condo block, In dark-blue combat fatigues and a Kevlar vest with 'Police' in Hebrew across the front and back. In one hand was a 223 caliber, carbine version of the Galil assault rifle. In the other, a holstered Sig-Sauer 9mm pistol hanging from a web-belt of magazine pouches.

He reached his personal car, which in his spare time was his personal toy, a rally-specification Datsun 1600 SSS coupe. He put his gear on the back and leaned his rifle against the passenger's seatback.

As he turned the key, he realized he hadn't even said a parting Shalom to Shaul Weizman.

The quick little Datsun raced up from the parking basement, squealed right onto HaGefen Street, and headed for the next northbound Highway 2 access ramp, just north of Havatzelet HaSharon.

TWENTY-SIX

South of Beit Yanai Lake
5:10 p.m.

Danny Lavi and Hani Sror had been doggedly following the Wanderers for a little under 10 minutes since the failed ambush at Olga. Keeping a safe-ish distance of about 150-yards. They'd been busy minutes.

Several more police cars had joined them. Once in a while Hani dropped back, waved an officer down, and ordered the man to close off a highway crossing. First Ha-Rav Nisim Street in South Hadera. Then the access road to the coastal Moshav of Mikhmoret. And just a minute or so ago, the 5720 highway junction at Beit Yanai.

Maybe police ahead of them were doing the same thing. Northbound traffic had reduced to a trickle. Unfortunately, they had still seen numerous vehicles shot at. Thankfully, as far as they could tell while speeding by, with no serious injuries.

The pursuit was down to just them and one other car. Danny was in the lead as the highway straightened after the S-bend right after the lake, the last long road stretch before the built-up area around Netanya.

Then the terrorists upped the ante. Two objects, trailing smoke, flew from the cavernous rear window and bounced along the road towards them. Danny just had time to think, *grenades!*

He planted the brakes and swung the wheel hard left, hoping to put some metal between him and the explosions. Unless they went off directly beneath him, in which case he'd have no chance. He gripped the wheel tight and prayed.

Hani was blocked by Danny's car. All he saw was just Danny's vehicle turn broadside in front of him. His right front fender speared in behind the center pillar. Both vehicles skidded along the road, locked together.

One grenade rolled off to their left and brought down a telephone pole, cutting off a good proportion of the phones north of Netanya. The other in the passenger's side front-wheel-well of Danny's Ford Cortina, with an orange flash that instantly turned to black smoke. It ripped the wheel off and lifted that corner up before dropping it back down. Crumpled metal dug into the road, stopping both vehicles after a few more yards.

Hani felt only the jolt of the seatbelt tightening across his chest. He was unhurt and thanked his stars he'd been wearing it. He flicked the release catch and leaped out to help Danny.

Danny was doubled over, holding his left arm against himself, but didn't seem to be bleeding.

"Are you okay?" Hani hollered through the shattered driver's window.

"Not sure. Broken arm, I think. Sore back."

"Let's get you out."

The driver's door was caved-in and un-operable. Hani ran around to the passenger side, marveling at damage to the right-front while passing. A giant wearing steel-capped boots might have kicked it with all its might. But the metalwork had absorbed the grenade's power and shrapnel. They were lucky beyond belief.

In another minute they were both in the other police car that had pulled up safely behind the wreck. They ordered the officer to oversee the scene, then headed back fast for the nearest hospital to get Danny some attention.

At Havatzelet HaSharon, two miles north of Netanya, Lev Shachar and five other policemen were standing beside Highway 2.

They didn't know it, but they had missed Assaf Hefetz, racing by on the parallel dirt road, by just moments when they'd arrived in a hurry from the south. Their black-and-whites were parked haphazardly in the lanes. They planned to position those more strategically once they had the highway laid with road spikes.

Beside the highway, a line of tall trees spring leaf stretched away in a perpendicular line. Australian blue-gums; the trees that old-hand kibbutzniks' said 'made Israel,' with their ability to find water where there was none, while also drying out the marshiest swampland.

The tree-line offered perfect concealment from vehicles coming down the long straight that began just around the bend. Unfortunately, it worked both ways. They couldn't see what was coming either.

They no sooner started dragging out long strips of Caltrops, four-pointed metal devices that always landed with a two-inch spike pointing upright, when they heard the thuds of two explosions followed by the faint mangling of metal, to their north.

Lev spun in his tracks. Weighed his options. He'd expected to have more time to set the trap. Now at a guess he had one, maybe two minutes. Just not enough time to lay the spikes, get the cars positioned properly, and find safe firing positions.

And if they did manage to stop the bus, he realized the tree line was a disadvantage. If the terrorists managed to get off the bus, the trees would make great firing cover for them too. It made the decision for him. Better to fight another time and in a place with greater advantages.

He hollered at the others to drop what they were doing, leave the car doors and trunks open and run to the coastal side of the highway where there was about a two-foot drop off.

They barely made it to and drew pistols, before the bus careered around the bend amid a strange rushing of air, the roar of its overstressed engine, and screech of distorted tires.

Shlomo saw the police cars and took his foot off the gas pedal. Dalal shouted and jabbed her AKM painfully into his arm. That didn't stop Shlomo from hitting the brakes hard.

He couldn't steer around the police cars at the speed he was going without risking turning over. The mass of metal beneath him juddered down to a more controllable speed.

Fifty yards out, Khaled said, "The cars are empty! The yellow-bellied Jews have run away!" Exuberant shouts echoed him.

Then Tariq saw a policeman peer over the road edge and fired, kicking up tarmac chips. Jalal saw bullets strike and emptied his magazine too, also hitting nothing. "Go through! Go through!" screamed Dalal, jabbing Shlomo again.

They were already straddling the verge when he turned the wheel to obey. The policemen thought the bus would go over the edge and roll on to them. They hugged the ground.

But the bus's fender struck one police car and shoved it aside like flotsam. It rocked on its suspension before pulling back into the lane under lumbering acceleration.

At the rear window, Rami and Hiza'a had plucked more grenades off their vests. As they sped away, both lobbed them, smoking, in the direction of the sheltering policemen. The devices exploded with a flat spanging noise on the hard road surface, but did no harm.

The time was 5:13 p.m. The terrorists were through and only 23 miles from downtown Tel Aviv. But the motley brigade of defenders forming to Lev's south had gained what was so desperately needed. A precious minute or two of time.

As the tortured sound of the battered Scania faded, he hauled one of his men up by the collar and then led them in a lumbering dash to the cars that were still drivable. The company did three-point turns and roared off south in pursuit.

The nearest hospital to Danny and Hani's crash-site was Hillel Yaffe Medical Center off HaShalom Street in Hadera. About half way back to where they'd started the chase at Olga.

Though famous as the Israeli center for organ transplants, it was also a fine accident and emergency hospital. There, tragic footnotes to the destruction so far, were playing out.

Maya Sosensky with her arm splinted, and her aunt Batya draped in a bloody police blanket, were being helped from a white ambulance onto gurneys. In moments they were on their way indoors with a paramedic supporting Batya's plasma drip.

Only then did the back doors of another ambulance open. The torn bodies of Katy and Joseph were wheeled much more sedately toward the morgue.

A policeman in the hospital foyer, who'd accompanied the ambulances, had a police-emergency telephone cabinet open and was cursing. Calls being patched through from the Israeli National 100 Emergency Number had overloaded Hadera station's lines. He couldn't get through. It was the same for every station. Communication was at a standstill.

All the while in the distance, the faint sirens of other ambulances gradually swelled, carrying other injured and deceased from far and wide.

Almost simultaneously, at the A&E entrance of Rambam Hospital on HaAliya HashNiya Avenue on Haifa's waterfront, two private vehicles slewed to a halt at ragged angles. The occupants had jumped out, shouting for help.

The first carried small Naama Hadani, picked up by a passing ex-IDF army medic who thought she might still have a chance. Within moments, a flood of orderlies and nurses arrived. A doctor checked Naama and indeed felt a faint pulse. She was rushed into the theater, but lost her fight before anything could be done.

The other vehicle was the Tel-Orens' bullet-scarred station-wagon. Sharona was helped out of the back seat, the side of her dress crimson from holding Omri against her. She was screaming for help. The orderlies didn't wait for a gurney, instead helped her husband directly to surgery. A harried looking doctor checked Omri's condition, but could only look sadly at Sharona. A nurse reached out in comfort, but couldn't prevent her from collapsing in the driveway.

She was helped to a waiting room, to sit crying inconsolably in the loving arms of two of her remaining children.

Back at Hadera, Danny had his broken forearm straightened and put in a cast. He insisted on only some pills for the pain. They set off tenaciously back south with Hani at the wheel of their borrowed black-and-white.

They weren't giving up now. No chance.

TWENTY-SEVEN

5720 junction, four miles northwest of Netanya
5:17 p.m.

Assaf Hefetz pushed his quick little Japanese coupe, using every ounce of grip from its fat knobby tires, as hard as he could along the winding country road south of Havatzelet HaSharon; slowing only to run the gauntlet of mongrel dogs around the house-bus encampments at Shoshanat Ha'Amakim and Tsukei Yam.

At the junction of the 5720 and Highway 2, two things happened almost simultaneously. Assaf saw a traffic officer had the on-ramp blocked off and was standing in the road holding up a white-gloved palm. And as the Datsun nose-dipped to a halt 10-yards in front of the officer, Adam's anxious voice poured out of the car-radio.

The traffic officer stood his ground, but popped loose the safety strap over his .38. It hadn't yet registered on the man through the dust caking the windshield, Assaf was in full combat gear with Yamam in yellow Hebrew letters across his tactical vest.

Assaf slapped his warrant card with its distinctive blue Star of David, against the windshield with his left hand, and drew the radio microphone with his right.

"Assaf. Yes Adam."

"Ah, boss. Phew." Assaf's normally cool and calm right-hand man sounded like a huge weight had lifted. "Things have changed. Where are you?"

"Fifty-seven-twenty and the Two. Traffic has the north on-ramp blocked off."

"No matter. You want to come back south. The bus is almost at Netanya."

"Shit! I must have just missed it!"

"Yeah, well, Sharon desk sergeant says they still have a couple of moves they can make south of there, I think at Kfar Shmaryahu and then Glilot, but it's a running battle. They've gotten through everything that's been put up so far."

Adam rattled off the rest of the circumstances as far as he knew them.

"Dammit!" cursed Assaf. "Any word if they're bringing our men from Beit Shemesh?"

"I know the request has gone to the top of the Army, but I don't think it matters now. They'd never make it in time, even by heavy chopper. No Two-Six either. Same problem."

Assaf wasted no time on spilt milk. "Okay, I'm going to stay clear of the Two for now. I'll take the fifty-seven-twenty east to the railway line and come south down the service road. Once you know where they stop the bus, vector me back west from there."

He reached down and cinched the center buckle of the four-point safety harness as tight as he could.

The Netanya black-and-whites, commanded by Daniel Shiller with Hamzah Arslaniyyun at the wheel, had quickly gotten past the red and white bus travelling sedately south. Then they'd put on some real speed, passing several cars and a meandering farm truck.

The bus-driver may have wondered what the panic was about, but probably didn't think it involved him. The police had steadfastly looked the other way. If they hadn't, they would have seen 'Ali Baba's Magic Carpet Tours' on the bus's side. Maybe also, that its plush little curtains were drawn for the comfort of more than 30 Turkish tourists.

With the time ticking past 5:19 p.m., the policemen pulled up in train at the crossroads of Ha-Ma'apolim Street and the Two, and hustled to lay down spike-strips.

But they hadn't given a single to how they'd separate the chaff of private vehicles, from the wheat of the terrorists' bus, once they controlled of the highway. Shiller assumed his NCO knew what he was doing. But Arslaniyyun had come up through regular beat policing.

He hadn't a clue and just mimicked what his boss did.

In a couple of minutes, they had the highway sealed off.

Disastrously.

The southbound lane was nearly double wide, with a generous outside verge. Cars started bunching up two abreast at the spike-strips. The innocent bus joined the jam.

Meanwhile, traffic from the two side streets was backing up also. And loudly. People who'd been inside observing Shabbat all day were busting to get about their business. Thwarted, they honked and shouted.

The collective thought was *enough already!* One outraged elderly man in a derby-hat barged up on the inside, slapped his hand on the roof, and called out, "Let's get the show on the road Heahhhh!" in a thick New York accent.

By then the misunderstanding was obvious to the police, from the decals on the tourist bus. Schiller was about to order his men to undo the roadblock, when the real terrorists' bus arrived, then several more cars and a truck. Then Lev Shachar and his men.

The five Netanya officers realized the mess they had made for themselves, and the danger they were in. They could be mowed down any moment. They hastily retreated behind their line of vehicles. It wasn't much of an improvement. They'd be shooting over each other if a gun-battle broke out.

Lev knew instantly this was a catastrophe in the making. The trapped terrorists were sitting in a sea of easy targets. Rifle muzzles moved at window openings, but curiously, weren't yet firing, as they had been virtually the length of Highway 2. Perhaps they were overwhelmed by the sheer number of targets. But that surely wouldn't last. His biggest fear was the terrorists rolling grenades under the jammed mass of vehicles. Spilling gasoline, trapping people in flaming steel coffins. Too awful to contemplate.

The terrorists were on the outside of the lane. The verge beside it was wide. Perhaps if given the chance, their desire to reach the killing zone of Tel Aviv would override any urge to cause mayhem here. He resolved to get to the other end of the roadblock and open it up. Problem was, getting there meant passing right by the hijacked bus. Hellish risky. But he had to take the chance. Lev outlined his idea to his driver.

The man blanched. “You’re *meshuggah!* (nuts) It’s suicide!”

"Just keep everyone else in the cars. Whatever it takes. I'm going now."

With his sidearm holstered, and empty hands, Lev lowered himself out of the passenger's door and took cover behind the car in front. Around him he caught glimpses of confused faces, some children, behind dusty window-glass.

If this all goes horribly wrong, I’ll never forget these.

He shook that off and judged the distance to his best midway shelter point. A stake-bed farm truck, down to its axles with sacks of alfalfa. It was perilously close to the terrorist's bus. Still, from there he'd have a clear view ahead, and could pick the right moment to run for it. He'd worry about the rest after that.

Lev got up on his toes, and upper body bent right over, began a fast shuffle along the center-divider.

In Jerusalem at 5:20 p.m., General Eitan’s Adjutant phoned Haim Avinoam to say he could have the chopper he requested, if he still wanted it.

"Well, thank you very much," Haim replied sarcastically. "That would have been a huge help twenty minutes ago. But even a Yas'ur won't get Yamam here in time to make a difference now. Yes, I’m sure you did the best you damn well could!"

He broke the connection abruptly. Well aware he’d pay a price. Word would travel back and Rafael Eitan was not a man to forget slights, even to his staff.

Still, though the military's 20 minutes of tardiness had been infuriating, the airlift request had always been a long shot. As any army or police commander will tell you, the major problem when an enemy is rushing at you, is information comes faster and faster, giving you less and less time to make tactical decisions, let alone strategic ones. This had been a textbook case.

Haim recapped the situation in his head, trying to think what more he could do. Communications were largely restored. His Ops Supervisor was now feeding him regular updates. If only those around Ma'agan Michael had communicated better instead of jumping to conclusions, the connection between the boats and the hijacking would have been obvious. A lot of wasted effort would have been saved. Resources that might have made all the difference before this spiraled.

Well, no point griping over things I can't change.

At least armed volunteers were flocking to rally points. More were being recruited while waiting at transport stops to return to their units after weekend leave. Haifa Chief Karel Kohler had pledged to take some under his wing as soon as it was clear where the terrorists would end up.

And Haim, on his own initiative, had provided one other bit of help. Though mindful of risking the wrath of the Tel Aviv police districts' prickly commander, for stealing his resources; he'd reached out to a personal friend; Commander Nissim Levi of the *Redivim*, the National Police Bomb Disposal department. As a result, two bomb-destruction vehicles were on their way up Highway 2. British Landrover flat-bed trucks mounted with machine guns. Seemingly anachronistic equipment for any force policing civilians, but there was good reason.

IEDs weren't common, but not unknown either. One type was the M15 anti-tank mine, 20lbs of destruction removed by night from the fields lining the Golan Heights, transported by farm truck down into Israel proper, and set into the highway where IDF armored vehicles might be on the move. Another was the M18 anti-personnel Claymore mine, set up with a tripwire on one of the heavily patrolled border roads.

The fix was usually the same in both cases. Call in the Redivim to explode it from a safe distance with a massive stream of gunfire. Since the horizontal-firing Claymores were packed with ball-bearings, the guns had protective shields of half-inch steel.

Yes, overkill in normal circumstances. But this situation isn't in any sense of the word normal.

Avinoam hoped they would do more good than harm, as he strained to think what more he could do.

His phone trilled. The panel light showed an internal call.

"Tikva Moret here, Commander," said the female operations center supervisor in cockney accented English. "Officers 'ave the bus pinned down at Kfar Shmaryahu."

Good news at last.

Avinoam strode to the wall-map and traced down to that point. It wasn't a bad place either, the first of several intersections, but still in a relatively open area.

Moret immediately burst his bubble. "Yes, but it's a cock-up. They 'ave it snarled up in a traffic jam surrounded with people in cars."

"How the fuck did that happen?"

In her role the past three years, through the Savoy atrocity and a number of other major events, Mrs. Moret knew her pithy boss well, and could call a spade a spade in her own right.

"It's fooking bedlam down there, sir. We should count ourselves fooking lucky they got it stopped at all. Anyway, a traffic chief inspector is trying to let them through. There are two other stops being put together further south, at Ha-Ma'apolim Street and then by the Herzliya Country Club at Glilot."

Avinoam checked. Glilot was another 500 yards after Ha-Ma'apolim. Then there was nothing else before Tel Aviv proper. They truly were down to their last couple of options.

Yehoshua.

"There's something else."

"Yes?"

"The road-block at Ha-Ma'apolim is just a jeep with a heavy automatic weapon. They are requesting permission to fire if it gets that far."

That should certainly halt the terrorists, Avinoam mused. *But at what cost among the civilians aboard? The alternative, though, is a running battle that might continue for hours.*

"Tell them it's up to them, but disabling fire if they can."

"Yes sir."

Which left Haim with just one more call to make. Experience told him it would be unpleasant. Rattling the cradle for a dial tone, he dialed Tel Aviv. A young voice answered and passed on the call. Then a deep and resonant one said, "General Tyomkin."

"Commander Avinoam from Jerusalem Ops here General. It's now distinctly possible the terrorists might cross into your district."

"Yes, Chief Superintendent Nadav has been keeping me informed," the General pronounced

Talking to *Nitsav* (Deputy Commissioner - formerly Police General,) Moses Tyomkin, the 48-year-old chief of the Tel Aviv police district, was always an ordeal. A man of undetectable political or people skills, Tyomkin had been passed over as Commissioner when Haim Tavori got the job. A snub intended as a nudge toward retirement. Instead, the embittered Tyomkin had insisted on his pick of the district commands. The pompous shit even insisted on being addressed by the old term for his rank. He'd been a thorn in Haim's side ever since.

"May I ask what resources you are committing?"

Tyomkin was silent for a few moments. *If they don't want me calling the shots in Jerusalem, fine, they can do it themselves. But they can't have it both ways. I'm not denuding my town of officers, on a busy Saturday night, with the World Youth Yachting event in town.*

"I'll make those arrangements with the Sharon commander. If I need any help, I'll let you know. Good day."

Need any... of all the stubborn sons of...

Haim took a long, deep breath and shook his head in sorrow. There went the last source of support, for what would soon to be beleaguered defenders. He could only pray it wouldn't be needed.

God, I can't even broadcast a direct warning to the North Tel Aviv residents. Commissioner Tavori thinks it might cause a panic. It's up to the men in the field now, and God help them!

TWENTY-EIGHT

Ha-Ma'apolim Street Junction, Kfar Shmaryahu
5:22 p.m.

Lev reached the shelter of the overloaded farm truck, but as he crouched behind a back wheel, there was shouting from the terrorists' bus. The faces of armed figures turned in his direction. Bullets followed, ricocheting off the tarmac where he'd been.

He figured they'd seen movement, but hadn't gotten a good look at him.

The next stretch to the road spikes would be more hazardous. He considered the options. They were all bad. Take the direct route up the middle of the traffic jam and hope he beat reflexes? Or zig in and out of vehicles, risking the lives of those inside? Either way, he was endangering those within the thin sheet metal shells of their cars.

In the IDF and all his police life, rule number one had been to protect the civilian population. Endangering this way went against all his instincts.

But he was committed now.

He got up and ran as fast as he could, trying to put the tourist bus between him and death. Gunfire spat before he'd gone three yards. Something briefly stung his thigh.

Then he was passing the terrorists' bus itself. Close enough to smell the stink. His head within feet of their guns. He counted on their having to switch windows to aim at him this close.

Now he was in full view of what had been the windshield. The shooting was deafening. Bullets punched nearby metal with an odd bashing sound.

Two more steps.

He dived behind the shelter of the tour bus like a base-runner sliding headlong into second.

But there was still no time to relax. He got up and ran to the road spikes. Grabbed a foot-wide strip with hands lacerated by the road. It was heavier than he expected.

He saw uniformed bodies behind police cars. Shouted in his Australian twang, "Are you stupid here you fucks? Gimme a hand, for fuck's sake!"

Two young constables uncoiled and raced toward him. They were briefly in view of the terrorists, but drew no fire. With their added strength the Caltrops were quickly hauled into a pile.

The verge was open.

The three policemen flattened themselves against the sheltered side of the tourist bus, with Lev praying the terrorists would take the bait.

The Scania revved up, nosed out of the traffic and accelerated along the outside. Lev glimpsed the driver, head bent over the wheel by the muzzle of a Russian assault weapon, held by a woman in green fatigues with her face framed by a short, tangled hair-style. The bus veered into the middle of the intersection and accelerated south.

Lev emptied his lungs in a vast sigh of relief. But it wasn't over for him yet. He still had the snarled traffic across west central Israel to untangle.

A mile and a half down the highway, facing north in the middle of the Abba Eban intersection in West Herzliya, was a Landrover gun-truck manned by two nervous officers from the Redivim.

The junior member, Sergeant Enoch Gavni, was up on the bed manning the post-mounted M60 machine gun.

His partner, Master Sergeant Shem Vilinsky, was at ground level behind the equipment, with his M1 carbine to his shoulder.

Dalal and others, swaying in the aisle of the Wanderer's bus, saw this weapon from more than two hundred yards away, and knew there was little they could do about it except bully their way through

It was Khaled this time, who moved his boot to help hold the gas pedal down in case Shlomo was tempted to slow down. All others aboard, fearfully aware of the paper-thinness of the metal that surrounded them, hunched low.

Muttered phrases of prayers in Arabic and Hebrew were heard over the sound of the wind.

Watching the giant bus charging toward him, Enoch, a fair shot with the gun in his sweaty hands when the target was motionless, realized this was a whole other kind of duty. He looked left and right, calculating the amount of room the bus had to get around him. Going through him didn't bear thinking about.

A son of orthodox parents, the daily declaration of faith, *Shema* prayer, played in his mind. *Hear, O Israel, The Lord is our God, The Lord is one...*

Left hand over the top of the gun-butt, he traversed the weapon, making sure it was free-moving. Then his racing heart stopped for one dreadful moment. They'd made a dreadful mistake facing the Landrover north. He would be shooting over the top of the cab. Not a problem with stationary targets at a distance. But his orders were to shoot out the tires of one rapidly approaching, while avoiding firing into the passenger compartment. Because of the height of the cab roof, he would quickly lose his ability to depress the muzzle of the M60.

Instead of waiting for the bus to get close, he panicked and commenced firing when the target was still more than a hundred yards away.

Baba'a had faced machine gun nests as an Al-Asifa commander in the early days in Beirut. He'd told his fighters many times, "Get in under the machine guns where they can't aim at you, if you don't want to get cut to pieces at a distance." He hollered over the road-roar, "Get in close! Charge him! He won't shoot at the kāfirs! Sister, make him do it!"

Enoch's first chatter of fire tore up the roadway, wide and yards ahead of the hurtling bus. The ricochets screeched away over the roofs of apartment buildings in the background.

He cursed, grasped the pistol grip tighter. The juggernaut was much closer and accelerating. The next rounds ripped at its undercarriage but missed the tires. Then it was too close. His third attempt raked the cabin-area. His nerve broke. He dropped down on the truck-bed to await the collision.

The copper-jacketed .30 ammunition punched through the thin metal of the bus. Some struck seat-stanchions and body framing, and deflected wildly.

Tariq grasped his throat and made a guttural sound. Freed one red hand and stared at it incredulously. Then flopped down in the aisle. A slug struck Josef Kheloani with an audible thump. He sagged soundlessly and lifelessly sideways in his bonds.

Other slugs ripped arbitrarily at the packed hostages. Sometimes passed through to find second and third targets. But taking no more lives.

A second later, the vehicle heeled like a yacht in a storm as Shlomo swerved around the bomb squad truck.

In the truck-bed, having miraculously felt no crushing impact, Enoch leapt back to his feet with the bus fishtailed crazily away from him.

He spun the machine-gun on its swivel, pointed it after the bus, and held down the trigger. But turning the gun around had kinked the ammunition belt. The M60 chattered only another couple of seconds before jamming.

One of those last bullets punched through the bus's metal skin and the frame behind Avi Perets's right elbow and used the last of its energy to bury itself in his upper arm.

By then the target had straightened and was fast receding. Gavni and Vilinsky struggled to get the Landrover turned around to go after it.

At 5.25 p.m., Adam's voice came over the radio just as Assaf was rounding the east end of the airport on the eastern fringe of Herzliya, 2 miles from Highway 2. Adam rattled off an update. Assaf listened intently.

Adam and Raffi were in route to Aluf Meir Amit Boulevard, a new industrial area in Ramat HaSharon, on the back side of the ridge that paralleled Highway 2 at Glilot. Assaf knew the area from briefings at the nearby Israeli Intelligence and Terrorism Information Center.

"We've roped in a few soldiers too," Adam added.

"Make sure they have ammo." said Assaf. "What's the plan from there?"

"It's a short trot over the hill to Glilot. They're putting up a last-ditch road barricade at a gas station just north of the Herzllya Country Club."

"I'll see you there in five."

"Rallying point is a construction shed on the top of the hill."

"Got it."

Assaf made it inside that time. Vehicles were already parked nose-up on the slope, including Adam's Jeep CJ 4X4. He glimpsed Adam's lanky figure beckon him on with a big sweep of an arm, before it disappeared over the scrubby crest.

Hefting his gear, Assaf dug in his boots and scrambled after him up the crumbly slope.

The badly shot-up Wanderers' bus lumbered away from the machine-gun-ambush intersection just on 5:32 p.m., with Shlomo wrestling the now barely responsive steering-wheel.

Behind Shlomo was a cacophony of cries and groans. The air seemed thickened by the smell of blood. Much of that had come from the terrorist that Zvi Eshet had shot, who'd bled out from his wounds despite the woman-terrorist's attempts to help him.

He glanced back once and saw another one was down now also.

The sharp-faced bastard who'd spoken over the tour-guide system. Tarik or something.

Shlomo smiled to hear him choking on his last breaths.

As the bus passed an obscuring line of trees on the left, the highway kinked left and straightened again, Shlomo saw something ahead there was no avoiding.

He put all his weight on the brake pedal, anyway.

TWENTY-NINE

Glilot, 5.5 miles north of down-town Tel Aviv
5:34 p.m.

When Assaf's head cleared the ridge-top, he was looking out over the last open strip of coastal land before urban North Tel Aviv. Between him and the tanker-berth oil-tanks along the shoreline, the many-times-fought-over Sharon Plain was less than a mile wide.

Highway 2 followed the foot of the ridge below, wider and bounded by steel crash-barrier-ribbons on stubby wooden posts, but still only two lanes.

In the left-background was the Herzliya Country Club sports complex and then the start of the sprawl. Directly ahead was an expanse of fields of thigh-high vegetation, crisscrossed by medium-height, evergreen tree-lines. Parts appeared marshy, with a deep drainage ditch running away to the north. A scrubby knoll rose in the middle of one field.

Below and on this side of the highway, the slopes of the ridge were under industrial-strength development. A plethora of white survey pegs suggested perhaps a shopping mall and parking lot. At his two o'clock also this side, were a couple of established highway-side businesses: a Sunoco gas station, and north of that a used car lot with perhaps two dozen vehicles in front of a sales-shed.

The gas-station forecourt was alive with police activity. Mixed-uniformed men were also scavenging the construction site for planks, trestles, and concrete blocks, to reinforce a roadblock of police cars parked nose-to-tail. A hundred yards or so up-highway were the shiny strips of road-spikes, also spanning both lanes.

Just past that, the highway kinked slightly inland; anyone rounding that bend would be unsighted by more trees bounding the north edge of the used car lot until too late. *Certainly, they won't get through that,* he thought, *if they do make it this far south.*

It all should have been reassuring, but Assaf's main reaction was a bad feeling. Given a choice between fighting them here or in the streets of Tel Aviv, he'd take it. But it was hard to imagine a worse place for an ambush. Just too much off-road cover.

He'd trained and fought in numerous similar scenarios. The chances of holding the terrorists aboard once they were stopped were slim. Not that that was even desirable, since they would be mixed in with their hostages. But once loose among this terrain, their capabilities would multiply.

The biggest negative was the tree lines. Each tree was thick enough to conceal an armed man. He shuddered at having to flush out terrorists among those, and from any number of bolt-holes in the open. A nightmare, especially with night approaching.

He focused back on the blockade. There were about 15 men manning. Mostly police from their blue uniforms, though they seemed to be taking orders from an army officer dressed in the green fatigues and gray beret of a combat engineer. The intention was clearly to back up the road-spikes with gunfire from the barricade, taking advantage of the open ground beyond to protect civilians. There weren't too many ways to slice this *matzah* loaf. He'd have done the same also, if tasked with making the best of this bad situation. Still...

Assaf heard himself being hollered at. He looked left along the ridge-top, to the construction shed where Adam had said they should meet. Adam and Raffi seemed to have brought along half a dozen soldiers, from a mixture of brigades judging by beret colors. Two even wore the khaki Australian-style slouch hats the Special Forces boys liked. *They all look competent enough, at least.*

Adam was beckoning him urgently. He was about to step in that direction, when there came the unmistakable thudding of heavy machine gun fire to the north. It was answered by Kalashnikov fire, another sound Assaf would recognize anywhere.

Below had turned to a frenzy with men running to their posts around the gas station.

Assaf ran as fast as he could toward the construction shed.

Shlomo could only cling to the wheel, using it as leverage on the brake pedal, as the Scania skidded out of control, toward the road spikes.

He felt no fear. Only inevitability. He was either going to die or he wasn't. It was out of his hands.

The woman terrorist was screaming at him. He kept his brake-foot hard down. What could she do? Shoot him?

They were crabbing inexorably sideways. Then he remembered the lives of all the innocents behind him were in his hands. If he gave up all control, he would probably roll the bus. He began fighting hard to turn into the skid.

Gravity sent Dalal and Khaled staggering helplessly forward. They had to grab the windshield frame to avoid going out through the space.

Fate added a macabre touch. Hussain's blood-crimson body came loose from its seat-row, and followed in their wake, leaving a ghastly trail until it too thumped against the front metalwork.

Behind them voices shouted and screamed in all pitches. The road spikes disappeared beneath the front of the bus, blowing out its tires with a thumping sound, and turning it instantly into an un-steerable missile.

Then gunfire erupted in a rolling roar, from the gas station forecourt on their left quarter, and behind the roadblock of vehicles. The visual effect was a billow of smoke laced with brilliant flashes.

The Scania shuddered as bullets hammered its undercarriage. Shlomo's brake pedal went flat to the floor. The bus dropped onto its front rims. There were several seconds of harsh sound as steel gouged at concrete, then a crunch as the right front hit the outer crash-barrier and began scraping along it.

They skewed out slightly at the rear, rebounded a couple of feet off the crash-barrier, then stopped in a haze of smoke and steam, amid a stink of hot oil and spilled coolant.

Shlomo yanked back the door-operating levers beside his right knee. The front doors opened instantly.

He leapt up and ran down the step, anticipating a flood of escapees following his example. Hurdling the hip-high road barrier, he veered out into the field, legs pumping. The ground was uneven under the long grass. He stumbled and almost fell, but made it seven or eight more yards before gunfire clattered behind him. Bullets zipped by him and slapped at the seed-heads.

He dared to hope. *I'm going to get away. I am.*

There was an almighty thump in the middle of his lower back. He tumbled headlong, felt his skull strike a clod of earth, then nothing more.

But Shlomo had run for his life completely alone. The front doors were cable-operated, but the rears were hydraulic. The fluid lines had been destroyed by the lashing gunfire or impact with the road. They didn't open. The hostages were trapped on board.

Thirty seconds of quiet passed before a voice spoke up from near the front. It was Haviv Ankwa, the Moroccan-Jewish Egged driver, dust-covered and bleeding where flying fragments had ripped at his exposed skin. He was speaking Arabic.

"Please. Let me talk to them. Let me tell them what you want."

Baba'a, hunched in the middle of the aisle, made eye contact with Dalal in front.

"Please! You want something, right? Tell me what it is and I will ask them. There is no need to fight. Let me tell them!"

Dalal shrugged back at Baba'a. Glanced down the aisle where Ramz and Hiza'a were agreeing. Not that their votes were required. Apart from some distant calling back and forth, things were quiet in the direction of the blockade.

Why not?

She called out, "No shooting. We will try to bargain!" Held out her hand toward Baba'a, working her fingers.

Baba'a felt in his pocket and found the folded paper Jihad had given him on the beach. The list of demands. He balled it up and threw it to her.

She said something to Khaled, who leveled his AKM menacingly on Haviv. She eased carefully down the aisle, reached in and untied his hands.

Haviv rubbed his wrists while looking at Dalal for instructions.

None of the hostages said anything. They could all have been patrons in a movie theater, watching a feature politely, except this scenario truly was life or death.

Dalal scanned the piece of paper so she could give Haviv a summary, then said, "Tell them we will come out if they put down their guns too. We will release hostages only with guarantees of safe passage, along with comrades we will name. This is a list."

Haviv waved it away. "No, first they need to know you will not shoot if they don't. I will tell them that, and we will make an agreement, then you can tell them more."

Dalal leaned back, body language to tell him he could go.

Haviv got up, still keeping his upper body below the level of the windows, and called out in Hebrew, "Coming out. Do not shoot. Coming out!"

He rose slowly to his full height, hands raised. Walked to the front doorway. Took one step down, then a step to the ground.

He was sweet, clean, open air.

THIRTY

5:37 p.m.

Assaf had barely enough time to throw himself flat on the ridge-top beside his comrades, before the bus appeared. Then the volley of fire lashed at it. He'd watched, cursing, as a man appeared and ran southwest into the fields, before going down in a hail of bullets. He understood, though, why the defenders at the blockade held fire. They had no way to protect the runner without firing directly into the bus.

Now another man stood up inside. From some head-nods, he seemed to take some instructions, before edging his way into the open with his hands held high.

Assaf had that really bad feeling again. Those at the barricade would be on hair triggers. But a single person wasn't a threat. It could be a messenger. Anything!

He was about to shout, "Don't shoot!" when there was a sputter of gunfire from behind the cars. The lone man clasped his midsection and crumpled.

There was a thunderstorm of return fire. The remaining glass in the bus's left side windows flew outward on the wings of copper-jacketed bullets. The fire was returned full force by the defenders. The last chance of preventing a slaughter had gone down with the fallen man.

Then five figures grasping multi-colored packs, and rifles, spilled from the far side of the bus, and fanned out beyond into cover in an obviously planned move.

Assaf's worst fears had come true.

The exit-and-scatter move had been agreed between the terrorists while Haviv Ankwa was making his appearance, in case the negotiations failed.

Jalal, Khaled, Rami and Wael had no intention of surrendering. Fayadh's thoughts were the opposite. Throwing aside his equipment, he ran until he reached the knoll rising out of the field beyond the center line of trees. Then cringed down behind it.

Meanwhile, three of the other escaped terrorists found cover behind trees, in hollows in the ground, anywhere with protection and a line of sight to the blockade and gas station. They propped their weapons on their packs and furiously continued firing.

Wael tried to make it behind one of the trees south of the bus. It meant covering a few yards of exposed ground. He was too slow. Fire from a couple of policemen with carbines marched toward him and then up his body, dropping him lifeless on the highway-flanking dirt road.

Assaf and his men on the ridge added their weight to the battle also, but picked their shots carefully. They didn't expect to hit any of the now-well-hidden terrorists, but were determined to prevent them getting away.

Some defenders and terrorists had tracer rounds mixed into their magazines. The two-way fusillade was punctuated by searingly bright streaks against the early twilight. Red from the Israelis, traded with green from the terrorists.

The gunfire lasted for another eight minutes despite regular shouting of "*Hafsakatesh! Hafsakatesh!*" (Cease fire,) from soldier-in-charge, Lieutenant Colonel Yaacov 'Yaki' Pirst. He'd been plucked from a taxi stand and shoved into the role when things first began moving at breakneck speed. Finally, a number of people reloaded at the same time, and decided not to keep shooting at targets they couldn't see, and it petered-out.

The hostages were at the end of their endurance. They'd been battered, brutalized, and subjected to unimaginable horror for an hour and nearly ten minutes, under the gun-muzzles of monsters. They'd had to endure the roller coaster of expecting the bus to crash through the guard rail or roll over, then of surviving to see Shlomo Zait and then Haviv Ankwa shot down like dogs. And just now the roaring gunfire; not knowing when a bullet might take another loved one. They were desperate to get off the bus at any cost.

One of the most desperate was Yossi Hochman. Rebecca had finally gotten his hands free. She'd been assuring him she and the children were okay, but he didn't believe her, and he was right. In fact, the boys were fine, but she'd been hit by a spent machine-gun bullet in the lower back. Though she was still able to move her legs, she'd been bleeding steadily for several minutes.

"We have to go, Rebecca. We can't stay here!"

"No, they will come and rescue us, I'm sure of it."

It wasn't just her wound. She'd seen the rage in the eyes of the terrorist she'd defied. She was certain he would single her out if she tried to get up and kill all her family. No, their only hope was a rescue, like at Entebbe.

Then she saw Baba'a say a few words to Ramz. She sobbed out loud and hugged the two boys tighter to her breast. "They are going to kill us."

Yossi had seen it too. "Maybe they're going to surrender," he whispered back.

"They never do that," Rebecca hissed. They are going to kill us. I know it!"

Dalal, Hiza'a, Baba'a, and Ramz knew their time left aboard the bus was short. They fully intended to carry out the no-survivors pact made at Es Saksakiye. The hostages were useless now, except as a diversion. Slaughtering them would surely bring rescuers running as wide-open targets. It might even distract the enemy long enough for one or more terrorists to slip away.

They gathered backpacks. Checked the loads in their AKMs. Baba'a and Dalal moved to the front and waited on their knees in the gore. Baba'a nodded at Ramz.

Ramz swung without hesitation toward the rear of the bus and raked the people huddled in the right rear with a murderous burst. Princess Leibwitz and Meir Segal jolted and jumped with the impact. He switched aim to the left, and Tzyona Luzia-Cohen and her husband, Avraham, died in each other's arms.

The storm of fire also killed the two children still hiding underneath those seats, Ytzak Ankwa and beautiful little Liat Gal-on, the six-year-old to whom Dalal had given the candy bar.

Gun emptied, Ramz reached up to his vest for grenades. He intended to throw them and follow the other three terrorists out the front door during the five seconds before they exploded. He expected Hiza'a to carry on the killing while he pulled the pins. But Hiza'a hesitated.

Ramz had just pulled the first pin when Yossi Hochman came up out of his seat and shoulder-charged him, slamming him back against the left-side seats. The live grenade flew from Ramz' hand, deflected off a seat stanchion, and lay spinning on the floor. Right beside Rebecca's feet.

Yossi didn't think about himself. Only of obliterating the man threatening his family. While enormously strong and fit, Ramz outweighed him by at least 25lbs of muscle. The huge Arab put all that power into getting back upright, while the Israeli fought to take away the AKM. Ara was an expert with it from his paratrooper days, if he could only get it free.

Yossi wasn't fighting alone. Two rows of seats forward of Rebecca, Abraham Shamir had leapt up and rushed at Hiza'a. They collided chest to chest. Abraham clawed at the larger man, trying to get a grip and throw him down. He missed the web vest and his fingers scrabbled against clothing, but Hiza'a had been holding his AKM loosely. It came easily into the Israeli's hands. Abraham reversed it, but the Arab was too close to shoot at. He smashed Hiza'a in the face. And again. The terrorist was helpless in the face of the Israeli's ferociousness. He reverted to trying to protect himself, but each thudding blow drove him further down into a row of seats. Reversing the AKM again, Abraham jammed the muzzle into the terrorist's chest and pulled the trigger. Hiza'a's body sank away. He turned with the gun leveled, looking for the other two terrorists, but they had melted away down the front steps.

Yossi at last had Ramz' AKM in his hands. He fired it into Ramz' head. One-two.

An instant later an almighty force hammered his lower body, lifting him up so his back hit the ceiling, then dropping him brokenly back into the aisle.

Ears ringing, but fully conscious, he numbly turned his head to the seat-row where Rebecca and the children had been. There was just a jumble of lacerated upholstery, and twisted tubular steel. The pockmarked wall was a solid smear of red.

Yossi looked up the aisle. His workmate Abraham was lying below the torn-up dashboard, shaking his head.

Yossi tried to move, but his lower body seemed disconnected. He looked down. His legs resembled the tentacles of a bright red octopus, twisted into crazy boneless shapes.

The pain and realization hit him and he screamed.

At points north and south of the battle area, men from every cadre of the IDF and all branches of the police had been answering Haim Avinoam's Kol-radio call out for over 40 minutes. The northern point was near the aborted Kfar Shmaryahu roadblock. The southern one at Namir Avenue, where Highway 2 ended. Those men had been listening helplessly to the tantalizingly close and regular, crackling of different calibers of small arms fire. They were desperate to get into the fight any way they could.

Command had changed frequently, as more senior or experienced officers took over from lesser ones, but that was now settled. And after some, “Hello? Hello?” efforts to find an available frequency, a radio-net- covering the roughly 800-yard circle enclosing the operational area, was also in place.

The plan was to move in as soon as properly coordinated, with a four-directional pincer movement, or even sooner if things audibly escalated.

Haifa’s Karel Kohler would advance from the north along the coast, then form a cordon to make sure the terrorists didn’t get away across the fields. His 2IC was a regular army officer, Major Yehuda Caplan. Many of his assault volunteers were senior men, including

Netanya commander Samir Hanina, Daniel Shiller and several soldiers.

Hadera's Daniel Shrof, backed up by Netanya Sub-Inspector Shochat Moses, would lead some constables down the west side of the highway, using the ditch for cover. Taking point would be 22-year-old Ya'akov Gaz, a marine commando from the *Shayetet 13*, the Israeli version of the U.S. Navy Seals.

Hani Sror and Danny Lavi would lead a group that included Army Sergeant Ben Soshan, Golani-Brigade Private Ori Karen, and no less than the head of the police shooting team; Master Sergeant Raphael Levy with a Remington 700, .308 sniper rifle. They would move along the side of the ridge, to the trees bordering the used car lot.

Coming up from the south was one big sweep of people, including Constable Asher Nimi and a half dozen soldiers, and Sharon Chief Superintendent Alisha Nadav and a mixed group of PCs from his and the Hadera station. Also, along would be a number of army medics, who would surely be needed, judging by the regular noise from the battlefield.

The police had their .38 Smith and Wesson service revolvers, and a few of the newer-issue 9mm Browning Hi-Power pistols. Their main shoulder weapon was the WWII-vintage .30 M1 carbine, while a few officers had 9mm Uzis, and fewer still, like Assaf and his Yamam people, the Galil .223 assault rifle. The soldiers uniformly carried Colt .223, M16 Armalites.

At 5:46 p.m. there came a heavy exchange of fire, followed by the muffled thud of a grenade going off in an enclosed space. This was escalation without a doubt. Terse instructions to "Move in! Go!" crackled over the radios. The assault teams ported arms and double-timed toward the battle sounds.

THIRTY-ONE

5:47 p.m.

The grenade bulged the bus's roof upward, directly above the middle seats on the highway-facing side. But with its force constrained by sturdy steel-framed seats and bodies, it did relatively little sideways damage. It did its worst work downward, ripping a cavity the size of two fists in the plywood and Formica flooring.

Directly underneath was the Scania's fuel tank. White-hot steel shards tore the tank open, spilling and then setting alight the many gallons of diesel fuel inside. Flames licked up tentatively through the hole. Smoke began filling the interior.

Though their captors were gone, the threat to those left aboard had been replaced by perhaps even greater danger. A fear of burning alive flooded minds.

There were ten people alive forward of the explosion point, including the shockingly injured Yossi Hochman and stunned Abraham Shamir.

Yossi somehow superhumanly dragged his maimed body the few feet to the front doorway and fell out onto the road. Fighting off shock, he pulled himself a little further away so as not to get trampled. Then tore off his shirt and tied the sleeves around his thighs before passing out.

Sixteen-year-old Marie Shamir was the first passenger in the forward section on her feet, from where she'd been curled two rows forward of the sickeningly flesh-splashed area. Bruised and deaf, she ran down the aisle to help her father. Finding a strength that she'd never known, Marie dragged Abraham to the ground outside the front doors. He rolled over, groaning. She got him up and pulled him around the bus's front and across the highway to the gas station forecourt.

Also close to the front, Monique Ankwa was frantic with worry about her heroic husband. With two-year-old Missy clamped in her arms, she yanked her middle daughter, Talia, upright. Her oldest, another Anat, followed. Monique assumed Ytzak would be right behind them, not knowing he had died under the seats at Ramz' hands. At the foot of the step, there was no sign of Haviv. He should have been right there. Monique let go of her two older girls, imploring them to, "Run! Run!" They sprinted sobbingly across the highway toward the gas station. Clinging to Missy, Monique went left around the front of the bus. She saw Haviv sprawled there and dropped to her knees.

Out through the front door behind the Ankwas came businessman Yehuda Basterman, followed by Arza Tazor and her boyfriend Gilad Gantz, all travelers from the 901 bus.

Several policemen got up behind the barrier and encouraged them on, but had to dive back down immediately because the terrorists now had a bead on this activity and opened up. Benenson fell, shot in the back and died within seconds. Gantz staggered from a leg-wound, but stumbled on into safety with his partner.

Meanwhile Monique found Haviv was alive, but in terrible pain. Through her anguish, she knew there was nothing she could do for him, and she had Missy to look after. With the child in the crook of her arm, she ran after the others. Within a few steps she felt a blow, as if something had struck her arm, but no pain. It wasn't until all she was lying behind shelter that she looked down and wailed. Little Missy was dead.

Galvanized by this first wave of escapees, a half dozen policemen rushed to the bus, using the now steadily burning side as shelter from steady gunfire from the fields.

They beat on the metalwork; shouting, “Get out! Get out!” Two exposed themselves to grasp Yossi's unconscious body by the shoulders, while trying not to look.

Others grabbed Haviv's arms and legs. Doubled-over, they half-carried the horrifically wounded men toward shelter, leaving a red trail, stumbling with the weight, bullets tugging at their clothing, and stinging from ricochet-chips flying up from the tarmac. All made it untouched.

Back inside the fire voraciously consumed plywood and plastic, forcing those still aboard, further to the rear away from the heat and toxic smoke. Their options were shrinking rapidly. They could climb out through the window-holes, brave the flames to reach the front doors, or somehow force the rear doors open. To do nothing was to die horribly.

But there was still selflessness aboard.

One of the least physically injured families was the Hadanis, Joseph and Lavan, and after Naama's murder at Ma'agan Michael, their surviving daughter Tiva.

They had also taken in and been trying to comfort Eran Bosknitz, who'd been weeping over his dead parents. Joseph picked Eran up in his large hands, talking soothingly to calm him, and lowered the boy out through a window-hole. The boy had the awareness to pick himself up and run toward the car yard.

Out in the fields, all the terrorists cared about was killing anyone they could, even an obvious child. They blazed at his small form from two or three firing points. Amazingly, he made it untouched and threw himself down behind the row of cars.

This attention had increased the danger for the Hadanis, but they still had to get out immediately. Joseph vaulted out through the same ragged hole and reached up and pulled Lavan and Tiva down after him. Then, right behind them, he saw little Junior Meshkel. Not realizing the boy's family was still aboard, Joseph lifted him down. But Junior was desperate to get back to his parents. He ran away, around to the exposed side of the bus.

The Hadanis couldn't stay there and try to coax him back. Flames were climbing up the outside now, and the heat was too great. The trio bolted away across the highway toward the car yard, trailing smoke from singed hair. But no shots came after them. A struggle inside had drawn attention away.

Coughing from the foul air, Samaritan Jeffrey Shapiro was throwing his weight against the rear folding doors. They wouldn't budge. Avi Perets joined him, though nursing his right arm. Then Egged Paymaster Shim'aon Glotman, despite favoring his bleeding right leg. Abruptly, the doors folded aside.

Tischner and Perets fell through the opening onto the ground, which, in the insane arbitrariness of war, saved their lives. Bullets flew above them. Shim'aon was framed in the doorway. He was hit several times and fell backward, motionless in the aisle.

Then from the crest poured a hail of suppressing fire. Assaf's men were the only defenders able to do so. Those at the barricade were right-then moving positions away from the thick smoke. It was frustrating work. They no sooner pinpointed one target, when fire blasted from another location. While they concentrated on that threat the first terrorist quickly changed trees or foxholes.

Into this hell on earth stumbled more people, faltering and falling, then rising and trying to run. First out the back door was Chaima Aharonowitz, clinging to Tali. At their heels was Na'omi Alichi hugging her school backpack. They were instantly mown down by Jalal, part way down the tree line. The two girls died instantly. Chaima lay writhing.

Judith Haas emerged next, struggling to drag out her smoldering husband Gid'on, the first Wanderers' driver that day. His initial wounds had stopped bleeding, but he was so weak he could barely keep his feet under him. The pair fell down immediately. It saved their lives also. Gunfire aimed at them only ricocheted away.

Judith got Gid'on back up just as Avi Perets clambered down from the rear, holding his left hand clamped against his right arm. The other Judith, Judith Zait followed him, towing Nathan, the only one of her sons she'd been able to find. Avoiding the bodies of Chaima and the two girls, the trio veered left to join the Haas's. All climbed the guardrail and stumbled southwest out into the fields.

Judith Zait un-knowingly passed close by her fallen husband Shlomo, the first hostage shot at Glilot.

He lay invisible and paralyzed from the waist down in high grass, waving weakly. She went right by.

The five collapsing in a moaning huddle.

The suppression fire from Assaf's group on the hill, and policemen who'd found firing points out of the path of the smoke, was at last having an effect. Brush barely had to twitch before bullets poured into that position.

Keeping the terrorists' heads down was crucial, because flames had spread across virtually the whole left side of the bus. The heat was hellish: the air unbreathable. It drove out the last still aboard and able to move. The confused, the grief-stricken, mothers with traumatized children, and those who'd stayed with incapacitated loved ones; all poured out the rear door with surely only seconds to spare.

Lily Glotman had been cut by glass chips in numerous places, as had her son Eitz and daughter Anat. She'd tried to follow her husband a moment before he was shot, but Anat wouldn't move. Now torn between throwing herself down on Shim'aon and stepping over him to get out, she'd chosen to save her children.

Else Shwin and Simcha Cohen from bus 901, had tried to get Matilda Ashkenazi up, but she was unconscious and too heavy. Barely able to breathe, they'd had to save themselves. With them was Leah Geffen, who had a lower side wound, but still the strength to drag little Efraim.

Following those four were Ben and Rachel Meshkel, dragging eight-year-old Issac. They had been vainly calling for their six-year-old, Junior, not knowing he was already outside.

Lastly came the Gal-ons, who'd been frozen with shock since watching their daughter Liat slaughtered under the seats by the hateful Ramz. Yet somehow Gil had managed to rouse himself and get Shoshana on her feet.

The forlorn throng drew air into burning lungs and struggled over the uneven ground and through the cloying vegetation toward the knoll.

But one more horror remained to unfold. Little Junior Meshkel, from the cover of some thick grass, saw his parents and ran shrieking towards them. He got within ten yards.

Rami has just reloaded his AKM and lifted his head to find a target. Seeing the cluster of people coming toward him, but fearful of death from above, he didn't aim, just jerked up his weapon and fired briefly, before ducking down again. The bullets missed the main group, but struck the little boy who fell flat on his face.

There was nothing his parents or any of the others could do, but fight onward in search of safety.

THIRTY-TWO

5:52 p.m.

To Assaf, on the ridge-top, it seemed impossible to credit that only 17 minutes had passed since the bus had first hurtled into sight. But he was more concerned only he and his people had any idea where the terrorists were. That mental picture needed to be acted on quickly. Dusk was settling fast.

One was certainly dead. The body was in plain sight. But counting the pair who had slipped out of the front doors just before the explosion, he reckoned there were still six terrorists on the loose.

Some were probably wounded. He'd sensed his own shots were on target several times, though nothing showed for it. Those enemies were within a 75-yard semi-circle, extending northwest from the bus. But continuing to fire at them from this distance was out of the question with the hostages scattered among them.

Ammunition for his Galil carbine was low, anyway. The soldiers with him had M16s of the same caliber, but barely a full magazine between them. There was a metal box-full in his car, about a three-minute scramble there and back.

He scanned the skyline, judging the light, and decided he'd have to make time. Leaving Adam and Raffi with orders to keep the terrorists pinned down if they saw any, he backed off the ridge-top and speed-walked down to the Datsun.

When he arrived back in position with the ammo, the situation had changed dramatically. While he distributed cardboard boxes, he saw armed men approaching from several directions. Multiple groups in single file. Police and IDF personnel it looked, maybe 25 or so. Then more entered the fields from the country club complex.

While still half a mile out, they were all advancing into deadly danger. Adam moved up beside him, also looking worried. "Can't just let them walk into it boss."

Assaf agreed. "We need to signal them to back off somehow until we can flag the Arab's positions.

Wish we had some smoke markers we could wave." Adam said.

Standing up waving, outlined above the skyline, when one of those Arabs down there is an outstanding shot? No thank you. He shook his head.

"Not many other options."

"Nope, I'll have to go down there."

Adam canted his head at his boss. It was the right call, though that didn't reduce the danger. But he'd have expected nothing less. Assaf wouldn't think about the risk. Just his duty. Leading from the front. Which was why Adam would follow the man anywhere. He asked hopefully, "You and me both?"

"No, I need you here," said Assaf.

Adam would cover him no matter what, and Raffi's steady, unflappable presence was reassuring.

"You Raffi and the soldiers cover. If I flush any out, shoot the shit out of them!"

Assaf had underestimated his people's effectiveness. Most of the terrorists were injured. The hollows and trees had protected them from ground level, but not from above.

Jalal, in one of the tree lines, had lost a lot of blood. Khaled in the scrub closer to the highway was wounded in the backs of both legs and could only squirm from place to place. Rami had a hip wound, and Dalal one to her left arm. Only Fayadh and Baba'a were unhurt, but for very different reasons.

After flinging away his Kalashnikov and pack, he'd kept crawling to the rear of the knoll. He'd been lying there ever since with his arms over his head, begging Allah for the chance to surrender.

Baba'a had also kept going after diving to the ground, but in search of a better fighting position. Now he was kneeling at the muddy bottom of the ditch, using it as a slit trench where a bend protected him from view from the north. He was aware Dalal was near him.

He had spare magazines laid out on the bank and had rapped each one on his AKM to make sure it would feed smoothly.

Assaf was ready to make the unprotected zig-zag run down the bare face of the hill, and across the construction site to the barricade. Taking a last look around the area, he saw soldiers from the south had reached some hostages. Distressed people were meeting them with arms outstretched. He counted seven, most limping or clutching injuries. A small victory.

Men from the north were spreading out along the shore as a backstop. Good tactics. If all those advancing had similar situational awareness, they could form a tight cordon, and wait the terrorists out. But that was too much to expect.

With a parting nod at Adam and Raffi, Assaf lifted his Galil to his chest and started down the face of the hill. His first aim was to reach the smoke-wall drifting east up the hill. To his surprise, he wasn't shot at getting there. He held his breath while running through it, then turned left and ran down the rear of the gas station.

Yaki Pirst, beet-root-red and ash-streaked, motioned him over and they knelt. "Thanks for the backup," the Colonel wheezed.

Nearby, people were tending to someone recovered from the bus. It seemed impossible that the charred shape was human, but what must be the chest was moving. The people around him or her had soot-black faces and hair melted into clumps. One slapped at a spark glowing in his tunic.

"The rest still aboard are gone," Yaki said with fathomless sadness. "Eighteen. Nineteen maybe."

Assaf felt a cold and rising anger. "What do you plan to do," he demanded.

"Plan? Do?" Yaki said, indicating other injured sprawled around. "Wait for reinforcements. Pray to God there are others out there we can still help."

Assaf said forcefully, "I'm going out there."

"You're crazy!"

"It's just got to be done."

"Let's make up a patrol." Yaki looked around to see who was available.

Assaf put a hand on the soldier's arm. "If we go out there in force, we'll just continue this shooting war. I know pretty much where they are. If I'm alone, some may surrender. If nothing else, I can signal their locations to those coming."

Pirst moved his head slowly from side to side. *Surrender? To one man?*

"At least take a couple of men to watch your back." *Or pull your dead ass out of there.*

Two immediately volunteered. Assaf also agreed to men standing by to help any wounded he found. He and his two bodyguards were still only halfway across the highway, when there was the muffled but unmistakable 'crump!' of a grenade from the direction of the knoll.

They walked faster.

Out in the field, Rami had been changing locations. On his belly. Sluggishly because of his through-and-through wound. After, thanks to Allah, shooting down the three women who'd emerged together, he'd been hit by a shot from the hill. But the bleeding had stopped, and he still had mobility, with effort.

He was also moving carefully because he was hunting. Trying to get close to some whispered talk and weeping he'd heard. It was a chance to kill more Jews. He heard them again. Only yards away. He dragged his backpack to him and felt for a grenade.

The one in tears was 14-year-old Anat Glotman. Now the shock of seeing her loved warrior-poet father shot down was wearing off.

Her mother, Lily, was whispering to her from nearby. "Life must go on. People love us. They depend on us. Be strong."

Right next to Anat was a five-year-old boy. The little Geffen boy, Efraim. He was virtually catatonic; shivering and teeth chattering from witnessing the brutal murder of his unhinged father. His mother Leah was trying to get through to him from where she also lay nearby, but he seemed unaware of her. It was the same all around her, Anat was sure, but she didn't dare lift her head to see.

An object struck her shoulder, painfully, and dropped beside her. It was metal and oval and leaking smoke. She dived away from it. The ground jolted her like she'd been kicked.

She looked at where she'd been, and saw Efraim lying still and sightless. Riddled with grenade shrapnel. Around her others were groaning from fresh wounds. But somehow, she'd been spared.

Assaf and his two flank-men climbed over the near crash barrier, and knelt down in the lanes at a bearable distance from the bus's radiating heat. He looked south and saw a group cautiously approaching up the east edge of the highway. To the west, smoke still drifted above the knoll where the explosion had been. More friendlies were advancing down the highway from the north, and there were men in the trees above the car yard. If an impermeable ring around the area wasn't possible, he supposed this was the way he would have done it too. A measured advance from all directions. With a pathfinder, of course, in this case himself.

Then he realized the group following the drainage ditch south was approaching far too quickly into the jeopardy of the uncleared operations area. They were too far away to hear a warning shout. He tried waving them back with arm motions.

It seemed that might work for a moment. They stopped. Looked confused. Then started forward again. Assaf cursed. He'd have to get closer where they could hear him. He stood up.

A single shot cracked out.

Ya'akov Gaz the naval commando was growing increasingly uncomfortable, as his team approached the blazing bus along the drainage ditch. Also, extremely vulnerable, since he hadn't had time to bring his Kevlar gear.

He looked back at his team leaders, Shrof and Moses, questioning whether they should slow down. They were coming up on a bend in the ditch. An ideal place for an ambush if you were an armed man with your back to the wall.

We should spread out here. We're close enough. Take up holding positions. Wait for the other groups to close the net. We're not flushing game-birds here.

But the two leaders kept coming, and after all, Gaz had volunteered to take the point. He took a few more steps and reached the bend. A bright flash ended his existence.

Ya'akov's body pitched down the bank and into the mud.

THIRTY-THREE

5:57 p.m.

During the moments after Ya'akov Gaz's murder, Assaf blamed himself. He couldn't have done more to prevent it, but still felt a total failure. He'd glimpsed wild tangled hair as the shooter fled his position and dived into heavy cover. Shots snarled down from Adam and the men on the ridge, ripping where the terrorist had waited in ambush. Uselessly.

Assaf had had no clear shot. The fallen man's companions were in his line of sight, and the hostages could be anywhere beyond. He cursed out loud at his helplessness. *A man lives or dies. We think we make a difference, really, but we're just grains of sand.*

He looked on somberly as the body was brought up out of the ditch and placed carefully down. A coat was laid over it. Then the hunt resumed. That group moved toward him again, with gun muzzles sweeping the scrub.

A flock of black-billed gulls cawed overhead, bound inland to roost. It lifted him out of all this dreadfulness for a moment. Then he motioned those with him to follow, staunched his shoulders and headed round the right side of the bus.

The heat was uncomfortable, but he ignored it. He was more worried about the firelight affecting his vision.

The vegetation was beaten flat by foot traffic. There were bodies. Two young women, and one older. And to the left, a young boy. Fury infused his every cell. But the older woman was blinking rapidly and making soft sounds. Assaf raised a hand to his followers and squatted again. Called back across the road for medics. Several rushed where he pointed. They started attending to Chaima Aharonowitz.

"We still have gunmen on the loose!" Assaf warned.

"Right, let's get her back across the road then," one replied in a weary voice.

Assaf tried not to think of the families who'd soon be learning of their loss, if they weren't also lying somewhere about.

As he stood again, he checked the load in his Galil out of habit. A full magazine and one in the chamber. He kept it to his shoulder as they advanced.

His companions' nervous movements were distracting, but he knew they couldn't help it. He was skin-tinglingly aware of being silhouetted against the fire, but there was nothing he could do about that either.

Damn you, concentrate. Look for movement.

A tree line separated him from thc knoll, though he could see it clearly enough. He intended to use the trees to get closer. Warily. A terrorist had been shooting accurately from there earlier.

He moved ahead, scanning left and right.

Then came excited shouts from Commander Shrof's group, still inbound in sweep-formation along the ditch. They raced ahead a few yards and converged on something on the ground. Someone. They didn't know then they'd captured Khaled, so weak from wounds he couldn't lift his weapon. They kicked it out of his hands.

Assaf was just yards from the first tree-line. There was movement among vegetation at the bole of a tree. He trained his gun. Shouted, "Stand up and come out!"

The movement became an arm holding a Kalashnikov. Swinging it toward him. The form of a man solidified behind. Assaf fired a three-shot burst into the center-mass and ran forward. Found a large Arab on his back in salt-stained and blood-spattered fatigues. He stirred the body with his foot. Lifeless. He picked up the AKM and heaved it a few yards away, just the same.

Terror-stricken in his hollow, Fayadh watched as the big Israeli policeman killed Jalal. He'd also seen the Shrof group approaching, having lost one of their men.

He was being hounded from two directions. But there were comforting noises nearby. Quavering voices. Occasional sobs.

He'd known his slim chance of survival depended on his mingling with the hostages. There they were. He huddled even lower. Praying to Allah for his mercy.

Assaf stepped through the trees into full view of the knoll; a low, roughly circular hump of rubbish and vegetation maybe 40-yards across.

There was a movement amongst that. He swung up the Galil. Then saw a woman's face. And a child's. He'd later learn they were Lily Glotman, hugging young Anat, while staring beyond him at what had been the bus, her husband's pyre.

A couple emerged. Embracing. Gil and Shoshana Gal-on. And another. Rachel and Ben Meshkel, with Issac clinging to his father's thigh. Faces ravaged by the loss of beloved children. Then Leah Geffen emerged with the blood-sodden body of Efraim in her arms, doubly devastated. Behind her came Else Shwin and Simcha Cohen from 901. Strangers until this day, they clung to each other inseparably.

"Are there any terrorists here?" Assaf bellowed. "Quickly. Have you seen any?"

Anat Glotman turned mutely in her mother's arms. Pointed a shaking hand to a few yards away. Fayadh rose from the grass, pleading in Arabic, holding his hands out before him in supplication. Assaf felt only disgust for the creature.

Then Rami arose like a demon from some bushes ten or so yards further away. His baby-face was contorted into a snarl of hatred. His AKM was at the aim.

The sight of the traitor Fayadh, plus 14 Jews including three policemen, was too tempting to ignore. He took his time. Savored the moment. This would be his last act for his homeland. Triumphant martyrdom. The main threat was the big bull-necked policemen who'd killed Jalal. The rest would be easy.

Then he saw Assaf reacting faster than seemed possible. His Galil was almost level. Rami frantically hauled back on his trigger. Both weapons fired together.

Rami was smashed backward by three high-velocity bullets, dead before his back struck the ground. But his Kalashnikov rounds had also been on target. Several expended harmlessly on Assaf's vest. One struck just above and to the left of it.

Assaf reeled away. Dropped to his knees, broken shoulder drooping and rapidly turning red.

Adam screamed as his boss fell. Thought only of getting down there to help. He ran in the direction of the construction site, Raffi followed in his wake.

The smoke pouring east had thinned now the flammable parts of the bus had burned out. The men in the northeast tree line, looking south, were on edge. Straining their eyes in the now quite poor light for targets.

Sniper Raphael Levy saw a figure running. *Surely a defender would be moving cautiously? It must be a threat.*

He drew a bead, then led the movement a few inches. His rifle seemed to fire itself. The Kevlar-penetrating bullet drilled through Adam's vest and into his upper chest, sending him tumbling.

Raffi changed direction and ran to Adam's aid.

People were rushing to help Assaf, confirm Rami was dead, take the sniveling Fayadh into custody, and calm the newly hysterical hostages. Most turned east at the sound of Levy's shot, to see if there was a new threat.

Baba'a, in a marshy tangle near the ditch with Dalal, took it as his best chance. He hauled Dalal up by her tunic, and both ran in the direction of the highway. Dalal immediately fell behind. Baba'a grabbed her arm and dragged her along with him.

He had no illusions they were buying more than a few additional moments. Any chance of escape had vanished the instant Hussain first opened fire, not much more than an hour before. The dream of a glorious attack on Yáfa the despicable Zionists would never forget was long gone. His last hope was to take as many with them as possible.

But Dalal was unarmed. Baba'a had less than half a magazine left. Yet if they could grab fresh weapons, they could still go down fighting. A movement registered in his left peripheral vision. It was nine-year-old Moti Zait screaming for his mother. He hadn't seen her shepherded away to safety earlier.

Baba'a saw only a threat. Not a child. He shoved his AKM out at arms' length and loosed off half his remaining ammunition. A round struck Moti in mid-stride and drove him down dead in a small heap.

They were just feet from the highway. Baba'a tightened his grip on Dalal's arm and tried to move his legs harder. Faster. They reached the crash-ribbon. Scrambled over it. Picked up the pace again. Dalal gasped harshly.

There were a number of defenders at the far edge of the road, but confusion was in their favor. With the haze of smoke hanging in the air, and the element of surprise, they had a real chance of grabbing fresh weapons and causing havoc.

What they were seeing ahead was a field ambulance station, with injured laid out being helped. Among the helpers was 22-year-old Sergeant Yaakov Segev of the *Heil HaRfu'a*, the IDF Medical Corps. Plucked from Highway 4 while heading back to his base-hospital after leave, this would be the paramedical instructor's last tragically unlucky day.

He'd just jabbed a morphine pen into the thigh of a man with horrible leg injuries, when he heard thumping boots on the roadway. Two Arabs in muddy and disheveled military kit, one tall and shaggy haired, the other a stumbling woman, came charging at him out of the gloom.

Either side of Segev police and soldiers scrambled for their weapons.

Baba'a blazed straight ahead until his AKM clicked empty. The soldier before him crumpled. He flung the empty weapon aside. Next in their path were two troopers helping a female hostage. They'd laid their M16s down while they worked. He stared hungrily at the loose weapons. If he could just close his hands around one of them.

Rifles stuttered behind them. Bullets whipped by. There were two painless but powerful thumps in his upper back, staggering him. Dalal was wind-milling beside him also. Dead on her feet. The weapons he'd coveted were lifted and aligned until he was staring at little round black holes in the ends of tubes of steel, no more than six feet in front of his face.

The holes were perfect in their symmetry. He couldn't take his eyes off them. There was a flash brighter than the sun. Then all light vanished.

The last synapses to register in Baba'a's exploding brain were the heat-pops from the fire, and the sirens of emergency vehicles racing up darkening Highway 2.

THIRTY-FOUR

Jerusalem
Monday, September 21st 1980

On a shining fall afternoon two and half years later, a number of vehicles, both private and official, made the turn off Jerusalem's Highway 60 onto Clermont-Ganneau Street and into the *HaMemshala* (governmental complex) on the slopes of Mount Scopus.

At the security entrance of the six-story, Jerusalem-stone, Israeli National Police Headquarters, the drivers were directed to special parking. The visitors signed a commemorative guest book at the guardhouse. The women received bouquets. Several delightfully dressed small girls had pretty rosettes pinned to their frocks.

They were guided along 50-yards of enclosed walkway, to an enormous foyer with a broad mahogany reception counter.

The walls were cream, the ceiling panel-lit and the floors tan. The walls boasted a progression of police recruitment posters, a visual history back to British occupation times when a fez was standard issue. One area was reserved for photographs and biographies of the six Police General Commissioners of the modern era.

The guests were greeted warmly by numerous officials in full parade-dress uniforms, then ushered to a semicircle of seating in front of an alcove backed by stylized brick-paneling. 'Remembrance and Heroism,' in Hebrew and English, stood out across the brickwork.

Last to join in, pushed in a wheelchair by his elderly parents, was a handsome man with longish hair, a muscular upper body, and a blanket covering his withered lower half.

A silver speaker's stand had been set up, faced with the blue multi-pointed Star of David and flanked by the flags of the Israeli State and National Police. Just on 2:00 p.m., a man in a pale blue uniform with the crossed leaves and stars of Israel's 7th Police Commissioner on his lapels, came from a side room and took his place behind it.

Herzl Shafir, 51, was lofty, with a finely sculpted face and intense eyes, and moved with the confidence of a past IDF Major General. Yet there was a studiousness about him. He'd been summoned back from PhD studies in the U.S., only recently, to take up his present job. This had surprised some of his peers, since he could be emotional and speak intemperately. Profoundly spiritual, he wore a small Yarmulke, as did most men present.

Shafir shuffled his notes while peering over the top of thin-rimmed glasses. He greeted and thanked all attending. Then announced, "We have an unusual situation here today, ladies and gentlemen.

Despite policy, it's been agreed to include both civilian and serving recipients in today's ceremony. We don't like to do this. Much as we'd like to hold our people's good deeds up for the accolades they deserve, presenting awards in public risks painting targets on their backs. Our officers know and accept that. However, by unanimous request, we have made an exception today. I just ask of you gentlemen of the press present," he laughed, "and ladies, that you respect the need to protect the safety of our men."

Shafir squared the edges of his notes and sipped from a glass of water.

"A little over 30 months ago our nation suffered a great evil, which would have been immeasurably worse, but for the heroism of a few, and the ultimate sacrifice of some whose families are present today. I shall not recount all the events of 11th March 1978. They are well-known as the Bloody Bus Affair. In the interests of time, I will deal only with the facts of each citation as I issue it, beginning with serving personnel."

On cue, a uniformed woman constable stepped into view bearing a tray covered in white satin. Shafir said, "I first call on

Superintendent Lev Shachar of the traffic police to rise. Superintendent?"

The recently promoted Shachar got to his feet, and stood with his hands in front of him, fingers fidgeting with the braid edging of his peaked cap.

"Superintendent Shachar coordinated a delaying action to gain enough time for others to create a roadblock on Highway 2. Then when civilians were inadvertently caught up in it, he exposed himself at great personal risk, to separate the terrorists from those in peril. For his actions that day, he is awarded the Police Distinguished Service Medal."

Lev donned his cap and squared his shoulders, then moved to stand at attention before Shafir. The big chief pinned on the blue and white ribbon and menorah with olive-branch, of Israel's second highest police honor, before shaking Lev's hand.

After a snappy salute, Lev returned to his seat, face pink with pride.

Adam Shmuel, now a Chief Inspector, accepted the same award for, "Providing support to his commander, the head of Yamam, and working to keep the loss of life to a minimum before himself being severely wounded."

When now-Chief Superintendent Assaf Hefetz rose from his seat, he received a wry grin from the commissioner who further broke protocol by asking, "Assaf my dear friend, what possessed you?"

Returning the grin, since he and Shafir were indeed close friends, Assaf replied simply, "I couldn't just stand by, Sir."

"And you actually drove yourself to hospital after being shot, in that little rocket-ship of yours?"

"I didn't want to distract from the mopping up, Sir."

Shafir just shook his head, smiling. "Be that as it may, to paraphrase what was once said about the founder of our country's special forces, Ord Wingate, by his British commander, 'When I read this, I don't know whether to embrace you for your courage, worry about you stealing my job, or court-martial you out of hand for your recklessness."

Holding up the red ribbon with blue stripes above a triangular menorah with twin olive branches, Shafir said, “I know only that we are the better for having you, and with the thanks of the nation, I award you our highest police honor for bravery, the Medal of Valor.”

The civilian awards added a somber sense to the proceedings. The first two were awarded posthumously.

Of Haviv Ankwa, Shafir said, "He volunteered to be a mediator between the terrorists and the security forces, and after being shot, continued to move ahead under heavy fire. After completing his mission, he died of his injuries on the way to hospital. His daughter Galit, two years old at the time, and his son Ytzak, ten, were also tragically killed in the catastrophe.”

His Distinguished Service Order was hung around the neck of his bereft widow, Monique. Their only surviving child, Tali, clung timidly to her side.

When Zvi Eshet's name was announced for his posthumous DSO, his wife Rita, along with his young son and daughter, stepped forward to receive the honor.

"With complete disregard for his own safety, and with true love in his heart for his friends and colleagues, Zvi broke loose of his bonds south of Netanya and stormed the terrorist next to him, seizing his weapon and killing the terrorist in a struggle. During this action he was killed by another terrorist."

Then the last recipient, of the highest civilian award Israel can bestow, the Medal of Courage, was pushed forward by his parents.

Shafir broke protocol again, abandoning his podium wet-cheeked to lay his hand on Yossi Hochman’s shoulder.

"I can read out the official statement, Yossi, but words cannot express what is in my heart. I can barely comprehend, let alone feel the pain of losing the love of your life, Rebecca, and your young sons Roi and Ilan. And that is without even mentioning the terrible pain of the physical injuries you suffered.

I can only liken it to having handfuls of your soul wrenched out. I will simply say that this Nation has survived its travails so far, only because of the willingness of citizens like you to stand up when called, and give everything that we as a people may have, everything.

You are a true hero, Ari, and no one has given more. along with the gratitude of a nation that loves you, please accept this honor. And may God keep and watch over you forever."

EPILOGUE

Tunisia
Friday, April 15th, 1988

The tall sky in which the Deputy Chief of the Israeli Defense Forces circled like a demigod, had been so clear and blue earlier, that from the windows of his Boeing 707 AWACS aircraft, he'd been able to see all the way north to the Turkish Bosphorus, while also watching heat lightning dance the crests of Libya's Nafusa mountain range, deep in Africa.

That was fitting, since his name, Ehud Barak, meant 'Bearer of Lightning' in Hebrew. And today he would strike a blow for his country worthy of his name.

But now it was deeply dark. The cabin was lit only by the blue glow of consoles manned by the best and brightest young men and women of the IAF's 120th Tactical Reconnaissance Squadron.

Ah, to be twenty years younger, thought Ehud, as he watched them work.

They were monitoring a stealth gunboat, ferrying 24 members of the Sayeret Matkal to the waterfront of the city of Tunis.

In charge of the operation on the ground was the unit's deputy commander, one of the IDF's elite warriors. A semi-orthodox Jew named Nahum Lev; tall, blond, serious, with the reputation of a fearless daredevil.

Near midnight, six Shayetet-13 frogmen went ashore. They secured the area and linked up with Mossad agents who'd entered Tunisia days before on the passports of kidnapped Lebanese fishermen.

A number of Sayeret Matkal troopers, an attack team of eight including Nahum himself, and two back-up teams, following in a number of rubber boats. They slipped aboard Mossad-supplied vehicles and drove to within 300-yards of a villa in the suburb of Sidi Boussaid. It was a villa they knew intimately, having replicated it in Israel, and spent many hours rehearsing a silent assault.

Around 1:45 a.m. Saturday morning, the AWACS plane began jamming all communications near Sidi Boussaid, except the commandos' own. Then in a move reminiscent of a scene in the movie 'Munich,' Nahum, arm in arm with a trooper disguised in a dress, heels, and blond wig, stepped out into the street.

They rollicked up to a guard in front of the villa, waving a map and a box of chocolates, pretending to seek directions to a party. When the guard looked at the map, Nahum shot him in the head at point blank range with a silenced pistol he produced from the chocolate box.

The troopers then set about their designated tasks like well-oiled machines. Some locked down the area, while the main team forced entry into the villa's basement. Inside were another guard and a gardener unlucky enough to be spending the night. They were also killed before the shooters began working their way up through the villa's three floors.

They cornered Abu Jihad at the top of the stairs, along with Intissar, who was holding two-year-old Nidal, and 14-year-old Hanan beside them. He was armed with a pistol, having been tipped off, but had stayed too long watching video coverage of the Intifada in Judea & Samaria, which he was orchestrating.

The four-commandos shot him numerous times, but spared his family, which was more than the evil little man ever did for anyone else.

Fingerprints and photographs were taken before the commandos withdrew the way they had come, burned their vehicles on the beach and sailed home to Israel without suffering as much as a stubbed toe.

Aboard the soaring AWACS plane, Major General Barak heard the code words proclaiming complete success. While the aircraft broke orbit and banked gracefully east toward the Israeli coast, he smiled blissfully, doffed his headphones, settled back into his plush leather seat, and shut his eyes.

Barak imagined himself at the keyboard of his Yamaha grand piano. Playing Brahms. Joyful.

Sonata Number One maybe.

He gestured with his hand as if conducting.

Jihad was buried six days later at Yarmouk. Israel denied having anything to do with his death until November 1st, 2012, when they confirmed the details given in 2000 by Nahum Lev, to the daily newspaper *Yedioth Ahronoth* (Latest News,) before Nahum's accidental death in a motorcycle crash.

Modern Day

Naama Hadani was buried in a full military ceremony in Haifa on a day too beautiful to waste on death.

Six soldiers carried her small casket. There was a 21-gun salute. Her father Joseph was released from Ichilov Hospital early so he could attend.

It set off a tragic time of deep mourning in Israel.

The last person rescued alive from what would soon be known as the Bloody Bus Affair was Matilda Ashkenazi from the 901 bus. Tragically, she died 19 days later in hospital from burns. At the end, 15 Israeli bodies remained aboard the burned-out bus. Five children and 10 adults. It was more than two weeks before the forensics were complete. Those people were separated from the terrorists' remains, and their grieving families took their loved ones home. The final death toll was 37 with more than 80 wounded.

After Assaf withdrew from the battlefield and drove himself to hospital, Commander Shrof took charge of the mopping up. Fayadh and Khaled were taken to Sharon Station. Chaima Aharonowitz, Shlomo Zait, Yossi Hochman, Haviv Ankwa and Adam Schmuel were also taken from the scene in ambulances, to various hospitals, around 6:00 p.m. By then the game of political musical-chairs was well under way.

Yaki Pirst was replaced by Police General Tyomkin as the overall crime-scene commander. General Moshe Joseph of the Carmeli Brigade took over next. Ownership swung back to the police when Commissioner Haim Tavori arrived around 6:20 p.m. Finally, a helicopter deposited Rafael Eitan on site at about 6:30 p.m., and it remained under IDF control from then on.

But before Tyomkin arrived, Yaki could not believe that one of the dead terrorists was a woman, despite the feminine features. He had Dalal's upper clothing loosened. A black bra convinced him it was true. Inflammatory photographs of the half-naked Dalal would later make it into the displaced-Arab' press.

That same vitriolic press claimed Yaki was actually Sayeret Matkal Commander Ehud Barak, whom they hated for his successes at Entebbe, and with Operation Wrath of God (the revenge for the Munich Olympics murders). It was even claimed he'd been seen spitefully firing a pistol into the dead bodies. Mr. Barak was nearly 7,500 miles away at the time, at Stanford University studying for his Masters of Engineering: Economic Systems Degree.

The search of the terrorists quickly turned up the document Dalal had offered to Haviv Ankwa before he took his tragic steps beyond the bus. It confirmed a major Tel Aviv beach-side hotel was the main target. Forces were immediately sent to guard local hotels.

Listed among the Arab prisoners the terrorists had hoped to free, was Kozo Okamoto, sole survivor of the Japanese 'Red Army' kamikaze attack on now Ben Gurion Airport in May 1972.

By then Glilot's thickening darkness prevented being sure that no terrorists had escaped the scene. The Glilot-Rash HaSharon area was shut down for two days while a yard-by-yard search was conducted. Only after reliable results began to flow from the interrogation of Fayadh and Khaled, was the curfew lifted on the night of March 13th.

The next morning, Israel went to war in South Lebanon with Operation Litani. They suddenly had an uncanny understanding of Arab strong points and troop positioning. The IDF deftly outflanked their opposition, and by March 17th could have rumbled all the way up the Bekaa Valley into Beirut had they so chosen. When they withdrew on the 21st they had inflicted over 2,000 casualties. Too many of them civilians. They had lost only 20 soldiers.

It took 18 more months to bring Fayadh and Khaled to trial before a three-officer military court. More than enough time to wring out every bit of information they had. On October 25th, 1979, they came before presiding Judge, Colonel Aharon Alpern, for sentencing. Fayadh had regained his bravado and interrupted proceedings several times with shouts of, "Long live a free and independent Palestine!" This despite the fact there was no such thing and never had been. They were sentenced to life imprisonment with absolutely, positively, under no circumstances, any possibility of release.

Unfortunately, that sentence wasn't fully served. Coincidentally, one of the prisoners released with Fayadh and Khaled in a prisoner exchange in May 1985 was Kozo Okamoto, so in a sense they achieved that one of their original goals.

Since then Fayadh has been in Jordan and more recently Algeria, living off his fame by appearing on Al Jazeera TV, where he once referred to Gail Rubin's murder as "human experience." Essentially: "Shit happens. It was war!" As recently as May 22nd, 2013, he was on a hunger strike protesting that the so-called Palestinian Authority hadn't followed through on a promise of a job. It's understood the PA has since appointed him an 'advisor' to shut him up.

Meanwhile Khaled, who calls himself Khaled Abu Usba now, is an esteemed (by some) member of the also so-called Committee of the Palestinian National Liberation Movement, based in Ramallah, Judea & Samaria. Their leader is Mahmoud Abbas, Yasser Arafat's successor as Chairman of the PLO.

It's a pretty fair bet the Arabs think the rat was the other guy.

As for other facts:

The massacre of the residents of Damour on January 20th, 1976, was one of the foulest atrocities of the Lebanese Civil War, but it at least helped alert the western press to what was going on.

The cold-blooded murder of the captured Christians, however, depicts only a few of the many thousands of murders that occurred during the ethnic cleansing of Central Beirut during 1977-78, by militias of primarily displaced-Arabs, affiliated with Fatah.

As for the lost and those who love them still:

Naama Hadani has since been immortalized in two fine folk songs by Simon Ophir and Motke Lebanon, and had a tree planted in her name by the Jewish National Fund in Philadelphia.

Gail Rubin's body was taken home by her parents and interred in section 52M of New York's, Union Field Cemetery. Her epitaph reads, 'Psalmist with a Camera.' Her plot is not a shrine today, like Jim Morrison's in the Père Lachaise Cemetery, Paris. But those who have been privileged to see some of Ms. Rubin's photographs, will say she created at least as much beauty in her lifetime within her art-form, as Morrison did within his.

Dov and Rina Bosknitz were interred at Haifa's Sde Yehoshua Cemetery, also called Joshua Field., On the south side of Mount Carmel, their resting place gazes out over the always patient Mediterranean. In February 2013, Danny Bosknitz left the following message on their grave, which translates from Hebrew:

'Dear Mom and Dad, it is your memorial in a few days, but I don't need that to want to be with you. It's Saturday night and I've just come back from a Shlomi Shabat concert at the Haifa Convention Center. You would have loved the show. I hope you are proud of who I have become. I love you and miss you. Your son who is older than you.'

Hanoch Tel-Oren, after a year of Feldencrais Integration treatment under therapist Yochanan Rywerant, recovered the use of his right hand and returned to his calling as one the greatest concert flutists of all time. Then went on to a second career inspiring generations of students at the Music Academy of Jerusalem's Karmiel Conservatory. He and Sheena's marriage couldn't survive their grief, however. When Hanoch died in 2005, Kol Israel devoted a program to his haunting music. Omri is still beloved in Israel.

The old warrior, Tuvia Rozner, also received a full military funeral at Joshua Field in honor of his years of service to his country.

Katy and Joseph Sosensky went together back to Ashdod, where they had spent so many happy years after the maelstrom of their youth. They lie peacefully in the Old Cemetery on the other side of Moshe Sneh Boulevard from the historic Gimel Quarter.

Amnon Drori, so huge in every way, and with all his experience as a commando, yet so unlucky to have been in the wrong place at the wrong moment, was received back to the Krayot by his wife Ruth “and their three children and laid gently down in Haifa.

Na'omi Alichi, who was so looking forward to starting her National Service in the IDF, also rests at Joshua Field. An award is still given out in her name each year, to the top senior at Haifa's private Beit Hasefer Hareali High School.

Tali Aharonowitz, who never got home to share her Tel Aviv experiences with her host of friends, is there as well.

Of the drivers, Gid'on Haas survived despite wounds he received during the first confrontation at Ma'agan Michael and later as the bus was charging south. He is now retired in Haifa. Avi Perets, who first saved and then defended his passengers so selflessly, was still with Egged recently, and quite a character around the bus museum in Holon.

Shlomo Zait, however, never recovered the use of his legs. It's impossible to know how much more pain and destruction might have been wrought if not for his quiet courage and steadiness. Rina and Nathan recovered from their minor wounds while Moti found peace from terror at Joshua Field.

The broken-hearted Meshkels took Junior's body home to Tiberius, where he had been born and had loved to toddle and play with his parents along the lake-shore.

Selfless Malkah Leibwitz' funeral, also at Joshua Field with full military courtesy, was a family affair that she would have loved, attended by her husband, brother, son, and numerous grandchildren.

A number of people have said fit and capable Tzyona Luzia-Cohen could easily have saved herself, but it was completely in her character, and a tribute to her love for Avraham that she would never have left him. Together today, they fulfill the prophecy she made at her mother-in-law's grave so shortly before their own passing. They rest at the cemetery in Holon, incidentally close to a 9/11 monument that is anonymous compared to the one in New York, but which matches it in horror: the murder of 6,500 Jews from the Stolin Ghetto, in the Belarus forest on Rosh Shoshana eve, September 11th, 1942.

In comparison to the sad solemnity of some, the Haifa funerals of Josef Kheloani and Meir Segal were joyful celebrations of the long lives of both great and much-loved men, attended by multiple generations of their families down to their smallest great-grandchildren.

Yehuda Basterman the Tel Aviv businessman, never saw Manchester or got to continue expanding the family business. He lies in the Kiryat Shaul cemetery almost within sight of Glilot.

Otari Mansharov, the quiet and reserved Russian-born carpenter about whom little else is known, went home to Acre where his wife Tamir put him to rest.

Liat Gal-on, so beautiful in her pictures and so loved in life for her soaring spirit, must have been so confused by the contradiction between Dalal's act of attempted kindness and the evil being perpetrated all around her. She will be remembered always at a memorial in the library of Tchernichovsky Elementary School in Carmel.

Shim'aon Glotman the soldier and scholar, was taken home to Haifa to lie at the German Templar cemetery. His brother Adam later published a book of his poetry about Israel's landscapes and people, adding the inscription:

'This book of poems is in memory of a young life, which stopped in the middle and left a trail of memories and pain that forever will be.'

The grenade explosion spared Yossi Hochman's life while doing ghastly damage to his legs. He only had a fifth of his blood remaining when he arrived at Ichilov Hospital twenty minutes later. His pulped right leg was immediately amputated, and a few days later, most of his left one. Yet due to his extreme will to live, he recovered enough to attend Rebecca's and the boys' funeral at Neve Yam on March 30th.

He has never accepted his injury as a limitation, only as an opportunity forced upon him. He decided that if he couldn't live with the loss of his family, he wouldn't get better, and that mindless anger against something that no longer existed wasn't an evolved attitude.

For the sake of his family's memory, he needed to get up and truly live. And smile again. On discharge from hospital, he moved out of Neve Yam into his own place in Atlit, not wanting to be a burden on the community. He was up on prosthetics within a year.

The Israeli Ministry of Foreign Affairs and Defense took him on a world tour, speaking about living with terrorism. No one could be better qualified. Then he went back to Egged for a period as Director of Culture and Sports.

Waypoints, since then, have included Chairman of the Hapoel Haifa football club, Director of Israeli Veterans Affairs for Haifa, and Board Member of the Mount Carmel Hospital. He still takes every opportunity to be at the bedsides of maimed IDF personnel.

He has also completed over 100 scuba-dives, using prostheses fitted with flippers, yet he has never considered seeking selection for the Disabled Olympic or Maccabiah Games. He just doesn't see himself as crippled.

As he is fond of saying, "Life is stronger than anything else."

As for the defenders:

Lev Shachar went on to a sterling police career and retired as a Chief Superintendent in 2006.

Adam Schmuel tired of the sit-around-and-wait-for-bad-things-to-happen side of the anti-terrorist business and resigned in

1982. He now runs a successful security equipment supply business in Tel Aviv.

Assaf Hefetz went on to become Commander of the Police Central Intelligence and Investigations Unit, fighting organized crime and drug trafficking, and then climbed onward through the rankings until becoming the 12th Commissioner of Police. He implemented numerous far-reaching organizational and operational changes to combat terror attacks, before retiring in 1998 to commence a high-profile speaking career.

While it is IDF policy not to publicize the names of members killed during domestic operations, so as not to fuel terrorist propaganda, those of the two IDF members who fell trying to reinforce the police that day, Ya'akov Gaz and Yaakov Segev, are engraved on the monument beside Highway 2 at Glilot.

Also, every *Yom Hazikaron* (Memorial Day,) *Reshet Gimmel,* the music channel of Kol Israel, devotes a program called 'Very soon we will all be transformed into song,' to compositions by fallen soldiers. Ya'akov Gaz's poems set to music are frequently played. For instance:

> You can wait for me at the neighborhood coffee shop with latte coffee and a cake on the side
> You can wait for me with all the love, but you will wait alone
> I am going out just for a moment
> Don't say why I didn't warn you earlier
> I only went out for a moment
> And the tears flow by themselves, to the warm grave.
> - 'ISRAEL, A NATION OF WARRIORS,' by Moshe Katz

As for the dead terrorists:

Most are known only by the kunyas they adopted for the operation, or as anonymous fighters from the ranks of the displaced-Arabs involved in the Lebanon civil war, driven to serve the cause the way they did.

Dalal Mughrabi, however, 39 years after her death, still remains one of the great enigmas of the Middle East conflicts. Trained nurse, caregiver, and fierce fighter. Family-loving terrorist.

An implacable murderess who was reputedly kind to children. A well-known tramp in a society where that kind of behavior could get you stoned to death. A warrior-woman who put the surrounding men to shame on the battlefield.

She has gone on to capture the imagination of her 'nation.' There have been more than 30 public squares, schools and parades named after her. Recent honors include the Palestinian authority funding the Dalal Dancing Group for Popular Arts, East Jerusalem's Al-Quds University naming a soccer team after her, and a 'Shahida of the Homeland, Dalal Mughrabi' award being given to the Governor of the District of Hebron.

She left the following inscription in a photograph album at her parent's home in Sabra, perhaps while on leave after the training at Damour:

> Because I loved my country's sky and the faces of the children, they killed me.
> Because I loved the wheat fields and the warm sun.
> I'll put the revolution on the sand of my homeland Palestine,
> Between the trees and the flowers.
> I will dance because I am the source of the revolution which will never finish, and from my blood I will irrigate the land of my homeland, Palestine.

Ten of the eleven dead terrorists, including the drowned Ahmed, whose body was recovered on the northern Israeli coast later in March 1978, were buried unceremoniously at an IDF military cemetery believed to be located on the Ashdod Naval Reservation.

They were later to be included in the 199 sets of remains Israel agreed to transfer to Hezbollah on July 16th, 2008, in exchange for the bodies of IDF soldiers Ehud Goldwasser and Eldad Regev. However, DNA testing failed to find Mughrabi's body among them. The excuse offered by officials was that her coffin might have been 'swept out to sea by underground currents,' which did nothing to quell rumors that her body was mutilated after her death.

A few days after a mass release of Arab prisoners by Israel on November 23rd, 1983, some from Ktzi'ot Prison in the Negev where Fayadh and Khaled may have been doing their time, 'Karem Osman' was found stabbed to death in an alley in the bar-infested Strovolos district of Nicosia, Turkish Cyprus.

And of the remaining masterminds who also harnessed the anger of these young people and turned them into monsters?

Azmi Zrayir, the fanatical South Lebanon Fatah Commander, dropped out of sight in 1982 and is believed to have died in that year's Israel-Lebanon *Milhemet Lebanon Harishona* (Operation for Peace in Galilee.)

Abu Iyad remained active within the PLO and actually quite accessible to the media. The English writer David Yallop, in his quite excellent book, 'To the Ends of the Earth,' describes several amiable interviews with him throughout the 80s.

Iyad was never, however, to overcome the enmity between him and Abu Nidal. Yallop says he was in the habit of offering Nidal Group members sent to kill him jobs as bodyguards on the 'keep your enemies closer' principle.

He was assassinated, along with two other senior Fatah figures, by a fellow displaced-Arab named Hamza Abu Zaid, who had been masquerading as a trusted bodyguard, in Tunis, on January 15th, 1991.

AUTHOR'S NOTES

The Author and Avi Perets beside the Wanderer's bus. Holon, Tel Aviv, March 2014.

When setting out to write about an immense tragedy such as this, you feel entrusted with people's lives.

I'm additionally honored to have been allowed guest entry to a unique and marvelous culture: Judaism. Since much of my research material is available only in the only extinct language ever to be resurrected and adopted by a modern nation--Hebrew, I've needed a lot of translation help, for which I'm very grateful.

I carried this story around, literally as newspaper clippings in my wallet, for more than 35 years, until I was looking through my repository of ideas for one more short story for a collection, and decided to write it.

That was since the morning of the Monday after the tragedy, when I was having breakfast in the student cafe of Princeton University with my girlfriend Mikhail Innerfield and our friend Josh Minkin. I turned over a copy of the New York Times and the story was all over the front page. I read avidly and in horror, found it inconceivable and deeply moving, and said so.

Josh said, "You simply have no idea what it is like there."

Josh, I hope now I do know, a little anyway. Thank you both for setting me off on this journey. I hope you are well.

But is this story exactly what happened? Of course not. This is truth-inspired fiction. Events such as this are a tight collection of microcosms, totally true only to each involved. What is true, is that the terrorists lived that way, and were recruited, trained and delivered to their destination, in that way. Whom they murdered and how they died, is true.

This has been my attempt to honor those victims in fiction as I would in real life, with respect and a plea for forgiveness for any fact I have gotten wrong. Now as a human being, I only have to deal with why.

We know Abu Jihad was desperate to prevent the united front against Israel, (Egypt, Syria, and Jordan) being split. That threatened his entire bloody empire. And he'd had success before finding people to do his dirty work, notably with the Savoy Operation.

But what caused those young people, particularly a disco-dancing dilettante like Salaam, and an apparently kind-at-heart woman like Dalal, to unleash such evil on so many innocents, while throwing their lives away in the process? And once involved, what hold could have been so strong, that it was impossible to gather the moral strength to turn back in the interests of common decency?

I believe a large part of the answer lies in their unique upbringing. This second generation of displaced-Arabs, the true children of al-Nakba, was influenced uniquely in three ways:

Firstly, being born so soon after al-Nakba, they were bombarded from birth with the awful tales of relatives expelled from lands and homes

Secondly, Israel's behavior while subduing the occupied territories seized after the 1967 war, was extremely counterproductive. There's no doubt they were heavily provoked, but there's plenty of blame to go around. It reinforced the worst tales being told by relatives. to impressionable minds. at that precise time a hundredfold and drove enormous numbers into the armed resistance. Just as the more recent, and horribly misguided, US 'War on Terror' has turned multitudes of Middle Easterners against my, in large-part, fair and just, home nation.

But mostly, the Lebanese Civil War provided the perfect infernal training ground for those many disaffected young men and women. And people like Abu Jihad provided the opportunity to strike against the evil bogeymen of their childhood and youth. Overused term or not, but it could be described as a perfect storm.

What I struggle most personally with, is what happened to common human decency during all this? Was Fatah so revered that once inside the machine, escape was impossible without abandoning one's entire identity? And how can any such force or influence be so strong as to subsume one's entire humanity?

As a westerner, Josh was right, I can probably never completely understand, though this work is my concerted attempt.

For those with further interest, there is much more to know.

On the west side of Highway 2 opposite Glilot's Cinema City Mall, accessible from an overbridge, is the official monument to the event, erected with funding from Sara Perlman and Egged, who hold a memorial ceremony there every year.

Another good place to look is on the English translation website of the Israeli National Monument to Civil Victims of Terror. Be prepared to be saddened and horrified.

DC-10/1/2020

ACKNOWLEDGMENTS

I am beholden to too many people in writing this book to name them all, but I am particularly grateful to the following. Thank you MapQuest Open for the maps. In Israel, I am deeply grateful to Natan Taig in Jerusalem for facilitating so many important contacts and for spending hours with me on Skype. Also, to Avriham Perets at the Egged Bus Museum in Holon for sharing his knowledge, and Yossi Hochman and his daughter Orya for their living example of the triumphant power of life. Across the globe, I owe a debt to my terrific beta readers, Addie Greene, Kerri Harris, Lori Fluker, Scott Skipper, Dave Edlund, and Roly Rogers, And in New Zealand, many thanks to Rinat Miezeles for her indispensable assistance with translation, and once again to my brilliant editor Dawa Rowley for so deftly turning my semiliterate scratchings into grammar. Last but never least, thanks to my family for their love and support.

As always, all successes I owe to the people who have assisted me. My mistakes are all my own.

www.ingramcontent.com/pod-product-compliance
Ingram Content Group UK Ltd.
Pitfield, Milton Keynes, MK11 3LW, UK
UKHW041635190726
13854UKWH00006B/2505